T0010614

Obsidian Tide

Praise for
Obsidian Tide

"McSpadden has created a unique and magical universe that is every bit inventive as it is captivating. *Obsidian Tide* is a gripping fantasy adventure that will instantly pull you in and keep you hooked until the very last page."

—**Ashley Mansour,** International Best-selling Author

"Fantasy lovers, your next great read is here. Get ready to be swept away by JoAnna McSpadden's *Obsidian Tide*. Through McSpadden's expert storytelling, readers will be immersed in the world of the Akarian Empire. Told in dual point of view from the perspective of Liam, the Emperor's nephew, and Princess Katerina of Esterine, betrothed to the Emperor's heir, readers are front and center on the royals' quest to save Akaria from illness and harness their magical abilities. The journey is a dangerous one filled with powerful enemies and ancient magic. But, through Liam and Princess Katerina, readers will discover that perhaps the greatest journey of all is breaking free from society's expectations and forging an authentic path of self-discovery."

—**Jessica Reino,** Author, Author Coach and Senior Literary Agent

"*Obsidian Tide* has everything you would want in a fantasy—a seemingly unachievable goal to cure an incurable disease, magic, friendships made through an epic quest and a hint of budding romance. JoAnna wove together a story full of magical adventure that will keep you turning pages and leave you wanting more."

—**Louise Davis,** Author of *Haunted By You*

"A rich and detailed world with a fresh twist, *Obsidian Tide* is a journey that will leave you wanting more."

—**Susan Shepard,** Author of *The Curse of the Winter Lord*

"*Obsidian Tide* is truly a magical read! With each turn of the page, you find yourself completely enthralled in the world of Akaria and the characters. JoAnna's attention to detail allows you to immerse yourself completely to the point of not being able to put it down … and that is the understatement of the century!"

—**Carmen Seda,** Bookstagrammer and Social Media Influencer

"If you're looking for a book with elemental magic, redeemable characters, and dark secrets all packaged together in a grand adventure, then look no further than *Obsidian Tide*! Full of all the twists and turns you don't expect, McSpadden has created a world that is both satisfying and unique, weaving an enchanted story on every page."

—**Erin Huntley,** Author, Freelance Editor

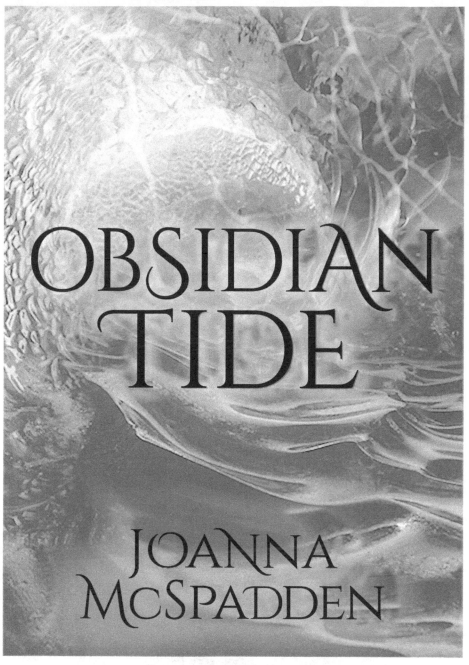

OBSIDIAN TIDE

JOANNA McSPADDEN

NEW YORK

LONDON • NASHVILLE • MELBOURNE • VANCOUVER

Obsidian Tide

© 2024 JoAnna McSpadden

All rights reserved. No portion of this book may be reproduced, stored in a retrieval system, or transmitted in any form or by any means—electronic, mechanical, photocopy, recording, scanning, or other—except for brief quotations in critical reviews or articles, without the prior written permission of the publisher.

Published in New York, New York, by Morgan James Publishing. Morgan James is a trademark of Morgan James, LLC. www.MorganJamesPublishing.com

Proudly distributed by Publishers Group West®

Publisher's Note: This novel is a work of fiction. Names, characters, places, and incidents are either products of the author's imagination or used fictitiously. All characters are fictional, and any similarity to people living or dead is purely coincidental.

A FREE ebook edition is available for you or a friend with the purchase of this print book.

CLEARLY SIGN YOUR NAME ABOVE

Instructions to claim your free ebook edition:
1. Visit MorganJamesBOGO.com
2. Sign your name CLEARLY in the space above
3. Complete the form and submit a photo of this entire page
4. You or your friend can download the ebook to your preferred device

ISBN 9781636982403 paperback
ISBN 9781636982410 ebook
Library of Congress Control Number: 2023939111

Cover Design by:
Rachel Lopez
www.r2cdesign.com

Interior Design by:
Christopher Kirk
www.GFSstudio.com

Morgan James is a proud partner of Habitat for Humanity Peninsula and Greater Williamsburg. Partners in building since 2006.

Get involved today! Visit: www.morgan-james-publishing.com/giving-back

For Scott
My dreams became your dreams and, my love, we did it.

I

Tonight was to be the beginning of a story so grand that it was widely promised to be recorded in the history books forever. Never before had Esterine royalty stepped foot in Akaria, but on this magical spring night that was about to change. The Esterine royals were to meet with the Akarian emperor to solidify the most powerful alliance of the known political world. And the setting of such a meeting was, of course, the most extravagant party of the year.

And Liam was late.

He felt his wrist for the familiar ticking of his watch as he walked up to the massive ballroom doors. He gave the two guards a half smile and they looked at each other for a moment before they each grabbed hold of a handle and pulled the doors open in front of him. Liam strode forward, pulling at his collar and forcing a convincing smile to break across his face. He rolled his shoulders into a more confident posture and entered the bustling room.

He wished he was invisible as he brushed past the full ball gowns and finely tailored suits, feeling the stares and hearing the whispers in the crowd. He tugged at the cuffs of his own magnificent white and red filigreed suit, scolding himself for not considering the traffic in the city tonight before leaving his manor. He should have known better. He had no one to blame but himself and now he would have to face the consequences.

The room glowed with golden accents throughout the trim in the walls and the sparkling gold suits of the waiters as they wove through the crowd with an assortment of light refreshments. As to be expected, all the wealthiest people in Akaria were here; the excitement and intrigue was palpable among them. Emperor Shadox's parties were always glamorous affairs, but on this historical night it was clear he was aiming to impress even more than usual.

A hand clapped Liam on the shoulder and he jumped in surprise. His body tensed in apprehension until he turned his head and saw a familiar smiling face.

"Holy Tykos, don't sneak up on me like that John," Liam said with annoyance, but undoubted relief.

"I've been looking for you everywhere," John said, his smile waning as he looked around them. "You're cutting it kind of close, don't you think? I know you're not the type to want a special entrance, but you've certainly got one now."

Liam looked down. "I know, I misjudged my timing," he admitted.

"Well your uncle is not going to be very happy about that," John said as he pushed Liam forward and they strolled casually through the crowd.

"I know," Liam said with a wince. "I know."

"You have to stop being late to important events," John said with a chuckle, but Liam did not think it was funny. His stomach churned. "I tried to cover for you when I went up to greet your uncle, but I don't think he bought it," John told Liam.

Liam sighed and stopped when he spotted the large dais at the far end of the room. A golden throne and a few grand chairs stood tall above the crowd. His uncle, the emperor of Akaria, sat supremely on his throne, his crisp military uniform a perfect depiction of his formidable presence. His brow was creased as he conversed with members of his Imperial Council who huddled around him. Liam noticed his uncle's right hand squeezing into and out of a fist, a familiar sign of his displeasure.

"We could probably sneak you up there," John suggested as he eyed the dais himself. "The Tykerials know who you are after all."

Standing around the dais, in their green and gold armor, were several Tykerial Guards. Liam knew he was soon expected to stand amongst their prestigious ranks, and though he admired them, he felt a wave of nausea hit him at the thought.

"Yeah, perhaps," Liam said as he thought about how he might get around the Guards to the back of the dais.

Liam's eyes scanned the dais and fell on the willowy man standing next to his uncle. His uncle's most trusted advisor, Edward, was in many ways the emperor's opposite. His sleek dark hair and muted clothing stood in stark contrast to the golden haired, brightly clothed emperor next to him. Edward never seemed to like Liam very much and he would surely take great pleasure in pointing out Liam's tardiness. Liam turned his face away from the dais before Edward could spot him.

"It looks like the old skeleton has it out for you tonight," John said, noticing the searching eyes of the advisor.

Liam sighed and nodded. "Indeed. He won't let me get away with this."

He glanced over to the seat next to his uncle's and caught the gaze of his brother's bright eyes. Anthony looked every bit as regal as an heir to an empire like Akaria should in his white and gold suit. He flicked his dark hair out of his face and cracked his trademark smirk at Liam. Liam self-consciously pushed his mess of red curls around on his head. His brother's perfectly kept sable-colored hair had always made him envious. Anthony casually tapped their uncle's chair, and pointed his head toward Liam in the crowd.

"Well, so much for a quiet entrance," Liam said. "I guess I'll just get this over with."

"Sorry friend," John whispered, patting Liam on the back. "Good luck."

Liam moved his gaze to the ground and walked up to the front of the dais. His nerves tightened and a flutter of anxiety moved through his body as the whole of the dais's occupants and those in the surrounding area turned their attention to him. He brought a shaking hand into a fist over his heart and bowed his head as he knelt to the emperor.

"Your Majesty, Emperor Shadox. I …"

"Get yourself up here," his uncle commanded.

Liam stood up quickly and shuffled up the stairs onto the platform. Keeping his eyes down, avoiding the many stares he could feel on his back, he came to stand in the spot Edward had just vacated for him. The emperor stood from his throne and Liam sucked in a deep breath before looking up into the sharp blue eyes of his uncle's frowning face.

"Is everything all right? Do you feel ill?" his uncle asked, lifting up one of Liam's arms and looking him over.

"Oh. I'm well, yes," Liam stammered. He managed another forced smile and a small embarrassed chuckle as the Imperial Council members watched their interaction.

Emperor Shadox exhaled as he let go of his arm. His body relaxed before turning away.

"Good," he said, waving off the council members from the dais and then directing his eyes back to Liam, promptly taking his signature stern furrow that Liam was all too familiar with.

"I thought you may have misunderstood my instructions due to some illness or ailment," the emperor said quietly, folding his arms behind his back, "for I do not recall instructing you to arrive to this festivity late."

Liam nodded as he glanced downward to his watch to fiddle with it.

"You nearly missed the introduction of the Esterine royals. I just gave word to move forward with their announcement, despite your absence. Their king is not known for his patience and I had to keep him waiting until you showed up! We need to solidify this alliance if we ever expect to get the granite we need to build strong enough walls to hold off the giants in the north," Emperor Shadox said before he glanced away from Liam, back out to the crowd with a reassuring smile.

"I'm sorry, Your Majesty, I tried to be here," Liam tried to explain. "You see my hansom cab it …"

"I don't want to hear any more excuses from you," the emperor said, raising his hand for Liam to stop. "I know it's been a rough year, but if you would just live in the palace and …" he said with a sigh.

Liam's stomach knotted at the mention. His uncle was the only father he'd ever known and as the second son in line for the throne, much was expected of him. Much of which Liam had been falling short on, including moving up through the ranks of the Tykerial Guard to eventually take over as commander. It killed him to know he'd messed all that up last year by getting disqualified from the Tykerial Guard exam.

"With Anthony officially being named Princep last month and his imminent betrothal to the Esterine princess, it is more important than ever for you to be here to protect the future of this empire," Emperor Shadox explained softly to him.

Liam glanced over at his brother. Anthony sat back comfortably in his chair, looking out at the crowd. His eyes squinted slightly as he smirked and nodded at someone. He reminded Liam of the many paintings of the fire god, Farran, with his charismatic gestures and charming attitude.

"I understand that you aren't sure anymore, but I know the Guard is where you belong," Emperor Shadox continued, grabbing Liam's shoulder to regain his attention. "You may think you want to do more for our beautiful capital city of Gilderon, but your rightful place is here. With your brother and with me."

"Yes, Your Majesty," Liam agreed with a solemn nod.

The emperor tugged on his suit jacket and straightened his tie. "Now, please do your best to put aside your fears and act like the future Tykerial Guard Commander I know you are."

Liam nodded as his uncle took his seat again. Liam then stepped toward the chair that was meant for him on the dais next to his brother. He sat and looked down at his watch. It was a simple, silver-rimmed watch with a white face. The silver filigreed pattern that laid behind the black numbers and hands defined its elegance. His uncle had told him it had once been his father's watch when he gave it to Liam as a gift when he graduated from Hetikan Academy four years ago. Liam pushed aside the knot growing in his chest as he thought back to that day— when he had the whole world ahead of him; no regrets, no disappointments, just a life full of potential and opportunity. Things had felt so different then.

Liam took a deep breath and lifted his head up. He looked around the room, searching for a particular face. A face that would calm him, a face that he had come to adore in the last few months. His eyes searched for only a few minutes before they found her: Caroline Morningfire.

Her fair blond hair was pinned up behind her head with two curling tendrils framing her face. The deep red of her gown made her stand out among the many other blue, black, and purple ball gowns. She held herself confidently as she conversed with another girl. She glanced in his direction at that moment and gave him a shy smile before flicking her blue eyes back to her companion quickly. Liam grinned to himself, letting the distress and nerves of the night roll off him. He allowed himself a genuine smile as he shifted his glance away from her. He couldn't wait to dance with her tonight.

He was imagining her touch when the trumpets began to blare from the balcony above the room. Liam's heart pounded with anticipation as he glanced over to his brother. Anthony looked over to him before they rose from their seats at their uncle's cue. Emperor Shadox squeezed his hands into fists before relaxing them and standing up straight with his hands down by his sides. Anthony smoothed down his white and gold patterned vest and Liam was surprised to see a glimmer of anxiety there. Anthony was always the confident, charismatic one, but in this moment, Liam could see his brother was nervous.

Tonight, Anthony would meet his bride-to-be, the Princess Katerina from Esterine. The royal family had traveled across the difficult Dalgradian Ocean, from the continent of Isavaria to their continent of Elusira. Everyone in attendance was dying to see what this family would be like: how they would act, how they would look, how they would dress, and how they would speak. After the initial meeting tonight, the negotiations for the marriage agreement would commence, and the wedding date would be set.

When the trumpets ceased, the whole room fixed their eyes on the doors atop the grand staircase that led down into the center of the ballroom, waiting with immense anticipation. The doors slowly opened and an announcer in a long-tailed coat stepped forward.

He bellowed out to the crowd in a most impressive voice, "Presenting, His Royal Majesty, King Nikita Xandrova and Her Majesty Queen Eva Xandrova of Esterine."

2

A large, burly man stepped forward past the announcer with a tall, slender woman on his arm. The couple came to the top of the staircase and looked out at the crowd with raised chins. It was immediately clear to Liam that this family had made no efforts whatsoever to conform to Akaria's norms. The king's long white hair and bearded face was improper enough, but it was nothing compared to their attire, which held paramount importance to many Akarians. Liam could hear the whispers of gossip and amusement making their way through the room, though everyone kept pleasant smiles plastered on their faces.

Unlike the suits and ball gowns they wore in Akaria, the Esterine royals wore long, straight-cut garments in a deep red color, heavily embroidered with gold and silver threads. King Nikita Xandrova's high-collared garment came down past his knees where they were met by tall black boots. He wore a sash around his waist and thick golden chords buttoned together horizontally across his chest, while the queen's garment had another layer of fabric that laid upon the main dress, hanging from her shoulders like a cape. The most impressive piece, however, was the queen's large, beaded headdress that rested on her intricately braided bed of blonde hair. Two strands of beads hung down from the pointed headdress next to her face, brushing the tops of her shoulders.

The announcer's voice called out above the muted whispers of the crowd and announced the next members of the Esterine royal family. "The Royal Princesses of Esterine, Princess Katerina and Princess Anya."

This was the moment everyone had been waiting for. The excited murmurs and whispers ceased in the suspense. Liam tried to catch his brother's eye, but both Anthony and Emperor Shadox kept their gazes fixated on the top of the stairs. When Liam turned back, the whole Xandrova family was descending the staircase. His eyes briefly glazed over the younger, smiling girl and fell on the princess beside her. The Princess Katerina.

It was clear to Liam by the white and gold of her dress that she was the one dressed to match the Princep tonight. She floated gracefully down the stairs in the strangely straight-cut gown, the beads dangling from her large round headdress shaking slightly as she held her head high. Her dark hair made her stand out from the rest of her fair-haired family as it cascaded from her headdress in one long braid resting on her shoulder.

As he watched, Liam felt a flutter in his chest—an uncomfortable, pulling sensation. He ignored the sensation as best he could, but the feeling grew stronger as the Xandrovas, and his time to interact with them, drew nearer.

The strange flood of anxiety continued, causing Liam to breathe more heavily as he followed behind his uncle and brother, stepping off the dais to greet the foreign family. He stood as still as he could manage, digging his fingernails into his palms as his uncle and the Esterine king embraced.

His uncle's voice rang out in a loud boom, causing Liam to close his eyes in a wince. "My nephews and I welcome you, our most honored guests, to the kingdom of Akaria."

The trumpets blasted again overhead and Liam had to clench his fists harder to overcome the flood of pain that invaded his head.

The emperor continued, "As our season turns to warmer weather, it is truly a perfect time for you to visit Akaria. We are overjoyed to host you."

King Xandrova smiled, though it was an unnatural smile. "We are honored to be here tonight, we thank you for the care you have shown us," he replied in a heavy accent.

"We look forward to the night's festivities and getting to learn more about the empire of Akaria," Queen Eva said, with a much lighter accent. Liam noticed that his uncle's gaze only lingered on her momentarily before turning back to the king.

"You will not be disappointed," Emperor Shadox promised the king before stepping back, motioning for the boys to step forward and stand by his side. "May I introduce my chosen heir and nephew, Anthony Farotus, the Princep of Akaria."

Anthony bowed to their guests, wearing an expression of quiet confidence as he did so.

"And my nephew, Liam Farotus," Emperor Shadox said with less luster, Liam noticed.

Liam bowed to the guests, forcing his focus off the pulling, anxious feeling in chest that refused to subside. He hoped his shaking hands were not noticeable to anyone else.

The king and queen bowed their heads in their direction politely. The Esterine king then turned slightly and held out a hand toward his daughters.

"May I present, the Princess Katerina of Esterine, my eldest daughter," he bellowed.

Liam watched as the dark-haired princess stepped forward, confirming her as the Princess Katerina. He clenched his hands into fists and his heartbeat increased as she stepped up in front of Anthony, her eyes locked confidently onto his.

She dropped her gaze only to curtsey low to the three of them. She extended her hand out to the emperor first, allowing him a polite kiss, before turning to Anthony. Liam could see Anthony was pleased as he took the hand of his bride-to-be, kissing it gently and giving it a small squeeze. Then it was Liam's turn for a greeting.

She extended her hand out for Liam to take. He tried to steady his own hand before taking hers, but did not succeed. The feeling in his chest was painful now, his vision getting spotty. He clenched his jaw tightly before leaning over to kiss her hand.

He focused his attention on a beautiful opal ring she wore on her middle finger. The ring seemed to have a swirling green glow to it and as he stared at it, the pain in his chest began to lessen. He carefully pressed his lips into her knuckles, briefly grazing the edge of the ring on her petite hand.

A sudden, sharp pain flooded his head. He squeezed his eyes shut, forcing himself to stay standing to keep from making a scene. Hundreds of eyes were watching him right now.

He straightened up slowly, too slowly, as Katerina pulled her hand away from him. His vision began to close in, so Liam closed his eyes. The pain seared through his entire body, starting at his head and flowing down through his limbs, but he needed to stay standing. He worried that the pain would never pass. His chest heaved up and down as he fought to calmly make it through the episode.

"And my youngest daughter, the Princess Anya," Liam heard King Xandrova say.

Liam opened his eyes and his vision cleared just in time for him to see the younger princess come forward to curtsy and greet them. She smiled brightly as she did so, emanating a radiance of joy and easiness.

The second princess stepped back behind her parents, and the pulling sensation in his chest slowly lessened. Only a slight headache remained. He wondered to himself how a simple greeting could have given him such anxiety.

Emperor Shadox spoke again. "Here in Akaria we like to celebrate important events with good food, good drink, good company, and of course good dancing. I hope you are all up for the festivities."

"We are eager to partake in your festivities," King Xandrova nodded, but did not look as eager as he proclaimed. Liam could see why his uncle had been worried about impressing him tonight.

Emperor Shadox smiled and gestured to the dais, inviting them all to take their seats. The orchestra started up a slow song as the Akarian nobles scrambled amongst themselves to find their partners for the first dance of the evening.

Emperor Shadox placed a firm hand on Anthony's shoulder with a nod and a smile and then gave a stern, but pleading look to Liam as he turned to take his throne in the middle of the dais next to the Esterine king and queen. The emperor didn't dance much anymore, and Anthony was the one that everyone would be watching tonight anyway.

Anthony turned to Princess Katerina and bowed. He extended a hand to her, inviting her onto the dance floor with him. She curtsied and accepted his hand, letting him lead her into the center of the room, over a star pattern etched in the marble floor, symbolizing the almighty light god, Lumos. Anthony faced the princess and the two took their position for the first dance as the rest of the floor filled with excited party guests.

The orchestra's song turned to an upbeat waltz and Liam snapped to attention as he frantically looked around for his dance partner, Caroline. He quickly found her in the crowd and took a moment to simply smile warmly at her, noticing again how exquisite she looked tonight. She returned his smile and the two joined the rest of the couples on the dance floor.

Liam and Caroline turned themselves around in a circle before walking to meet each other, as the dance required. Liam shook off the odd episode from before as he walked up to Caroline. He felt his shoulders finally relax when their hands touched. They fell into the proper hold easily and twirled together with the rest of the guests on the floor. He watched the lights dazzle in her eyes and felt very lucky that he was the one she was dancing with.

"You look beautiful tonight," Liam whispered into her ear.

He could see her smile at his comment. "You look very handsome yourself, even if you were a bit late."

Liam groaned. "Yes, well, not terribly late," he said quietly, more to himself. He twirled Caroline under his arm in unison with the rest of the dancers on the floor.

"How do you like the suit?" Liam asked when she stood before him again.

Caroline glanced at his jacket briefly and smiled. "It's perfect. I can't believe you remembered what I said."

"Of course I remembered. I promised you I would wear the perfect red to match you tonight," Liam said, catching the scent of her sweet perfume as she moved around him. "And I promised I would dance with no one else."

Caroline smirked, stepping back in front of him. "I appreciate that," she giggled silently before moving back into the dance hold. "I'm sure it will be hard for you to resist. After all, it only took you a few months to finally ask me."

Liam laughed as he admired the angles of her face and her genuine smile, allowing himself to dream of a future with her when he caught a glimpse of his brother behind her.

"So, what do you think of the new arrivals?" Liam asked, eyeing the princess as Anthony held her and gently spun her around the dance floor.

She shrugged. "They seem quite odd. The way they dress is very … unattractive."

Liam nodded and glanced back to the princess. Her headdress swayed slightly as she moved. Anthony seemed to be guiding her movements, but clearly enjoying the opportunity to do so. The Princess Katerina had just arrived in Akaria earlier that day so it was no surprise she hadn't memorized the proper steps yet.

The searing pain in his head returned as he forced his attention back to Caroline. He winced and sharply turned his head from her, disoriented by the pain. He missed his next turn and felt a light pull on his arm as Caroline tried to subtly remind him. He quickly turned back to Caroline and saw the perturbed look on her face. He gave her an apologetic look, praying quietly to Farran, who was also the god of dance, that he would be able to get through this gracefully.

The headache continued through the rest of the song and the ending finally drew near with a waltzing circle. Liam kept his eyes on his beautiful partner, focusing on anything but the growing pain. With one final spin, Caroline's eyes left his and the pain became too much. He was forced to shut his eyes tightly and grabbed the sides of his head. He tried to get back into the dance, but only managed to bump into someone behind him. He flashed his eyes open, his face already red with embarrassment to see he had run right into Caroline, ripping the bottom of her skirt. She stumbled slightly and turned to face him to end the dance. He looked up at her in panic, but she didn't meet his eyes.

The music stopped and she stepped farther from him to join in the applause. He stared at her, trying to get her to look at him so he could apologize, but she refused to return the glance. She exited the dance floor, smiling at the crowd but without looking back at him, the red in her cheeks apparent.

Liam squeezed his eyes shut in regret and left the dance floor by himself. He hoped he hadn't hurt her, but he knew he had embarrassed her. He scolded himself for letting the pain detour his actions so much. He had been so close to making it through the dance. Sweat dripped down his neck as he stumbled toward one of the side walls, hoping to remove any attention from himself. His mind felt scattered as he gripped the wall, trying to regain his composure.

A waiter came by with small skewered sausages, but Liam waved him away. He winced as the pain continued to cut through his head, unrelenting and sharp. True concern bubbled up within him. What was happening to him? He needed to get some air before he broke out into a full-blown panic attack.

He headed for the open doors in the back of the ballroom that led out to an open balcony. He hoped few people had escaped the party out there just yet and he could be alone.

He stepped out into the fresh night air and breathed a sigh of relief. The pain in his head immediately melted away. He moved to lean on the railing when he saw a bright figure off to one side of the balcony.

"Your Majesty?" Liam asked as he approached the man in golden military attire. "What are you ..." Liam began to ask as the man turned, but he didn't get the chance to finish before his uncle's legs crumpled beneath him, collapsing him to the ground.

"Uncle!" Liam exclaimed and darted over to him.

Liam turned his uncle over onto his back and listened for a heartbeat. Liam felt his own heart racing as he confirmed his uncle was still breathing.

"Emperor ..." Liam begged as he shook the limp figure. Emperor Shadox fluttered his eyes open and he lifted his arm slightly before losing consciousness.

Liam looked at his uncle's arm. A pang of fear shot through him as he noticed something strange poking out from underneath his long sleeve. Liam hesitated, looking around to be sure they were alone on the balcony, before pushing up the sleeve. When he saw what was hiding beneath the sleeve, he quickly lowered it.

Prominent gray lines had sprouted on his uncle's fair skin beneath the golden fabric, jagged and raised. Liam had seen these marks before. He had heard what agonies they caused, but it didn't make any sense for his uncle to have them. Only Isavarian witches were known to have these marks. Fear and confusion rushed through Liam as his mind raced. What secrets was his uncle keeping from him?

Liam made sure his uncle's sleeve was completely covering the marks before he yelled for help. Edward raced out onto the balcony, his eyes wide with fear when he saw the emperor on the ground. He darted back into the ballroom and returned with several Tykerial Guards.

Liam fell back as the Guards pushed him out of the way to lift the emperor off the ground. Liam watched as they carried his uncle way. He hadn't realized he was holding his breath until Edward turned to him.

"I will handle this. Speak to no one about what you saw," Edward said with furious eyes.

3

Katerina's eyes ached with fatigue as she was escorted through the lavish palace corridors to her rooms by a group of Tykerial Guards. Her father had insisted they accompany her back to her rooms on her first night in Akaria. She stifled a yawn as she thought about the respite of the bed that awaited her.

The Akarian maids assigned to her upon her arrival hadn't attended the festivities tonight and she was glad they would have everything waiting and ready for her when she opened the door. Sadness gripped her heart when she realized she wouldn't be seeing familiar faces behind that door tonight. Her father had refused to let her bring her own ladies from Esterine. She would have to navigate this new country without her only friends.

Tonight was just the beginning of the new faces, new customs, and new pressures to impress. She had always learned new languages and historical facts quickly, but this was an entire life she would have to learn. And she would have to do it all without a single friend or someone she could trust. Her shoulders sagged as her entire body felt the weight of it all.

The guards stopped in front of the double doors that led into Katerina's private chambers. Katerina dismissed her escorts with a nod and reached for the doorknob. She pushed open the door and felt the tension melt off her body as she walked into the room. She was pleased to find that indeed her maids were waiting to help her get ready for bed immediately. They looked tired themselves, still in the same gray uniforms and white aprons from earlier.

Madeline, the head of her new maids, looked especially tired with her red-brown hair frizzing out from beneath her white ruffled bonnet. She greeted Katerina with a weary smile and Katerina decided she would let her disheveled appearance slide for tonight. Katerina sat down on the seat in front of the mirrored vanity and removed her own earrings. Madeline ordered some of the other maids to get the bath ready, to turn down sheets and close the windows. Then Madeline and another maid, whose name escaped Katerina, began unpinning the large headdress from Katerina's hair. Katerina watched as they worked, their hands moving quickly but precisely. She supposed she would probably only wear a headdress like this a few more times in her life.

"Did you enjoy the party?" Madeline asked, with a polite, but forced smile.

"Yes, it was a nice celebration," Katerina responded primly with an accent. She appreciated Madeline's effort to build rapport, but she hoped she wouldn't try too hard tonight.

"That's good, Your Majesty," Madeline said. She and the other maid lifted the headdress off her head and took the braid out of her hair to comb it.

Katerina's eyes watered and her chest tightened. It had been years since anyone besides Katya or Nadia combed out her hair. Katerina waved the girls off and instead directed them to help her remove her tall boots. She then stood for Madeline to begin unbuttoning the back of her dress. She shrugged off the ornate dress and the maids pulled it off her body carefully. Katerina stood in a thin slip when she felt Madeline reach for the clasp of the necklace she had worn underneath the dress.

Katerina grabbed at the back of the necklace. "This always stays on," she said as kindly as she could manage.

Madeline only nodded and turned away from her. Katerina looked down at the aquamarine stone set inside a cage of twisting silver. Given to her by her father when she turned sixteen, this necklace had belonged to her real mother. She hadn't taken it off since.

An aching pain rose in one of her shoulders and she felt the nausea start to set in.

"That will be all for tonight ladies," Katerina said to her maids as she hurried behind the dressing screen.

"Very well, Your Highness. The bath is drawn and your fresh towel is on the rack," Madeline said.

Katerina hunched over in pain as she listened for the maids to exit her private rooms. As soon as she heard the door shut and latch, she grabbed the bin and heaved into it. After nearly emptying her stomach of the dinner she had eaten earlier, she sat back on the ground and slid her slip off her right shoulder to glance down at it.

Black veiny lines radiated from a circular dark patch of skin over her heart. The lines had reached across her chest now, scarring her with a trail of gray skin beneath the lines. The black lines were beginning to crack, revealing a faint blue glow. The damning evidence.

The Obsidian Streaks.

Katerina sighed as she remembered the first time she saw signs of the dark circle over her heart. She hadn't wanted to tell anyone. She was so afraid of what it meant. She knew the magic she held within, the magic she couldn't seem to control, would only continue to make them worse. Of course, she wasn't able to keep the marks a secret for long.

He had promised to help her and it was such a relief to hear someone say that. But he was gone now and she needed to find help here. She needed to keep her magic under control to keep the lines from spreading.

Most importantly, she had to keep this curse from her father. She knew her father would see her as nothing but an affront to God if he knew what she was. If he knew that she held the power of the Well within her, he would undoubtedly treat her as he treated all the other witches in Esterine—she would be imprisoned at best or executed at worst. It wouldn't matter that she was his daughter. His belief that the witches should no longer exist was too strong.

Katerina contemplated not bathing and just getting straight into bed, but she knew she couldn't do that. She would feel much better after a nice bath. Katerina shrugged off her slip before stepping into the warm water of the bath. The water had cooled just enough and she was able to sink down into the warm water in one motion. She laid her head back on the rim of the tub and took a deep breath in and out. She let her body float in the water, urging herself to forget the Streaks, the new people, the pressures of the coming days, for just a few minutes. She imagined the lines on her shoulder disappearing underneath the water, making her whole and strong again as she sank herself deeper and deeper into the bath.

Suddenly, the door to her outer chamber burst open and she heard some-one run in. Her stomach dropped and she felt a deep rush of dread and sudden anxiety. She quickly reached for the towel rack next to the bath, but her magic decided to react with her. A gust of wind, brief but powerful, flew through the room knocking the towel rack out of her reach. She cursed to herself, scrambling to reach for the towel on the ground now. She couldn't let anyone see her shoulder. It would be incriminating evidence of what she was and what she was cursed with.

"Kat? Kat where are you?" a familiar voice called.

"Anya," Katerina said with a heavy sigh, and through gritted teeth called out, "I'll be out in a minute."

"Oh I'm sorry, I didn't mean to disturb you! I didn't think you'd be getting ready for bed already."

"Why would I not be getting ready for bed at one in the morning?" Katerina muttered to herself as she stood up from the warm water and leaned over the edge to grab the towel. "I'll be out in a minute."

Katerina dried herself off quickly and moved behind the dressing screen. She took the nightgown hanging there and pulled it over her head. She gathered her hair in a wet heap over her shoulder as she walked into the bedroom apprehensively. Anya was leaning out of the window that Katerina was sure her maids had just closed. Anya was still in her party attire minus her small headdress, though it appeared she had rolled up the bottom of her dress and had it tied to just above her knees. Katerina rolled her eyes and sat on the bed with a huff, grabbing a pillow to hold in front of her in the now chilly room. Anya turned to her with a glowing smile.

"Tonight was amazing, wasn't it?" Anya asked, taking a seat next to her sister on the bed. "The dresses they wear here are quite interesting, don't you think? I think they look awfully heavy, but so beautiful. Do you think you'll have to wear one for your wedding?" Anya looked at Katerina with big blue eyes.

Katerina nodded, squeezing the pillow in front of her. "Yes, well I would imagine so," she responded tersely.

Katerina wasn't sure why Anya was in her room right now. The two of them hadn't been close in years, and had drifted even further apart since Anya's incident with the Lodarine prince that had ultimately landed them all here. The immaturity of her younger sister was often too much for Katerina to deal with. Anya was sixteen after all, she should be able to behave by now. They had gotten along when they were younger, but so many things had changed since then. Katerina had changed and it was time Anya did too.

"Do you think Princep Anthony will take you around the city a bit tomorrow?" Anya asked, looking at her sister with hungry eyes.

So that's what she wants, Katerina thought. "Something tells me Princep Anthony will be quite busy with his own plans tomorrow."

"What do you mean? Don't you think he's great? And handsome?" Anya said, crossing her legs underneath herself on the bed.

Katerina felt her annoyance growing with her settling in. "He's very great and handsome. And he knows he's very great and handsome. However, he's not the type of man who's going to make time to take two foreign princesses around in a carriage."

"I think he would! I don't think you give him enough credit. You never trust anyone anymore, but I think you can trust him. He has such nice eyes," Anya said, swooning at the thought.

And you trust people way too easily, Katerina thought to herself.

"Nice eyes. Sure," Katerina agreed begrudgingly, saying anything to get her sister out of her room.

"What happened with the emperor tonight, do you know?" Anya asked, cocking her head to one side.

Katerina looked away from Anya, trying to contain the bile she felt rising up through her throat. "They said an old battle injury flared up on him or something, I don't know. But it's really none of our business why he had to leave so suddenly," she said rather curtly.

"Well, I was only asking because it seemed quite mysterious …"

Katerina couldn't hold her anger in any longer as her sister continued to prattle on. She was so tired and Anya's words only continued to remind her of how Anya's frivolity had ruined her life. Multiple times. She felt a heat rise in her chest and then a sudden discharge of energy. The candle sitting on the bedside table immediately flared up into a tall column of fire. Katerina's eyes widened in surprise as she stared at it, alerting Anya to something amiss. Anya snapped her head toward the candle just as the flame slowly came back down to a normal height.

"What was that?" Anya exclaimed as she stood up quickly, turning to look at the candle.

"What?" Katerina asked naively.

"You didn't see that?" Anya asked, pointing at the now perfectly ordinary candle.

Katerina shrugged and forced a yawn, though she was shaking with nerves. "See what?"

"The candle, it just …" Anya said looking back at Katerina. Then she shut her eyes and laughed. "Never mind I guess I just … maybe I'm just tired."

"It has been a very long day, with all the events from the arrival, to the lessons, and the party. We should probably be off to sleep. Tomorrow is going to be another busy day," Katerina said, standing up to usher her sister out of her bedroom.

Anya wrinkled her forehead and nodded. She looked back at the candle once more, eyeing it carefully and then shaking her head. Katerina walked over to the door and was relieved when Anya followed her.

"Well, I suppose I will go then. Goodnight," Anya said, walking through the door and glancing back.

Katerina knew her sister wanted to be invited to stay, but she just couldn't fake it with her tonight.

"Goodnight," Katerina said softly and closed the door behind her sister.

Katerina's heart clenched in her chest as the sad look in her sister's eyes replayed in her head. Their time together was quite limited now. Katerina squeezed her eyes shut and whimpered before walking slowly back into her bedroom. Right now the most important thing was ensuring the success of this marriage agreement. Esterine needed a favorable deal from the Akarians and she would not let anything stand in the way of that, not even Anya. She couldn't risk telling her sister her secret and having her spill it to their father like she had in the past. She would find someone here to help her control the magic. They didn't hate the witches here like they did in Esterine, and she should be able to find someone. She couldn't have any more mishaps like what just happened with the candle.

Katerina crawled into bed and sank down underneath the covers. She willed her body to relax as her mind wandered to all those times she had better control over the magic. She smiled as she remembered the way his eyes had lit up when she lit that first candle for them. The fun they used to have in the mists she would create for them to hide in and run through. Mikhal hadn't minded. In fact, she felt it drew him closer to her. They had shared so many secrets, the two of them. She remembered his arms around her, the touch of his lips, the way he held her in those stolen moments at night.

Katerina shook her head.

No, I can't think about that anymore, she told herself. *Those days are over.*

She turned over and forced her thoughts to Anthony and her future as an Akarian empress.

4

Liam was back in the golden ballroom. Everything seemed brighter, with more yellow and white in the decorations than he had remembered. The room was full of guests and Liam was up on the dais, dressed in the green and gold armor of a Tykerial Guard. He felt a surge of pride as he looked over to the man who stood beside him. Liam's heart swelled when he saw it was his father next to him, beaming at him with a pleased smile. They both turned to the dance floor to see Anthony twirling around with a blonde girl in a silver dress that Liam didn't recognize. Everyone in the crowd smiled with approval and Liam found himself automatically doing the same. Everything seemed right with the world in that moment.

Trumpets sounded and the figures of Anthony and his partner faded away. A staircase was suddenly visible in front of Liam, ending in the middle of the open floor. Gracefully, Caroline glided down the stairs in a magnificent maroon gown. Her face was glowing and her eyes were set on Liam.

Liam instinctively moved forward to stand at the bottom of the stairs with an outstretched arm. She placed her hand in his and he noticed an opal ring on one of her fingers. The milky ring with green swirls seemed familiar to him, she must have worn it before. He curled his fingers around hers and led her out into the middle of the now busy dance floor. Without waiting for a proper start, Liam started gliding across the floor with Caroline in his arms.

Then a strange noise blared through the air. Everyone stopped and Liam looked up onto the dais. Instead of seeing his father there like before, he saw a frightening scene of large, winged men bursting through the glass windows. Aurens.

They yelled as they rushed into the room, quickly overtaking everyone present. Liam looked around frantically but he couldn't find his father, his uncle, or his brother anywhere. He was then pushed forcefully to the ground and his hands were tied behind him. His vision went black.

When he awoke, he found his wrists and ankles chained to a cold stone wall. He looked at his bonds curiously and pulled against them. To his surprise, they immediately fell away. He shook off the bonds and then pushed with all his might against the barred dungeon door. It bent away from its frame and gave in to his pushes. Liam was free, but he had to find his family. Where did the Aurens take them?

A dark corridor stretched out in front of him and he stepped through the darkness. Liam walked slowly until he finally came upon a blue door with a teardrop ornament hanging on it. He turned the knob and pushed the door open.

He peered into the room and widened his eyes in surprise when he saw what was inside. Books, swords, tea pots, different colored rocks, and shields all floated in a sea of pure blackness in front of him. He stepped forward into the room to investigate further and realized too late that there was no floor in this void of a room. He began to fall, but a hand reached out and grabbed him.

An old man, unfamiliar to Liam, lifted him back into the room. The room with the floating items was gone now and instead he sat on the floor of a room lined with bookshelves. He turned to thank the man who had saved him, but he couldn't see anyone in the room with him anymore.

Someone was calling his name now. It was a whisper, but Liam could still hear it.

"Help me … Liam …" a woman's voice whispered.

He looked around but couldn't see anyone. His heart raced and his anxiety rose. Someone needed help. Was it Caroline? Maybe it was his mother. Could he do something to help her?

Liam stood up quickly and grabbed the handle on the only door in the room. The door melted away like liquid in front of him and he found himself outside, wind blowing fiercely around him.

"Liam, please …" the whispering continued in his head.

There was a weeping sound behind him and Liam spun around to see who was crying, only to find himself in a field on top of a hill. The sky was dark and gray, as if a storm were coming in. The dark gray clouds, heavy with water, rolled overhead unnaturally quickly. There was a strike of lightning in front of him and then Liam saw her.

A woman stood on top of the next hill. He saw the outline of a cape waving behind her in the strong winds. Liam ran to her as fast as he could, reaching out to the woman.

"I'm coming!" he shouted as he ran. It felt like he was running slowly, though he was giving it all he had as the distance seemed to stay the same between them. His feet slipped on the wet, blue-green ground and he gradually, clumsily made his way up the hill.

He finally got to the top and could see her clearly. She had her back to him but he could see her gray dress billowing furiously and her fiery red hair blowing wildly in the wind.

"I'm here," Liam said with an outstretched hand. "I'm here. You don't need to …" he began as the woman turned to face him. Her red hair whipped around her face as she snapped her eyes open, revealing glowing white eyes, piercing through Liam and causing him to stumble backward.

Liam jolted awake with a sudden flinch of his body. He was drenched in sweat and his heart was pounding against his chest. He let out a long exhale and unclenched the blankets in his hands as he realized it was just a dream. He let his eyes stay shut for a moment longer, hoping sleep would take him again. His body begged for more rest as his heart rate slowed back down.

He had never had a dream like that before, at least not that he could remember. It had seemed so real and he still felt scared. And that girl with the red hair—he felt like he knew her somehow, or maybe he used to know her but he had somehow forgotten about her. Was she supposed to be his mother? He couldn't remember much of her face besides her white glowing eyes.

He laid there for another few moments before giving up on sleep and reaching out to grab his watch off his nightstand—but there was nothing there. He peeked his eyes open slowly and realized he was not in his own bedroom.

Then he remembered the horrifying truth: his uncle had collapsed last night and had to be carried away by Tykerial Guards in the middle of the Xandrovas's Welcome Ball.

Liam shot up and awkwardly slipped off the tiny couch he had occupied overnight in his uncle's sitting room. He found himself slightly tangled in the small throw blanket he slept under last night and knew it was no wonder he hadn't slept well. He stood up when a severe, sharp pain seared through his head like it had the night before and the world shifted beneath him. He held on to the plush cushions as he pulled himself back onto the couch. His vision blurred and was blacking out in the corners as he moved.

"Whoa there," Liam heard Anthony's voice chime out from somewhere nearby. "Take it easy, my poor heart can't take any more family members going down this morning."

Liam looked up at his brother's voice and waited as the room slowly came back into focus again. Anthony was already dressed in a crisp dark gray suit and appeared to be as pristine as always. Liam looked down at himself and saw he was still wearing the long button-up shirt and his white dress slacks from the night before. The shirt was half untucked and incredibly wrinkled, causing Liam to groan. His vest, tie, socks, and suit jacket lay on the floor next to him in a pile on top of his shoes.

"Sorry. I'm fine, I just stood up too fast," Liam explained, bringing his hands to his head, hoping to ease the pain still gathering there. The solace of the warm couch and blanket still called to his senses.

"Well, you look positively ragged," Anthony said with a chuckle as he threw the suit jacket over to Liam.

Liam shook his head, slowly putting one arm through the jacket sleeve and then the other. "It was a long night on this tiny couch," Liam explained, trying to make himself more presentable. He hated being sloppy.

"I'm sure it was. I bet now you wish you had your own quarters here in the palace," Anthony paused before adding, "and you know we would have such fun together." Anthony smiled mischievously at his brother.

Liam simply shrugged and put on his shoes. They did have fun, but they also got into a lot of trouble as Liam recalled. He didn't have the time or patience for such things anymore.

"Some fun would do you some good, you know. You seem so tense lately," Anthony said as he sat down next to Liam on the couch.

"Have you seen him since last night?" Liam asked, changing the subject and turning to look at his brother.

Anthony shook his head and combed his dark hair back with his hand. "No. He's still sleeping. I've been waiting for nearly an hour for an update from the physicians. They should be out soon."

"An hour?" Liam asked, fumbling to put his watch back on his wrist.

Anthony nodded and looked over to the closed doors of their uncle's private closet.

"Where is Martin?" Liam asked, looking around for their uncle's chief butler when the doors to the private closet slowly opened.

Anthony jumped off the couch and strode over to the man who emerged—and it was just the man they were looking for—Martin.

"So, how is he this morning?" Anthony asked the tired-looking old man, craning his head to get even a glimpse of his uncle through the crack in the door as it closed.

The butler bowed toward Anthony. "Emperor Shadox is in much need of some rest this morning."

"What is it?" Liam jumped in to ask, concern bubbling up in his chest. If he was honest with himself, he had hoped last night was some fluke and that his uncle would be miraculously better this morning. There was no way what he had seen—the dark lines stretching down his uncle's arm—could be what he thought they were. His uncle couldn't possibly have the horrific, deadly disease of the witches. The two boys stared at the butler, waiting for an answer.

Martin sighed. "It does appear that the emperor has a condition that has progressed to a very serious point. We believe he has contracted …" he hesitated to continue, "The Obsidian Streaks," he finally confirmed, looking up at the boys with worried eyes.

Liam's heart dropped into his feet. So it was true. But how could it be? The disease only infected Isavarian witches. Though these witches were rare in Akaria, Liam knew about the horrible curse they carried. They migrated from their homeland of Isavaria over a thousand years ago, when their power source, the Well, dried up. They came in search of power and hope, but instead, they found themselves entangled in war and disease. His uncle wasn't an Isavarian witch … was he?

And even worse than how he might have contracted the disease, was the fact it was incurable. It meant that it was the end. It meant, it meant … Liam couldn't even fathom what it all meant.

"That doesn't make any sense …" Anthony said incredulously. "Are you sure?"

Martin stood straighter and looked up at the ceiling. "The physicians say his markings are different in color than the other cases they have seen, but he appears to have the fatigue, the weakness, the nausea, the vomiting, the chills, the shakes …"

Martin was only halfway through his rough explanation when Anthony had apparently had enough. Without looking at the butler or waiting to be properly brought in, Anthony pushed past the man and crashed through the private closet doors.

25

Liam sighed and shook his head. Anthony never was one to follow rules.

Martin nodded curtly in frustration before lazily gesturing for Liam to go ahead into the room. Liam walked through the private closet and into his uncle's bedchamber on the other side of the room. When he entered the bedroom, he saw his uncle slowly swinging his legs over the edge of his large bed. A dark red canopy hung over the bed, shadowing his uncle's face at first. Physicians surrounded him, trying to get him to lay back down, but ceased their efforts when they saw the boys enter.

Liam immediately brought his eyes to his uncle's arms, but they were wrapped carefully with thin cloths. The emperor looked smaller than Liam had ever seen him look before. He looked so fragile and weak as he tried to move away from the doctors.

"Uncle Philip?" Anthony questioned softly as he walked slowly over to the bed.

Emperor Shadox turned his tousled blonde head toward Anthony as he approached, squinting his eyes to help them focus in the dimly lit room. Liam stepped forward with apprehension. It was very intimate for them to be in their uncle's bedchamber and it didn't feel proper. He hoped their uncle would not be angry with them for barging in unannounced.

The emperor grunted and put weight on one of his feet. Anthony rushed forward to assist him, grabbing him underneath his arm. Liam watched with discomfort, expecting their uncle to throw Anthony's hand off him. It was really Martin's job to help him out of bed, but the emperor allowed the assistance to continue.

"Leave us," the emperor said to the doctors gawking behind him. His voice was weak and raspy. Liam didn't like the sound of it.

The doctors quickly shuffled out of the room, shutting the doors behind them.

Emperor Shadox shrugged Anthony's hand away and shook his head. Anthony reluctantly let go, allowing him to stand on his own. The emperor shuffled slowly over to a big armchair sitting over on the other side of the room as Liam and Anthony watched with concern.

Anthony hesitated and looked over at Liam, his eyes swirling with a fear that Liam had never seen in them before.

"They are saying you may have contracted the Obsidian Streaks, but I can't see how that's possible," Anthony said, turning his head back to their uncle.

Emperor Shadox dropped himself clumsily into his chair, letting out a groan as his body slammed against the fabric.

"That makes absolutely no sense. The quacks …" their uncle replied with a clear ring of anger in his voice. "I can tell you I am no Isavarian witch. If I were, it would have made ruling this kingdom and fighting in all the wars a lot easier …" he trailed off with a sigh before pointing back over to his bedside table. "The pipe," he commanded.

Liam was suddenly unfrozen and he rushed over to pick up the pipe on his uncle's bedside table to bring it over to him.

"The lines," Liam said in a shaky voice as he handed the item to his uncle. "They said they are a different color?"

His uncle ignored his question and took the pipe from Liam's hand. He lit the end of it and took a big puff from it before responding. "That is what they are saying," he said, not looking back up at his nephews.

"So this is something different then?" Anthony asked.

Emperor Shadox sighed and put his head back against his chair. He looked up at the boys with tired but intense eyes.

"My Streaks appear to be gray in color, while the witches have darker Streaks. They turn a nasty black color before they start to crack and show the blue glow of the power that resides within their bodies. I have a lot of the same symptoms so they think I must have the same disease, though they say it is a mystery as to how it will progress in someone without the power of the Well." He put his pipe to his lips again and looked away from them out of the window.

Liam looked over to Anthony, waiting for him to say or do something. What could they do? As far as Liam knew, this disease had never touched non-magical humans before.

Emperor Shadox exhaled a puff of smoke and reluctantly looked back toward the boys. "I need you both to continue with things as usual," he said as sternly as his weak voice would let him.

Liam squirmed a little at the thought. Continuing through his day as if nothing were wrong seemed a tall task.

"How can you expect us to do that? Shouldn't we …" Anthony complained, but their uncle held up a hand to silence him.

"Anthony, you will continue with your tutors. Edward will handle the bulk of the negotiations with the Esterine king, but you need to be by his side now. We need to show the king we are committed," he said as he looked at Anthony seriously.

"The negotiations? But I ..." Anthony whined.

"You will take the lead on all negotiations soon anyway. This is a perfect opportunity for you to get some real experience. The Esterine king is eager to return to Isavaria with the troops we've promised to help him fight his neighboring country, and it is important that we get the necessary amount of granite from the Esterine king in a swift and efficient manner. We cannot afford to wait much longer to build this wall in the north. We must protect our boundaries and I don't want to keep wasting our resources constantly fighting off the giants. And there's more and more reports of packs of the two-headed wolves ..." their uncle paused to cough. It was a low, deep cough that unsettled Liam. Emperor Shadox swallowed hard and looked back up to Anthony.

"The Esterine king cannot know about my Obsidian Streaks. He despises witches, as you know, and we can't risk him getting suspicious and pulling out of the deal. He can only know that I am indisposed by an old injury for a time."

Anthony grimaced, but nodded. Liam knew his brother would not like being shut up in a council room all day. Though it was probably time he got used to it.

"And you," their uncle said, looking over to Liam. "You will continue with your training as usual. The Tykerial Guard exam is coming up in less than a month. You will not disappoint me this time."

Liam nodded. This order was no surprise to him. If his uncle wanted things to go back to normal, he would obey his wishes.

"But what about you?" Anthony asked. "What are we going to do to make sure you get better? This disease ... it has no cure."

Emperor Shadox looked away from his nephews again and took a deep, ragged inhale. "I will take a few days to gather some strength back. I feel I can manage a recovery well before a wedding date is set."

Liam looked into his uncle's eyes. There was determination in them, but also a deep tiredness. Liam knew his uncle would push with all his strength to fight this disease.

"I have the best physicians in the land treating me and scholars looking into how this disease could have been contracted. Isavarian witches with this disease live many years after contracting it. It may not have a cure, but we have some time to figure that out," the emperor looked back to the boys and gave them a slight smile.

"Now, go. Leave me to rest. Have Martin send for Edward as you leave," their uncle said with the flick of his hand in the direction of the door.

Liam and Anthony nodded and bowed before turning to leave. Liam felt his heart drop as he walked away from his uncle. He looked back at the man in the chair before he exited the room. His uncle had always been such a rock, such a sturdy and important part of Liam's life. He had ruled over this massive country for longer than Liam could remember. He downed rebellions, took care of the poor, won battles, passed important laws, expanded the empire more than anyone else, and had kept his country safe in times of war. Liam was terrified to think of what this world would be like without him.

5

Katerina pushed the blueberries around on her plate, stifling a yawn. Staring down at her food, the familiar dull ache in her shoulder persisted. She longed for the freedom to slump in her chair from the pain. What a relief it would be to not have to hide her pain anymore. A polite murmur of conversation took place around her at the long dining table where she sat with her family. It was odd for them to all be together for breakfast. They dined together for dinner in Esterine when she and Anya were brought to the palace for holidays, but never in the morning. It had been more than two years since they'd dined together at all. Two years since the night the Aurens came.

Katerina squirmed slightly in her chair, shaking off the memory and longing to stretch her neck from side to side and to yawn freely. Instead she sat with her back straight, respectfully taking each bite of food. Servants hovered around her, asking if she wanted anything more or anything different. Katerina was irritated and exhausted by all the attention and interaction already. She felt the skin on her face sag as she wished she could be permitted to take her breakfast in private, like she always did at home. She knew this change was coming, but it was more difficult this morning than she had been expecting. At least her father had insisted they still wear the traditional clothing of Esterine. It was a small comfort, but at least she would have one thing she was familiar with.

"Anya, dear, take that flower out of your hair while we're eating," Queen Eva said admonishingly.

Katerina looked over to watch her sister remove the white flower she had gotten from God only knew where.

"I suppose the marriage agreement negotiations will proceed today as planned?" Eva asked, looking over to the king.

"Yes, they will," the gruff voice of Katerina's father answered, his face scrunching into a scowl.

King Nikita Xandrova had always been a large and intimidating man to Katerina. With his broad chest and full gray beard, he gave off a clear impression of being dangerously strict in his ways. He sat now with stern eyes, cutting the meat he must have insisted be prepared for him—for Katerina had learned that they didn't usually serve meat in the mornings here.

"We will continue the negotiations and get this marriage agreement signed swiftly. The emperor has assured me that his advisors and heir will be able to handle the meetings while his injury heals. It is not ideal, but we don't have any time to waste."

Eva nodded. "Indeed. Perhaps dealing with the advisors will be better for us. I know a few of them share our beliefs on certain important matters."

King Nikita huffed. "Yes. There are few who see the true way of the Light. And with the emperor's failing health, Katerina may even be empress of this wretched land sooner than we had hoped," he said, turning his eyes on Katerina.

Katerina kept a pleasant smile on her face as she felt the eyes of her stepmother and sister turn to her.

"You will show these people how to truly practice The Way of the Light. You will be their pinnacle, their role model, and their empress. I expect you to take charge of drawing out and ridding this kingdom of the few witches who still survive here," her father said, almost spitting at the mention of the witches.

He wants to rid of world of me. The thought invaded Katerina's head.

"Yes, I'm sure Katerina will make us very proud here. She always has done everything we expect from her," Eva said sweetly, sipping her hot tea delicately.

Even though Eva wasn't Katerina's real mother, she was the only mother Katerina had ever known. She was a kind mother figure to her, though a little distant. Katerina knew that a lot of expectations were put on Eva when she took her mother's throne and tried to never hold that against her. Eva had always been compassionate toward Katerina and supported her even in her most rebellious hours.

"The Obsidian Streaks are prevalent among the witches in Akaria as well. They will be easy to spot," Eva said almost nonchalantly.

Katerina's shoulder burned. She dared to glance at her father and saw his eyes flash with hatred and anger. No matter how many times she saw those eyes, they would always make her shrink into herself.

"The numbers may be decreasing, but it's still an unnatural existence," Nikita continued fervently. "We all know it's against God's will that they continue to practice the magic that He has long removed from this world. It was clear when the Well ran dry that the Age of the Well was over and we humans no longer deserved access to that magic as we entered into the Age of Faith where we now must have reliance on God. And yet they still practice, they continue to feed their tainted blood to their infants, hoping that the ritual takes hold."

Katerina had heard this rant over and over again throughout her life, but it still made her stomach turn with fear. It was one of her father's greatest passions—to rid the world of the heretical witches, cleansing the world of magic, and making way for the next age, The Age of Awakening, in which new gifts would descend upon the people, straight from God once again. But many believed that could not happen with the magic from the Well still being pursued and used.

"This disease they carry is clearly God's way of plaguing them for their insolence. The filthy, faithless scum," he slammed a fist on the table before he continued. "When Katerina is the Empress of Akaria, she will deal with the witches much more efficiently than Emperor Shadox has. Together we will get closer to ridding the world of magic."

Katerina could feel her father's eyes on her as her heart beat quickly in her chest. She prayed her father couldn't see right through her, right through to the scar forming across her chest, cracking and revealing what she was really was. Chills ran down her arms as she turned her head toward him bravely and watched as he straightened his sleeves, recovering from his tirade. She wanted to assure him of her commitment, but she knew she had better stay silent.

"The emperor is most unequipped to handle the heathens here," the king said with a sigh. "That is why it is so important for Katerina to be strong in The Way of the Light."

Katerina nodded once toward her father. She felt ashamed and unworthy when her father spoke like this. She hadn't asked to be a witch, someone must have performed the ritual on her when she was a baby. She had survived it and her father had apparently no idea it had occurred. The tea in her cup steamed more than usual. She shook herself from her melancholy at the sight, dispersing the steam quickly with her hand.

"I heard the emperor even allows one of the witches to live on his palace grounds," Eva said quietly shaking her head.

Katerina's eyes flashed with interest at this piece of information. *A witch, living on palace grounds?* she thought to herself. That could be her answer.

Nikita sighed. "It's worse than I thought over here. The witch must be removed if they expect an Esterine Princess to reside here. There's a good deal to discuss with these Akarians still and this will need to be added to that list. I have at least been assured that we will get the troops we requested for our war back in Isavaria. Enough to crush our Lodarine neighbors easily."

Katerina saw her sister shift in her seat and look down at the mention of their Lodarine rivals.

As she should, Katerina thought with annoyance.

Eva nodded and turned back to her tea. "Yes, that is very good. When do you expect we will have a wedding date?"

Nikita smiled. "It is my hope we'll be celebrating the wedding feast in just a few weeks, after the heathen celebration they have coming up. The emperor won't consider a wedding until after that, which is, I suppose, the one concession I will have to make."

"An Akarian holiday? How exciting!" Anya said, clapping her hands together. She was clearly over any regret the subject of the Lodarinians.

Katerina wanted to roll her eyes or sigh, but instead she said, "I suppose they will have some gaudy display for this festivity," hoping to please her father with such a comment.

"Yes, it will most likely be a lavish occasion. Crealum is their most celebrated holiday, I believe," Eva said sweetly. "You will both need to be properly prepared and dressed," she said, looking over to the girls.

"A new dress?"

"Of course."

Katerina and Anya spoke at the same time, with clearly different sentiments. Katerina controlled her eyes from rolling again and forced a smile to cover her annoyance. It was obvious they were only half related sometimes.

"Yes of course dear," Eva said with a smile to Anya before turning to Katerina. "We may not celebrate in Esterine quite as extravagantly, but they will no doubt be expecting their new Princepa to participate properly. It will likely be the first time you are presented formally as the Princepa. It will be very important for you to make a good impression on the people at this event. I'm sure you know there are some who are not so pleased with the arrangement the emperor has made. And even though we all know their so-called "gods" are really just the true God at work, we must do our best to show humility and acceptance at this event. You two will need new Akarian-style dresses, dance lessons, etiquette lessons, and a brief history lesson on why they observe this day the way they do," Eva said, turning to look toward her husband.

Nikita's face darkened. "I don't know about …" he started to say, but Eva placed a gentle hand on her husband's arm and looked him in the eye.

"We discussed this dear, and you decided the history lessons and the dresses would be an important part of Katerina's transition," she said softly, stroking his arm.

"It sounds like such a glorious time!" Anya interrupted with an excited smile and dreamy eyes. "Well, not so much the lessons, I suppose."

Her father chuckled once from the head of the table. "Anya, you're my little speck of light, aren't you?"

Katerina's stomach turned and she felt jealousy rise quickly within her. She was always the one with all the responsibility and pressure. She would excel in the lessons and the etiquette training, while her sister received praise in her frivolity and childishness. Katerina still blamed Anya for what happened with Mikhal and it was Anya's fault they were even in this war with Lodarine, and Katerina was being married off to the highest bidder to fix her mess.

"They will have their new dresses, of course," Nikita relented.

Eva smiled brightly and took her hand off Nikita's arm. "Oh, and didn't you have some other news to tell the girls this morning, dear?"

Nikita looked dazed for a moment and then shook his head to bring his focus back to reality.

"Other news?" he asked, looking confused. Eva nodded at him and he seemed to remember. "Ah yes, that."

Nikita put down his utensils, took his napkin from his lap and set it on the table. He stood up from the table, signaling for everyone else to stand with him.

Katerina was glad breakfast was cut short. Nikita led his family into the room next to their private dining room. Tykerial Guards stood at either end of the room next to each set of doors.

"I've made some arrangements with Emperor Shadox to make sure you girls are looked after and protected properly while you are here."

Arrangements? What could he have done? Katerina wondered with growing suspicion.

"Along with the maids you received upon arrival, you have both been appointed personal guards. Special guards. Guards I know I can trust," he flicked his hand toward the Tykerial Guards standing next to the far set of doors. They each grabbed a hold of a handle and pulled the doors open.

Katerina lifted her eyes to see the new guards coming in through the door and she sucked in a surprised breath.

Taller and more muscular than all the other guards, with horns protruding out of their black hair, two dark figures came through the doorway. Tykens. Non-human beings with a propensity for strength. Their kind was one of the four ancient races that the Akarians called the Lumenaros—believing they were each created by one of their Light Gods. Katerina knew, however, they were all created by the one, true God. These Tykens would indeed be quite reliable guardsmen. They were known to despise humans with magic.

Katerina eyed the Tyken who came to stand in front of her. He stood tall with one hand on a sword that was hanging from his belt. His chest was bare with just straps across it, holding a long sword on his back. His skin was dark like tree bark and tattooed with white designs that made him look primal and dangerous.

Her father turned to her first. "Katerina, this is Kona. He is a high Tyken Protector here in Akaria. The emperor has them work alongside his Tykerial Guardsman to protect the capital city in various ways. He will be tasked solely with your constant safety until further notice. He will guard your rooms and escort you to certain important events. He will have eyes on you at all times," King Nikita explained with a satisfied smile.

Katerina looked the Tyken in the face. His dark brown eyes didn't meet hers as he sank to the ground in a kneel. Even while kneeling he was almost just as tall as the human Tykerial Guards. She took a small breath and then smiled in acceptance.

She listened to her father introduce the next guard to her sister. Anya looked much more dismayed at the appointment. Katerina smiled slightly to herself. At least Anya wouldn't be able to run around and do anything stupid now.

Katerina's new guard would make things harder for her, but perhaps she could find a way to use this new acquaintance to her advantage. She was taught the Tyken language years ago as a child when her father brought a group of them to court, hoping to create an alliance with them against the witches. She knew the language well still and she knew what they considered important. Her first mission in Akaria would be to befriend this Tyken. She would need to either win him over or figure out his weaknesses if she was ever going to be able to find the witch she needed to help her control her powers.

6

Liam inhaled the crisp morning air, letting it fill his lungs completely. He had been anxious to start the day this morning and had gotten up with the sun to start training. He hadn't been able to complete his usual morning routine since the night the Xandrova's arrived, and his muscles were ready for action again. He had returned to the city manor that he called home these days briefly to grab a few things and to inform the head housekeeper of his prolonged absence. He had agreed to Anthony's offer to stay in the palace temporarily while their uncle was sick. Staying in the palace allowed Liam more time for his training as well as a close proximity if anything happened to the emperor, but he also felt more on display.

No one was around besides the groundskeeper when he arrived at the palace training grounds. Liam looked up at the rising sun and was pleased to have a run in solitude before the Tykerial Guards arrived for morning training.

He stretched briefly before taking his hour-long run. He thought through the list he had made of the things he needed to work on today. There was still so much he needed to improve on before the exam in a couple of weeks.

The exam would be broken into three parts: a fitness portion, a skills portion, and a written exam. In the first two days they would test his endurance, strength, and agility in a series of challenges and obstacle courses before the fitness portion would conclude with a long-distance run. Then, if his numbers were good enough, the next three days would focus on skills such as archery, wrestling, and sword fighting. He had arrived too late to participate in the first day last year and was disqualified from continuing. He would not be late this year.

As he reached the end of his run, a small ache crept into his head again. He squeezed his eyes shut in denial, ignoring the pain. He didn't have time for distractions like headaches.

He opened his eyes and continued through his usual training regimen. His schedule was optimized to the highest degree and he got through his strength training and the agility obstacle course efficiently and quickly. He felt confident and strong today, breezing through his usual training with surprising ease.

He stood at the end of the agility course, having completed his final run, breathing heavily with his hands on his hips when Anthony walked up in a sleek all-black training uniform.

"There you are little brother," Anthony said with a smile. "I had a feeling you'd be out here."

Liam stood up, surprised at the appearance of his brother. "I suppose it's a safe bet. You're up early."

Anthony shrugged. "Yeah, I just needed to get out and actually do something this morning before being stuck inside a council room with Edward all day," Anthony grimaced.

Liam nodded. He did not envy Anthony's position. He believed Anthony would make a great emperor, if Anthony wanted, but lately, Liam wasn't so sure that was something Anthony really desired. Anthony would never admit that though, even if it was true. Anthony knew that Destiny had chosen him as the next emperor, just like Liam was chosen to be the next Commander of the Tykerial Guard. They knew what was expected of them, regardless of how they felt about it.

"Are you training with Dante?" Liam asked, eyeing a tall brown-haired man who sauntered into the training arena. He was one of Anthony's best friends and one of Liam's least favorite people. He walked around with an arrogant smile now, his Tykerial Guard crest prominently displayed on his chest.

Anthony turned to look at Dante too. "Nah," he said with a flop of his wrist. "I thought I'd train with you today." Anthony smiled at Liam.

"Oh," Liam said, surprised. "Well, I was supposed to meet John …"

"Oh, come on now. You know I'll give you a better workout than John will."

"It's not that, I just already told him I would …"

"He'll understand. Come on," Anthony waved his arm for Liam to follow him.

Liam scowled. He supposed John wasn't here yet anyway. He could spend a few minutes with Anthony.

Anthony walked over to the sparring area.

"You don't want to run the obstacle course first? Warm up a little?" Liam suggested, pointing back to the start of the course.

Anthony turned to look at the course with disgust. "No, no. I don't think so …" he said and turned to look back at Liam with an eager smile. "I want to get down to the good stuff."

"Sure, the good stuff," Liam said with irritation and followed his brother to the fencing strips of the sparring area.

At Liam's insistence, they each strapped on leather armor and put on helmets before grabbing a couple of training rapiers. They walked into one of the fencing strips and just as Liam feared, everyone was lining up to watch them.

Anthony walked a few paces away from Liam as Liam brought his thin blade up in front of his body. Anthony echoed his movement and made the first lunge toward Liam. Liam easily parried the attack, their swords clinking together. Anthony tried another strike, but again, Liam defended comfortably.

They stood apart again, concentrating on each other's movements as they circled. Liam tried a lazy strike next and allowed Anthony to block the blow. Anthony smiled and nodded as he stepped back. Then Anthony lunged forward again with his sword outstretched and Liam caught the metal rod with his own. The two swords clanked together, and they continued through the motions. One move after the other, they each tried to throw the other off balance or trick the other into going a different way.

Their swords came together again and Liam tried not to appear too triumphant as he relieved Anthony of his sword with a flick. The blade clattered to the ground, leaving Anthony wide open. Liam lunged forward, but that annoying, searing pain shot through his head again. Liam squeezed his eyes shut for only a moment, but it was long enough for Anthony to gain the upper hand. Anthony ducked under Liam's arm and spun around, putting his hands on the ground and kicking one of his legs out toward Liam, and swept Liam's legs from underneath him. Liam fell hard onto the ground, knocking the air from his body.

Anthony removed his helmet and stood over Liam who was flat on his back on the ground and laughed. The few others that were watching them seemed to get amusement out of the scene too.

"Well, it seems you do need to train some more if even I'm beating you," Anthony said, brushing the dirt off his hands.

Liam stood slowly with a grunt, irked at what just happened in front of an audience. "You aren't supposed to attack without a sword. We're fencing, not wrestling," Liam said through gritted teeth.

Anthony laughed again. "Ah, yes. My mistake. I can never remember all the silly rules. We were just having some fun anyway. It's not like we were in some serious competition."

Liam rolled his eyes and felt a strong burn of anger flood his body. He quickly shook it off. He didn't want others to know how angry he had gotten, and he should have expected as much from Anthony.

Liam stripped off his helmet and walked out of the sparring pen.

"Let's go again?" Anthony asked. "You can't just walk away after being beaten like that, right?"

"I told you, I'm supposed to meet John."

"Oh, come on now. Just one more round. I'll get you and John into the races this weekend if you stay. We can all go. It'll be fun. We could all use some fun after this stressful week."

Liam sighed with closed eyes. He didn't care about the antiquated chariot races, but he knew Anthony would not let him just leave. He could do one more round, if they hurried.

"Fine, one more round," Liam agreed and walked back into position.

Anthony smiled and threw his helmet a few feet away.

"Helmets on, come on," Liam said, pointing to his brother's helmet before putting his own on.

"Nah, we don't need helmets," Anthony said, removing his leather armor. "I can't see or move around in that stuff. Forget the rules and all your planned, structured training. Let's have some proper fun. You're not supposed to do headshots anyway, right?"

"Right," Liam agreed apprehensively. "But fencing can be dangerous when …"

"I'm willing to take my chances," Anthony flashed a smirk at Liam.

"All right then," Liam said, returning the smile. Maybe this would be fun after all.

Liam removed his own helmet and armor, widened his stance, and nodded to his brother. Anthony smiled widely before he swung hard at Liam. Liam moved out of the way with ease, focusing on Anthony's every move.

"You used to be more fun," Anthony said playfully as they walked around in a circle. "You remember that time in academy when Dante and Logan sent you and your friends out looking for those two-headed wolves?"

"I think you were included in that group of convincers as well," Liam said, keeping his eyes on Anthony's feet.

Anthony laughed. "What ever happened to the Liam who was eager to find those wolves? The Liam that took risks and had fun?"

Liam shrugged. He didn't want to admit that he had only gone along with it because he didn't want to be left out. Breaking the rules and putting himself and his friends in danger had given him so much anxiety. "I suppose the damage I did to my foot that night acted as a pretty good lesson."

The memory of the pain caused Liam to wince a little as he pictured the long scar that ran from his ankle down to the bottom of his foot. The thin, white line cut through the circular birthmark he had on the sole of his foot.

Anthony rolled his eyes and advanced toward Liam, the blunted point of his blade tapping Liam in the chest. Liam stepped farther away from Anthony, realizing that Anthony was cleverly distracting him from paying attention to his distance.

Swords clanged together as Liam continued to defend Anthony's attacks, blocking and stepping aside. Anthony smiled as he picked up his pace, thrusting and advancing and spinning around with flare. Liam kept defending, but he felt he was only barely keeping up. With all the training he had been through recently, he should easily beat his brother who had only been sitting in council rooms talking.

What is going on with me this morning? Liam thought as he felt his frustration start to climb.

The headache flared again, searing its way through Liam's concentration. Liam took a deep breath and tried his best to ignore the pain. He lunged forward with great force, throwing all technique and patience aside and going for sheer strength and force. However, just before Liam's blade was about to prick Anthony in the chest, he pulled up, worried about hitting Anthony without any protective gear, and Anthony thrust Liam back with a strong shove.

Liam was knocked backward and almost stumbled to the ground. His frustration culminated into a full burst of anger. His headache was too much to ignore now and he grabbed at his eyes. He felt something inside himself shift, something seemed to click into place under his chest. He felt a surge of energy vibrating through his limbs and could barely control his own body as he let out a yell and threw his sword to the ground at Anthony's feet.

The metal sword hit the ground, tip first, and shattered into a million tiny pieces.

The anger subsided as quickly as it had appeared, leaving Liam feeling weak and exhausted. Liam fell to a knee, breathing heavily. Liam stared down at the metal pieces that used to be the thin rapier on the ground. Anthony's eyes were full of astonishment as he glanced down.

"What in the four gods just happened there?" he asked Liam in a stunned tone.

"I … I don't know. I guess you cracked it or bent it or something," Liam offered, grasping for any kind of logic.

"I mean, I'm strong, but I'm not *that* strong. I can't crack a metal sword," Anthony said, crouching down to examine the sword pieces. "It's broken into a thousand little pieces. I would expect it would only break in half if there was some fault in it." He looked up at Liam, his face full of confusion.

Liam shrugged and scratched the back of his head. "There must have been something wrong with it already," he continued to insist.

The pain in his head melted away and his vision and mind cleared. Fatigue gripped his arms, and his legs almost buckled beneath him as he tried to stand. Liam looked down at the sword on the ground and realized with a tinge of fear that there was nothing wrong with that sword. There was something wrong with him.

7

Katerina walked out of the dark room that had been set up for the Esterine visitors to have their religious services. She blinked her eyes rapidly
to adjust them to the bright sunlight that was streaming through large
windows that lined the long palace corridor. As expected, her new Tyken guard
protector was waiting for her, looking like a pristine, but intimidating statue. He
would escort her to her next lessons where her father had deemed it appropriate
for her custody to be traded off to her new gaggle of maids.

Katerina curtsied in farewell to the rest of her family as she split off from
them and turned toward Kona again. She tried not to let her eyes linger too
long on his strong, bare chest as she walked in front of the towering figure. They
walked together to her next appointment, in which she would start her Akarian
etiquette lessons.

She would normally be excited about sitting down and going through lessons
in which she would learn about and memorize some rules and traditions, but she
found herself distracted by her larger mission. She needed to find her way to the
Isavarian witch before her symptoms became too much to hide. And she needed
to make her first move today.

Katerina slowed her step to allow her guard to walk almost next to her and
exhaled loudly.

"Such a lovely sunny day, isn't it?" Katerina asked the Tyken in his native
language, Tyk.

Kona's face slowly curled into a surprised smile as he looked down at her.

"It is, Your Highness," he agreed, responding in Tyk as well. "Forgive me, your knowledge of the Tyk language is quite surprising. That is not a normal thing to know around here."

"Thank you," Katerina said, smiling at him and lifting her chin up in pride. It had been a while since she'd used the language, but she still remembered enough of it. She continued the conversation in Tyk. "It's come back to me quite easily. I wish I was as comfortable with the Akarian language. I imagine it's going to be a bit difficult to take in all this new Akarian culture, especially in a language I'm not very comfortable with," she said, looking up at Kona.

"You manage the Akarian language quite well, Your Highness," Kona said, resuming his stiff guard posture.

Katerina turned away and pursed her lips. The hallways were sparsely populated this morning, though there were still plenty of people to stop and stare at the Esterine princess as she walked by in her long, straight gown and casual headdress. When they were finally clear of any big groups and there were no other Tykens in sight, she took a big breath in.

"It would be so much easier if I could just learn all these Akarian things from someone who spoke my first language. You know?" Katerina asked, still sticking with the Tyk language.

Kona glanced at her but didn't offer any response.

Then Katerina got to the point. "I have heard there might be someone who speaks Isavarian living nearby. Do you know about them?" She knew the Tykens prided themselves on their honesty and she hoped he would uphold that virtue now.

Kona thought for a moment before answering. "I know of him, yes. He lives on the palace grounds, out in the forest behind the gates. I believe he was an old friend of the emperor and he is now permitted to live there. I am unaware of the extent of his language abilities, however."

Katerina felt hope rising in her chest. "Do you think you could take me to him? To see if he would be interested in helping me?"

Kona shrugged. "I could take you there. Though you know I am only on duty after dinner through the morning. There may not be much time for you …"

Katerina waved a hand, refusing to let this opportunity slip away. "Oh that's fine, we can go in the evening. After dinner."

Kona nodded, though he did not look pleased at the notion.

Katerina smiled triumphantly before realizing one more thing.

"My father would likely not approve of this excursion …" she lingered over the sentence and looked up at Kona. She stopped in front of the door to her lessons with her maids.

"My duty is only to keep you safe," Kona answered before his face turned up into an unexpected smile. "And besides, parents may think they always know best, but I find that is rarely the case."

Then he bowed to her and waited for her to enter through the doors. Katerina smiled at him, surprised at his easy compliance, but grateful that her father had shackled her to someone like him.

The sky was painted with bright oranges and reds as the sun began to set. Katerina clutched at the soft traveling cape that hung around her as she walked beside Kona through the cool spring evening. She wore a maid's dress instead of one of the new fine dresses she had gotten earlier today. Kona too wore uncharacteristic attire. He wore simple black pants and gray shirt with a traveling cloak that nearly brushed the ground. They remained inconspicuous as they walked through the back doors of the palace, and continued through the outer grounds beyond the fences.

Katerina felt a sense of exhilaration as they trekked through the darkening forest, Kona holding out a lantern to light the way for them. She had been able to get out of her rooms easily with the Tyken guard by her side. Her new maids had barely looked up from their evening sewing as she was escorted away.

"So this Isavarian," Katerina said, breaking the silence. "You've met him before?"

Kona shook his head slightly. "No, but Alexander Kusovo was a very well-known witch around here. I haven't heard anything about him for years, though, until you brought him up. We were all told to leave him be out here."

She glanced over, forcing herself not to stare at this beautiful creature beside her. The white tattooed lines on his hands glowed against the darkness of his skin in the dimming light. She knew the Tykens all received different markings, meaning different things, but she was never taught what they each meant. She wanted to ask him, but worried he wouldn't appreciate such an intimate question from her. He stood towering over her, a few feet taller than she was, his strong presence easing Katerina's anxiousness as they continued through the dark.

"Are you excited for Crealum this year?" Katerina decided to ask, hoping to keep her mind away from what dangers might be lurking in the darkness around them.

"Crealum is not something the Tykens celebrate," Kona responded tersely.

"Oh, I didn't realize ..." Katerina responded, a blush rising on her face.

"The appearance of the Alumetris tree and the powers it brought to the humans of Elusira was not a blessing for most of the world, including the Tykens. We don't celebrate it."

Katerina knew the Lumenaros factions of this continent and the humans had a quite combative and difficult history and realized quickly she must have hit on one of the sources of this hostility.

"I see," Katerina said quietly.

Kona hesitated before speaking again. "We have a much better holiday coming up though. Tysella. We celebrate it about a week after the Akarians celebrate Crealum, beginning on the first of the month. It is our most celebrated holiday."

"Oh," Katerina said with a smile, pleased that he decided to continue the conversation with her. "What is Tysella like?"

Kona smiled, lowering his lantern a little. "It is a multi-day celebration for Tykos, the Land God. There are all kinds of festivities that honor and represent Tykos: feasts, contests, gifts and ..." his face fell a little before he finished, "lots of family time."

Katerina inclined her head, interested in the familial strain that had crept up in his voice now and in their conversation from earlier. "You aren't fond of going back to your family?"

Kona shrugged and let out a long sigh. "I don't usually travel home for the holiday anymore. The Tykens here, we celebrate on our own. It's just too long of a trip back to Tulneria and I have duties here now. Which, of course, my mother is not happy about, but my mother and I don't see things the same way most of the time anyway. She's not pleased with my decision to stay here in Akaria and work with people who are not of our kind."

Katerina had wondered how common Tykens citizens were in Akaria. She had noticed a few around the palace, while they never had any in Esterine. The only time she really had any interaction with the Tykens before had been in brief interactions when they participated in political and trading meetings with her father and his advisors. And then, of course, they had been there with the Aurens the night Mikhal disappeared …

"It should be up here around this boulder," Kona's voice said, breaking into her memory before it could run away. "We should approach with some caution, there have been some reported sightings of two-headed wolves in these parts lately and the patrolled trails end here."

"Two-headed wolves?" Katerina asked. "Aren't they supposed to prefer colder weather?"

Kona nodded. "Usually, yes, but it seems a few packs are starting to migrate south now. Like the giants have begun to do."

Katerina nodded, she knew about the giants already, it was the whole reason the emperor was even entertaining the idea of a foreign heiress to his empire. She wondered what was causing this migration of the more dangerous species.

Kona led them through another few feet of wooded forest before they turned into a wide clearing after passing a large boulder. A small round hut lay in front of them, the chimney smoking. Someone was home. Kona drew his sword from his belt, but kept it low to his side.

Katerina stayed behind Kona as they slowly and cautiously approached the structure. Katerina looked around in the semidarkness, looking for any signs of movement around them. Kona led her up to the door and then turned his back to the hut, standing facing away from it.

"I'll give you your privacy and stand guard out here, Your Highness," Kona said, taking a wide stance and grounding the tip of his long sword in front of him.

Katerina nodded nervously and took a deep breath as she walked up to the hut door. She balled her hand into a fist and raised it to the door. She knocked loudly three times and then stepped back to wait for an answer. She shook her leg nervously for a few moments but there was no reply. She knocked again, listening intently for any noise beyond the door. Finally, she heard some shuffling from within, but still no one came to the door.

Katerina scowled and put her hands on her hips. She continued to knock on the door, hoping to force an interaction through sheer annoyance. She heard more shuffling from within and then the sound of many chains and locks being undone. The door opened a crack and Katerina stood up straighter, ready to greet the occupant with a polite greeting and charming smile.

A man's face appeared in the crack of the door, a few feet lower than Katerina had expected to see it. She tilted her head down, adjusting her gaze to meet the man's face. Kona hadn't mentioned he would be shorter than she was, but she tried not to look surprised.

"Holy fire on ice! Do you know how rude it is to keep knocking on a poor man's door like that?" the man demanded. She could barely make out the man's face in the darkness, but she could see he had a scraggly beard. His voice was both tired and intensely irritated. His sunken eyes glared at her.

"Oh … well … I am looking for Alexander Kusovo. You see I …" Katerina replied clumsily.

"I'm not him, not anymore," the man said and slammed the door shut.

Katerina's eyes widened at the ill-mannered greeting and scowled in frustration.

"Lord Kusovo, please!" Katerina yelled, unsure what she should say to sway him out of his hiding place again.

No answer came from within and Katerina crossed her arms in a huff. She turned away in anger and stubbornness when the flame in Kona's lantern rose. She took a deep breath in and calmed the flame back down to normal. This reminded her of the importance of her visit, and she walked up closer to the door. Placing her hand on the splintered wood, she spoke quietly and gently to the man she hoped would hear her inside.

"Please, sir. I need your help," she said quietly. A soft breeze blew through her hair as she let her fears wash over her. "I can't go back without some relief."

The door swung open and Katerina quickly leaned away to avoid falling forward.

"There's nothing I can help you with. Now please …" he began to say as he waved her off indifferently.

Katerina knew she had to be fast if she was going to convince this man to speak with her properly. Without saying word, Katerina threw her cape behind her shoulder and brought down the fabric of her simple gown, exposing her shoulder, the cracking black lines, and the blue glow that lay underneath.

The man's eyes widened, his gaze frozen on her shoulder. Closing his tired eyes to break the stare, he muttered something unintelligible under his breath before flinging open the door with a deep sigh, signaling for her to enter his humble home.

Katerina quickly covered her shoulder and turned to glance at Kona, who hadn't moved from his post, before stepping into the small hut. She had never seen such a small and cramped living space. A small fireplace with a pot hung over the dying embers stood in front of her as she entered. A straw bed with a ragged pillow and a torn blanket was stuffed into the far corner next to what looked like another room, or perhaps a closet, closed off with a tattered sheet.

A cluttered table with only one chair stood in the center of the space, separating the fireplace from a wall of books and scrolls that reached from floor to ceiling.

Katerina took a quick look around before her eyes found the man in the dimness of the hut. She found his wild white hair in the darkness as he got around the room in a wheelchair, trying to find a clear space to set his candle down on. He wasn't short, he was simply a person with a disability. Katerina wondered why Kona hadn't told her this as Alexander turned his wheelchair back toward her and scowled.

Then she saw them. The horrible cracking black lines going up and down both of his arms.

He doesn't even bother to cover them, Katerina thought with wonder. She almost envied this freedom, even if his case was more advanced than her own. He must be able to help her.

"Now I don't have any food to offer ya, so don't ask," Alexander said harshly as he wheeled around the table to the wall of books and scrolls. He glanced behind his shoulder for a second then said, "The Obsidian Streaks. I can give you something for the pain, but I'm afraid that is all."

Katerina stood awkwardly, trying not to stare at all the clutter around her. *What were all these books? What information did they hold? Spells? Potion recipes?* she wondered, highly intrigued.

"Thank you, I appreciate that," Katerina started, forcing her focus back to the man in the wheeled chair, "but what I really need is for you to help me control the power."

Alexander stopped rummaging around and turned to face her, a confused look crinkled his face. "Control the power?"

Katerina nodded. "It's becoming a danger and I never know what I might do. I'm afraid I will …" *Be exposed,* she thought to herself, but instead she finished with, "hurt someone."

Alexander shook his head, still looking bewildered. "I don't meddle with that stuff anymore. The magic from the Well is dangerous and you shouldn't be messing with it either. It'll make those lines grow much faster if you don't just give it all up now. That's what I did. And it cost me plenty …" His eyes flashed to the back of the room. "Quite a lot."

He turned back to grab the bottle he had been searching for, wheeled back to Katerina, and handed it to her.

His white hair is proof enough of his advanced magical abilities, she thought to herself as she hesitantly took the bottle from him. *He knows how to help me. It is clear he wants to help me with the Obsidian Streaks, what exactly is holding him back? How can I convince him? I will not be leaving here until he agrees to help me.*

"Thank you for this, but you need to teach me how to control it," she demanded.

He continued to shake his head. "You need to go to someone else then," he said as he turned away from her.

"Who else is there to go to?" Katerina asked in a shaky, raised voice.

A gust of wind blew through the hut, gentle at first, but as he continued to wheel away from her, dismissing her, the wind grew stronger. She would just have to show him then. She let her fear go. Pots and pans fell from their places on the shelves and the loose papers that had been lying in various places took flight and scattered throughout the room.

Alexander turned back to look at her. His eyes danced with curiosity, shifting back and forth quickly as they surveyed the mess.

"I tried to tell you," Katerina said in an irritated tone, quickly moving to pick up the papers that she'd tossed about.

"That was you? You did that? Without saying a spell?" he asked her, his tired eyes now full of surprise and wonder.

"I'm sorry, I didn't mean to," Katerina half-lied. "That just tends to happen when I get … well, you know, scared." She placed the papers back on the table in a stack. "I don't know how you had them …" she started to say.

"Xevron's souls …" the older man cursed quietly, using the name Katerina remembered as the Akarian god of death. "Let me see your Streaks again," he said, his faced furrowed in intrigue.

Katerina hesitated, she didn't like others analyzing her scars, but she knew she couldn't refuse if he was actually interested now. She released her cloak to the ground and slowly leaned down to reveal her shoulder to him again.

"They haven't cracked much yet, and they haven't invaded your arms? Not even to your elbow?" he asked, examining the lines on her skin.

Katerina shook her head. "No, they aren't that far along yet."

"And has this always happened to you? You've never needed incantations to do magic?" he asked, stroking his beard and looking her in the face now.

Katerina shook her head. When she had used her magic before, before Streaks appeared, it seemed so natural. Mikhal had been helping her, but when he left, she was suddenly on her own. She felt the weight of her necklace fall out into the open as she continued to lean over. She straightened her posture and pulled up the shoulder of her gown again. She grabbed at her necklace, playing with the charm between her fingers absently.

"That necklace," he said, pointing to the gem she now held in her hand. "Where did you get that?"

Katerina looked down at the necklace and opened her hand, displaying the glowing blue jewel in her palm.

"It was my mother's," she said, looking up at him.

"Your mother's ... your mother was a Volkev?" Alexander asked, still staring at the piece in her hand.

"Yes. My mother was Queen Ivana Soless of Esterine, a descendent of the Volkev line," Katerina explained. The Volkevs were once a politically powerful family in Isavaria, but it seemed this bloodline was more important to Alexander than Katerina could have guessed. She watched him closely now, hoping this new bit of information would help convince him to help her and not turn her away faster.

Alexander only stared at her, looking at her intensely, but saying nothing.

"I am Princess Katerina Xandrova of Esterine," Katerina confirmed confidently now in her native Isavarian tongue. "Will you help me?"

Alexander looked away from her. He took in a deep inhale before answering. "You come from a lineage of very powerful witches, one that hasn't been seen on this continent of Elusira in hundreds of years. You could be the key ..." he said trailing off. "The missing piece ..."

A powerful line of witches? Katerina wondered with excitement. *I knew my mother had to be a witch.*

"The key to what?" she asked.

Alexander looked up at her again and wheeled closer. "The key to healing us all." He looked at her with hungry eyes now, eagerness flared where apathy once was.

"How can I be the key?" Katerina asked, her mind flooded with questions.

"I believe there is only one thing in the entire world that can heal our people of the Obsidian Streaks. And that thing is protected by powerful magic. Powerful magic that only a Volkev witch can break through."

8

Liam relished the feeling of the warm sun on his face. Caroline's white glove held gently onto his arm as they walked leisurely through the large park. Liam inhaled the scent of fresh spring air and actually felt at ease as they nodded to other couples that passed by. Caroline had been correct in her assumption that the park would be a social place today with the weather finally warming up again. The trees were beginning to turn green and the park would soon be one of the few natural escapes in the city.

Liam was relieved he had packed the gray suit that matched Caroline's lavender lace dress so perfectly, or so she told him. He looked over to Caroline, who held her lavender parasol over her shoulder primly, her blonde hair pinned up perfectly. He noticed the easy look in her bright eyes and smiled. He enjoyed seeing that comfort and delight in her demeanor. He felt he didn't see that in her much anymore.

She caught him looking at her and turned her eyes away with a shy smile. "I'm so glad we were able to do this," she said.

"Me too. It is such a wonderful day," Liam said, forgetting his recent headaches, weird dreams, and the failing health of his uncle.

Caroline nodded to another couple as they passed and sighed. "I do wish we were able to see each other this weekend though."

Liam squeezed his lips together. "I know, but I promised John we would go to the races."

"I know, and you are such a good friend. It's just—well, you know—you will eventually need to stop doing things like that and spending time with people like John."

"What do you mean?" Liam asked, a sinking feeling arose in his stomach.

Caroline avoided looking at him. "Oh, I just mean when you're a Tyker- ial Guard … and perhaps when you have a family of your own." She paused. "Besides, we will need to be seen together at some big evening gatherings with- out your friends if we're to be seen as an official couple." She turned to smile sweetly at him.

Liam smiled back. "For instance, at your father's birthday soiree?"

Her smile widened and even made it up to her eyes this time. "Yes, for instance. But I thought an event before that would be a perfect time to officially attend our first one together, as a couple."

Liam looked down, his brain scrambling. *What is today?* he wondered. *What's coming up?* His lack of sleep was really starting to affect him.

Caroline sighed and continued. "Like the Crealum Ball perhaps?"

"Oh," Liam said with a shake of his head. "Of course, of course, yes."

Caroline removed her hand from Liam's upper arm to set it on her parasol and looked over to him. Liam stopped walking and turned to face her. He reached for one of her hands and she gently placed it in his.

"Caroline Morningfire, would you do me the honor of attending the Crealum Ball with me?" Liam asked properly, bowing slightly over her hand as he did so.

Caroline smiled shyly. "I would love to, Liam Farotus."

Liam squeezed her hand, wishing he could lean in and kiss her in that moment. He had never publicly courted someone before and he'd never taken anyone to the biggest holiday party of the year as his date. He wanted to show her how much he cared for her, he wanted to show everyone in the park, but he knew she wouldn't want him to do anything so improper. Instead, they turned back into their walk- ing posture, Caroline placing her hand back on his arm.

"Now," Caroline said, holding her head a little higher as they walked by the lake in the center of the park, "I assume we'll be in the traditional first dance this year and that we'll be honored to be among the group that represents the gods. Which god shall we pick?" Caroline asked without glancing at Liam, and she con- tinued before he could respond. "I was thinking Tykos. It would be a good symbol for you, I think, since he represents the strength and endurance of the Tykerial

Guard and the Earth Alumenos. And then of course he's also the god of marriage, which I think …"

The Earth Alumenos. It sure would be nice to have the power of gods like they once did, he thought. *To be blessed by Tykos himself with immense strength that could make me nearly invincible in a fight. The strength that could shatter even the strongest …* Liam's arms prickled with chills and his mind flooded with an idea. His attention faded from Caroline's voice. *Could it be? No … surely it couldn't. The Alumenos lost their powers hundreds of years ago. But still, could it be that I have somehow awakened some of this power again? The power was only lost, not destroyed.*

Liam thought back to that morning. He had another strange thing happen to him when he woke up from one of his fitful dreams: he had thrown the sheets off in frustration and they had flown across the room, which had only annoyed him at the time, but was that another sign?

"Just make sure you're not late this time," he heard Caroline say, shaking him from his thoughts.

Liam scrambled to jump back into the conversation. "Of course, of course, I wouldn't …" Liam stopped walking and rubbed his forehead. "Do you remember learning about the Lumos Gems?" he asked clumsily.

Caroline laughed, looking around with confusion in her face. "Well, of course. They held the long-lost remnants of the great powers of the Alumenos." She turned to look at Liam, her eyes narrowed. "Why? They don't have anything to do with Crealum. If you want to do something with the Gems, it's best to wait until the next holiday, Peralum."

"The Gems were hunted for many years, weren't they?" Liam asked, looking at Caroline but not really seeing her.

Caroline looked perturbed. "Yes, but none were ever recovered. Why are you being weird right now?"

Could it be possible? Liam wondered to himself. *Could the earth stone have been found without it being widely known? Could I have come in contact with it? Could that be the reason for my headaches and my incident with the sword yesterday?*

"I'm sorry," he said, dropping Caroline's arm. "I just remembered, I told my uncle I would see him this afternoon before my evening training. I'm afraid I have to head back to the palace."

"Now?" Caroline asked, her face falling and Liam's heart twisting at the sight. "But we only just got here."

"I'm sorry," was all that Liam could say as he looked pleadingly into her eyes.

Caroline huffed and looked down to the ground. "I suppose you can't disappoint the emperor."

Liam led them back toward their carriage waiting for them at the front of the park. "Let's have tea tomorrow?" he asked, hoping to make some kind of reparation.

Caroline nodded once in agreement. "But not at that place you took me before that serves mostly cheese things. I can't have that kind of stuff anymore. We need to go somewhere with proper biscuits. I'll send you a list of places."

Liam smiled and nodded. "Of course."

Liam rushed into the dimly lit palace library. The familiar smell of old parchment and leather wafted through the air as he frantically searched the shelves. He was acutely aware that it had been years since he enjoyed the quiet solitude of the library. He used to love it in here. He glanced over to the faded green overstuffed chair in the corner that used to make him feel so safe. Right now, however, he didn't have time enjoy it.

Turning back to the bookcases—everything he had been taught about Crealum and the Alumenos flooded back to him. A thousand years ago, in the midst of a continent-wide war, the sudden and mysterious appearance of a magical tree, the Alumetris, created the Alumenos. Much like how the Well was the source of the Isavarian powers, this tree granted four humans abilities beyond anyone's imagination. Their powers were eventually stolen from them and stored in four magical stones that were scattered around the Elusiran continent.

His hand stopped on an old, tattered hardback book with the words "The Alumenos Awakening" scrawled on the spine. He carefully pulled the book off the shelf, his hands shaking slightly.

He opened the book and flipped through the thin pages. Inside, his eyes scanned over the pictures and explanations about the appearance of the Alumetris, the gifts the original Alumenos were gifted; the elemental powers of Water, Earth, Fire, and Air, corresponding to each of the Light Gods: Revira, Tykos, Farran, and Aurelia respectively. He continued through the pages and passed the description of each power and each god. Then he turned to the page about "surges."

His stomach twisted as he read about how the subsequent generations of Alumenos experienced "surges" when they began to come into their powers, manifesting in different ways for each type. Liam's heart rate increased as he read about the Earth Alumenos surges—increases in physical strength. These surges were also known to bring on ailments like headaches, mood swings, and fatigue.

Liam turned the pages eagerly and his heart dropped into his stomach when he saw the symbol. A symbol so familiar to him he could hardly believe what he seeing. Staring back at him on the page was the same spiral symbol he had on his foot. His birthmark. It was true. He was an Alumenos Awakening.

"What are you …" a voice said from right next him.

Liam jumped out of his skin and dropped the book to the ground. He turned to see his brother's face staring over his shoulder, smirking at him.

"Good Tykos, Anthony," Liam said with exasperation.

Anthony laughed at Liam's reaction. "I said your name twice. Did you not hear me?"

Liam sighed and bent down to pick up the book.

"So what are you reading so intently?" Anthony asked as he snatched the book from Liam's hands.

Liam rolled his eyes. "I was just looking for …"

Anthony took the book from him, looked it over, and shoved it back into Liam's chest. "Have you been in here all day? I've been looking for you everywhere," he asked, apparently no longer interested in Liam's previous answer.

Liam straightened the pages. "I was with Caroline earlier," he said.

Anthony scrunched up his nose. "Oh, Caroline, right," he said with clear distaste. "Why are you reading about Alumenos stuff?" Anthony said, pointing back at the book.

"I …" Liam's face curled into an uncontrollable smile. "I …" he looked down and chuckled. "You're not going to believe this," Liam said, looking back up to Anthony.

"What?" Anthony asked, smiling.

Liam just looked at Anthony for a moment, trying to decide how to answer.

"Don't tell me you think you're Alumenos or something," Anthony said, eyeing his brother suspiciously.

Liam shrugged and looked away. "I mean, actually …"

Anthony let out a roll of laughter. "Are you serious? You're being ridiculous! Why would you even think that?"

Liam shrugged again and walked away from Anthony. He waved his arms around as he continued. "My birthmark is in this book, Anthony. And I've been getting these headaches, these dreams, what happened with the sparring sword …"

Anthony crossed his arms and looked at Liam with quizzical eyes.

Liam sighed and touched the bridge of his nose with two fingers. "I feel different …" Liam mumbled to himself. Then he looked up quickly and opened the book again. "We need to test it," Liam decided, flipping through the book.

"Test it?" Anthony asked as he came closer to Liam.

"Yeah, they used to do these tests on the Alumenos. It unlocked their full powers and helped them learn to control the surges, or something …"

"All right," Anthony said with a chuckle, crossing his arms. "What's the test then?"

Liam found the right page and stopped reading when he saw what it said.

"What is it?" Anthony asked again.

Liam rolled his head back and handed Anthony the book.

Anthony laughed a hearty laugh again, waving the book around. "You want to bury yourself alive? Oh, come on now."

Liam squeezed his eyes shut and shook his head. He agreed it sounded insane. But how else would he know for sure?

Then suddenly the doors to the library crashed open and two Tykerial Guards rushed in, their armor clanging together as they moved.

"Your Highnesses," one of the guards addressed them with a quick bow. "You two must come with us immediately."

9

Liam's feet pounded against the marble floor as he ran behind Anthony. He realized he was still holding the book he had been reading as they dashed down the familiar palace corridors, drawing interest from everyone they passed. The emperor had called for them to come to his chambers immediately and Liam couldn't help but feel a shadow of fear creeping over him at this request. This could not be good.

Anthony led them quickly, rushing through the four Tykerial Guards that stood in front of the doors leading to the emperor's private chambers. They both burst into the rooms with a clatter.

Martin, the butler, stood in front of the bedchamber doors and looked up from his conversation with one of the doctors when the boys entered. He sighed and dismissed the doctor along with the other servants that stood around the room and turned to the boys, clasping his hands together. Liam watched as the doctor and servants shuffled out of the room in a flood of black uniforms. He did not gain any comfort from the look on the doctor's face as he avoided looking at the boys.

Anthony walked toward the bedchamber doors when Martin stepped in front of him.

"We received a message that the emperor had called for us," Anthony said sternly, clearly annoyed at the formalities they had to jump through with Martin to be able to see their uncle.

The butler nodded. "Yes, your uncle has indeed called for you …"

"Well then we should be allowed in!" Anthony yelled. Liam could hear the concern and fear in his brother's raised voice.

The doors to the bedroom opened behind Martin and Liam's eyes quickly darted to see who was emerging, tucking the book under his arm. He was not so thrilled to see it was Edward.

"What are you doing in here?" Anthony asked, his hands clenching into fists by his side.

Martin moved away from the bedroom door, allowing Edward to approach the boys.

"The emperor called me here, of course," he said in his usual sinuous tone. He held his hands behind his back and stopped in front of them. "I want to warn you," he said slowly, looking at the boys with serious eyes. "His condition has worsened quite a bit since you last saw him. You should be prepared when you enter. I'm sure you know, he doesn't want pity or sad eyes. He has called you here to tell you both something very important."

For once Anthony didn't say anything as he narrowed his eyes at Edward. Liam nodded, his stomach turning with fear. The adrenaline from his recent discovery hadn't even worn off yet and now even more stress was pulsing through his entire body.

Edward nodded and walked past the boys, out of the emperor's rooms. Martin moved forward then, opening the doors of the bedroom for them. The boys followed the butler inside, allowing him to announce their arrival to the emperor. Then the butler quickly took his exit, closing the doors behind him and leaving the boys standing in the middle of a dark, warm room.

Liam's heart sank when he saw his uncle. He laid in his large bed, clearly too weak to stand and could barely sit up on his own. Papers and books were lying all over the bed on top of him—typical that he would continue to work through his illness. The gray lines on his arms were exposed this time and Liam's stomach twisted at the sight. The veiny lines cut into his skin, looking like tree roots, taking over his body. Emperor Shadox's chest moved up and down rapidly as he tried to take more air into his lungs and sweat dripped off his face as his eyes fluttered open.

"Liam …" the emperor's voice cracked. "Come," he said, reaching out a hand to Liam.

Liam hesitated for a moment and looked at Anthony. He saw the same fear that he felt in his chest apparent in his brother's eyes—the fear that threatened to paralyze him in this moment. He didn't want to get any closer, but he forced himself to take a step. He moved slowly through the heavy air over to his uncle, squinting his eyes in the near darkness of the room, beginning to sweat himself.

"Your Majesty, I'm here," Liam said as he approached. He pulled the book out from under his arm to give his hands something to hold on to while fighting the urge to turn away from the sick man and weep like a child.

Emperor Shadox swallowed slowly and opened his mouth to speak again. He paused and glanced at the book in Liam's hands. "You are reading about Alumenos?" he asked, having to stop to catch his breath. "So you know then?"

Liam hesitated and looked back at Anthony.

"Tell me," his uncle spoke again, causing Liam to look back at him, "what happened during training yesterday?"

Liam looked down to the floor. He knew his uncle was only interested in one thing about his training yesterday, but he still didn't totally understand what had had happened himself. "I lost my temper," Liam admitted.

"And you broke a sparring sword into pieces?" the emperor rasped out.

Liam nodded. "Yes, sir. I shouldn't have lost my temper, but …" Liam began, but then broke off when he didn't know how to explain what he thought actually happened.

The emperor nodded and looked away from Liam. Liam saw a sadness in his face that surprised him. The emperor closed his eyes for a short moment and waved a weak hand over to Anthony signaling him to approach as well. Anthony came forward swiftly and grabbed the emperor's hand. Emperor Shadox opened his eyes and pushed himself up to sit upright in bed.

"It is time you both know something," Emperor Shadox said hoarsely through this swollen throat. The boys exchanged nervous glances and Liam's anxiety began to rise, his heart rate quickening. He grabbed at his watch to feel the reassuring ticking again. What his uncle was about to tell them could very well change everything.

"You boys have a magical heritage," he said, looking up at Liam with red, tired eyes. "You, Liam, indeed have Alumenos blood in your veins."

Liam couldn't help the smile that grew on his face. A gentle vibration flowed through his body. He had been right after all. He really was an Alumenos Awakening. His gut spiraled with excitement. This would completely change his life, and possibly the lives of everyone in Akaria. Magic was returning to humans. Liam's mind raced with the possibilities before his uncle's voice forced him to stay focused on the conversation.

"That is one of the reasons I was so interested in finding the Lumos Gems all those years ago," Emperor Shadox admitted.

Liam was sure his face betrayed his surprise and confusion at this confession. He had no idea that his uncle had once sought the Lumos Gems. *Why did I never know this?* he thought.

"When the Tykens from Tulneria joined our forces in the war against Wenstetter, I was able to learn from them where the Water Stone was hidden. The Healing Stone. I immediately thought about how the power within this stone would not only be a miraculous find for healing the people of Akaria, but it could also bring back the magic of the Alumetris. So, after I had secured our victory in the war and you boys were enrolled in Hetikan Academy, I put together a team to go after the stone." He paused and sank back down into the bed. "But we failed to retrieve it. We failed so miserably."

He looked back up to Liam. "However, I think you, Liam, will be able to recover it. I take it you have started to discover some changes within yourself."

Liam nodded, holding back his smile. It didn't seem like the right time to smile. "I have, sir. And I believe I may be an awakening Earth Alumenos." His stomach fluttered at the words as he remembered the pages of the book. It felt so odd to say out loud.

The emperor squeezed his lips together and nodded slightly. "I believe that to be the case, from what I've heard. And I think, even with just your surge powers of strength, you can complete this quest. You could be the piece we were missing before. And as much as I hate the idea, as much as it pains me to ask it of you … I am asking if you will try," he said and looked back up at Liam, his eyes full of deep sorrow. "Holding the Water Stone may be my only chance at survival now. This disease," he looked down at his arms and the ugly gray Streaks that now ran all the way up and down his arms, "it's progressing in me much faster than it does in the witches. They are able to live for years after the lines begin to appear, but I …" the emperor stopped. "I don't know how long I have."

Liam's stomach turned and his head ached again. He covered his concern with a deep inhale and forced back the tears that threatened to burst from his eyes at the thought of losing his uncle. "Of course, I will try …" Liam said, wanting to reach for his uncle, but hesitating to do so.

"And I will go too," Anthony said as he released his uncle's hand and stood up, a firm and determined look on his face.

Their uncle shook his head. "No. Anthony, I need you here. Edward will be regent while I'm sick, but if I …" Emperor Shadox swallowed before continuing. "I need you here, learning, continuing the negotiations with the Esterine king and taking on as much as you can from Edward. You may need to take over my throne sooner than we imagined."

"But I can't just let Liam go out there alone …" Anthony tried to argue.

"He will not go alone …" their uncle started to explain but a cough rose in his throat and his body convulsed violently as he tried to regain control and speak again. Liam watched helplessly as his uncle suffered, a desire to help him burning within him. When the coughing stopped, the emperor closed his eyes, truly exhausted.

His voice, even weaker than before, croaked out a final instruction. "Take this to Alexander Kusovo, the Isavarian Witch," he said to Liam, searching the piles of papers that laid in front of him. He grabbed a small, crumpled piece of paper and held it out to Liam.

Liam took the note from his uncle and glanced at it. It was written in some language Liam didn't recognize. He folded the note carefully and nodded to his uncle.

"He will tell you more about the stone," the emperor said breathlessly.

Anthony turned on his heel and stormed out of the room. Liam watched his brother go, not surprised by his behavior, but for once, he thought he might understand how he felt.

"I will do all I can, Uncle Philip," he said, purposefully not using titles or proper etiquette. It could be one of the last times he spoke to his uncle and he wanted him to know he saw him as more than a title, more than the emperor. Philip Shadox was the most important man in the world to him and even though it terrified him to go on this mission, Liam would not let him down.

10

Katerina let a strand of dark hair fall into her face as she scanned the page of an old book. She turned the page and the smell of old parchment and ink wafted toward her. Numerous spells, incantations, and potion recipes laid before her, scribbled into a book by another witch a long time ago. Her face cracked into a hungry smile as her mind raced with all the opportunities held within these pages.

She knew the Isavarian Witches were once very powerful when they had access to the Well, but she had no idea the depth of what they were capable of—what she could be capable of, even now. All this knowledge was spread out right in front of her, and somewhere in all of this was a spell that would help them find a cure for the Streaks.

Alexander hadn't revealed much more about his plans for finding the cure in their first lesson, but Katerina had learned it was better to let him get to that when he was ready. She had come here to learn how to hide herself, she only really needed to know how to control her abilities, but there was now an undeniable pull to know all she could about her powers. And now that there was a chance for a cure, she might actually be able to pursue learning more.

Alexander had dozens of books like the one in front of her now. Books that held the incantations and ingredients for spells that could do amazing things, such as shrink and grow items, tame animals, and create portals to transport people across the world in seconds. And even beyond that, since spells could not alter human bodies, there were recipes for potions that could turn someone invisible, disguise someone's appearance, and help someone sleep. The list went on and on and she wanted to learn them all. The idea of all the freedoms they could give her lured her in. The short evening visits to Alexander's hut suddenly seemed vastly insufficient.

A thin wooden rod slammed down on the page in front of her before she could turn another page. She removed her hands from the book quickly and snapped her head up to see the scowling face of Alexander glaring at her from across the table.

"Are you listening or am I wasting my breath?" he asked, his face scrunched into a scowl and his arm stretched across the table, holding the wooden stick that had gotten her attention.

"I'm listening," Katerina nodded eagerly, and then with a smile she mumbled, "for the most part."

Alexander was not amused with her honesty. He brought his wooden stick back across table and laid it down on the edge.

"What will happen if you dehydrate and continue to use magic then?" he asked, crossing his arms.

Katerina looked away from Alexander. "Something … bad …" she said, dragging out the words.

"Very good, yes, that's what I was just saying, 'Something mysteriously and generally bad will happen to you …'" Alexander said, rolling his eyes and shaking his head.

He then scowled again and reached across the table to drag the spell book away from Katerina. He shut it forcefully and a puff of dust escaped the book as it closed. Katerina eyed the book for a moment, aggrieved at having it taken away from her.

"You must understand this before we continue our lessons. I cannot teach you anything until you get how important this is."

"I just need to learn to control it," Katerina snapped back. She couldn't help the annoyance that ran through her at his tone. "I don't need to know all the little details …"

"You do need to know," Alexander cut her off, looking at her with wide, serious eyes. "By all the gods, how daft are you? You have no idea how any of this works, do you?"

Katerina sat quietly with her hands in her lap and looked at the ground. Tears threatened to escape to her eyes as a wave of disappointment flooded through her. No one had spoken to her like that in a long time. She hated that she was just sitting there, being reprimanded by a man who secluded himself from society and lived in such a small and cluttered space. However, deep down what she hated more was this feeling of failure. She was clearly failing at this.

"I see the hunger in your eyes, I know it's in your blood to practice this magic. You can't escape this power as easily as you might think," Alexander said, a little softer in his tone this time.

He exhaled and pushed the book off to the side. Then he pulled his mug to sit in front of him and whispered something to himself. Katerina looked up slowly and felt curious as she watched Alexander wave a hand over the mug and the blue glow shining through the Obsidian Streaks on his arms intensified. The water inside rose out of the mug in little droplets. He put his hand down and still the water danced gracefully above the mug.

"Water is very important to Isavarian Witches. It is where our power lives. The water from the Well, it lives inside our bodies now. If you ignore it, if you shirk the importance of it and refuse to obey to limits of your body …" Alexander paused and gently let go of the spell, causing the water to fall back down into his mug. The blue glow on his arms dimmed. "You'll end up like Davi," he said seriously.

Katerina's hair stood up on her arm as a chill ran through her. Her first lesson, just a few days ago. She remembered the horrifying sight of the poor woman, so sick she didn't even remember who she was anymore. She didn't seem awake, although Alexander explained this was the state she was always in, just staring into nothing.

"Davi pressed past her limits," Alexander continued, his voice straining. "She had no choice, really. It was ultimately my fault, but …" he stopped and looked down to the ground. He cleared his throat before continuing. "She nearly called forth a DarkHeart. You remember what that is, don't you? From our previous lesson?"

Katerina nodded slowly. The most destructive and evil creatures known to mankind, the DarkHearts were pure demons. According to scriptures, thousands of years ago, it was the summoning of DarkHearts that had led humans into the Age of Darkness. Eventually, God gave them the Gift of the Well, ushering in the Age of the Well, and it was the only thing that could stop the DarkHearts from destroying the entire world and everyone in it. Katerina remembered the drawings Alexander had shown her of these demons ripping themselves out of the bodies of their summoners. An Isavarian Witch still had the ability to summon them into the world.

"DarkHearts are very dangerous to call forth and the Obsidian Streaks make it even easier for them to peek through the veil from the other side. The Streaks make us weaker, they almost siphon the water and the magic from us," Alexander explained.

"But the SoulFires," Katerina asked, focusing her eyes on the white-haired man in front of her, "they are good. So why can't we just as easily call them forth?"

"They might be good, if they even exist. They are impossible to summon anymore. Only a pure Isavarian witch could do so, and none of us are pure anymore. Not since the Well ran dry.

"So, I'll ask again," Alexander said, firming up his demeanor. "What is the importance of water?"

Katerina sat up a little straighter. "Water is what carries my magic through my body. If left depleted and I do magic, whether on accident or not, it could leave me vulnerable to calling a DarkHeart."

"Right," Alexander said with a nod. "Except, I still can't figure out how you're 'accidentally' doing magic." He said with a wave of his hand. "Davi was one of the most talented witches I had ever taught. She was powerful and dedicated, and still, even she didn't affect the elements around her like you do."

Katerina shrugged. "I used to be able to control it more, but then … the Streaks …" she looked away and shook her head. "I don't know, I just feel so …"

"You let your emotions rule you!" Alexander said pointing at her. "That much is clear!" he continued, pounding the table with every word.

Katerina frowned at his sudden outburst. She hated that accusation.

Alexander sighed and softened his shoulders. "But so do I," he admitted. "We both must remember, however, that our emotions are simply signals. They bring our attention to what's happening around us and inside us. They move us to react in some way and it's our job to recognize the signal before we react. For you, your emotions are manifesting around you through the power of the Well for all to witness. It's quite difficult to step back and see the truth in a situation when our emotions flare, but it is vitally important for us to try."

Katerina sat quietly, shifting her eyes away from Alexander as he rolled away from her. She knew he was right. She often let her emotions overcome her. She never thought there was any other choice. She couldn't control how she felt, but she saw now that she needed to be able to control how she reacted.

"But anyway, back to business. What are the steps to successfully completing a spell?" Alexander asked over his shoulder.

"Intention is first," she said confidently, shaking off the heaviness of his previous comments. "Then the incantation, the hand gesture, if necessary, and finally the release of the magical energy. Spells direct magical energy through an object or the elements around you. Unbound spells must be held with concentration and intention lest the magic disperse. They can be very powerful, but they don't last like bound spells," Katerina recited perfectly.

She waited for both confirmation she was correct and praise from Alexander, but he didn't acknowledge her answer at all. He instead continued to gather up odd items from around his small home. Katerina watched as he picked up a candlestick, a plate out of the sink, and a teapot off the makeshift stove.

"Now," Alexander said, arranging the gathered items in a line on the table in front of her, "Show me. I want you to light this candle, summon this book, and shatter this plate," he said, pointing to each of the items. "And if you manage all of that, pull the water in this teapot out in a light mist."

"What about a bound spell?" Katerina asked, looking over the items with disinterest. "It seems spells that hold would actually be more useful to learn since they are more permanent. Isn't the spell I need to learn for the cure a bound spell?"

Alexander shook his head. "We start small with the unbound spells. These are what you must learn to control first. Binding a spell is more difficult, breaking an enchantment, even more so. And besides, I thought you didn't need to know more than how to control your weird elemental bursts anyway."

Katerina tilted her head and held back a smile. She nodded and leaned toward the items. Alexander pushed a small book over to Katerina instead of the big one she had been looking at earlier.

"If you don't remember the incantations, you can look them up in here, but that is all you may look at in this book," he told her pointedly.

Katerina took a deep breath in and nodded in determination. She had done most of these things at some point in her life, apart from shattering the plate. She thought she should be able to complete these tasks with ease.

She looked at the book he wanted her to summon, took a big gulp of water from the glass on the table, and stood up from her chair. She smoothed down her simple gray maid's dress and twisted her mouth in thought before reaching out a hand for the book. She set her intention to summon the book in her mind and quickly pulled her hand back toward herself, repeating the summoning word, "*Vyzyvat*."

The book shot toward Katerina's head with a speed she hadn't expected. She ducked out of the way as the book flew through the air and hit the wall of the hut behind her. Pain in her shoulder flared and she grimaced as she slowly looked back over to Alexander, ready to be scolded.

Alexander sighed and turned his attention away from the book on the floor. He rubbed his eyes in anguish before speaking in a much softer tone than Katerina had expected.

"Why did that happen?" Alexander asked, focusing his eyes on her again.

Katerina looked back at the book behind her and thought about the sequence Alexander had repeated for her.

"I didn't wait for the words before expelling the power?" Katerina guessed. She walked over to retrieve the book from the ground, trying to avoid the disappointed eyes on her for just a moment.

"You didn't concentrate. This is what I've been trying to tell you," Alexander exhaled in an exasperated tone. "You clearly need more preparation. You need to learn to focus. You need to be mentally strong to be able to do these spells. You need to be able to feel the energy pulsing within, all through your body. Your emotions will cloud your mind if you let them. You need to be able to observe your emotions objectively. Once you recognize your emotions and the energy of the power, only then can you control it." He waved his arms around as he spoke.

Katerina nodded solemnly, clearing her eyes of the water that pooled there. She took her seat across the table from him again and looked up at him, waiting for the next instruction. Alexander shook his head at her and started to gather up the books he had put on the table for their lesson.

"We're done for today, come back in a few days after you've taken some time with yourself. I can't stress how important it is …" Alexander began to say and Katerina's shoulders drooped in dismay.

She didn't want to be done. She had only memorized a few silly words so far and she still didn't think she could control her power reliably. If he wouldn't show her how it was done, she would have to convince him by showing him how much power she was holding inside.

Katerina stood up quickly from her chair again and looked at the candle still sitting on the table. She tuned out Alexander's droning and complaining and concentrated on nothing but the candle. She set her intention, to light the candle, to call forth the air and heat from around them to come together to form a flame on the wick. Then she whispered the fire word, "*Ogon*," and felt the power within her gathering in her hands. She clenched her fists together as the heat grew and then when she felt she couldn't hold it any longer, she opened one hand and spread her fingers out over the candle. The power that had gathered in her palms slowly faded and she watched the candle begin to flicker and sputter, the fire trying to attach itself to something to remain burning. A flame shot up in the air, strong and burning brightly.

She smiled and let the power continue to stir within her. She could feel the magic, recognized its warmth, and let it invigorate her. She turned to the only book Alexander had left on the table and repeated the summoning word, *Vyzyvat*, commanding her power to do her intention. The book flew across the room to her, landing perfectly in her outstretched hand. She then turned to the plate that Alexander had placed on the table and stretched a hand out toward it.

"*Razbit*," she said with certainty and the plate shattered where it stood with a loud crash.

She smiled as the power continued to grow within her and she turned away from the table, to the rest of the room. She locked her eyes on the heavy pot over the smoldering fire and decided to impress.

"*Levitirovat!*" Katerina commanded and the pot lifted itself from its metal stand and hovered in midair.

Katerina felt her power waver and a sudden ripple of exhaustion gripped her. She let the power fade from within and the pot clanged back down on the stand and she released the spell. Her shoulders relaxed and she took a deep breath in before turning to Alexander with a satisfied smile. She had forgotten what a rush it was to intentionally call upon her power.

Alexander sat with wide eyes as he looked over to the pot on the fire. Still holding a stack of books in his arms he looked back at Katerina in astonishment. She waited for him to say something, hoping he would agree to continue their lesson today. Instead of the praise Katerina had been hoping for, Alexander frowned.

"You are quite talented," he said, "but stunts like that will only make the Streaks grow faster and make you more susceptible to the DarkHeart."

Alexander set the books back down on the table and looked at Katerina. Katerina sighed in frustration. *What does he want from me? Why is he always so sporadic with his teaching?*

"We will get you where you need to be. I just think we need to take things a little slower. I have big hopes for you, you know that," Alexander said.

Katerina felt a tug on her heart as she looked into his tired eyes. She could see how much he meant that.

Then Katerina's nerves nearly jumped out of her body when loud, incessant knocking came from the front door. Without waiting for an answer, Kona burst in. His eyes serious and sharp.

"Your Highness, I'm sorry to interrupt, but there's someone coming."

II

"I told you I could handle this on my own," Liam said as his boots crunched through twigs and grass in the darkening light. "You didn't need to come along."

"I know," Anthony said, outpacing Liam as he eagerly pushed forward through the trees, lantern glowing before him. "But if I have to miss the real adventure, at least I can be there for this part."

"It's not 'an adventure,'" Liam said with a sigh, holding his own lantern up higher. "It's more like … more like an errand."

The thought of going on a quest like this made Liam's stomach turn and muscles tense, but he had no choice. It was his duty to not only follow the emperor's orders, but to also do everything he could to save the life of his uncle.

"Call it what you want, but it's certainly more fun than council meetings and negotiations," Anthony said with a laugh, still pressing onward through the dark forest path.

"Don't you have one of those in the morning? A meeting with the Esterine King?" Liam asked.

Anthony shrugged. "It's not *early* in the morning though," he said with a wave of his hand. "The Esterine family has to do their religion stuff or whatever first. So I can stay up as late as I want." He smiled smugly.

Liam rolled his eyes and winced slightly as the muscles in his legs twitched. He'd been using training as a distraction lately and he may have overdone it. He suddenly felt a gentle vibration in his stomach and he curiously focused on the sensation. As he focused on it, he felt it grow. The soothing feeling encompassed his body and he felt the strength in his body increase. He continued forward on sturdy, strong legs. He smiled to himself, enjoying the sensation.

"Do you know who this Kusovo person is? Or why Uncle allows him to live on palace grounds out here?" Anthony asked Liam without turning to look at him.

"I have no idea," Liam responded. "I suppose he was a friend of our uncle's at one point or another."

Liam had only been slightly surprised to find that Anthony had stormed out of their uncle's quarters to immediately seek out where this Alexander Kusovo lived. Liam easily assumed that Anthony would have spent the night pouting and drinking away his sorrows with friends, but he hadn't. Liam now saw that Anthony was just as worried about their uncle as he was. Anthony had come straight to Liam once he had the information, but what surprised Liam the most was that Alexander Kusovo lived on the palace grounds, out in the forest beyond the gates.

They eventually came upon a small hut in the middle of a clearing. Made of thin pieces of wood and a thatched roof of grass—it was exactly how Liam had imagined a house in the woods would look.

"Is this it?" Anthony asked, approaching the structure.

Liam sighed in frustration. "Yeah, this must be it," he said.

"Some important guy lives in this?" Anthony chuckled. "All right then," he said with a shrug and strode up to the door confidently.

Anthony knocked on the door in a cheerful manner. The boys could hear movement and shuffling inside and then the clicking of locks and chains being removed from the door.

"Who's there? What do you want?" a man's voice asked in a hostile tone as he swung open the door.

Liam couldn't help his surprise when he looked down to see a feeble older man in a wheelchair staring up at him. It appeared they had surprised the man. His white hair and beard were wildly unkempt and his wrinkled face turned from concern to surprise and eventually to anger as he took in the sight of the two boys.

"Um, right, yes … we're sorry to disturb you, sir," Liam hesitated to say, but the man shook his head.

"No, nuh uh," the man said firmly, pushing the door closed.

Anthony grabbed the edge of the door quickly and held it open before it closed on them completely.

"Are you Alexander Kusovo?" Liam asked as amiably as he could manage with his curiosity peaking.

"Why?" the man asked, crossing his arms.

"The emperor sent us. I'm afraid we have a very important matter we need to discuss with you. It should only take a few minutes of your time," Anthony said seriously and calmly.

The man looked up at them with a scowl. His eyes scanned them carefully. He looked tired and much older than Liam had expected. This man had been through a great deal, that much was clear.

"Please, we must speak with you about something of utmost importance. The future of Akaria depends on it," Anthony pleaded dramatically.

Liam looked at Alexander hopefully. Alexander's eyes locked onto Liam's, and he grumbled to himself and turned his chair around. Liam heard him mumble something about a violation of privacy and how his house had apparently become a common area now, as he left the door open behind him and wheeled back into the small cabin.

Liam ducked into the small hut and felt rather uncomfortable in the intimate disarray of this man's home. Books lay strewn about the room and dishes were piled up in the sink. Alexander began clearing off the table in the center of the room, ridding it of the books and papers that were stacked there.

"I only have the one chair, got my own here you see," Alexander said gruffly. "So I suppose you'll have to fight over it."

The boys looked at each other, but neither took the semi-offered chair. Liam wondered if he should offer to assist the man as he wheeled back and forth through the room, holding stacks of books on his lap, but he seemed to move rather easily through his task. Liam glanced at the open book still on the table and saw that it held a recipe of some sort, though the ingredients were nothing he would ever put in any stew. Alexander slammed the book shut and glared at Liam. Liam cowered away from the table apologetically.

Once the table was cleared of books and papers, Alexander came up to the table and rested his hand on top of it.

"So what is this 'important matter' that you came to talk to me about? Is it about Princess Katerina?" Alexander asked, interlacing his fingers together in front of him calmly.

Confused by the mention of the Princess Katerina, Liam wrinkled his forehead and shook his head.

"No, sir, why would it …" Liam began to say, but Anthony decided to jump in to explain.

"It's about the emperor himself," Anthony declared, moving into the empty chair to take a seat in front of Alexander. "I am Anthony Farotus, Princep of Akaria, nephew and heir to Emperor Philip Shadox. And this is my brother, Liam Farotus."

Liam crossed his arms and stepped up behind Anthony. He tried to stand as authoritatively as he could, channeling his Tykerial Guardsman training. He just felt awkward as he stood behind Anthony with his arms crossed and his face set in a stern frown. If Anthony wanted to do all the talking, he supposed he would let him. He was better at that stuff anyway.

"The emperor has fallen ill. Very ill," Anthony looked Alexander in the eye as he spoke and paused before continuing. "He appears to have the Obsidian Streaks."

Liam's chest tightened at the reminder of the horrible disease. He watched as Alexander's face fell from its scowl and twisted into bewilderment.

"The Obsidian Streaks?" he asked. "Well, now that's impossible," he said with a doubtful chuckle. "And I know a thing or two about the Streaks." He pushed up the sleeves on his jacket, revealing the horrific black lines that ran up and down his arms.

Liam's stomach tightened at the sight of the disease again and he took a step back. He couldn't take his eyes from the cracking lines and the dying skin on the man's arms. A soft blue glow radiated from the lines and Liam was forced to cease his staring when Alexander pushed his sleeves back down.

"We thought it was impossible too," Anthony continued, sorrow clear in his voice, "but it appears we were all wrong. He has the Streaks. I've seen them, and while they are not quite the same color as yours, he has all the other symptoms the Streaks bring. He's getting worse every minute, the disease wreaking havoc on his body so quickly. His condition has progressed far faster than any case we have ever heard of. We don't know how long he has left."

Liam felt a lump growing within in his throat as Anthony spoke. The reminder of his uncle's condition threatened to melt down the strong demeanor he had forced himself to portray. Anthony paused and the boys stared at Alexander anxiously as he sat in silent thought, probably trying to decide whether to believe them.

Anthony continued. "We need to find the Water Stone. The stone with the power of the Water Alumenos. It's the only hope we have to heal the emperor," Anthony revealed calmly and seriously. "And he told us you would know where to find it."

Alexander's eyes widened and he looked from Anthony up to Liam, and then back down at Anthony.

"He told you about the Water Stone?" he asked, squinting his eyes.

Anthony nodded. "Yes. And he believes we can retrieve it."

Liam rolled his eyes internally at Anthony's use of "we."

"And what makes him think that?" Alexander said, a chuckle escaping his throat. "Just because he thinks he needs it now? I tried to get him to go back years ago and he wouldn't do it. Not after what happened last time." His voice shook with emotion. He removed his hands from the table and rubbed his legs as he spoke. "Now he wants to send a couple of boys? You two are certainly not ready to fight such a beast."

"A beast?" Liam asked, watching the man and his reactions closely. His uncle had mentioned they failed miserably, but it seemed the failure had cost Alexander much more than pride.

"He didn't even tell you what was guarding it?" Alexander asked incredulously.

"Well, he is sort of in the middle of dying," Anthony snapped. "He didn't get that far into the story."

"He sent us here, to you, to learn more," Liam said more gently.

Anthony sat back in his chair and crossed his arms, clearly perturbed. Alexander allowed a laugh to escape his throat as he looked up at Liam with a glimmer of animosity in his eyes.

"The stone is guarded by a dragon. A very old, strong, and powerful rock dragon," Alexander revealed haughtily.

Chills ran through Liam's body, prickling their way up each of his arms. He grabbed onto that gentle vibration within to keep himself standing.

"A dragon?" Liam asked as Alexander turned his eyes away from him.

"So what?" Anthony asked in his customary arrogant tone. "People used to take down dragons all the time. For sport."

"Yes, that is certainly true," Alexander said with a single nod. "It was a sport that brought me great riches and fame once."

"You? You were a dragon hunter?" Anthony asked, leaning forward again.

Alexander nodded and sat back in his chair, folding his hands in his lap. "Oh yes. My team and I were the very best. We had taken down countless dragons and other monstrosities, like packs of two-headed wolves and even a giant. Our fame and reputation as beast slayers were exactly what brought Philip to us. We knew Garrock would be a challenge, but we never doubted that we could take him down."

"Garrock?" Liam asked, remembering the name. "The dragon guarding the Water Stone is called Garrock? Then that means …" Liam's memory sparked with recognition of a lesson in one of his history classes years ago. "You were a member of the Mighty Four?"

Alexander only shrugged and looked down in answer.

"Your encounter with Garrock ended dragon hunting in Akaria forever," Liam said, remembering what he had learned many years ago about dragon hunts being outlawed by his uncle after a terrible incident.

"Your uncle and I were the only ones to leave that cave with a shred of ourselves still intact," Alexander said. "We had the beast cornered. He couldn't move. We had him paralyzed and all we needed to do was pluck that blue stone from his skull. But we wanted the kill, and the alagon sword didn't work. Stabbing the dragon didn't bring him down. Alagon is the only metal known to man that will pierce a dragon, but we were left stunned and helpless with no weapon. The dragon became death itself and we knew nothing of what we were really facing. We had no chance." Alexander's face hardened with the memory. He stared past Liam as he continued. "It was the worst day of my life. If your uncle hadn't pulled me from the wreckage, I would have lost more than just the use of my legs. Though, in reality I did lose more than that." Alexander looked down at his hands. "Much more."

Liam remained silent, unsure what to say next. The pain was so clearly displayed on the man's face in front of him. Liam hoped Anthony would know what to say better than he did, but it seemed even Anthony couldn't find the right words to say.

Alexander inhaled sharply and looked back up. "We couldn't defeat him and you won't be able to either. No one can. Not yet. Philip shouldn't have sent you here. I told him what we needed to defeat Garrock, but he wouldn't listen."

"So it's possible. There is a way to defeat him?" Anthony asked carefully.

Alexander nodded slowly with a menacing smile. "We need the key. The spell protecting Garrock is a 'lock and key' spell. And the key is a sword called Velios. The magical flaming sword is untouchable by human hands while it remains under the protective, blood-bound enchantment," Alexander explained. "I found this out much later, in a song the Fairies had written. For years I had searched for the answer, and when I had finally found it, your uncle just shut me down. He wasn't interested in helping anymore." He sighed. "I suppose that's because we have no idea how to find this sword. It was hidden away ages ago when the spell on the dragon was first created by the Lumenaros and none of them would ever give up that information to a bunch of humans."

Suddenly, a high-pitched cry pierced the air. Liam smacked his hands over his ears to drown out the terrible, ear-wrenching sound. He watched as the candles set around the room flickered. Liam's heart raced uncontrollably fast and he felt the adrenaline of the sudden fright pulsing through his body. Anthony jumped up from his seat and put a hand on the small dagger he kept tucked into his pants, as he looked around for the source of the screeching.

"Xevron take me ..." Alexander whispered and wheeled over to a small table that stood next to the straw bed in the far corner of the room. Alexander opened the loud drawer in the small table, and snatched a piece of bundled cloth and quickly closed the drawer again. In his haste he fumbled the item he had picked up and a small piece of black rock slid out of the cloth in his hand.

Alexander cursed again as the rock bounced onto the floor in front of him. Without hesitation, Liam moved across the floor quickly to pick up the rock for the older man. Liam examined the smooth black rock as he picked it up off the floor and offered it to Alexander.

Alexander glared at Liam but took the rock from Liam's palm with the cloth, clearly not wanting to touch the thing with his own bare hands. Then he rushed into a room partitioned behind a tattered sheet. The wailing continued and gusts of wind blew through the cabin. The pots hanging above the dwindling fire swayed and banged together loudly.

Then Liam heard a muffled scream and the whole cabin began to shake. The pots hanging on the ceiling crashed down to the ground and the dishes in the sink, books on the shelves, and the clothes on the bed slid onto the floor. The wind continued to blow through the room and papers shot across the room as they fell from the shelves out of the falling books. Liam and Anthony crouched down to crawl beneath the table to shield themselves from the chaos.

Liam and Anthony remained under the table until the quaking slowly subsided and the screeching grew quieter and quieter. They looked at each other, both of them quite disheveled now, before slowly coming out from under the table.

"What was that?" Liam asked in a whisper with wide eyes.

"I have no idea," Anthony said as they stood up. "No wonder his house is a mess, though," Anthony added with a nervous chuckle to himself.

Liam ventured closer to the tattered curtain. "Sir? Is everything all right?" he called out to Alexander.

"Don't take another step! I've got it under control," Alexander called out from behind the curtain.

Liam hesitated and took a step back. Then he changed his mind, deciding the man may need help and stepped up to the curtain. He peered through one of the holes in the sheet and immediately regretted his decision as his eyes fell upon a disturbing sight.

Alexander held a frail woman upright in a small bed as he held the cloth with the stone in it to her forehead. She was frighteningly thin and Liam watched as her eyes closed and her head lolled backward before Alexander laid her gently back down on the bed. The skin on her arms were a sickening gray color and covered all over in black veiny lines, cracked down the middle, exposing a very faint blue glow. The Obsidian Streaks.

Liam quickly stepped back away from the curtain and quietly hurried back over to where Anthony still stood. Liam felt sick as he realized his uncle was headed for a similar fate as the woman behind the curtain.

"What? What was it? What did you see?" Anthony whispered.

"I'm … I'm really not sure …" Liam said, eyes still wide, looking at the ground. "It was a person, but a pretty withered one." Then Liam looked up at his brother. "She had the Obsidian Streaks, Anthony. A very advanced case."

Alexander emerged from behind the curtain with an angry look on his face, forcing Liam's attention away from his brother. Alexander violently threw an empty bottle on the ground at their feet and pointed to the door.

"That's it, show's over. Time to go," he said in a raised voice. He motioned to the door. "I have my own problems to deal with right now."

"Sir, please, you must tell us more …" Liam began to plead, but Alexander shook his head as he wheeled himself over to the door to usher them out.

"There's no more to tell. I can't help you," Alexander said definitively.

"My uncle wouldn't have sent us if there wasn't a good reason he believed we could do this now," Anthony chimed in.

"You see … things have changed, I'm different …" Liam said, pleading to Alexander to listen. He had to get Alexander to tell them everything he knew. What could he say to get this man to trust him?

"Everyone thinks they're different. We thought we were different too," Alexander said, not looking at the boys. "But that sort of thinking tore my sister apart. Her Streaks grew at an alarming rate due to the amount of power she used to try to save us. Now she is barely clinging to life and doesn't even remember who she is … or who I am," Alexander said with a crack in his voice. He looked back up at Liam. Pure despair in his eyes. "I have no way to help her. I have resorted to using the very thing that all witches despise. The rock that originally surrounded the Well and drains our power and our strength. Obsidian itself. You don't want to be where I am now. Having lost nearly everything precious to you. Unable to do anything to help."

Liam's face softened. "I'm so sorry," he said. "I can't imagine the pain you've been through because of this stone, but if you just tell us where to find the stone …"

"Your uncle may be selfish enough to send you two out on a suicide mission, but I certainly will not do that," Alexander said angrily.

"It's not that …" Liam said exasperatedly. "I'm different. I really am. There's a reason he has faith in this mission."

Alexander huffed. "And why do you think that so fervently, boy? What silly stories has your uncle told you?"

The words caught in Liam's throat. He still felt ridiculous even thinking the words he was about to say out loud.

"I'm an Alumenos," Liam finally said as evenly as he could muster.

After a brief pause, a smile split through Alexander's anguished face and a laugh heaved out of his chest. He laughed for a few moments before turning a scowl back on Liam and shaking his head.

"I can prove it," Liam said, lifting his eyebrows.

Liam looked around the room, but there was nothing heavy enough to convince Alexander beyond a doubt. Liam grabbed a lantern and hurried out the open door, motioning the others to follow him. He looked around, the moon bright in the sky, surveying the trees as he waited for Alexander and Anthony to join him outside.

Liam locked his eyes on a thick tree standing at the edge of the clearing. He looked down to the ground and squeezed his eyes shut. *Oh please Tykos, let this work,* he prayed as he approached the large tree, setting his lantern down on the ground beside him.

Liam took a deep breath. He reached inside and felt for that vibration of power in his gut. He paused, feeding the vibrations, feeling the power start to culminate within him and his body begin to hum. Then he moved quickly and confidently, ramming his fists into the tall column of wood. A loud snap echoed throughout the clearing. The tree tilted, but still stood upright. Liam felt heat running through his arms as he pushed the tree over and watched it split and tumble to the ground.

The feeling was so intoxicating, he didn't want to stop there. He was curious just how far his strength would go. He moved over to the fallen half of the tree and squatted next to it, wrapping his arms underneath the trunk. The bark cut into his skin as he lifted the massive trunk up. He grunted as he lifted the tree clear over his head. He felt a pulsing all over his body as the power sustained his strength and he held the tree above him like it weighed nothing.

Satisfied, Liam set the tree back down onto the ground carefully and let the power and the vibrations fade, the tingle of the power leaving his limbs. He looked over to Alexander and Anthony as he pushed a red curl out of his face.

Anthony wore a huge smile on his face as he shook his head in disbelief, but Alexander looked frightened. Liam worried he had gone too far too fast, but then Alexander smiled and broke into a soft chuckle. Liam smiled with relief and jogged back to them.

Alexander continued to laugh for a few moments as Liam approached. Alexander grabbed Liam's arm when he got close enough and looked Liam in the face. A sparkle of a tear sat on the edge of the man's tired eyes.

"Thank all the four gods, I can hardly believe this," he said as emotion poured out of him. "This is a miracle. Do you realize that my boy?"

Alexander turned away from Liam and quickly wheeled back into his hut. Liam and Anthony followed, Anthony jabbing Liam in the ribs playfully with a proud smile as they went.

"I never would have believed we would have a chance like this. Not in my lifetime, anyway. Both an Alumenos and a Volkev descendant, here in Akaria, with me, at the same time. She's not quite ready and we'll have figure out that disenchantment spell sooner than I thought …" Alexander continued to ramble as he faced away from the boys and began gathering up books again.

Liam felt his knees buckle briefly. He felt a wave of fatigue set in as he stood there. His arms felt heavy and he stumbled over to the lone chair in the room to sit down. He sat down carefully and smiled as Alexander continued to babble about all the possibilities. Liam was relieved to have convinced him that they had a shot at recovering the Water Stone.

"So you will help us find the sword? And tell us where to find the Water Stone?" Liam asked in confirmation. He was sure he would hear the answer he wanted.

"Well, Xevron's souls, of course. We need to find the sword's location and I will have to go with you," Alexander said as he turned back to look at Liam. "The stones are well hidden and well protected. The Volkev witch responsible for creating them and hiding them never wanted them to be found or used again. It will be a difficult journey …" Alexander's face fell and he slowly shook his head. "But I am in this chair now and I have to take care of her. She can't be alone. I don't see how …" Alexander said sadly, his eyes searching the air for some kind of answer.

Anthony walked up to Alexander and knelt down to be face-to-face with him.

"I will make sure your sister is taken care of while you are helping with this quest. She will come to stay in the palace," he assured the man.

"I really don't know, I don't know if anyone else can handle her episodes," Alexander said wearily.

"We have the best doctors in the country at the palace and we can call whoever else you want to come in and help as well," Anthony guaranteed him.

"The best thing you can do for her is to find this stone," Liam broke in.
Alexander looked up at Liam. "This could actually bring her back to me …"
Liam watched as thoughts turned in the man's head.

"I have to have her back. She was so magnificent, so kind. She deserves to live out the rest of her life," he finally said. "I can call in a few favors with some other witches. I can't let this opportunity slip away."

Liam and Anthony looked at each other. There was a sense of nervous triumph in the shared look. They could both feel what this meant. Though it was success, there was still a mystery to solve before they could even start the journey.

"I will have guards sent today to bring your belongings and your sister to the palace," Anthony said as he stood up from his kneel.

"There is one more thing I feel I should you should know," Alexander said with a finger in the air. "It may be difficult to work out, but ..." Alexander hesitated. "We will need the Princess Katerina."

12

The covers shuffled noisily as Katerina rolled over again. She had tossed and turned for hours now, but still sleep would not take her. She flipped herself flat onto her back and threw her hands down in frustration, letting out a sigh. She peeked up at the clock on the wall and whimpered.

Time did not care she couldn't fall asleep and was rudely still moving forward. She needed to be ready for morning service in just four hours. The clock kept ticking away as she stared at it, her heart thumping loudly in her chest and her mind racing with the information that had been dumped on her this evening.

Kona had warned her of the unexpected arrivals in enough time for her to hide in Davi's bedroom. She couldn't let anyone know she was sneaking off into the woods at night to learn magic. She was surprised to hear it was the Princep and his brother that had come to see Alexander, especially at that hour. She listened intently as they revealed to Alexander that the emperor seemed to have the Obsidian Streaks and was dying quickly. But that wasn't the most shocking thing revealed tonight.

There was a Water Stone. A healing stone that held the miraculous ability to cure anything and everything, even the Obsidian Streaks. She had of course heard of this Water Stone, but it was always just an Akarian legend. She knew the stone was supposedly hidden away over 500 years ago when a group of Isavarian witches stole all the powers from the Alumenos, creating the Lumos Gems, and scattering them across the world. And tonight, Katerina learned that she was part of this story.

Izolda Volkev, Katerina's ancestor, and her sisters were the witches behind the Lumos Gems and the protection spells that had kept them hidden all these years. It was believed, but never written, that Izolda likely led her sisters to imprison the Alumenos powers when rumors of an Ultimate Alumenos began to spread. The Alumenos had always been a great force and they led the many kingdoms of Elusira back then. But an Ultimate Alumenos—an all-powerful Alumenos with all four of the powers from the Alumetris and the ability to create more lines of Alumenos—was something Izolda could not let happen. She acted out of fear and desperation. She wanted revenge for how they had oppressed her husband and his people, the Noxenos. She had wanted security for her family. Now, Katerina had a real chance to obtain the Water Stone and use it to save Izolda's own people. A chance that could only be realized if Katerina played her part.

Katerina gave up on sleep and threw the blankets off. She swung her legs over the side of the bed and sat there for a moment, looking down at her chest and tracing her finger along her black, cracking lines running across her chest and onto her shoulder. This could all be gone. She could be cured.

She had wanted to burst into tears when Davi's episode happened right next to her. She had wished Kona was with her in that moment to shield her from the afflicted witch, but he had stayed outside. As the cabin shook, she hid her face in her hands and huddled in the corner, but she had already seen the horror. Chills ran up her arms as she remembered. She didn't want to end up like that. She couldn't let her Streaks take her like that.

Katerina slid off the bed and rummaged through the drawer in her nightstand. She pulled out a clean sheet of paper and a pen and opened the window next to her bed. The moon was close to full tonight, which would give her enough light to see as she sketched. She set the paper on the windowsill and let her mind wander freely as her hand moved across the page, the familiar strokes calming her nerves.

She thought back to Izolda. Izolda and her sisters had used many spells in her defeat of the Alumenos: a linking spell, a siphoning spell, and a sealing spell. They linked all the Alumenos together and then slowly siphoned each of the four powers into magical stones.

Katerina decided to draw the four captured Alumenos, one of each kind, hanging chained on dungeon walls. She added wavy lines across the page, coming from each of them to signify their powers leaving them as the witches siphoned their powers one by one. Then she sketched the four stones, each with a different symbol.

Then Katerina flipped the piece of paper over and drew the flaming sword, Velios. The weapon that was forged as the key to defeating the monster guarding the Water Stone, the ferocious rock dragon Garrock. Garrock was the lock around the stone and Velios was the key that would unlock the spell. The flames danced brilliantly in Katerina's mind—the flames that rendered it untouchable until the protection enchantment on it was broken. And Katerina had to be the one to do it.

She stopped drawing and stared at the picture. Her blood, her Volkev blood, was needed to break the enchantment on Velios. Alexander told her that she would only be needed to break the enchantment on the sword, she would be kept far away from the dragon fight itself. In fact, he was quite adamant that he would let her nowhere near it. And while that was a relief, once they figured out where the sword was located, she would have to go with Alexander and Liam, the emperor's timid nephew, to break the enchantment.

Katerina looked up into the moon's light. She had been filled with both excitement and terror after hearing this. Her father would be so angry if he knew. She had no idea how they would convince him to let her go somewhere without him, but she had turned down adventure before because of her fears, and she didn't want to do that this time. Every day since Mikhal left she had regretted not going with him. A sharp pain swelled up in her chest as tears formed in her eyes.

She needed to get out of this room. The room felt suddenly very small, and despite the open window, she couldn't breathe.

She grabbed her traveling cloak out of the wardrobe and whispered the flame spell to quickly and easily light the candle that sat on her bedside table. She quietly opened the door to her bedroom and tiptoed through the dark room, holding her candle out in front of her.

She unlatched the door leading out into the hallway and peeked her head out of the doorway. She was comforted to see the familiar shape of Kona standing next to the door.

"You should be asleep, Your Highness," Kona said, looking toward the hallway.

"I know," Katerina admitted as she stepped into the hallway and closed her door behind her. "But I couldn't sleep. I think I just need to walk. I need to clear my head."

Kona sighed and then nodded. He hadn't heard all the details of what Katerina learned tonight, but he had to know that it was something life-changing. Katerina was grateful that he hadn't prodded her for answers on their way back to the palace; she didn't know if she could have coherently explained anything to him at that point.

"I know a good place," he said with a slight smile and waved for her to join him as he walked down the dark corridor.

The hallway was lit with only few candles in the chandeliers and the moonlight shining in through the windows. Katerina grabbed her cloak around her tightly as they walked silently. Kona came to stop in front of a small door set into the outer wall of the palace, nearly eclipsed by a large column.

"Go through here and all the way up the stairs," he instructed as he opened the door for her. "I'll give you thirty minutes. If you're not back by then, I'll come up and get you." His eyes never stopped scanning their surroundings.

Katerina nodded and smiled gratefully at the Tyken and slipped through the door. Inside she found a staircase that wound upward in a narrow spiral. She stepped up the stairs, letting her hand drag across the wall as she walked carefully up each step.

Soon she came to another door and opened it slowly. The door did indeed lead her outside and Katerina was relieved at the sudden burst of cool fresh air that filled her lungs. She extinguished her candle and set it down as she walked out onto the high tower overlooking the backside of the palace. She looked out over the forest behind the castle and the small lake that sat in the center of it all. She leaned on the edge of the stone and watched as the moonlight rippled on the water.

Then she heard a noise from behind her and her calm immediately vanished. She turned quickly and saw someone standing and looking out the other way over the city.

"Who's there?" Katerina demanded. She felt the breeze start to pick up around her with her sudden fright.

The figure jumped. Katerina had apparently startled them as well. The person slowly turned and as his face came into view, she realized with relief that she recognized that unruly red hair. She smiled and relaxed, letting the breeze flow back into its natural state.

"Oh, I'm so sorry, Your Highness," Liam said, his eyes turned down and his hands raised in front of him, palms exposed.

"It's quite all right," Katerina said with a laugh. "It's my fault. I didn't know anyone else was up here."

Liam lifted his head to look at her and smiled a crooked smile at her before looking down to the ground again. "I shouldn't be up here anyway, but I couldn't sleep. This used to be one of my favorite places to sneak off to when I was a child," he said as he looked out over the edge of the turret, toward the city.

"I can see why. It's beautiful. Not to mention, very peaceful," Katerina said, glancing at the view.

Liam turned back to Katerina. "Well, please do enjoy it. I'm sorry I disturbed you. I'll let you be in peace," he said as he moved toward the tower door.

"Oh, no, please," Katerina said, stretching her hand out. "Will you stay?" He turned back to look at her with uncertainty, so she added, "I wanted to ask you something."

Liam flicked his eyes up at her, keeping his head lowered. He seemed very kind, although cripplingly shy. Katerina cringed internally about having to deal with his awkwardness as they traveled together, but maybe she could get him to loosen up a little. She could likely get him to trust her with a little effort. He lifted his head up fully and smiled at her. A very nice, charming smile. And then he nodded, waiting for her question.

"This quest for the Water Stone," she began. "Alexander tells me that you will be going with him to find it?"

Liam nodded and came to stand closer to her. "Yes, Your Highness. It is a great privilege to be seeking this stone for Akaria," he said. He hesitated before asking, "You've already spoken with Alexander then? Did he say anything about what you …" he stopped.

Katerina smiled and turned back to the outside edge. She placed her hands on the stone. "Yes, I spoke with him. He told me that because of my bloodline, I would need to be present for him to break the enchantment on the flaming sword once we know where it is." She looked back at him, and invited him with a gesture to stand next to her.

He inched a little closer and set his elbows down on the ledge. "Do you think that's something you would be willing to help us with?" he asked timidly, unable to keep his eyes on her.

Katerina dropped her smile and sighed. "I want to … but right now, I don't see how I could," she said before turning to look at him again. "I'm not exactly free like you are."

Liam chuckled and shook his head. "Free? That's a nice thought, but I'm anything but free." He looked out over the landscape, letting his eyes glaze over with thought.

"Well, you're certainly freer than I am," Katerina said. "You get to go out there and be anything you want. You can go on this adventure freely and you don't have to worry about messing up a great alliance and dooming your country in a war or saying the wrong thing in a council meeting or wearing the wrong color to dinner. I guess that's the luxury of being second born …" She let the last words sit in the air between them.

Liam shook his head again but cracked a smile. "That's not how things are at all for me. Destiny has my path laid out for me just as much as she has dictated Anthony's. For instance, my uncle insists that I join the Tykerial Guard. It's the rightful place of the second born to lead the Guard someday."

"Is that not what you want?" Katerina asked, feeling horrible for assuming he was as frivolous and unshackled as her own sister.

Liam let out a big sigh. He appeared much more relaxed now. "I don't know. I thought it was. But last year …" He trailed off and then shrugged.

"What? What happened last year?" Katerina asked.

He turned toward her and didn't drop his gaze this time as he told her his story. "I was on my way to the Tykerial Guard exam. I was coming from the training ground a few blocks away. I thought they had a better archery range and I had been doing some last-minute training there. I was running a little late, so I decided to take a shortcut. I knew the shortcut would take me through some sketchy areas and small roads, but I figured it was worth it. I was hurrying through an alley when I smelled the smoke. Then I heard screams. I ran toward the sound and saw that a small bakery had caught on fire."

Liam paused to swallow hard. The emotion in his eyes, Katerina couldn't place. She wasn't sure if it was anger, sadness, regret, or fear, but he was clearly in agony at the memory.

"Townspeople gathered around the small building, some ran for help, and some threw small buckets of water onto the fire, but the flames were too much. It would take them too long to extinguish it all. I saw a little girl screaming for her father who was apparently still inside the burning building. I knew I didn't have time to stop. They were already alerting the local guards. But the girl, she just kept screaming. I couldn't let what happened to me happen to her." Liam's eyes darted away from Katerina as he continued. "My parents were lost in a fire when I was little too. I wasn't there when it happened, and I was much too young to remember any of it, but I still have to live without them every single day. I didn't want that for her, not if I could do something about it. So I ran in."

Liam took a deep breath.

"Did you find the father?" Katerina asked, concern building in her chest.

Liam shook his head. "It had been too long. I couldn't get through. I showed up to the trials with ash on my clothes and a shadow of regret hanging over me. I didn't make it in time and I was disqualified from the exam. This year will be my last chance. I can't let my uncle down this year. Especially not now. Not with him …" Liam cut off, wincing.

"Not with him being so ill," Katerina finished for him. "Alexander told me about that."

Liam looked at her with surprise and then just nodded.

"It's just sometimes I feel like I could do more. The Guard is great and it is really important, but I don't know. I've just seen that there are so many people out there, even just in Gilderon alone, that need real help. My uncle didn't have a choice in sending me on this quest for the Water Stone. When I get back and he's healed, he's made it clear he still sees me on the Guard. He wouldn't understand if I told him I wanted to do something else with my life." Liam looked out over the horizon. Then he turned to look at Katerina with a smile, trying to lighten the mood. "For instance, he wouldn't want me running off to fight in your father's war."

Katerina laughed. "Oh, I don't blame him one bit there. It's a stupid war," she said, resentment creeping up into her words.

Liam chuckled, apparently assuming she wasn't serious. "It seems like a pretty important war if he's willing to marry off his eldest daughter for soldiers to fight in it."

Katerina's face darkened as she gravely told him her own story. "No, you see, my sister was betrothed to the Prince of Lodarine, Isavaria's second largest country. And it was by choice. She thought they had a 'real connection.' She told everyone she knew how he proposed under the stars and how she knew it was meant to be and all that mush. But then we received word a few months later that he had married someone else."

"Oh, I didn't realize your sister was old enough to be married."

93

Katerina rolled her eyes. "She's not. Clearly. But my father obviously took issue with the way he believed his daughter had been treated. He had started to look forward to forming an alliance with Lodarine and possibly expanding his own kingdom and so he decided it was all a betrayal of the Lodarine king to let this happen. So the war between our countries started and then my father decided to pursue this alliance here with Akaria to gain the skilled troops he needed to take down his enemy. Esterine's standing army isn't going to be enough I suppose. So here I am, cleaning up the mess."

She looked up at the sky and stared into the night.

"I'm sorry," Liam said with genuine sympathy in his voice. "I'm especially sorry you have to marry my brother." He started to laugh.

Katerina turned to him and laughed.

"He doesn't seem too bad," Katerina said, still smiling. "It could definitely be worse."

"He's a good one. He'll make a good emperor," Liam said with a nod. "… and a decent husband too, I'm sure."

A silence spread between them and Katerina tried not to let the word "husband" cause her stomach to flutter nervously. She remembered Kona was waiting for her, but she had more to ask Liam first.

"There seems to be quite a few Tykens working here. I was surprised that the emperor is able to employ so many. It seems like an odd thing for them to want to do," she prodded subtly.

Clearly relieved with the subject change, Liam nodded. "Yes, it is a very unique situation. A few years ago, during the war with Wenstetter, my uncle was able to form an alliance with the Tykens. Both Akarian soldiers and Tyken soldiers from Tulneria fought against Wenstetter and when the war was over, some of the Tykens just stayed, not wanting to return home to their isolated forests in Tulneria. They preferred the life and opportunities in Akaria. Emperor Shadox found suitable places for them and they've been content here ever since."

Katerina raised her eyebrows. "Wow, that is pretty impressive. My father has tried to ally himself with the Tykens and the Aurens for years but has never managed it. My father believes they have similar goals, but just different tactics. He would invite them to our court every few months. He had me and the whole court learn their languages and customs as he tried very hard to impress them."

"You've seen Aurens?" Liam asked with awe.

Katerina laughed. "Well, of course. You haven't?"

Liam shook his head. "No, never. I was always told that they hated humans and didn't want to be associated with us in any way. They would never even think about coming around here."

Katerina smiled to herself and let her eyes glaze over as she remembered the beautiful, tall beings with huge, feathered wings protruding from their backs. "They are very beautiful creatures," she said.

Katerina looked down, shaking herself from the vivid memory of Aurens storming through the hallways, searching for Mikhal. A piece of hair fell into her face and she pushed the string back behind her ear mindlessly.

"That ring," Liam said suddenly, staring at Katerina's hand as it brushed back her hair.

Katerina looked down at her hand to see the opal ring she wore on her middle finger.

"You wore that ring on the night of your Welcome Ball, didn't you?" Liam asked. Without waiting for an answer, he continued. "Did it change color?" Liam asked, coming closer to her, his eyes fixed on the ring.

Katerina looked at the ring more closely. "I suppose it has a little," she said, still examining the ring. She looked up at him curiously. "That's a strange thing for you to notice."

Liam stepped back from her. "I remember touching it when I greeted you that night ..." he paused, clearly not wanting to continue his thought out loud.

Katerina laughed a little, trying to comfort him into trusting her with the truth. "Yes? And? I've touched it many times and I'm sure countless others have as well."

Liam let out a sharp exhale and squeezed his lips together. "You're going to think I'm crazy, but I think that ring might have a very special stone in it."

Katerina held the ring out in front of her and looked it over once again. "Special? I don't think it's supposed to be anything special. My stepmother gave it to me before we came over from Isavaria. She said she had purchased it from a traveling merchant earlier that day as a gift for me. She wanted me to have something to wear that would remind me of home and gifts are usually her way of comforting my sister and me."

Liam hesitated but couldn't take his eyes off of the stone. "I think ... I think that it might be a shard of the Earth Stone," he finally revealed.

Katerina laughed. "The Earth Stone? Like another Alumenos gem?"

Liam nodded, though he looked like he hardly believed it himself.

"How could that be? How would it have made it all the way to Isavaria? And then all the way to me? That would be quite fortuitous."

"I know," Liam said. "But I think the stone affected me in some way. I could feel it pulling me to it as soon as you entered the room. And once I touched it ... well, that's when I started feeling different and the headaches came," Liam said, staring at the ring, and added more quietly, "And the dreams started ..."

Katerina took the ring off her finger and set it down on the ledge.

Liam picked it up and turned it over in his fingers as he examined it. "This has to be it."

"So you are a Earth Alumenos?" Katerina asked, putting together the pieces of what Alexander had told her after Liam and his brother had left. He hadn't wanted to tell her about Liam, but he did imply there was something special about him.

Liam nodded and smiled at her. "My touch must have drained this stone of the power it held. I was reading about this earlier today. An Alumenos who touches the stone of their destined power, will have their powers returned to them. That's why the witch decided to hide them away so securely. All her efforts would have been in vain."

Then Liam suddenly looked embarrassed and quickly put the ring back down on the ledge. "I'm sorry," he said and backed away from her. "I'm sure that was too much information."

"No, no," Katerina assured him. "It's nice to know actually ..." she trailed off as she thought about what she wanted to say next. Could she trust Liam?

"I just ... it's not a ... I don't really want a lot of people knowing ..." Liam fumbled over his words now as he avoided her eyes again.

Katerina felt her body tighten and her breath quicken as she made the decision. A decision she desperately hoped she wouldn't regret. She had to tell him who she really was and what she could do.

"I understand. I understand more than you realize ..." Katerina said softly.

He turned to look at her, concern written all over his face. She watched his face transform into one of relief and compassion as he understood what she meant. Katerina smiled. She felt a kinship with Liam that she hadn't been expecting.

"I know a thing or two about keeping certain abilities hidden."

13

Liam squinted his eyes in the bright sunlight as he walked out onto the beautiful terrace balcony. He felt the bags under his eyes sag with fatigue and he did his best to straighten out the slightly wrinkled suit he was wearing. He had planned on stopping by the manor to get more clothes last night, but plans had changed.

His mind was fuzzy this morning from lack of sleep and he hoped he could keep it together for this important meeting. He was still flabbergasted by how much the world had changed for him in the last day. He was an Alumenos and Princess Katerina was an Isavarian witch. She had seemed surprised and relieved at his acceptance of her confession, but Liam knew how King Nikita would feel about it if he knew. He couldn't imagine keeping a secret like that from his own family; he had never been good at lying. Alexander had made it seem like they only needed her blood to disenchant the sword, but she actually would be playing a much bigger role. She had asked him not tell anyone about what she was, not even Anthony, and he had of course promised not to, but he was worried Anthony would just read it on his tired face this morning.

He rubbed his face quickly to wake himself up and saw Anthony standing at the far end of the balcony, overlooking the many buildings and people that made up the city of Gilderon. Anthony had invited him to this meeting last night after they had learned about the song the Fairies had written about the Lumos Gems weapons, and Liam was incredibly nervous about it.

He walked toward his brother as members of the Tykerial Guard watched him carefully. They surrounded the terrace, standing perfectly spaced with spears at their sides in their full green and gold decorative armor. Liam was sure they always wore their best for this regular meeting with the Fairies.

He felt more self-conscious of his wrinkled and plain gray and brown attire as he stepped up beside Anthony who wore a pristine white and gold filigreed suit.

"Thank you for including me in this meeting today," Liam said, still trying to stretch his suit straight.

Anthony nodded and turned to his brother. "It is my most important, not to mention most fun, meeting of the day. Edward would usually be leading this meeting, but it falls to me today with him picking up all the other emperor's meetings. I've been in these meetings before though. They'll drop off their payment as usual and then I'll invite them to sit for a drink, which of course they won't refuse, and then I'll find a way to ask them about the flaming sword, Velios. If the Fairies did indeed write that song Alexander found, these guys will know something. They are excellent gossips and especially loose with information after a little wine." Anthony smiled proudly and then finally looked his brother up and down. "Farran's flame! What happened to you?"

Liam continued pulling and smoothing his suit. "I know, I'm sorry. I guess I should have run home for a new suit this morning."

Anthony closed his eyes and laughed. "Well never mind that now I suppose. Perhaps the Fairies will get a good kick out of it."

Liam smiled slightly, already embarrassed. He'd never actually met a Fairie up close, though he'd seen groups of them from a distance at some of the bigger parties and holidays throughout the years. They were the creation of the Fire God, Farran, and therefore one of the most beautiful and playful creatures in the world. He turned to look over his shoulder at the long glass table that stood in the center of the balcony. Two tall-backed chairs sat at one end and Liam could see that there were tiny chairs, chaises, and pillows set around an arrangement of small tables on top of the larger one. The small tables held an assortment of tiny food portions, including pieces of breads, cheeses, and fruits, and of course carafes of dark liquid for their Fairie guests.

This has to work, Liam thought to himself as he turned to look back over the vast city below them.

He saw a spot of light off in the distance. It looked like a star shining brightly despite the midday light. It started off small at first and then slowly grew bigger and bigger. Liam felt his muscles tighten in his neck. That must be them. They were almost there. In just a few minutes he would be taking part in a very important political meeting with a Lumenaro faction.

He continued to watch as the ball of light turned into a bundle of many lights as the Fairies got closer. He looked over to Anthony, who stood firm and straight with a warm smile on his face as he watched their guests approach. The specks of light turned into tiny heads and bodies as they came closer to Liam's view. They hovered above the balcony and Liam was astounded by how intricately beautiful each of them was. Their features were perfectly defined and they each held a soft, warm glow about them.

"My friends," Anthony said, looking up at the floating lights. "Welcome once again to the kingdom of Akaria. It is a pleasure for me to receive you this month. My uncle is indisposed at the moment, so he asked me and my brother Liam, to handle our meeting this time. Shall we get the boring stuff over with then?"

A Fairie wearing a large golden headdress and a long, open red robe glared at Liam as he looked him up and down. Liam squirmed slightly and smiled sheepishly back at him. Then the Fairie nodded to one of the other Fairies beside him, apparently deciding to accept Liam as participant in this meeting despite his disarrayed appearance.

A group of five Fairies flew forward out of the vast group, holding a bundle of cloth between them. Anthony motioned to one of the Tykerial Guard officers standing nearby. Liam recognized the man as a legate officer from the helmet he wore as he came forward and proffered his hands out to the Fairies. They flew forward and gently placed their package in his hands. The Tykerial Guard legate opened the bundle carefully and Liam saw the twinkling of the diamonds from within the small package. The legate examined the contents carefully and then signaled for another Guard to come forward. The legate slid the diamonds into a wooden box held by the other officer and latched the box firmly before turning and nodding to Anthony.

Anthony nodded back to the legate and then dismissed him with a flick of his hand. The legate left the room with two other guards, taking the payment of sparkling diamonds with them as they went. Liam looked around at the remaining guards, trying to decide who was the highest ranked in the room now.

"Now that our tedious business is concluded, would you sit with me for a drink?" Anthony said to the Fairie leader and gestured over toward the long glass table. "I know you've come today to speak more about a renewal of our agreement since our alliance is near the end of its contract. We will need to discuss the terms of renewal before the New Year next month, but before we get to all that, I thought we should celebrate our long friendship. I've had a few things prepared."

"Indeed, a fine idea," the Fairie leader said in his small voice, a smile breaking through his stern expression.

Anthony motioned for them all to take their seats and the specks of light descended upon the glass table quickly. Liam followed Anthony over to their own seats and was soon sitting face-to-face with the stunning creatures. The Fairies' skin glowed with a warm yellow light that faded only slightly as he got closer to them. The Fairies eagerly took advantage of the chairs, chaises, and pillows that were laid out for them, and many of them immediately grabbed at the breads and cheeses and began pouring themselves generous helpings of wine.

Liam was intrigued by how much they looked like ordinary people this close up; that is if ordinary people were only a few inches tall and immaculately beautiful. Their skin was flawless, their brown and red hair swished back into impossible shapes, and the bone structure in their faces was something Liam had only seen portrayed in art. Their perfectly muscular physique shown through their open puffy shirts and vests, though Liam was sure they did nothing to maintain those flawless frames. The leader sat in the chair clearly laid out for him with its high back and golden flourishes and, slung back his open robe, revealing tight fitting pants and boots that came up to his knees.

"Liam, this is Lord Emilio of the Gustavon Volcano region," Anthony said as he bowed his head to the leader of the Fairies. Emilio tilted his chin back and raised his glass to Liam in greeting.

Another Fairie wearing a long vest and the same tight pants came to sit by Emilio, reclining on the chaise next to him.

"This is my brother, Diego," Emilio said in introduction with a thick accent. "He is a bit sloppy like your own brother there," Emilio said with a hearty laugh to Anthony, pointing toward Liam.

Anthony joined Emilio in laughter and nodded before taking a drink from his goblet. Liam smiled warily, trying to find the humor in the joke himself.

"We heard about the emperor's illness," Diego said, waving his cup in the air. Liam knew he was fishing for some answers.

"My uncle will be fine in a few days. It's just an old injury flare up," Anthony said with a shrug. "I trust our troops are doing well in protecting your lands? Nothing to complain about this time?"

Emilio shrugged and leaned back in his chair. "Yes, we have had no reason to complain since you sent that troop of Tykerials to whip your common soldiers into shape. It seems your most elite military forces will continue to be necessary in our lands."

Anthony nodded. "I'm glad that was all …" he started to say when Diego broke in.

"We hear this Princess Katerina will soon be your wife and Princepa of Akaria," he said with a sly smile.

Anthony nodded again. "Yes, that is true. We are working on the exact details of the agreement with the King of Esterine. The wedding should be very soon. You will of course be receiving invitations when the time comes."

"We have heard she is very beautiful, that one," Emilio said, eyeing Anthony mischievously.

"Her hair, dark as a raven's feather and skin pale and delicate like a snowflake," Diego added, looking up to the sky poetically.

Anthony chuckled and looked over to Liam with a knowing smirk. Liam had to return the smile. Anthony was right, they do love their gossip.

"She is lovely yes, though her features are not quite as extreme as you have been led to believe. This will be a very important alliance for us to solidify. As you know, we need to start work on the wall in the north as soon as possible."

"Ah yes, the problems in the north," Emilio said, dropping his smile. "Soon we too will need a new contract to have your troops protect us from the giants and the wolves if they keep coming south." He shook his head and rolled his eyes.

"They are running rampant up there, the pack of two-headed wolves," Diego said, his eyes glazing over as he imagined the sights. "The Crimson Ravagers as some call them. Driving away the giants and even other wolf packs. Very dangerous it is."

This is it, Liam thought. This was his opening. He felt his pulse quicken and his face heat up as he found himself saying, "I wish we could do something about the source of the problem." He looked to Anthony for support, but Anthony only nodded, letting Liam be the one to bring up the sword.

"If only we had Velios. Then we could maybe do something about it," Liam finished clumsily. He leaned back, trying to look as nonchalant as he could, even with his heart pounding loudly in his ears.

The Fairies both looked at him quizzically. Liam worried he had ruined the whole thing and offended them, but then they broke into laughter. Liam tried to smile as their echoing laughter both relieved and confused him.

"Now what would you do with that sword? It would burn the crap right out of you!" Emilio said through his laughter as he looked over to Liam.

"That sword would do no good against the Crimson Ravagers anyway, that sword is only for the dragon," Diego said before donning a mocking voice. "Oh excuse me terrifying two-headed wolf pack, but I do believe I have this flaming sword that you happen to be impervious to. If you would please just back off and go back to your empty lair, that would be great," Diego stood and mocked, acting like he was holding and swinging the sword. "Did I mention I have this sword that is burning right through me?" He burst into laughter.

Emilio's laughter continued to roll. "Can you imagine it? We'll just walk right up to the Tykens and ask for it too!"

They continued to laugh with each other. Liam caught on to the mention of the Tykens and glanced over to Anthony. Anthony darted his eyes to Liam and nodded slightly before joining in the laughter.

"Yes, I'm sure those bunch of stuck-up forest dwellers would be happy to give it to us," Diego said, his laughter dying down. "That is, if they haven't already given it up to the 'all-powerful' Aurens," he said, his laughter ceasing and his eyes rolling.

Emilio's laughter faded and he gave out a big huff and took another swig of his drink. "Pompous winged brutes ..." he muttered quietly.

Anthony leaned back in his chair casually. "So I take it the Tykens and Aurens are not among your favorite creatures to be around?"

"Nah," Emilio said disgustedly.

"Not for many many years now," Diego agreed.

"Did they do something to harm you all?" Anthony asked, concern plastered on his face.

"Well, no, not exactly," Emilio began, looking up to the sky in thought.

"It was all our fault, if you ask them," Diego chimed in with a scowl.

Emilio sighed. "We misplace one stupid magical chain and everyone gets all upset about it," he said rolling his eyes. "It's still enchanted, it can't be used by anyone or anything anyway. We never asked to be the guardians of it to begin with."

"And it's not our fault the Tykens made the accursed thing so big. It was much too large for us to keep moving around with and they knew we didn't like to stay in one place for too long," Diego complained.

"A magical chain?" Liam dared to ask, hoping they would elaborate more. *This must be another one of the enchanted weapons that help guard the Lumos Gems*, Liam thought hungrily to himself.

Emilio only waved his hand in the air. "Enough about the chain. Ancient history that is."

Anthony glanced at Liam and then back at the Fairies who were refilling their glasses with the pitchers of wine on their table.

"We are fortunate to have a partnership with some of the Tykens of Tulneria, but their chief, Inola, still has something that belongs to my uncle. She never gave it back after the war ended. I had hoped we might get your assistance in the matter at some point …" Anthony began to say. Liam assumed his brother was completely making this up, but he found it hard to tell for sure.

"No, me temo que no," Emilio said with a chuckle, slipping into his native tongue. "That is not in our contract."

"The Tykens will not give up anything if they have deemed it valuable to them anyway," Diego said hatefully. "You will probably have to get it back the old-fashioned way."

"What's the old-fashioned way?" Liam asked, leaning forward with interest.

"The Tykens," Emilio explained, taking a moment to spit to the side. "They pride themselves on honesty, tradition, strength, and whatever other nonsense righteousness that Tykos embodies and whatnot." Emilio waved his cup in the air in a circular motion. "But the only way I've ever seen them give something valuable away—unless it was taken by force, which I have only witnessed happen once—regardless of their so-called 'generosity' and 'honor,' is to win one of their contests."

Diego laughed. "Yes, they will give you anything you want if you win one of those."

"A contest? What kind of contest?" Liam asked.

"They are usually contests for testing strength or gardening or something, I don't know," Emilio said with another roll of his eyes. "Stuff that no other being could beat Tykens at anyway."

"Do they have contests often?" Anthony asked, tilting his head in thought.

"No, not without an occasion," Emilio said, his words beginning to slur.

"They will have contests over their Tysella holiday though. That's for sure. They always have contests for that," Diego said, his eyes beginning to droop.

Liam shot a glance at Anthony and they smirked at each other.

"It would be interesting to know how one goes about getting an invitation to these contests," Anthony said thoughtfully, sitting back and shrugging, clearly trying to look unconcerned with the answer.

Emilio jutted his lips out as he thought. "Well, it is a holiday and they love to taut their generosity and family values. They would have to let you in if you released and escorted their soldiers back to Tulneria for the holiday."

Diego nodded. "Yes, but you'll need a proper invitation to stay," his words slurring together.

Emilio nodded in agreement, his eyes unfocused. "Ah, yes, of course. Someone will need to invite you to stay publicly to the court. If you can get that, they'll have to let you stay. In the name of hospitality and honor or whatever," he said and stuck his face in his cup.

"They wouldn't like that at all!" Diego said, beginning to chuckle.

Emilio agreed and the two burst into a long roll of laughter again, holding each other's arms.

Liam smiled at Anthony, satisfied with this information. This was perfect. A Tyken strength contest was just the sort of thing he was equipped for these days, if he could learn how to reliably call upon his powers.

"Well, Liam Farotus, how would you feel about representing Akaria in the Games of Tysella this year?" Anthony asked Liam as the Fairies continued to laugh and joke with each other, no longer paying attention to them at all.

Liam hesitated momentarily before he picked up his glass and raised it to his brother. "It would be my honor, Princep."

They clanged their glasses together and Liam threw back the dark liquid, letting the strong alcohol sting his throat all the way down.

14

Katerina looked at herself in the full-length mirror. She mindlessly fondled the necklace around her neck as she narrowed her eyes to examine herself closely. She had spent the past few days working tirelessly in the evenings with Alexander and her eyes looked heavy with fatigue now. She thought her skin looked dull against the rich gold fabric of her magnificent dress. It had been requested by the regent, Edward, that she wear this color to match Anthony's suit, as it was customary for the highest ranked Akarians to wear gold on Crealum night. Edward thought it would send a clear message of their intent to make her their next empress. And while Katerina didn't have any personal input on the dress, she liked the high boat neckline and long sleeves that hid her Streaks well, and was actually fond of the full skirt with pick-ups all around it.

Her maids encircled her in front of the mirror, full of smiles and excitement about the night's festivities. They prattled on as they pinned up lose hairs, smoothed down her dress and tightened her corset. Katerina tuned out their usual prattle about boys they wanted to dance with tonight and who they might marry and how many children everyone wanted to have. Katerina wished she could be that simple. She wished that was all she wanted in life and that she didn't have this terrifying hunger for something more. It would make things so much easier.

The door to Katerina's chambers opened abruptly and she flicked her eyes to see the doorway in the mirror and was immediately annoyed when she saw the smiling face of her sister prancing in through the doorway with her maids trailing behind her. Katerina closed her eyes momentarily, trying not to let the fact that Anya should have waited to be properly admitted into her rooms irritate her too much.

Anya walked over to stand behind Katerina. She shrugged her shoulders up and beamed at Katerina as she continued to be primped and pinned by her maids. Katerina averted her eyes deliberately from the uncomfortable stare of her sister and smoothed down the dark hair on top of her head and was shocked when her eyes ran over a piece of hair that didn't match the rest. A gleaming white hair stuck out from her scalp and she very swiftly plucked it out. She glanced at the hair on her fingers and saw that it was indeed a single white hair. She knew her hair would turn this color as she continued to practice magic, but she had expected it to take years of practicing.

Katerina released the hair to the floor as Madeline came forward with some sparkling final touches on a purple velvet pillow. A simple golden headband, that would replace the lavish Esterine headdress on her head, lay on the pillow next to a pair of cream-colored lace gloves and a set of glimmering diamond earrings that Anthony had supposedly sent for her. Katerina allowed Madeline the honor of placing the headband on her head and she placed the earrings in her ears herself. Then Katerina turned back toward the mirror as she picked up the delicate gloves.

"Oh Kat," Anya began in their native Isavarian language as she stepped forward closer to her sister. "You look so beautiful."

Anya then gently fluffed Katerina's dress, looking at it with admiring eyes. Anya was dressed much more plainly, in a simple gray gown that covered every inch of skin beyond her face and gloved hands. Katerina knew it was not the dress her sister had pictured herself wearing on a night like tonight.

"Thank you, Anya," Katerina responded primly, pulling on the gloves.

Anya smiled at Katerina through the mirror and then pulled something out from underneath one of her braids.

"Here," Anya said, looking down at the item in her hand. "I thought you might like this for your hair," and she handed Katerina a small barrette with the face of a white owl on the end of it.

Katerina looked down at the piece, puzzled.

"It symbolizes the Air Goddess, Aurelia," Anya explained, pointing to the hair accessory. "I've been learning a lot about the Akarians this week and I think you would have picked her as your patron goddess if you were Akarian."

Katerina looked up at Anya, trying to decide how much interest she should show in something her father would have deemed heresy.

"She's really smart and beautiful and loves to read and follow rules," Anya continued to explain as she rubbed her hands together nervously in front of her. "She married the Earth God, Tykos and I think you're basically the perfect living example of her."

Katerina couldn't help it, her heart melted. She smiled at Anya and let the compliment sink in a little before turning back to the mirror and placing the small barrette into the side of her tightly wound bun. She smiled and turned her eyes toward her sister. Anya smiled back at her in the mirror and Katerina felt a tinge of guilt as she saw how accepting this amazing gift affected her sister. Maybe she shouldn't have shut Anya out so harshly lately.

"It looks gorgeous," Anya said, her smile genuine and warm.

Katerina opened her mouth to say something nice back to Anya, but couldn't find the words fast enough. Then the moment was over.

"But I do think maybe your old necklace doesn't quite match," Anya said pointing to the shining blue stone around Katerina's neck.

"It's fine," Katerina said sharply, still in Isavarian, holding the gem against her chest protectively.

"You'll be getting a new one anyway when your engagement to the Princep is announced," Anya said, moving behind her sister to unclasp the necklace without regard to Katerina's protest.

Katerina knew she'd be getting an engagement necklace, but she wanted this one on as long as possible. She wanted her mother there with her tonight and this necklace was the closest she had.

Anya's fingers reached for the clasp of the necklace and Katerina quickly turned and smacked her sister's hand away. Katerina glared at her sister and clutched at the bauble again.

"I said, it's fine," Katerina said tersely, anger filling her face as she looked into the shocked face of her sister. Regret spread through Katerina as she looked around to everyone standing around her.

"I was only trying to help ..." Anya said as the surprise on her face melted into a look of defiance.

"I'm sorry," Katerina said with a sigh. "But I don't need you trying to help me."

"At least I do try though. I, for one, actually care that we're sisters and that we're never going to see each other again after you're married!"

"Well you should have thought about that ..." Katerina began to say with a raised voice as she clearly remembered why she was getting married in the first place. Then she shook her head and calmed herself down. "Just let it go Anya. We aren't even full sisters ..." Katerina said quietly and turned back to the mirror for one final glance at herself.

Anya's irritation quickly turned to sorrow and she whispered back, "You're right Kat, I lost my real sister a long time ago."

Katerina watched Anya pick up her dress and walk out of the room. The maids watched the encounter with open mouths, unable to understand the words, but clearly understanding the sentiments exchanged. Katerina lifted her shoulders and let them fall as she exhaled sharply, then shook her head as if she could shake off the encounter. She longed to put her head in her hands and cry, but all the maids were staring at her.

Alexander's words rang her head again. *You let your emotions rule you.*

Katerina felt the guilt creep in. She knew she was being hard on her sister, but Anya always knew just how to annoy her. Anya hadn't known about Katerina's relationship with Mikhal, but she had been the one who told their father that she had seen him lurking around the palace. Once he had been found out, the Aurens came, and he had to leave. Then her affair with the Lodarine prince was why she was here right now; marrying a stranger in a strange land without her friends, without anyone. She wanted to forgive Anya, but Anya always made it so hard. They were so different.

Katerina looked up and examined herself in the mirror again, touching the pin in her hair lightly. She thought about removing it, but a polite knock on the door distracted her. Madeline moved quickly to open it. Katerina turned to see Anthony standing in the doorway with a bright, charming smile on his handsome face. He was dressed in a much more modest suit than Katerina had ever seen him wear, made of plain gold fabric with a white tie and a white shirt underneath. Katerina smiled amiably at him.

"Princep Anthony is here for you, Your Highness," Madeline announced properly to Katerina before skittering out of the way.

"The Crealum ceremony in the temple has concluded. May I escort you to the banquet hall for the feast?" he asked, stretching his hand out to her.

A part of Katerina wished she had been able to attend the Crealum cere-mony in the temple, just out of curiosity, but she knew her father would never allow that while he was here. She wondered what the ceremony entailed beyond the recounting of the story of the Alumetris and lighting of some candles, but she supposed she would have to wait until next year to experience this Akarian holiday fully.

Katerina nodded and bit her lip, hoping to dissipate the anger and annoyance that still flooded her body as she stepped forward carefully in her long dress. She curtsied low to Anthony and took his outstretched hand. He led her out into the hallway and the couple was escorted down the hall by a group of Tykerial Guards in ostentatious gold and green armor toward the banquet hall.

"May I say, you look very beautiful," Anthony said, turning his head to her as they walked.

"Thank you, Your Highness," Katerina responded with a smile, keeping her eyes in front of her.

Anthony took a deep breath in. "You're going to love the Crealum Feast. Crealum is the best time of the year in Akaria. I asked for a special performance. I think you'll really enjoy it." He looked at her with a gentle smile.

Katerina smiled back, finally turning her head to him, and nodded. He seemed nice enough and his eyes ... *no, don't think about his eyes*, Katerina scolded herself. She knew she had to marry this man, but it was only a business arrangement for them both. She knew it was better to keep her heart guarded. She didn't think she could survive another terrible heartbreak.

Anthony led her into the palace's largest banquet room. As soon as they entered the nearly empty space, Katerina's attention was immediately drawn to the blooming tree in the center. The Crealum tree. She knew it represented the Alumetris and it did indeed look truly magical. Its branches were full of green leaves and small white flowers. The beautiful tree was decorated with jewels and colorful garland hung from every branch representing the colors of the four light gods: blue for the water goddess, green for the god of land, white for the goddess of the skies, and red for the god of fire. The hanging lanterns and the candles placed around it gave it an aura of pure magical beauty.

Katerina and Anthony stood in front of the long table that was placed in the back and turned to face the entrance. They were soon joined by Edward, wearing an all-white suit and a woman that Katerina wasn't sure was his wife or not. They greeted each other with simple nods and smiles and readied themselves to receive the rest of the guests.

A small orchestra in the corner struck up a soft tune as Katerina's father and stepmother walked in, being deemed the next highest ranking in attendance. They wore their traditional Isavarian clothing, in dull gray colors. Katerina knew her father wanted to be clear that they were not, under any circumstances, celebrating the Crealum holiday tonight. Eva's gray and white beaded headdress jingled gracefully as they walked up to Katerina and Anthony. They greeted them and Edward, and then sat at the head table next to the seats Anthony and Katerina would occupy.

Then Katerina watched with a smile as the rest of the Akarian nobility filed into the room. They entered with laughter and excited chatter, walking up to greet the regent and the Princep briefly, before taking their seats at their designated tables. As they entered, Katerina noted that they were all dressed in their finest holiday attire of blue, green, white, or red, according to their chosen god during their coming-of-age ceremony.

Katerina tried to pick out any familiar faces in the crowd, but she noticed most of the nobility avoided her gaze. She was relieved when she saw Liam enter the room, dressed in all green, with a pretty blonde girl on his arm. Liam smiled warmly at her as they greeted them. It was nice to see a friendly face, though what she really longed for in that moment was to see a certain man in a wheelchair roll up to her and give her a sarcastic comment.

Then she saw her sister walk in, escorted by a nobleman Katerina didn't recognize, but she assumed he must be important. She would need to know his name soon as he was undoubtedly on the council. Anya did not glance over to Katerina as she curtseyed to the others and walked over to sit at the same table as Liam.

Once everyone else had taken their spots, Katerina, Anthony, Edward, and his wife, all turned to sit down at the head table. Anthony pulled Katerina's chair out for her and she had to push her skirts down as she sat. Anthony sat next to her and Katerina looked out across the magnificent room, noticing the Tykerial Guards dotting the sides of the room.

The sound of the orchestra mixed with the sound of polite chatter and excitement as the servants began to bring out the dishes for the feast. The dishes were each brought out to them first for Anthony to direct who should receive each one. Anthony clearly enjoyed the tradition immensely and she was happy to just sit and smile next to him. Once all the special dishes had been bestowed upon the tables, the servants brought out the rest of the traditional Crealum meal for everyone.

Anthony turned to Katerina and exhaled with feigned exhaustion. "Now that the business is taken care of, I have something very important to ask you," he said with a smile, his eyebrows raising, as he picked up his eating utensils and cut through his meat.

Katerina glanced at him sideways as she picked up her own fork. "Of course. What is it, Your Highness?" she asked, hoping his question would be more face-tious than serious.

"My brother tells me that you can speak Tyk. Is that true?" Anthony asked, placing a bite of food in his mouth.

Katerina swallowed nervously and nodded. *What else did Liam tell him?* she wondered as a flutter of nerves filled her stomach.

"Yes, fairly well," Katerina answered.

"That's perfect then," Anthony said with a pleased smile.

"It is?" Katerina asked curiously, still worried about where this might be going.

Anthony turned to look at her again, that annoyingly charming smile stretched across his face. "How would you like to represent Akaria as our new Princepa in the Tyken nation of Tulneria?"

Katerina couldn't control the surprise that washed over her face. "You want me to go as an ambassador to the land of the Tykens?" she asked, unsure what answer or reaction he was searching for. She glanced behind Anthony and saw her father's attention turn toward them.

"You see, I'm sending our Tyken Protectors back home to Tulneria for the Tysella holiday in a couple of days and since I can't go myself, I'd like for you to go in my stead," Anthony explained, loudly enough for her father to hear. "My brother Liam and a proper escort of Tykerial Guards will accompany you of course. We think it would be immensely beneficial for Akaria to send someone who actually spoke their language, and it may help you gain some favor among the nobility as you transition into your new role here."

Anthony paused and turned to look at Katerina, making sure she was looking him in the eye before he continued. "This trip will be *very* important to the health and future of Akaria," he said and then gave her a little wink.

Katerina received his message clearly and excitement flooded through her instantly. This excursion to Tulneria would have something to do with finding

Velios, she was sure of it. "I would be most honored to represent Akaria in Tul-neria. Thank you for the opportunity, Your Highness," she said, a smile growing on her face.

"Excellent," Anthony said, turning back to his plate. "So, what other hidden talents have you been keeping from me?" He smirked and Katerina saw the attention of her father fade away from their conversation.

Katerina smiled shyly and turned back to her own plate. "Oh, I don't think speaking a different language is really that much of a talent," she said, pushing some food around on her plate, the exhilaration of the previous conversation still pulsing through her and clouding her thoughts.

"Well it certainly is in Akaria," Anthony said, grinning at her, "but I guess if you won't tell me what else you're interested in, I'll just have to uncover that on my own."

Katerina felt her cheeks start to burn and was sure they were turning red. She hated that, but she hadn't expected Anthony to want to actually know her. Their conversation continued effortlessly and Katerina found herself enjoying herself much more than she had anticipated. They laughed together throughout the meal and she was surprised that Anthony hardly took his attention from her. Though they only shared some light banter and surface details, such as favorite pastimes and foods, they also uncovered some shared interests such as horseback riding and stargazing. It had been ages since she'd talked to someone like this.

Katerina glanced out into the crowd throughout their light conversation and noticed the glares and disapproving sneers that were thrown her way while Anthony wasn't looking. She knew a foreign Princepa wasn't everyone's idea of a perfect match, but she was surprised at how transparent some of the nobles were about it. They likely had daughters they had hoped to see on the throne beside Anthony instead.

Katerina couldn't eat another bite by the time their dessert plates were cleared from the tables. Coffee and tea were brought out while Edward stood and clinked on his champagne glass full of water to capture the attention of the attendees. He had a slight hunch in his back and his lips pressed into a thin smile. The music in the corner ceased and the room quieted as all eyes turned to look at him.

"It is such a pleasure to have you all with us. We have much to celebrate as a country this Crealum, but most importantly, we must celebrate our alliance with Esterine," Edward said as he looked to the Esterine King. "It is my privilege to announce that tonight, we not only have a wonderful holiday to celebrate, but also an agreement on the betrothal terms between the Princess Katerina of Esterine and our Princep, Anthony Farotus. The papers have been signed and tonight, we will complete the betrothal properly, according to our customs." He paused for a light round of applause that ensued from his audience.

Katerina masked the sinking feeling in her gut as she smiled out at the crowd proudly. Though this news was no surprise to Katerina—she had been told the day before—she couldn't stop the prickle of anxiety that ran through her chest. She had thought perhaps she may feel content in this moment, triumphant even, as her father had always told her a good marriage would be her biggest accomplishment, but that was clearly just a foolish fantasy.

She wasn't ready for this.

She wasn't ready to leave her entire life behind. She felt the power rising within her as nausea crept in. She took a deep breath in and concentrated on her breathing to keep her power under control, causing no disturbance or gusts of wind.

Anthony stood up next to her and buttoned his suit coat before he reached into his coat pocket and pulled out a small box. When he opened it, he revealed a beautiful white and green necklace. A wave of awe hit Katerina when she saw how beautiful and pure it was. She knew it was an Akarian custom to receive a necklace of these colors upon an official engagement, but she hadn't expected something so stunning. The necklace looked delicate and she realized the glimmering clear beads were actually diamonds as they caught the light in Anthony's hands. She had never seen so many diamonds at once. This necklace was worth a fortune.

"In Akaria we like to signify our marriage engagements with a token," Anthony said, taking the necklace from the box and holding it up for the room to admire. It sparkled exquisitely as he moved it, catching the many lights in the hall. The awe from the crowd was audible as they all stared at the piece.

Then Anthony turned to her and she stood up, along with her parents, for Anthony to bestow the gift properly. His light blue eyes locked on her turquoise ones as they stood face-to-face before she turned away and her stepmother came to stand beside her. Katerina controlled her impulse to grab ahold of her mother's necklace as her stepmother moved to release it from her neck. She pushed down the anxiety and held back her power with enormous effort as Anthony draped the new necklace around her now empty neck. She swallowed down a lump in her throat, willing herself not to show any emotion. Receiving this necklace made the agreement final. Her fate was sealed.

Her stepmother stepped back and Anthony finished clasping the new necklace with ease. She hesitated, before looking down to admire the new piece. She would wear this necklace on display every day until the marriage vows when it would be replaced with a ring. She eyed her mother's necklace in her stepmother's hands as the queen walked back to her seat with it. Eva gave Katerina a comforting smile as she carefully tucked her necklace into a handkerchief and softly placed it within a fold in her gown.

Then Katerina turned back around to face Anthony. He gave her a warm, gentle smile and she forced herself to smile back at him though she felt as if a small piece of herself had just been chipped away.

My emotions are just a signal, Katerina reminded herself. *I choose how I react.*

She felt the tension in her chest loosen as Anthony swiftly turned back to the audience of guests. "The emperor and I look forward to building a better world with strong allies like Esterine," he announced to the room.

"It is a great honor for me to officially announce the betrothal of the Princep of Akaria to the Princess of Esterine!" Edward's voice rang out jubilantly.

An eruption of cheers and applause emanated from the room as the nobles at least pretended to celebrate this news, whether they supported it or not. She glanced at her father and was relieved to see him clapping. Then Katerina thought she saw Anthony's hand inch closer hers, but he apparently thought better of it and instead silenced the applause with a placating gesture.

"And the good news doesn't end there," Anthony said with a smug smile. "I am also pleased to announce that we have received an invitation from the Tykens of Tulneria. They have invited us to their Tysella holiday to share in their festivities and mend our fractured relationship. With a solid partnership already in place with the Fairies of Gustavon, this invitation could be an enormous opportunity for us to expand our influence in Elusira and among the Lumenaros." Anthony paused and looked over to Liam. He took a deep breath before he continued calmly. "I will be sending our Tyken Protectors home for this holiday this year, but I, myself, will be unable to attend. Luckily, my betrothed, the Princess Katerina, has agreed to go in my place. She will represent Akaria and bring the Tykens a special gift. She is a fluent speaker of Tyk and she will surely impress and charm the Tykens for us all. And when she returns, we will be wed!" Anthony lifed his glass into the air to the congregation of nobles. The whole room burst into loud clapping and cheering once again.

Anthony took a long drink from his glass, emptying its contents, and smiled out at the adoring crowd. Katerina smiled sweetly and nodded, looking out over the people. A rush of pride filled her as she looked out into the faces of the people, each one filled with at least a touch of admiration and acceptance now.

15

Chatter instantly started up again throughout the grand hall as Anthony unbuttoned his suit coat and took his seat again. He nodded over to the side of the room and Katerina followed his gaze to see a man with an oddly flat, but floppy hat and curly brown hair. Katerina scrutinized his long, red brocade jacket with black buttons as he bent down to pick up a lute sitting on the ground next to him.

"I think you'll like this," Anthony said softly to her, leaning his head toward her slightly but keeping his eyes forward. "Colin Calfree is the best storyteller in Gilderon."

Colin smiled as he entered the floor in front of the head table and bowed low to the occupants. He strummed his instrument lightly and turned to face the rest of the crowd. He waited until the room quieted before he spoke in a loud, commanding voice.

"In honor of our Princep's official betrothal to the Princess of Esterine, the Princep has requested a very special performance," Colin announced proudly. "Ladies and gentlemen," he was almost yelling now, "it is my honor, my joy, my absolute pleasure to present to you—the story of the original dragon. An adaptation of the famous poem, Darian's Fury." He strutted out into the center of the open floor and played a jaunty tune.

Performers in masks streamed into the banquet hall, wearing elaborate costumes and carrying armfuls of props. Katerina glanced over to Anthony, who nodded and raised his eyebrows at her pleased expression. She smiled back at him and leaned back into her chair comfortably. She had heard about these sorts of performances, "masques" she thinks they were called, but she hadn't expected to actually see one. They were supposedly going out of fashion.

A blonde woman in a light blue and white stola stepped into the middle of the floor, smiling and dancing around gracefully. Colin stepped off to the side as she entered, strumming his instrument more quietly as he narrated.

"Oh Galina, sweet and innocent Galina, walked alone in the forest. She walked along so peacefully, not knowing what Destiny would bring her today," Colin said as the girl in the center danced and twirled and forced a show of happiness and innocence. She reminded Katerina of her little sister.

A strong, bulky man in a black and red toga entered from one side, stepping backward into the center of the floor until he bumped into the woman in blue. They stopped walking and slowly turned to look at each other.

"It was love at first sight. Love at first sight!"

The couple clasped hands and danced a fast waltz. The man spun the woman in and out skillfully and lifted her in a series of impressive moves. Katerina had never seen such creative and sophisticated skill in entertainers.

"Their love grew and grew, but she didn't know. Oh, she did not know! Just who her new paramour really was."

The couple stopped dancing and the man stepped back from the woman, holding her hand in one of his with his other hand on his chest.

"I am Darian. I am the firstborn son of Farran, the God of Fire, and Demexia, the Goddess of the Night," the actor spoke loudly.

The crowd chattered at this revelation with giggles and some feigned gasps as the woman pulled away from him, taking her hand from his, looking scared and worried.

Katerina felt herself slipping into a memory of hearing a revelation like that, but quickly pushed the moment away. She nearly jumped when she felt Anthony place his hand on top of hers. She looked over to him with surprise, but he seemed content with his gesture and didn't move his gaze from the performance. Katerina squirmed in her seat, glancing over at her father briefly, but allowed his hand to stay on hers. She knew the whole room was watching the pair of them just as much as they were watching the play.

"But worry not, my love! My sweet love, I will always love you. You are the truest thing in this world to me. You only have to trust me," the actor playing Darian continued.

The girl smiled and the two rushed back together and collided in a passionate kiss. Katerina pressed her lips together. She knew immediately that this story would not end well for Galina.

A woman in a sleek black and gold gown with long black hair and bright, dramatic makeup painted on her face, entered from the side. She ran up to the embracing couple and violently broke them apart.

"Oh no! Darian's wife-to-be, Zola the trickster goddess, has found them out!"

The audience gasped and then laughed again, the story too familiar for them to take seriously. The Zola actress danced around the couple, leaping and twirling in fury. Katerina looked over to her to her father again and wasn't surprised to see his face set sternly in a scowl.

Zola stopped next to Galina and pointed a long, curled finger at her.

"Be warned! If you continue this relationship with my betrothed, I will place a curse on you that you will never be able to escape! A curse so terrible, you will be begging Xevron to take you!" the actress shouted out before picking up her skirts and twirling back off to the side.

Galina fell to her knees and pretended to cry into her hands. Darian shook his fist in the direction of Zola. He bent down next to the crying girl and tried to comfort her, but she pushed him away. Darian took her hands and raised her up. The couple stood to face each other and then backed away from each other slowly, and exited the main part of the floor.

"From that day forward, Galina decided to move on with her life," Colin explained as Galina entered the floor again, this time holding the arm of another man. The man bent over to kiss her hand. "Her father arranged a decent marriage for her and Galina had accepted."

Darian entered again, pushing the other man away from Galina. Galina stepped between the two men with an arm outstretched to stop Darian from coming any closer.

"But why Galina? Why have you forsaken me and broken my heart?" Darian called out, falling to his knees in front of her.

Galina shook her head at him and walked back over to the other man.

"She knew they could not be together. Zola would never rest until she suffered greatly if she continued to be with him. Zola was known for her callousness and brutality," Colin explained as Galina walked away from Darian, looking back sadly, before continuing off the floor. "But Darian was determined to be with his true love. No matter what it took." The Darian actor stood up and ran in a circle. He ran to the far side of the room and extended his arms over a covered structure. Another actor removed the curtain revealing a wooden structure resembling a castle behind it. The audience murmured with awed expressions.

"Darian constructed a strong and beautiful fortress for Galina to reside in," Colin explained as Darian ran over to grab Galina's hand and brought her up into the castle structure.

Darian kissed Galina passionately, but then he left her in the castle alone. Galina's arm outstretched toward him as he ran away.

"Even with this mighty fortress, he still worried for her safety. So Darian decided to create something more. He created a new kind of beast, like many other gods before him had, to protect her completely," Colin explained dramatically.

Darian motioned for four actors to enter the scene, all dressed in different colors, and wearing streamers from their arms and legs, with reptilian masks.

"And the dragons were born!" Colin said with a loud, triumphant voice.

The dragon dancers danced around for a few measures as the orchestra in the corner chimed in briefly. The dancers wove through the crowd and danced up and down the aisles between tables as Darian remained in the center of the floor, waving his arms in the air and swaying around.

Katerina watched the dancers in their exquisite colors and she let herself relax, even with Anthony's hand still grasping hers. They never had such fun in Esterine, and she imagined her father would be sure to lecture her about fantasy and myths tomorrow.

But that was tomorrow.

The dragon dancers ran back to the center of the floor with Darian and surrounded the castle. The actor playing Darian ran back up into the tower and took Galina's hands in his. The girl smiled at him, but then slumped over weakly into his arms.

"Though the dragons kept her safe, they also kept her isolated in the fortress. Galina was a lonely soul in the tower. The visits from Darian were not enough. She longed for her freedom again and so Darian vowed to bring down Zola."

Darian walked down from the castle and grabbed a wooden sword from one of the other actors off to the side. The Galina actress reached her arms out over the side of the castle, looking anguished and sad.

Zola entered from the opposite end of the structure, walking slowly and con-fidently, head held exaggeratedly high. Darian forced his sword upward and over to Zola, telling his dragons to attack. The dragon dancers surrounded Zola, but she was able to push them away, one by one. Darian and Zola circled each other as four more actors entered, each wearing a different colored robe of green, red, white, and blue.

Katerina recognized these colors and assumed these actors would be portraying the four light gods: Tykos, Aurelia, Farran, and Revira. Behind Zola, entered five more actors in gray robes. Katerina wasn't as familiar with the Akarian dark gods, but she assumed these actors were portraying them. All eleven actors, portraying the pantheon of the Alumetry gods, ran at each other. It was choreographed chaos on the floor and Katerina didn't know where to look.

"The feud between Darian and his eventual wife Zola ignited the Divine War between the gods and all their creations. Chaos reigned everywhere!" Colin yelled out.

The floor cleared and Zola returned to the open floor with a man, who revealed a costume of black and gold beneath his gray cloak.

"Zola and her twin brother Zoli decided they too must create a new type of creature to give them an advantage and end this war. It would be something devious and mischievous, representing them for who they were."

Two children wearing long black dresses and pointed hats entered the scene out of the group of actors waiting on the side. The audience awed and laughed at the sight of the children on the floor.

"They created the Zomes, small little creatures of pure mischief, with immense power of manipulation and deceit. Zola sent them into Galina's tower, as they were small enough to remain hidden from the dragons."

The two children ran up into the tower, between the dragon dancers. The audience laughed again, enjoying the children. Galina smiled at them and looked down at them with hands on her hips.

"The Zomes befriended Galina, being the only other souls she had seen in years besides Darian," Colin explained. "They fed her lies and planted doubts in her mind easily, telling her: 'You deserve to be free!'" He said this last part in a high-pitched voice, before switching to a lower voice, "Darian doesn't love you!" Then switching to the high-pitched voice again, "You are his prisoner!" And again to the low voice, "He's stealing your youth!"

The children threw green scarves over the Galina actress. And Galina hugged herself and looked concerned. The little Zomes handed Galina a green wooden dagger before running down the castle stairs and off to the side again. Galina held up the wooden dagger, looking at it intently.

But Darian ran into the castle structure just then and Galina hid the dagger behind her back. Darian moved to embrace his love, and she allowed him to wrap his arms around her while keeping her arms and the dagger behind her back.

"Galina, confused and distraught, and still heavily under the influence of the Zomes, pulled the dagger of alagon metal from behind her back and stabbed it into Darian's chest!" Colin yelled in excitement.

The actress pulled the wooden dagger from behind her and stuck it into the breastplate of the Darian actor where it remained in place.

Darian looked up at her, face in agony. "Why would you try to hurt me? Are you so unhappy with my love?" Darian asked with pain in his eyes, arms reaching for her. The actress backed away from him. He pulled the dagger from his chest and glanced at the weapon.

"Darian knew the dagger must have somehow come from Zola and his heart was filled with hate and rage!"

Darian yelled in anguish and the dragon dancers filled the floor again and threw red scarves as they swayed back and forth in front of the castle. "His burst of wrath created dragon fire within the dragons while they also inherited the weakness for alagon," Colin called out seriously.

Galina ran from the tower into the center of the floor as Darian stood on top of the fortress, solemnly looking out over the floor. Zola entered again, a confident smile on her face, waiting for Galina.

"Darian decided to let Galina be free if that's what she really wanted and she ran right into the hands of Zola."

Zola pushed her hand toward the girl and Galina screamed in horror and dropped to her knees and fell to the floor, dying in front of Zola. Zola smiled and then laughed deviously.

Darian ran in from behind the castle.

"Darian heard her cries and ran after her, but he arrived on the scene too late," Colin said, quietly.

"Zola! What have you done!" Darian called out as he lifted Galina's head onto his lap. He hugged her and rocked her back and forth. "Please, don't die on me, my love!" Darian cried out.

"She was always meant to die Darian. She was only human after all," Zola said.

Galina reached her hand up to stroke Darian's face as the Zola actress walked slowly and proudly from the floor.

"Before her last breath, Galina assured him that she always loved him. If only they had been free to be together," Colin explained before she closed her eyes and her body went limp on the floor.

Darian called out in anguish with a long "No!" The actor pretended to cry while holding the body of Galina. The crowd was silent. Then Darian looked up to the ceiling and shouted out "Xevron! Xevron please! Xevron hear my plea!"

"Darian called out for the God of Death in his anguish," Colin explained as an actor in a gray robe entered the scene. The Xevron actor had on a long white wig and his face was painted all white as well with vertical black lines drawn on his face.

"Xevron answered his call and Darian begged him to save his love," Colin continued as the Darian actor raised his arms to the Xevron actor.

"Undo this evil that your daughter has wrought!" Darian yelled at Xevron.

The Xevron actor shook his head, but lifted his palm out from under his robes.

"Though he refused to resurrect the object of this Divine War, he did offer Darian a concession. Xevron offered to put the heart of Galina inside his first dragon, along with the good and light part of his own heart that he inherited from his father. They could be together for all time that way."

Darian looked back down at the girl lying limp in his lap, then back up at Xevron. He nodded his head once in agreement.

Xevron held up a finger and Colin explained in a gravelly voice, "This act would come at a price. One that Xevron thought was fair. Darian would need to promise to continue to bring him souls, every year until the end of time. Darian would need to embrace the dark part of himself and his violent wrath, and use it to invade the hearts of humans and send their souls to Xevron's own domain."

Darian stood up, kissed Galina gently on the forehead and laid her gently on the ground. He faced Xevron and held out his hand to shake, solidifying the deal.

Xevron lifted his arms in the air and Darian's back bent backward at an alarming angle, causing Katerina's eyes to widen. One of the dragon dancers with large wings strapped onto their arms, approached and ran in a circle around Xevron and Darian twice before stopping in front of the crowd. The dragon swayed back and forth before standing firm, wings spread wide. The other dragons joined the large dragon on the floor, forming a circle around the other actors, their fabric wings also spread wide. They swayed back and forth for a few moments, the orchestra joining in again and then the music stopped and they all cleared the floor, running off to the side.

Galina was standing now, wearing white instead of blue. Katerina was amazed at how she had been able to change right in front of everyone with no one noticing. Xevron walked slowly away from the couple. Darian reached out his arm to Galina and she took his hand in hers. They walked together from the center of the floor, arms intermingled, leaving the floor empty.

"For years after the fusing of the hearts, the war still raged on. The dragons remained impenetrable by any of the common metals. All the Lumenaros—the Tykens, Fairies, Rivens, and Aurens—worked tirelessly alongside humankind to fight off the threat the dragons posed to their homes and lives. No one was able to take down Darian's wrath and he was dubbed the God of War," Colin continued as the dragon dancers returned to the floor with actors portraying Tykens, Fairies, Aurens, and humans, holding swords and bows. They all fought against the dragons, but the dragons remained on their feet.

Then Anthony's hand slid off Katerina's as he stood up from the table. Katerina watched as he buttoned his suitcoat and strolled over to the castle structure.

What's he doing? Katerina wondered as she watched him, her hand cold now without his warmth. He put his arms through some straps, attaching a large wire frame covered with white feathers to his back. Wings. Katerina's heart wrenched. She couldn't take her eyes from him as he took a bow from one of the actors and stepped up into the castle. He remained confident, looking as handsome and as calm as he always did, even with the silliness of the play surrounding him.

"Azariah the Auren!" Colin yelled and pointed up to Anthony in the tower. The whole audience burst out with applause and cheers at the sight of him. Anthony didn't acknowledge the praise and looked seriously down at the dragon dancers.

"Azariah, the greatest and smartest hero of the time, figured out the dragons' secret. He crafted an arrow with a tip of alagon and was able to take down many dragons on his own."

Anthony fired blunted sticks with white scarves tied to the ends from his bow five times in quick succession over the dance floor. Katerina stared at him, letting him remind her of someone she had been trying so hard to forget. She finally tore her eyes away from him and she couldn't look back.

Below on the floor, the dragon dancers fell as the scarves hit them lightly, but the previously deemed Original Dragon remained standing. Katerina kept her eyes on the dragon as she saw another scarf fly through the air slowly, arching above the floor. The scarf made contact, and the dragon knelt, but did not fall.

"Even the alagon arrows couldn't take down the impenetrable Original Dragon, but the death of its comrades was enough to chase it away, ceasing its seemingly never-ending rage," Colin said as the dragon limped off the set.

Katerina quickly flicked her eyes over to Anthony as he stepped off the set. He then removed his wings and gave his bow to another actor as the masque concluded.

"The dragon still lives to this day, hiding away in the mountains, waiting for the day to strike his revenge on the people. Darian's darkness still envelopes the world with war and destruction, keeping his promise to Xevron to deliver him many souls."

Colin then ceased his strumming and there was a loud round of applause from the crowd. The actors all filled the floor, including Anthony, and bowed to the crowd before turning to kneel at the head table. Katerina stood along with the rest of the table and clapped along.

Do they all believe this happened? she wondered as she looked out into the crowd. Their faces were all smiles and cheer. She glanced over at Liam. His face portrayed exactly how she felt. Scared and worried. The story of an impenetrable dragon might have seemed inspiring to Anthony, but it was just foreboding to Katerina.

The actors cleared the floor and Anthony walked up to Katerina and extended his hand to her over the table. Katerina smiled politely and nodded. The masque had nearly made her forget about the traditional Crealum dance she still had to perform.

Her stomach turned with anxiety.

She had been practicing this dance of course, but she didn't feel ready. Everyone would be watching them, expecting her to be perfect. She knew how to suppress her nerves though and pushed them down with a deep breath. She walked around the table with her back held straight, keeping her eyes on Anthony.

She curtsied low to Anthony when she stood in front of him and put her shaking hand in his resolute one. He kissed it lightly and smirked up at her. He then led her to the center of the floor and the orchestra struck up the song. Katerina averted her eyes from his face as she turned to place her hands in the closed dance hold.

They moved together across the floor, stepping in unison: one, two, three. They would dance the first part of this first dance without anyone else on the dance floor, all eyes on them. The two of them, and their golden attire, symbolized the Light God, Lumos, bright and vast and alone in the universe before he created the other light gods.

Katerina kept her cheek turned away from Anthony, concentrating on the steps. Anthony spun her out and she let her skirts flow out from under her. She let herself smile as they came back together and moved across the floor again, though she still kept her eyes from his.

After a few measures, they were joined by four more couples, one at a time. These four couples, dressed in green, white, blue, and red, depicted the entrance of Earth, Air, Water, and Fire into the world. These were often very coveted positions and were only handed to those closest to the emperor. She noticed Liam among them, representing Tykos with his blonde companion. She knew she would soon need to know the rest of the faces out there too.

On the next crescendo, the rest of those chosen to dance the first dance, representing the entrance of humanity, joined in. Spinning around, filling up the space around Katerina and Anthony. Anya joined the dance with the nobleman she had been given permission to dance with, and even Katerina's maids were honored with a place in the dance tonight. Katerina relaxed a little as the floor filled up, taking eyes away from her. Katerina let her eyes meet Anthony's as they spun around each other, shoulder to shoulder.

Katerina held his gaze for only a moment before she tripped over the long lining of her new ball gown. Panic rushed through her and she felt her face start to burn with embarrassment. Anthony moved quickly in front of her, catching her in his arms and hiding her misstep. She was forced to look into his eyes again as he did so. Their eyes remained locked as she stepped back into the hold. Her stomach fluttered as she gazed into Anthony's crystal blue eyes and felt her shoulders relax a little at his charming smirk.

The song came to an abrupt end, but she lingered in his arms, letting the warmth and strength of his arms sooth her nerves. A smile broke across her face to match his. Then she snapped herself back into reality. She quickly moved herself away from Anthony and curtsied, turning her eyes down to the floor. She stood up from the curtsy slowly and then turned away from him, heading back to her seat as quickly as was appropriate. Her body thrummed with a kind of heat she hadn't felt in years.

She stopped and turned back to Anthony. She felt the high emotions dampen as she saw he had already bounded off into the crowd. He seemed to be in his element as he conversed with a group of men, drinks in their hands, laughing and prodding each other.

Katerina sighed softly. She had let her girlish emotions get the best of her and she would have to be more careful in the future, especially with someone like Anthony. She continued back to her seat and bowed her head reverently to her father who was looking at her with his customary stern look. She relaxed when he nodded to her—his form of praise—and she was happy she wouldn't have to dance anymore tonight.

16

"Tykos's beard!" Alexander exclaimed. "What do you think you're doing?"

Liam hurried up onto the deck, pushing Alexander in his chair up the ramp from their cabins below. It was nearly sunset and the ship had started to pull toward the shore of Tulneria. He had heard that they would be docking within the hour. He pushed Alexander up to the side of the ship so they could both look out over the serene sea. The shores of Akaria were long gone since they departed three days ago.

Liam had traveled by sea before, but this trip had felt excruciatingly long. He had mostly kept to himself during the last three days, learning to better hone his surges of power. He could always feel the vibration of power within and he discreetly tested his ability to use his new-found strength at will throughout the trip by lifting heavy things when no one was around and pushing his body in different exercises. He couldn't escape boredom with sleep because the dreams of the red-haired girl still haunted him. In these dreams he fought a plethora of strange monsters and they always ended with the girl reaching out to him, asking him to find her and save her.

He thought about asking Alexander what these dreams might mean, but Alexander was not much of a conversationalist. He liked to stay in his stately cabin below deck, next to Liam's, with his nose in some book he had brought and only scowled at Liam when Liam asked him about it. They had their meals with Katerina and her ladies in the royal accommodations above deck, but Liam was never

129

able to speak with her alone. So, Liam was left alone with his thoughts for most of the trip, contemplating his dreams, thinking up plans for how he would impress the Tykens and, of course, all the ways this mission could go terribly wrong. He was undoubtedly relieved to see the end of the long journey as the greenery of the lush southern lands of the Tykens came into view.

Liam watched in awe as the small ship entered a narrow channel of water, beautiful rocky cliffs passed by them on either side, nearly scraping the sides of their vessel. He had never been to the Tyken country, and he had to admit it was pretty thrilling. He looked over to Alexander, but Alexander only sat there watching their arrival with a stoic expression and bored eyes as if he came this way every weekend. Liam sighed, pity flooding his heart for the man who had once had a great sense of adventure.

It had been easier than Liam had expected to explain the addition of the old man to their traveling party. As an Akarian ambassador escorting the princess on a diplomatic visit, Liam needed to have his own groom for the trip—someone to wait upon and help him dress. Liam was sure that a disabled valet might seem like an odd choice, but it had been accepted without question as they boarded the ship. It seemed Liam's eccentric tendencies served them well this time.

The ship emerged from the narrow channel into a large bay and a world of pure beauty opened in front of them. A landscape of vibrant green and pink trees painted the horizon. The fresh scent of a large waterfall filled the air as it rushed down into the bay, a tall, spired building covered in roots and vines stood beside it. The unique building was massively tall with stained glass lining the outside of the spiraling architecture. It had three spires, a large one that sat in the center, glowing with a yellow light and two smaller ones on either side. Balls of yellow and green light emanated from the spires, giving a vibrant glow to the whole valley in the dimming sunlight. The balls drifted through the air, floating gracefully toward them. As the ship approached the shore, the specks of colorful light hovered in the air above them, filling Liam's vision with nothing but magical beauty.

Liam never wanted to forget this beauty and he paused to take in every detail that he could. He felt as if he could truly feel Tykos's presence here. He had no idea that the Tykens lived in such a beautiful place.

A gentle scent of lavender alerted him to Katerina walking up to the edge of the ship to stand next to him. Liam glanced over and saw Katerina had taken meeting the Tykens as an Akarian ambassador seriously. She wore a beautiful green gown with brown embellishments, her hands covered in lace gloves and her hair pulled up into an intricate bundle of braids. She looked every bit the Akarian Princepa she would soon be.

She made no attempt to hide her amazement at the lands she was seeing either. Her eyes welled up and she brought one hand to her mouth as she reached out into the air to try and touch one of the floating balls of light. Liam felt a flutter in his stomach until he looked down at the necklace on her neck.

Liam quickly turned his gaze from her to Alexander on his other side. Alexander continued to sit quietly, arms crossed. Liam thought he could see a slight smile warming up on Alexander's face at the scene, but then he just shrugged and looked down at the book in his lap.

"Have you ever seen anything like this?" Liam asked Alexander with a gentle smile.

"Humph," was all Alexander said with a shrug, not looking up from his book.

"Welcome to our home," a voice said from behind them.

Liam turned to see a familiar Tyken Protector approaching them. Liam had learned through Anthony that this Tyken had been in charge of Princess Katerina's safety and she had gotten him to extend them the public invitation to his people's holiday festivities.

"Kona," Katerina said, looking at the Tyken now and putting down her hands. "Your home is so beautiful," she said as she looked back at the shore again.

Kona smiled at Katerina before glancing over to Liam and Alexander.

"Tykos is very much present in our lands. We have been very fortunate to be able to keep the lands the way He created them," Kona said crossing his arms proudly.

"Why would you ever want to leave such a place?" she asked him wistfully, staring off into the distance.

Kona's smile faded a little. "The land is beautiful, but as with everywhere, the intentions of the leaders are not always agreeable." He trailed off, taking in the sight of the shore himself. "The spring season is truly a magical time to visit Tulneria."

"We are very grateful for your invitation," Liam said awkwardly to Kona.

Kona turned to look at Liam, concern written all over his face. "I must warn you again that the leaders of my clan will accept the public invitation when I ask for you all to stay in front of the entire court, but they will not like it. You should be on your guard," Kona said and then looked over to Katerina briefly before speaking more quietly to Liam. "After you all are permitted to stay, I may not be able to protect her here."

Liam looked over to Katerina who was pointing to the balls floating through the air and looking back at Alexander. Liam could see she was very nearly making him smile.

"She is more than capable of taking care of herself, I'm sure," Liam said, turning back to Kona. "But I will be with her at all times."

Kona nodded and shifted his eyes. Another one of the Tyken Protectors called out to him and he backed away from the group to begin to help with the ship's docking.

The ship came into the docking area and the ship's crew, along with the Tykens onboard, moved to dock the ship. Alexander wheeled himself quickly back down under the deck to get himself ready for departure. Katerina's ladies flooded around her, chattering with excitement as they checked her gown and her hair for anything less than perfect. The fifteen Tykerial Guards onboard grabbed their armor and helmets, looking very excited to be getting off the ship. Liam looked down at his plain white and brown suit and smoothed it out, his hands shaking slightly as he did so.

Liam closed his eyes and took a breath. *Tonight is just a party,* he reminded himself. *We have Tykerial Guards and Tyken Protectors with us. The Tyken Court surely wouldn't try anything sinister, not tonight. This is the easy part.*

He opened his eyes and watched the Tyken Protectors carry their bags of belongings and gifts off the ship and a group of Tykerial Guards carried the Akarian gift to the Tykens between them. The crew would stay onboard, but everyone else lined up to exit.

Liam heard the sound of Alexander's wheelchair behind him and he turned to see that the old man had cleaned himself up nicely and looked quite dapper in his black suit coat and bow tie. He had his long hair combed and tied back and he even seemed to sit up a little straighter.

Liam moved to help push his chair off the ship, but Alexander waved him off with a wild gesture and lots of protests. Liam stepped away from the old man, his arms up in surrender, as Alexander rolled in front of him, his face returning to its normal scowl. Liam checked that his watch was comfortably on his wrist before walking off the boat behind him.

The group of humans were led by the Tyken entourage into the great spired structure Liam had seen before. Once they were closer, he saw it was a large vine-covered tree that had been carved out and decorated. Liam looked around in awe as they stepped through a set of huge stained-glass doors.

It was dark inside. The hallways and entryway were lit only by a few small candles now, but it seemed the sunlight probably lit the rooms well through all the stained-glass windows during the day. The Tykens led them up a grand staircase made of dirt and bark. Alexander grumbled as he accepted the help of two Tykerial Guards to lift him and his chair up the staircase. They kept his chair aloft as they continued behind the Tykens through two large wooden doors. The doors had the symbol of Tykos carved on them and Liam realized this must be their place of worship. He bowed his head slightly and said a quick prayer to Tykos as one of the large doors opened for them to enter through.

They continued through a large open area and out the glass doors at the rear of the church. Colored balls of light filled the air behind the church and they walked through the magical lights into a large forest. Soon they came into a large clearing, decorated with an abundance of white flowers. The flowers hung from the branches above, laid gathered together on stumps, and were even scattered all over the long, tall wooden tables that stood about the clearing.

Liam had never seen so many Tykens in one place before and he felt very small as they continued to walk through the clearing. He looked around as the Tykens were mingling around the tables, food piled high on them. They all wore different white markings on their dark skin, and Liam was mesmerized by their beauty even as they grabbed the food with their hands and talked to each other with their mouths full. The gathering seemed like chaos to Liam and he noticed there didn't appear to be anywhere to sit, nor any plates or silverware. Their actions seemed primitive and off-putting, but also somehow liberating and beautiful at the same time.

Tykens turned and watched them as they walked through the feast scene and by a line of Tykens dressed in long shiny robes of different colors—The Tyken Council. They conversed with each other quietly, not noticing the trail of newcomers at first. When they finally noticed the guests, they ceased their hushed conversation and turned to face the visitors. The Tyken Protectors that had travelled with them from Akaria all knelt on one knee in front of them, digging their fists into the ground, a common sign of reverence that Liam had only ever seen done in the temples for Tykos. The Akarian humans remained standing, awkwardly, in the center of a hushed Tyken crowd.

After kneeling for a moment, Kona alone stood up from the group and a tall, female Tyken stepped in front of other council members. Her white eye-tattoos gleamed against her dark skin in a most intricate pattern. Liam had not seen markings like this on the Tykens in Akaria and he noticed she had a few on her neck. She wore a long purple robe with sleeves that touched the ground and her golden jewelry sat finely on her pristine skin. Her dark hair was braided and pulled up onto her head, while the sharp angles of her face gave her a very intimidating look. She was clearly someone important and Liam assumed her to be Inola, the leader of this Tyken clan and recent enemy to his uncle.

She gestured for all the Tyken Protectors to rise and frowned angrily as she turned to look at Kona. She addressed him tersely in their native Tyk language. Kona responded with a regretful but calm tone, bowing his head to her as he spoke.

Inola turned her head to the group of humans as they stood nervously behind their Tyken companions. Her face remained stoic as she spoke to Kona once again and then her eyes locked on the Esterine princess. Kona gestured to the humans as he spoke again to the Tyken leader. Her eyes flashed with rage as Kona spoke and she turned her furious eyes back on him. A murmur ran through the crowd around them.

The public invitation, Liam thought as he tensed up and looked around, wanting to avoid the gaze of Inola. Kona was right that she wouldn't be happy. He turned his eyes back toward Inola as her lips pressed together in frustration. He watched as she pushed down her anger with a deep breath in and forced an expression that somewhat resembled a smile directed to the human guests. It was one of the scariest smiles Liam had ever seen.

"We will accept the Akarian guests into our festival of Tysella," Inola spoke in the Akarian tongue, her accent thick but understandable. "Though I am sorry that we have no rooms prepared for them here," she said more quietly to the humans before raising her voice again, "This is a very important time for our people and I trust our friendship will bring honor to Tykos and his never-ending virtue of hospitality. Who do we have the honor of accepting here?"

Katerina stepped forward out of their group and knelt on one knee, her green gown puffing out around her. Liam was impressed as he watched her dig her fists into the ground and bow her head in a very Tyken-like motion.

She spoke loudly and clearly in the Tyken's native language. Liam assumed it was a very tasteful greeting and introduction, though he couldn't understand a word. She waited for the Tyken leader to tell her to rise. A piece of dark hair fell loose into Katerina's face as she continued to look at the ground.

Liam watched the shocked faces of the Tyken leaders turn to either more disdain or to amiable impression, but Inola's face remained stern and rock-solid. She said two words in Tyk, glaring at Katerina and Katerina lifted her head and stood up.

Katerina spoke directly to the Century leader for a few moments and then gestured over to the large box that was carried in by the Tykerial Guards. The guards came forward and opened the box in front of Inola. Liam watched as Inola's mouth twitched subtly into a small smile when she saw what was inside. Four golden statues laid in the box, each depicting a different theme of Tykos. One for family, one for growth, one for charity, and one for strength. Liam felt a chill prickle up his spine when he saw the last one.

Inola nodded to Katerina and the Tykerial Guards closed the box and carried it over to where the other council members pointed. Katerina smiled genuinely at Inola before finally saying something Liam could actually understand. "I'm so pleased you like the gift, and thank you all so much for this welcome," she said in Akarian, bowing her head to the Tyken council once more.

The Tyken leaders nodded their heads. Liam noticed one or two of them looked genuinely welcoming, but others remained skeptical. Still, they all forced smiles onto their faces and tried to embrace the spirit of hospitality that Tykos is known for.

Inola stepped forward without taking her gaze from the princess, and spoke in clear Akarian.

"You are welcomed into our city, as we welcome all of Tykos's creatures here." She forced a smile before gesturing to the crowd. "He would want all his creatures to celebrate him in unity. Enjoy the feast." She turned back to her group of Tyken leaders and the Tyken Protectors dispersed into the crowd, greeting loved ones and pulling out their own gifts to share. Liam supposed that was all the formalities that would take place tonight, but he still felt on edge.

"Well, all right then. I suppose we don't need an introduction or any kind of real hospitality," Alexander said grumpily.

Kona turned to his guests, a small group of humans surrounded by an escort of Tykerial Guards in the middle of a Tyken horde. "I've gotten the invitation for you stay, but it's probably best if you keep a low profile tonight. Enjoy the festivities from afar, don't engage with anyone and you should be fine. We want to show the clan that your people are not threatening and that you really are here to build a partnership once again," he instructed. He looked around nervously. "Stick to that area over there," he said, pointing to a region off to the side of the main aisle. "Tonight may be a little tense, but I'm sure the more everyone sees you mean only to bring our peoples together throughout the holiday, things will loosen up a bit. And hopefully by the time the final night of the holiday comes around, we can convince them …" He trailed off as he heard a group of Tykens calling his name. He smiled weakly at Liam and Katerina and sighed. He pointed over to the area he wanted them to go and then he turned to walk toward the other Tykens.

Liam watched as the Tykerial Guards dispersed, setting up posts around a wide area, but Katerina's ladies remained timid and glued together.

"An interesting selection of food for a feast," Alexander commented, looking around eagerly.

Liam looked around at the long tables of food, piled high with nuts, berries, dried fruits and meats. A few Tykens walked around with trays, carrying the same foods and pitchers of something purple. He wrinkled his face in disgust as he realized there were also some insects, large and small stacked on the platters. It was all food that could be found within this forest, Liam realized.

"Yes, very interesting indeed," Liam agreed, imagining what biting down on one of those insects would be like.

"Shall we get ourselves out of the middle of the aisle?" Katerina asked, looking anxiously over to the area Kona had pointed to.

"Right," Liam said, tearing his eyes from the food selections and ushering everyone over to an empty table off to the side.

The tables were high off the ground, almost too tall for even Liam to reach, but they surrounded the table anyway. Liam took another glance around the party. A group of Tyken women approached a couple of the Tykerial Guards with platters of food and drink. Liam sighed as he watched the guards help themselves. Some of them removed their helmets and began conversing with the Tykens. Liam tried to relax. It was a good thing that the guards seemed to be so relaxed and approachable, right?

"Kona's mother was not very pleased with his invitation," Katerina said as her eyes darted around the feast.

"His mother?" Liam asked, his head snapping over to Katerina.

"Yes, Inola is Kona's mother. It seems when Kona agreed to extend the invitation for us, it was not just about Akaria and Tulneria. He has mentioned a thing or two about not always getting along with his mother, and now I see this was possibly just another way of him asserting his independence," Katerina explained before biting her lip nervously.

"When are we getting something to eat?" Alexander asked gruffly.

Liam looked around. "There are a couple of waitresses coming this way now," he said, nodding over to a pair of Tykens carrying trays and walking over to them.

The Tykens stared at the humans as they bent down to offer them their choice of food and drinks from their trays. Katerina nodded to her ladies and each one took a turn to grab something gently and timidly off the tray. Meanwhile, Alexander scooped up a cupful of nuts and fruits and snatched a cup of wine. Liam and Katerina took their share of meats and cheeses, and Katerina thanked the Tykens in their language.

Liam felt uneasy as the waitresses whispered between themselves and backed away from the human group slowly.

"Woowee!" Alexander exclaimed, making Liam turn to look at him. Alexander scrunched up his face. "That is … that is … very good," he concluded with a real smile.

Liam laughed at this, but Katerina looked concerned.

"Should you be drinking something that we don't even know what's in it?" she asked, concerned.

"Nonsense! What could possibly be worse for me at this point?" Alexander asked with a laugh before taking another generous drink.

"This isn't a party for us," Katerina said in a whisper as her eyes darted about again.

"We really should try to relax a little," Liam said. "We don't want to appear as if we have something to hide. The games are tomorrow and we need to appear amiable until then so they'll let us stay." He turned his attention to his cup and lifted it to his nose to smell the liquid before taking a sip. It smelled sweet with a tinge of tart; it was some kind of fruit that he couldn't quite place. He took a sip and let the liquid burn down his throat as he swallowed. Despite the initial burn, the taste was amazing. It was like nothing he had ever tasted before.

Katerina looked at him, expectantly.

"He's right, this is very good," Liam laughed. "Maybe a bit strong, but very good. A sipping wine, for sure." Liam took another small sip.

Katerina smiled at him and took a sip from her cup.

"What is all that about?" Alexander asked pointing to something behind Liam, his words already beginning to slur.

Katerina and Liam turned to see what Alexander was referring to. A group of small Tykens were being paraded around the clearing in a line. Applause followed them and they each wore similar green robes and carried uniquely carved wooden staffs.

"The young Tykens received their first marks today," Katerina explained. "They'll be considered adults now."

"Their first marks?" Liam asked, intrigued. "Do they choose what marks they receive? What are they based on?"

Katerina shrugged. "I don't know all the details. I only know that the Tykos holiday is opened with the coming-of-age ceremony, which must have taken place before we arrived. The marks and their meanings are still a mystery to me."

Liam turned to look over at Alexander. His eyes blinked rapidly as he tried to keep them open and his head bobbed slightly. Liam looked down at his cup and decided to wait a few minutes before taking any more of the liquid himself. When he turned to suggest the same to Katerina, she looked upset.

"What's wrong?" Liam asked, worrying that she felt unsafe here.

"I just wish they wouldn't be so unkind to Kona," Katerina said quietly. "He's really a very kind soul and reliable protector. I've come to really trust him."

Liam turned to look over to where Kona now stood, surrounded by a group of rowdy Tykens. The other Tykens laughed and elbowed each other as Kona stood in the middle, rolling his eyes and smiling sarcastically.

"What are they saying to him?" Liam asked, unable to understand the conversation.

"They are ridiculing him for bringing us. Calling him unkind names for working for humans …" Katerina said uncomfortably and took another drink from her cup.

Liam watched Katerina and the hurt in her face was clear. Liam felt his stomach turn. He didn't like that look on her face. Then he felt something rumble within him. His power. He could feel it wanting to escape. It vibrated, a ball of energy sitting in his midsection, waiting to be released. He pushed it down, not wanting to make a scene, and took a big drink from his cup. Liam looked over again at the group. Empathy washed through him for Kona. Kona had done them a huge favor and Liam hated that it cost him so much already and he had no idea what else was coming.

One of the Tykens in the group caught Liam staring and Liam felt a jolt of fear as he quickly averted his eyes away from the group. Peripherally he could see the Tyken nudge another and point over to their group. Liam closed his eyes in regret, anxiety rising within him.

Oh no, Liam thought as the group of Tykens began to walk over to them.

They were standing in front of Liam in a matter of seconds and Liam was forced to be face to face with a huge Tyken as he looked Liam over, head to toe. The Tykens spoke to each other in Tyk, clearly not caring if Katerina could understand them or not.

Katerina tensed up and grabbed ahold of Alexander's shoulder, but he was snoring now. His head rolled over onto his chest and his cup nearly spilled its liquid as it sat in his lap.

One of the Tykens poked Liam's shoulder and chuckled. Liam felt his head begin to swim from the drink as he tried to laugh off the gesture with them as they chuckled together. He looked at Katerina, who gave him a subtle but serious shake of her head.

Katerina spoke up, speaking their language lightly and airily and raising her glass with a smile. She was clearly trying to take the focus from him and lighten the mood. *What was she saying?* Liam wondered.

However, her attempt to disperse the tension didn't work, and now their attention had turned solely onto her. She kept her face pinned in a small smile, though Liam could see the humor leaving her eyes as they talked more in her direction. Kona stuck an arm out to hold back the Tyken who was getting too close to her, but he pushed Kona's arm away forcefully before reaching out and picking up a piece of Katerina's hair, examining it closely.

Liam felt the rising of power within him again. Anger and fear seared through him as he felt his inhibitions beginning to leave and his power begging to be set free. His temper only continued to build as Kona smacked the other Tyken's hand away from Katerina. The Tyken turned to Kona, fury in his eyes, and yelled and pointed in his face.

Liam was about to lose all control and let his power escape him when he heard someone shout from across the clearing, "Hey! Keep your filthy hands off her!"

Liam turned to see one of the Tykerial Guards stomping over to them. It was most out of character for a guardsman to act this way. *Perhaps it was the wine?* Liam guessed. But then the guardsman removed his helmet and Liam's heart lurched into his throat.

Horror rippled through him, sobering up any intoxication he had felt up to that point. He rubbed his eyes with his hands to be sure he was really seeing what he was seeing, but when Liam looked again, he still saw the rustled black hair and angry blue eyes of his brother in front of him, his cheeks red with fury. It was Anthony.

Anthony barged into the group of Tykens and shoved the one who touched Katerina's hair backward. Liam quickly grabbed Anthony's arms to stop him from further altercation, but the Tykens seemed amused at this interaction.

"Don't ever touch her!" Anthony yelled fiercely, leaning closer to the Tyken. The Tyken smirked mischievously down at Anthony as he towered above him.

Liam could smell the alcohol on Anthony as he continued to pull him away from the large dark figure.

"All right then," Liam said, forcing a chuckle. "We should probably be going now. It's been a long day …"

He dragged Anthony down the path that led off into the woods. The Tykens watched them go, and to Liam's relief, they did not seem interested enough to follow them. Liam turned Anthony around and pushed him in the back once they were far enough away from the feast that they could only see a faint glowing from the lights.

"What in all of Xevron's souls are you doing?" Liam yelled as he held his arms out in question.

"What?" Anthony asked, stumbling to the side as he turned to face Liam. His eyes were unfocused and he swayed in place on his feet.

"What are you doing here? You're supposed to be back in Akaria!" Liam exclaimed, anger pulsing through him.

"It's not like I'm really needed there. Edward is doing all the hard work anyway. And I couldn't just let you guys have all the fun, could I?" Anthony said, laughing to himself.

"Fun?" Liam asked incredulously. "This is not *fun*, Anthony! This is serious! This is life and death and war and peace stuff!" Liam continued to yell.

He turned away from Anthony to take a deep breath in, clenching his fists tightly by his side. His power thrummed within him again. He really wanted to punch something.

Katerina arrived in front of him then, wheeling the sleeping Alexander through the bumpy forest ground with some difficulty. Her ladies trailing behind her, their eyes wide with excitement and fear.

Liam turned back to Anthony, having calmed down enough to refrain from punching his brother in the face.

"How did you manage to stow away without anyone noticing?" Liam asked.

Anthony shrugged. "I mean some did notice," he said and sat himself down on the ground. "Just not you. I have quite a few Tykerial Guard friends you know." His eyes drooped and his speech slowed as his face curled into a lazy smile.

Liam rolled his eyes. His frustration climbed again as he realized this meant that he was stuck with Anthony until they could return him and Katerina to Akaria, which could only happen after Katerina had a chance to disenchant the sword they hoped to receive from the Tykens. Liam looked over to Katerina.

"Come on, let's get these guys back to the boat and into bed before I destroy this entire forest."

17

Liam woke with a start from a shallow slumber. The mysterious girl still refused to relinquish her grip on his dreams. He lifted his head to see the first light of sunrise starting to stream in through the small window of his private cabin on the lower deck of the ship. He sat up slowly and waited for the headache to split his head open again. The headaches were always the worst first thing in the morning.

He sat there, wincing, as pain filled his head and his vision blurred. He could do nothing but wait for it to pass and soon it slowly faded and Liam's vision cleared. His brother laying next to him, snoring softly, still in the Tykerial Guard arming doublet he had worn last night underneath his armor when he crashed the Tysella feast.

A fresh wave of anger flashed through Liam, flaring the pain in his head once again, as he remembered the moment he saw Anthony's face under that helmet. Liam ran his hands through his hair and pulled at the curls. Today was the day of the Tyken games and the most important day of his life. The life of his uncle and the future of Akaria relied on him being able to win these games and request the sword as their prize. Liam knew Anthony's presence would only make the day more stressful.

Liam stood up from his small berth and tapped at Anthony's shoulder. Anthony groaned and rolled away from Liam. Liam swiped Anthony's thin blanket off him and Anthony whimpered pitifully. He rolled back over and fluttered his eyes open.

"Oh, right," Anthony said tiredly as he glanced at Liam through squinted eyes.

"Here, drink some water," Liam said with annoyance and tossed his canteen down at his brother.

Anthony sat up, blinking his eyes, and took a sip out of the canteen.

"Ugh," Anthony groaned. "It seems I may have drank too much of that Tyken wine last night."

"You think?" Liam asked, irritation spraying out with his words. Then he sighed. "Anthony, why did you have to sneak onto the ship? It's going to be hard enough for me today, and now …"

Anthony stood up clumsily and shoved the canteen back to Liam. "Look, I only want to help. I won't be in your way, I promise."

"How are you not going to be in my way?" Liam asked exasperated. "The Tykens are going to have their attention on you and I have to make sure that no one tries to do anything to you now. You do realize we are in hostile territory? And the fact that we didn't tell them you were coming … It looks horrible on us!"

Anthony shrugged. "Just don't tell them who I am then."

Liam sighed and groaned, rubbing his forehead. "Everyone we brought with us from Akaria knows what you look like, including the Tyken Protectors."

Anthony stood up and slipped on his boots. "Look, it's no big deal. Really. Just go about your business. No one is going to say anything or care about some reckless Tykerial Guard from last night."

Liam rolled his eyes and angrily got dressed. He barked at Anthony to bring Alexander up on deck with him when they were ready. He needed to get out of this stale air. He grabbed his suit jacket to cover his simple training tunic and stomped out of the small cabin and up the stairs onto the deck of the ship. He leaned over the edge of the ship, glaring at the beautiful bright green trees, feeling his power rise and fall within him as he waited for the others.

He was starting to feel calm again when he heard the wheels of Alexander's chair behind him and he turned to see Anthony had cleaned himself up nicely and was pushing Alexander toward him. Alexander's eyes looked even more tired than usual. His hair was disheveled and his face was a sickly green.

"All ready for today?" Liam asked Alexander with concern. Alexander only grumbled in reply and took control of his own chair to wheel himself up closer to the edge and looked out at the horizon with crossed arms.

Liam turned and looked up to see Katerina emerging from her rooms on the upper deck of the ship. Surrounded by ladies, he was grateful that at least someone in this group was put together this morning. She looked like spring itself as she floated down the stairs from the grand cabin in a light blue gown, covered in a floral pattern with pink and white flowers. She kept her traditional Isavarian braid today, but wore an Akarian style hat with a wide brim that shaded her face from the sun.

She descended the ship's stairs and dismissed her ladies before approaching the group of men alone. She immediately looked concerned when she saw Anthony and Alexander.

"Are you all right?" Katerina asked Alexander with concern, leaning over to look into his face.

"Good Tykos, leave it to a woman …" Alexander grumbled. "It's called a hangover. We're fine."

Liam chuckled and then dropped his smile as he looked over at Anthony. He checked his watch nervously.

"I was thinking … maybe I should go alone to these games today. It doesn't really seem like a good idea to have …" he started to say.

"You will not," Katerina said, putting her hands on her hips. "You will not go without me at least. It would be quite strange and rather suspicious if I didn't attend. Besides, I need to be there for when Alexander disenchants the sword."

Liam smiled. "Well, I doubt they'll just roll out the sword for me as soon as I ask for it."

"They will likely bestow the requested gifts and prizes on the last night of Tykos holiday," Anthony said, squeezing his eyes with his fingers.

"Still, I'm the official Akarian representative," Katerina said, dropping her hands into a crossed arms position. "I will be expected to attend all of the Tysella traditions."

"Yeah, the mating rituals, the forest walks, the gift-giving celebration, it all sounds so fascinating," Anthony agreed, smiling at Katerina. She rolled her eyes slightly and looked away.

Liam sighed and nodded. "I just don't want any more surprises or unplanned incidents. Today has to go perfectly," he said and squeezed his eyes shut briefly. When he opened his eyes again he saw Kona walking over to them.

"Kona?" Katerina asked. "What are you doing here? I thought we would meet you at the games today."

Liam didn't like the look of concern on Kona's face. "Slight change of plans," he said, avoiding making eye contact with her.

Liam's stomach fluttered nervously. *Great, something has already gone wrong,* he thought.

"I don't think it's a good idea for your whole entourage to attend the games today," Kona began and Liam's heart lifted with hope. Katerina opened her mouth to protest, but Kona continued before she could say anything. "I talked to my mother and she has agreed to allow a few of you to sit in the royal box with us, but we will only have room for four or five people. You'll have to sit way off to the side, but it's better than being around all the rowdy rabble. I think it could be dangerous to have any of the Akarians sit in the audience with everyone else."

Kona paused and everyone looked to Liam.

"Does everyone know about …?" Liam asked, pointing his head toward Anthony. Anthony crossed his arms and rolled his eyes.

Kona shook his head, eyeing Anthony with a firm stare. "Luckily no. The few Tyken Protectors that did see him have all agreed that it would be best to keep the identity of the rogue Tykerial to ourselves." He looked back over to Liam. "But he will need to tread carefully and not cause any more disturbances."

Liam stared daggers into Anthony and Anthony shrugged and nodded like it was the most obvious thing that he would behave like a real Tykerial Guard from now on. Liam looked at the expectant faces of everyone around him again. He knew Katerina was right that she needed to be there and he knew Anthony would not allow them to go without him either, not quietly at least. It would also be a relief that he wouldn't have to worry about any of the other Akarias learning about what he could do yet and the others would be safe in the royal box with Kona.

"Fine," Liam finally said. "The four of us will go, but Anthony," he said, turning pleading eyes onto his brother, "please keep your helmet on."

Anthony made a face at Liam and Kona nodded in agreement. Anthony walked over to give the order to the Tykerial Guard Legate to keep everyone on the ship until they returned. Though there was some protest, he eventually agreed to the order and handed Anthony a Tykerial Guard helmet and helped him with the rest of his golden armor. Katerina told her ladies they would have to wait on the ship today and before long, the small group shuffled themselves off the ship, Kona leading them.

They walked through the church entrance again into the Tyken's world. Then they easily followed the crowd of Tykens over to where the games were taking place. With every step, Liam's muscles tightened with more and more anxiety. Soon, a large oblong stone structure emerged in front of them. The bowl stadium looked much like the stadiums they used for Lumyball in Akaria, but with numerous arches and intricate cornices set into the sides of it, making it look much more majestic. Crowds of Tykens were piling in through the few entrances and Liam was glad they had Kona with him because the Tykens only spared them a few glances of amusement.

"The entrance to the royal box is just over here," Kona said as he pointed and led them over to one of the smaller entrances to the stadium.

Liam stopped abruptly in place and forced himself to speak up. "I was actually wondering where I would go to sign up to compete in one of these games. People can still sign up today, right?" he asked, trying to keep his voice from shaking nervously.

Kona stopped walking and turned to look at Liam with confusion. "You don't want to sign up for these games. They are not really the type of 'games' that you're used to," he told Liam shaking his head.

Liam lifted his chin, trying to look confident with an air of nonchalance, while keeping his eyes on Kona. "Yeah, I really do. I think it would be ..." Liam searched for a good word to use, "... fun."

Kona furrowed his brow at Liam. "These games are not 'fun,'" he said. "They are extremely dangerous, even for the Tykens who participate, and there are no mercy rules. You would undoubtedly be very hurt, if not killed." Kona's face told Liam that he was serious.

Liam shrugged. "Maybe. But I'd like to see for myself. How would I sign up?"

"You humans are up to something aren't you?" Kona asked, looking Liam up and down. Liam didn't answer and Kona shook his head and sighed. "I don't know what you're planning, but I don't want to know either." He paused to sigh again. "There isn't really a 'sign up.' You just go down in those tunnels over there and hope to get into a group. The games are mostly fighting and wrestling, with a few groups performing tricks sprinkled in. I suggest you try to stay to the trick contests like juggling or solo acrobatics," Kona pointed to some stairs that led down below the stadium.

Liam nodded and looked at the stairs. "Thank you, Kona." He removed his watch, placing it in an inner pocket in his suit jacket and slid it off, leaving him in just a light, lace-up tunic and trousers. He turned to Katerina. "You guys have fun. Be safe. And watch out," he said, pointing at the other two in their group with his eyes.

Katerina nodded. The concern and nervousness on her face did nothing to ease his own fears as he shoved his jacket into Anthony's chest and forced himself to turn and leave the group behind. He very much wished he could also just watch some fun and interesting Tykens wrestle and fight today.

He followed a couple of bulky Tykens down the stairs into the tunnels underneath the vast stadium, rolling up his sleeves with shaking hands as he walked. They soon entered a dark gathering area. Small stalls with raised latticed portcullises were set into the sides of the room and benches were scattered among the center. The space reminded Liam of the men's dressing rooms they had in school, though much dirtier and crude. Tykens of all sizes were gathered here, getting ready for the games to begin. They warmed up with stretches and exercises as Liam tentatively stepped forward. Eyes turned on him as he stood in front of the large intimidating group.

"Wrong place, human!" one of the Tykens yelled out in a rough Akarian tongue, causing a roll of laughter to erupt in the cave.

Liam clenched his hands into fists nervously.

"I wanted to see about entering the games ..." Liam said, his voice cracking embarrassingly.

There was a pause as the Tykens looked around at each other and then another roll of laughter ensued.

"You had better go back up into the stands now," a large Tyken with concern written all over his face said to Liam. He looked familiar to Liam and was likely one of the Tyken Protectors that had come with them from Akaria.

"I would like very much to participate in the games. How do I ..." Liam began to ask again. He could feel his face heating up and his power begin to vibrate as he spoke.

Then a familiar face pushed his way through the crowd and smiled wickedly at Liam. The Tyken who wouldn't leave them alone from last night. He said something to the kind looking Tyken, making him hesitate before looking back at Liam.

"This is Dekota," he said, pointing at the roguish Tyken who was looking at Liam hungrily. "He said that you may enter into his fighting group, if you wish. They have an open spot."

Liam shook his head. "Oh no, not a fighting group, I just want to try to …" Liam paused. He could likely win the fighting matches just as easily as the lifting competitions with his recent training and it would be so satisfying to take down this scoundrel of a Tyken with his own two hands. "All right then." Liam finished, nodding his head confidently.

Dekota smirked at Liam and led him over to his competition group. The Tykens all returned to their warm-up activities, though they didn't try to hide their sideways glances at Liam, as they all chattered amongst themselves and waited for the games to begin. Liam decided with hesitancy to remove his tunic to match the bare-chested Tykens. He was sure he was going to look absolutely ridiculous in the arena with his light skin and less-than bulging muscles, but he worried they would be able to use the extra fabric against him. He stretched along with the Tykens, trying not to make eye contact with any of them and keep to himself. He reached inside to stoke his power, making sure it was still there and that he could call upon it when he needed to. He could barely breathe as the realization sunk in that everything hinged on this performance.

Liam watched as other groups were called into the arena one by one as the games began. He could hear the roar of the crowd and the sound of grunting Tykens coming from outside. He stood waiting for his group's turn to enter, trying to concentrate only on the vibration and strength he felt within.

Finally, it was time for Liam's group to step into the arena. They all lined up in front of the gate that led into the dirt field of the bowl stadium. Liam's head felt as if it was floating off his body as the gates rose in front of him. He gritted his teeth and dug his fingernails into his palms and forced himself to step into the glaringly bright stadium with the rest of the Tykens.

The crowds cheered around them as their feet kicked up puffs of dirt with every step on their way into the center. Liam easily found the royal box, sitting high in the stands, covered with an overhang while the rest of the stadium was open to the elements. Inola sat on a large throne made of curving branches intertwining with vines and decorated with white flowers. She glared down at the contestants, Kona and her Tyken council sitting on either side of her. Liam searched the royal box for the shiny reflection of Anthony's helmet and finally caught a glimpse of Anthony and Katerina standing way off to the side, in the corner of the box. He hoped they wouldn't have a great view of what was about to happen.

Liam could hear all the whispers going around the stadium as he lined up with the Tykens, all towering feet above him, in the center of the field. He stood as straight as he could, desperately missing the soothing ticking of his watch.

Time is passing, it will all be over in a few minutes, Liam told himself.

Another Tyken came around to each competitor and had each of them pull numbers out of a sack to determine their first opponent. Liam reached into the sack to pull out his wooden chip. The chip had a symbol painted on it that Liam couldn't decipher. He held it up, searching for the matching symbol in the group. His stomach flipped when he realized he would be partnered with Dekota first.

Of course, Liam thought to himself, controlling the mixture of anticipation and dread that threatened to show on his face.

The line of contestants dispersed into the fighting pins. Many taking amused glances at Liam as he went over to his designated competing area, marked by a wooden sign with the same symbol that was on his wooden chip. Liam cracked his neck side to side, took a deep breath, swung his arms across his chest and outward a few times, and then bent his knees into a strong stance as he faced Dekota. The horn sounded and the games began.

Dekota lunged toward Liam swiftly, but Liam dodged him easily with a simple rolling maneuver. Dekota smiled and looked at the crowds around them. He nodded and yelled at the crowd to start cheering before lunging at Liam again. Liam let Dekota smash into him this time and he caught Dekota's waist in his arms. His arms didn't make it all the way around the hefty Tyken, but he gripped as tightly as he could and called upon his inhuman strength to keep himself standing. He felt the pulsing of his power in his arms as he tried to pull Dekota down.

Dekota tensed in panic before breaking free of Liam's grasp. He stepped back and glared at Liam suspiciously. Liam lunged forward this time, and the two bodies clashed together again. Dekota got his arms around Liam's neck and tried to take Liam down to the ground. Liam felt Dekota's force and energy and stoked his powers to counter it, keeping his focus on Dekota and ignoring the rantings of the crowd as best as he could.

Frustrated that Liam was still standing, Dekota let go of the hold and quickly pushed Liam backward with a kick to his stomach. Liam staggered back, the wind knocked out of his lungs, and knocking him to one knee. Before he could even catch his breath, Liam could see his opponent charging at him again, and it took all his might to stand up as quickly as his body would allow.

His instincts told him to dodge this massive enemy coming right at him, but he knew he had to stand his ground and prove himself. He braced himself for the full force of Dekota's weight and took a step forward just as Dekota slammed into him. Liam gritted his teeth as he held Dekota back, his arms barely reaching Dekota's shoulders. Fury flashed in Dekota's eyes and suddenly his horns were coming straight at Liam's face.

Liam had no time to react before Dekota's forehead rammed into his own. Liam saw nothing but black as he felt his body hit the ground, and the crowd roared in triumph as he struggled to regain his footing, shaking his head vigorously to recover his sight. Slowly, bits of light were visible again and he could see the blurry figure of Dekota soaking up the cheers from the crowd and strutting around prompting more cheers. He thought it was over, and maybe it was.

Liam felt inside for the rumble of his power again.

Where is it? Where is the power? he thought to himself in a panic. It had to still be in there, somewhere. He felt it flicker, but it seemed to be majorly depleted. He clearly had no idea how to use only what he needed at a time. He only knew how to flare it. He focused and pulled at the faint vibration within him again. *Tykos, please help me*, Liam prayed.

Liam snapped his head up when he heard the pounding of Dekota's footsteps approaching him. Dekota was chuckling to himself as he moved to pick up Liam. Liam reached within, willing the power to come back to him, but he couldn't even feel the faint pulse anymore. Dekota lifted him up by his neck and held him up so he could look him straight in the eyes. He was going to lose, and this terrified him.

Then Dekota stumbled backward suddenly, losing his balance and blinking his eyes rapidly as if they were full of dust. His grip loosened on Liam allowing Liam to slip from his grasp and land on his feet, stumbling slightly. His eyes were slowly refocusing, and he glanced over to where he believed Anthony and Katerina stood. They were still too far away for Liam to see them, but he thought he could see Alexander's head now too, leaning over the box. He must have done something to Dekota, Liam thought. He cheated for him. He should have lost, but he had a second chance now. And Liam was going to take full advantage.

He had to win this. He had to earn the sword from the Tykens. He had to do this or their chances of saving his uncle plummeted. Liam took a deep inhale and gathered himself, stoking that inner pulsating power and it flickered up again. Liam grabbed hold of that power with everything he had and just as the vibrations thrummed through his body strongly again, he looked up to see Dekota's fist swinging toward him.

The whole world seemed to fall away and it was just him and Dekota. Liam ducked from the swing and planted his hands firmly on the ground. Remembering a move that had taken him down recently, he kicked his leg out and spun around, sweeping Dekota's legs with a full flare of his power.

There was loud crack and Dekota yelled out in pain. Liam heard the Tyken's leg bones snap as he brought him down. Dekota's body bounced as it hit the solid ground, knocking the air from his lungs.

Dekota raised a hand in surrender as he rolled over onto his stomach, searing pain clear on his face. Liam stood up, his heart sinking at the sight. Dekota's face conveyed not only his pain, but his shock. Liam thought he saw something else painted there as well—utter fear.

Liam felt sick looking at the misshapen leg and turned away to look at the crowd. His hands shook by his sides as he wrestled with the realization of what he had just done. He had done it. He had won. But he had also gravely injured a Tyken in their own arena. This wasn't what he had pictured this moment to be like. He wished he could enjoy the victory, but he was far too nervous to see the Tykens' reactions. Would they let him continue in the tournament? Or would they punish him for being an outsider who injured one of their men?

Silence fell over the arena. Every Tyken in the stadium stood, looking down at him in amazement and confusion at what had just occurred. Even the Tykens competing in the ring with him stopped to stare. Three nearby Tykens moved out of their frozen shock and rushed toward Dekota to pick him up and carry him off the scene carefully as he winced and writhed in pain.

Liam looked up to Inola and the other Tyken leaders nervously. He could see her face clearly now as she stood at the edge of her box. Liam thought she looked scared for a moment, but then her face took on an expression of pure anger. She stared at him with fierce eyes, but didn't make a move or a sound. Finally, she turned her head slightly and whispered something to one of the Tykens beside her. He departed her side quickly and Liam looked around to the rest of the crowd again. The cheering and the chatter had completely stopped.

"It appears we have a very important person in our presence today," Inola called out to the masses from her box.

Liam saw the fear on Kona's face as he looked over to where Katerina stood and Liam's heart rate only continued to rise.

"The gift Tykos gave the humans many years ago started out as surges of strength that would grow into powers of earth and plant manipulation. We haven't seen a gift like that in hundreds of years," Inola said as she looked down at Liam.

Liam was suddenly exhausted as he let go of his hold on the inner pulsing. His legs felt weak, but he managed to stay on his feet, slightly swaying, as he bowed his head to the Tyken leader in reverence, hoping to appear humble, but strong.

"Tykens of Tulneria," she said loudly, "Tykos' gift of strength was never meant to stay in the hands of humans for long. They have proven that they cannot control it properly. They cannot be trusted with such power. They will always hurt others with it as we have seen here today. We have been lied to and manipulated by these humans into inviting them into our most sacred traditions." A large group of Tykens ran across the stadium's floor and gathered around Liam. "Seize them," she shouted with absolute venom, her eyes piercing Liam with hate.

Liam was rushed by a mob of Tykens. They grabbed his arms and kicked his legs out from under him. He hit the ground on his stomach, unable to gather even a sliver of strength to fight them off or struggle. His muscles refused to obey his desperate pleas and his stomach only fluttered with fear now. He looked over at where Katerina, Anthony, and Alexander stood but could no longer see them.

Completely powerless, Liam turned his eyes down and then his whole world went black.

18

Katerina felt her body tense with a sudden jolt of adrenaline as panic set in. She took a sharp breath in and her arms were forcefully and painfully pulled behind her back by the Tykens who once stood around her as allies. Wind picked up around her as she quickly darted her eyes down to Liam in the stadium. She didn't even try to control her fear, watching helplessly as Liam was kicked down and tied up by the towering brutes surrounding him. He had no power left and she couldn't risk revealing her powers to help him.

The breeze grew stronger and colder as she tried to pull herself free from the grasp of the Tyken who held her arms. Kona was promptly pushed out of the box, yelling and protesting as five other Tykens detained him. Katerina looked over to Anthony, but saw that he had been surrounded and could only struggle against the Tykens. He shook his arms fiercely, trying to pull away from their strong hold, but he only managed to knock the Tykerial Guard helmet from his head. His black hair tousled into his face and his bright eyes glared at a Tyken in front of him, his chest heaving with anger.

She snapped her head toward Alexander, worry clenching her chest. But he was sitting in his chair next to her, not struggling against the calamity whatsoever, with his eyes closed, whispering to himself. The hat on her head slipped forward and Katerina let a small piece of hope fill her chest as she watched him. His lips moved faster and faster, his eyes remained squeezed shut.

He's trying to do a spell, she realized. *He's going to get us out of this. Oh please, God of all creation, please help us. Give Alexander strength. He's our only hope. Please …*

Katerina closed her eyes. She tried to calm her emotions with a few breaths and put all her focus on her own powers. She could feel the turmoil inside. Waves of anxiety, fear, and hope all tousled within—control over her magic laid somewhere beneath all of that.

She heard heavy footsteps and dread filled her. The wind blew her hat off her head as she snapped open her eyes to see more Tykens pouring into the royal box carrying chains. The first one through the door moved straight over to the murmuring Alexander and threw a handful of dust into his face. Before Alexander could manage any kind of spell, his head fell forward limply and he was unconscious.

Katerina's eyes widened in fear. *No*, Katerina thought helplessly as she struggled harder against the strong arms holding her, but the same dust was sprayed into her face too. She fought the effects, ordering her body not to give in. She continued to squirm, but soon the effects were too much and she felt her body start to go limp and numb. She couldn't fight the influence of the drug any longer and she fell into unconsciousness.

When Katerina awoke, she was being jostled around in what felt like the back of a very old carriage on a forest road. She heard heavy footsteps outside, pounding the ground quickly and steadily. She didn't think it sounded like horses. The Tykens must be pulling her along in whatever box they had her in.

She tried to lift her head, but her muscles refused to obey. Her arms were bound behind her, and they felt too heavy to move. There was something else, however, that didn't feel right—she felt oddly still within. A strange silence blanketed her body, as if her heart wasn't beating or her blood wasn't flowing. And then she knew. Her power. She couldn't feel it.

She forced her eyes open wide and found she was lying in darkness, making the absence of her magic even more perceptible. Her eyes adjusted to the darkness after a few seconds and she relaxed slightly when she saw Anthony lying next to her. He was stripped of all his golden armor and unconscious. She could barely move her head, but she turned it enough to see someone else lying above her. Probably Alexander, she guessed.

What did they do to us? she wondered as she let her head fall back down with relief from the effort.

She focused on Anthony's face in the darkness. She used as much energy as she could muster to try to nudge him, but she could only manage to tap him lightly, which did nothing to alert him. She ceased her efforts and thought back to Liam. The Tykens had reacted so poorly to his powers, clearly threatened by him. Katerina wondered if she should be scared of him too. What he managed to do in the arena was terrifying to watch. And then, everything had suddenly gone wrong.

I should have done something, she thought to herself. *That's why I'm here. I should have tried to talk to Inola. I could have done a spell. I should have tried something. Anything.*

Katerina felt the regret and sorrow building up in her chest, threatening to escape through tears, until the pounding footsteps quieted down and the jostling ceased. They were coming to a stop and Katerina assumed it couldn't be anywhere pleasant. She closed her eyes tightly and felt the prickle of fear rising within her. However, this time, she couldn't feel the air being stirred up around her, not even a light breeze.

Light suddenly flooded the dark box she had been placed in and a set of strong hands grabbed hold of Katerina's ankles under her gown and pulled her out of the darkness. Katerina kept her eyes shut, feigning unconsciousness to avoid any more of that horrible dust being thrown in her face. Her limbs still felt incredibly heavy and she could do nothing to stop the Tyken from lifting her over his shoulder and carrying her away.

Relief from the chilling stillness she felt while inside the dark cage was fleeting as she was carried back into darkness. The sunlight on her skin suddenly gone as the air around her grew cold. She felt her stomach bounce uncomfortably on the Tyken's shoulder as he descended a long stairwell. She tried to remain limp and lifeless as she was taken through many twists and turns. Her head swam with questions and her skin tingled with worry as the Tyken carried her along in the dim lighting.

"Just put them in here for now," she heard a gruff voice instruct.

Then she heard the sound of a metal lock opening and a squeak of old hinges before she was dropped onto the hard, cold ground. They were dumping them into a dungeon cell, she realized. She had seen enough dungeons in her life to know. The bonds on her hands were released roughly and her arms fell to her sides, but still she did not move. Her arms remained heavy and her head swam. A deep pit in her stomach roiled with distress as she laid in the darkness of the cell.

What am I going to do now? she wondered helplessly, fighting back tears. *How had I failed this mission so miserably?*

She continued to lay on the cold stone ground, her face warming the stone beneath her cheek, and opened her eyes slightly. Two more Tykens entered the cell to drop Anthony and Alexander next to her on the ground.

What have they done with Liam? Katerina wondered, her heartbeat rising.

"This is where she wants them?" one of the Tykens asked.

"We'll be back to move them to more permanent cells later, but this puny cell should hold these three for now," she heard a voice quietly say as the metal doors clanged shut and a lock was shifted into place with a click.

Katerina shifted her gaze toward the doors and saw two large shadows standing at the door in the dim dungeon lighting. She quickly averted her gaze from them as they stared at their prisoners through the bars.

"It appears the Alumetris magic has returned to the humans," Katerina heard a Tyken say as his shadow turned away from her. "We must find out how this happened and take action to prevent the knowledge spreading too widely." The Tykens walked away from the bars, leaving the prisoners alone in the darkness.

Katerina saw a slight movement in front of her as Anthony stirred.

Oh, thank God. He's alive, Katerina thought to herself, sinking deeper into the floor with relief.

Once the Tykens had walked far enough away from the cell, Katerina placed her hands on the smooth stones beneath her and pushed herself up, wincing with pain in her shoulder and exhaustion as she lifted herself to a seated position. A sudden, suffocating grip of despair filled her chest as she looked around and saw the black, dismal holdings she had been dumped in. She lifted her chin to follow the cell's bars as they stretched from the ground up into the tall ceiling.

She curled herself into a ball, hugging her knees and resting her forehead on them. Her necklace swung forward and hit her thighs. She whimpered slightly as she reached to grab it and realized it wasn't the one she had been expecting. It was just the string of diamonds that Anthony had given her. Her mother's necklace wasn't with her. She didn't even have that comfort.

She let go of the necklace quickly and squeezed her eyes shut. She desperately wished that she could do something to get out of this on her own, but she was so weak, so tired. Maybe her father would send someone to rescue them. He wouldn't let his daughter, his best chance at solidifying this Akarian alliance, remain captured. Someone had to come for them. That is, if the Tykens didn't kill them first.

Anthony stirred again and groaned. Katerina looked up as he shakily lifted himself up into a seated position. He was nearly out of breath by the time he leaned against the dungeon wall next to her. The drug still affected him too.

"Hey Princess," he said with a weak smile as he turned his head to her.

Katerina felt a little warmer as she smiled back at him before she turned to look at Alexander. He still lay on the ground, his arms and legs sprawled out around him, breathing steadily, as if simply sleeping. He looked so frail and pale in the dim lighting. The powder they had thrown at their faces had clearly affected him the most. Katerina saw beads of sweat forming on his forehead.

"Do you think he'll be all right?" Katerina asked. She wanted to scoot herself closer to him, but still felt too heavy to move.

"Yeah, I think so. They sprayed us with mist herb. It's a common military tactic the Tykens like to use when they want to take prisoners alive. Usually for questioning. It may take Alexander longer to recover from the herb though with his health being as it is," Anthony said as he looked over at Alexander. Then he turned back to Katerina slowly. "I'm sure Destiny has a plan to get us all out of here though."

Katerina nodded, though she could feel her forehead still creasing with concern. She looked around at their surroundings again. Recognition bolted through her like lightning. Her heart sank into her stomach. She slowly and painstakingly crawled closer to the wall that Anthony leaned against and put her hand up to the wall to examine it closer. She stared at the smooth, glassy walls and she thought might be sick. The walls were made of obsidian.

"They've put us in an obsidian cell," Katerina said, trying to hold back the trembling in her voice.

"Obsidian cells?" Anthony asked as he turned to look at the wall behind him. "What does that …"

Katerina turned around and leaned her back against the wall. She took a deep breath and closed her eyes. She knew what obsidian did to witches like herself and Alexander. It was one reason, besides the fact the Streaks were hideously black, that their affliction was coined after the abhorrent rock. The Obsidian Streaks. All her father's dungeons in Esterine were made of the rock because it rendered witches powerless. Powerless and physically weak. Neither she nor Alexander would be able to do any magic while they were in here. And since they already had the Streaks, they would continue to get sicker the longer they stayed.

But how did they get so much of it over here? Katerina wondered. *I thought it was only found in Isavaria.*

"I need to wake him up," Katerina said, desperation clear in her tone.

Katerina placed a hand on the slick obsidian wall and tried to place her legs underneath her to stand. Her full gown made the process even more difficult than it would have been already.

"Wait," Anthony started to say as he reached over to her.

Katerina chose not to listen to his protests and continued to try to rise. She needed to wake Alexander if she could. She continued to climb her hands up the wall and straighten her legs as she rose. Her legs wobbled as she took her first step, but she continued over to Alexander by the metal bars of their cell.

Anthony sighed and grunted as he moved to stand. He stood up much more easily, the obsidian effects not weighing him down.

"How can we wake him?" Katerina asked, not taking her eyes from the sleeping form when Anthony was standing next to her.

"I don't …" Anthony began to say as he looked down at Alexander. "I'll think of something." He looked back at Katerina.

Katerina allowed herself to turn her gaze toward him. She looked into his face and she noticed his rumpled black hair. Her heart twisted with a sudden longing just before her head started spinning and she staggered backward.

"Whoa, are you all right?" Anthony asked as he grabbed onto one of her wrists to help steady her.

Katerina nodded, but her vision blurred. Nausea roiled up within her and the Streaks on her shoulder began to burn. The numbing effects of the herb had worn off so suddenly and she was beginning to sweat as dizziness settled over her. Her knees buckled and she felt herself start to fall. She expected to hit the ground, but strong, steady arms wrapped around her.

"Katerina?" she heard the muffled concern of Anthony's voice as she was lowered to the floor gently.

"We need to get out of here …" Katerina managed to say as the world continued to spin, darkness closing in from every angle. "I'm … I …" she struggled to find the words. "I have the Obsidian Streaks …" she forced herself to say before she let go and allowed the world to fall away completely.

19

Liam looked up at the roaring crowd in the arena. The faces were blurred and he couldn't make out any details until he turned to see a scowling Tyken rushing toward him. The Tyken slammed his shoulder into Liam's stomach and Liam stumbled backward from the impact before he felt his power flare. His body hummed with a warm sensation as the strength heated his body. He grabbed the Tyken's waist so he could easily throw him aside.

Then he saw another Tyken rushing toward him and soon two more came from either side. Liam glowered at them as he stood his ground, digging his feet into the dirt and bracing himself for another collision. He lifted a hand out to defend himself from the Tyken rushing straight at him, and he felt the bones of the Tyken's face crack in his palm, and the Tyken fell to the ground in agony.

More Tykens ran at him and he continued swinging and striking and kicking at each one of them as they came at him relentlessly. It seemed easy and he barely broke a sweat as he moved around the arena. Solely focused on surviving the onslaught, he felt no remorse for the Tykens that fell.

Once the attackers stopped coming, Liam found himself standing in a field of bodies. He looked around at the several Tykens lying on the ground in agony and his desperate sense of self-preservation waned, leaving him with a pit of horror in his stomach. He had hurt so many of them, and some of them quite severely. He looked around in shock at the scene, not wanting to believe that he had been capable of such an atrocity.

Then a large shadow came over Liam and he looked up to see Inola looming over him from her royal box. Her face was hard, nostrils flared, hatred pouring from her eyes. She lifted her chin and continued to look down at him with anger. She yelled something incoherent to Liam and pointed toward him accusingly. Liam felt his stomach drop as the ground beneath him suddenly gave way and he found himself falling into pure darkness.

His fall was abruptly broken as he landed painfully on a cold, hard floor. He winced in pain as he rolled himself over. He flared his power again so he could stand up and found himself completely surrounded by metal bars. He rushed over to the bars and grabbed hold of the chilled metal, pulling at them in frustration. And as he did so, the metal gave into his enhanced strength, and bent within his grasp. Without much time to wonder at this new ability, he bent the bars enough to free himself from the cage he had fallen into. He was able to easily walk out of the cell and into the empty blackness that surrounded him.

He continued to walk, though he could see nothing in front of him or around him. He stretched his hands out in front him, trying to feel for anything as he continued, until he heard something. A small voice was calling out in the darkness, and he realized with a sudden chill that it was his name the voice was calling.

Anxiety rushed through him and he walked forward more quickly, keeping arms outstretched, his pulse racing. When his hands met something solid, he ran his fingers along the cold, slick grooves to determine it was some kind of wall. He let the wall guide him through the dark corridors as the voice got louder and louder with each step, until the wall led him to a door with smooth blue markings that swirled around each other gracefully, reminding Liam of water. He reached for the glass doorknob and the door swung open at his mere touch.

Liam stepped into the room beyond cautiously. It seemed even darker inside the room, though Liam hadn't expected that to be possible. The blackness became more gray as his eyes adjusted to his surroundings and he gathered his bearings. The voice called out again, this time sounding as if it came from right behind him. He spun around quickly, straining to search the darkness for any sign of the source of the voice.

Then he saw her.

He saw her more clearly than he had ever seen her before. She floated in front of him in a glass cylinder filled with water. Her fiery red hair was spread out in every direction, softly flowing through the water and around her face. Her hands rested against the glass and her eyes looked worried as they searched the darkness. Her torso was feminine in shape, but smooth and solid in color. Her lower half was a shining, scaly fishtail.

She's a Riven? Liam thought in astonishment. He had never seen a real Riven before and was completely captivated by the sight. Rivens were few in number since they were all female and their existence was largely dependent on the will of the gods. He had read about their beauty, but he could never have imagined this.

Her top half was quite human-like, though her skin seemed to glow and glitter. Her tail shimmered in the midst of the darkness, swishing back and forth steadily. Liam couldn't take his eyes off her as he continued to move toward her, drawn to her like she was a beacon of light.

Finally, her eyes focused on him and her eyes softened from anxiety into relief. She smiled at him, a hopeful look on her face, as he stepped up to the glass case and put his hand opposite of hers.

"Liam …" her voice whispered in his mind. She didn't move her lips when she spoke to him, but he could hear her clearly.

"I've been dreaming of you. I've finally found you," Liam said, looking into her bright green eyes. He had seen her in his dreams many times, but a deeper familiarity stirred within him. He felt as if he'd known her all his life. He had never seen her face so clearly in his dreams before, but he had such a feeling of recognition as he looked into her eyes. "Who are you?" he asked in a whisper.

She blinked slowly and smiled at him again. "I am called Elyria. We must finally be close enough for me to reach you more easily. I can better control what I'm showing you in this dream now."

Liam squinted his eyes in confusion, lowering his hand from the glass. "A dream. Right …" He tore his eyes from hers and looked around. There was still only blackness surrounding them. When he looked back at her, the outline of the glass case had disappeared and she floated freely in front of him.

She nodded. "Yes, this is still just a dream. However, I am very real. The Tykens have me locked up in a room not far from the cell they put you into."

"Cell? They put me in a dungeon …" Liam said with dismay and anger swirling within. He looked down and away from Elyria as he remembered the truth. "You're in the dungeon too? Why would the Tykens lock up a Riven? Isn't that against some law of nature or something?"

The corners of her eyes fell and she looked away from him. "No, not when I am what I am. Not when I was freely given up because of the dangerous gifts that I possess."

"Dangerous gifts?" Liam's heart raced with equal excitement and terror. A Riven with magical gifts from the Alumetris was nothing Liam had ever heard about, but if it was true, maybe she could help him with his own gifts and help him get out of here.

"I was created with immense powers of varying abilities. Powers that I myself do not fully understand. It has been a terrible burden to bear these gifts all at once and especially in the magnitude they sometimes present themselves. My powers are the reason I am able to speak with you like this, but our meetings have been fragmented because this prison keeps my powers weak."

Liam nodded and let the realization slowly sink in. If this dream was one of her powers in practice, then that meant her powers were much different than his. Just as the Light Gods had granted the Alumenos their gifts, the Dark Gods had done the same for the Noxenos. These powers of dream-walking—they were of a more sinister nature, born of the darkness when the Alumetris was corrupted. She would have to be a Noxenos, and he had always been taught that the Noxenos were mortal enemies of the Alumenos.

"You're one of the last Noxenos then?" Liam asked, stepping away from her slightly, eyeing her carefully.

She simply nodded and looked down.

"How is that possible?" Liam asked looking away from her in thought. The Noxenos were supposedly banished from existence long ago. They had disappeared before the Alumenos lost their powers. And a Riven with Noxenos powers? That made even less sense.

Elyria raised her eyebrows a little, still not looking at him. "I don't know how I came to be like this. Many Rivens, Tykens, and Aurens have …" she paused shortly, searching for the right words, before continuing, "… studied my condition. But it seems no answers could be found. It is a curse I wish I could be rid of."

"A curse?" Liam asked. He hadn't thought of magical gifts as a curse before.

Eyria didn't answer and only wrapped her arms around herself, looking sullen and regretful.

Liam watched the Riven carefully as she floated in front of him and he felt a certain comfort being around her. He had always been taught Noxenos were a dark and evil people, but he didn't feel that could possibly be true with Elyria. She was indeed different and something must have been done to her to make her this way.

"They are keeping me here because they don't know what else to do. I admit that I am safer here in captivity, but I will never be cured while I'm here. I can never be rid of these horrible and tremendous powers that plague me while they keep me locked away like this. Even with my powers being greatly dampened, I still suffer from intense seizures. An irresistible desire to use my powers grows within me every second and when that pressure gets to be too much ... I can't control what happens," she explained to him, looking toward him again, swimming closer to him. "I can remain unconscious for days after an episode. It's a painful existence and I want nothing more than to be rid of this unnatural atrocity. I long for a cure."

Liam looked into her pleading eyes. "You're looking for a cure?" His heart dropped when he realized what she wanted. "You want the water stone. Is that why you've been reaching out to me?"

She looked away from him briefly before looking back at him. "I believe I do need the water stone, yes."

Liam thought for a moment. "But you came into my dreams before I even thought about finding the water stone. Before I even knew I was an Alumenos Awakening. How did you know I would be looking for it?"

"I have visions. Of possible futures. It's another one of my abilities. Seeing the future and dream walking are only two of the many Noxenos abilities I possess. I don't understand all that my powers can do yet, but I am sure about the visions." She paused. "And I know that we are connected Liam. I don't know how or why, but when you touched that fragment of the earth stone in that witch's ring, your Alumenos powers manifested and my visions of you began. It was like I had suddenly found someone I had been missing and I was able to connect to your dreams even though I'd never met you. I'd never been able to do that before."

So it was the ring after all, Liam thought.

"So we are connected," he said slowly, trying to understand everything she just said. "And you can see my future?"

"I can only see a few fragments, but I know that you're very special Liam. You're the only living Alumenos ... and I think you could be different, like I am. I believe it's possible that the Alumetris has connected us—the only Noxenos and

Alumenos with awakened abilities—and has given us both the gift to wield multiple powers. An Ultimate Noxenos and an Ultimate Alumenos. There have been legends of Ultimate Alumenos, but never an Ultimate Noxenos. I think that's why it's been so painful and so dangerous for me. But I've seen you wield the powers of healing in my visions of the future and I know you already possess the powers of strength. The Alumetris is creating a new beginning and I think the Noxenos powers are meant to die with me. You see, you are my only hope to becoming cured and banishing these powers for good."

Suddenly the ground beneath Liam faltered, causing him to fold over to catch himself. He looked down and saw that the floor he stood on was becoming liquid. He was sinking slowly. He snapped his head back up toward Elyria. He felt a sharp prickle of fear shoot through him when he saw that she was bent backward at an alarming angle, her eyes glowing. And then, she began to shake.

"Elyria!" Liam yelled, stretching out his arm to her as he continued to sink. "Elyria, what is happening?"

A strong wind blew all around him and Elyria spun. Liam covered his face from the violent wind that lashed against his face. He peeked through his arms and squinted eyes and watched as Elyria was torn away from his view. She faded quickly into the abyss that surrounded them.

And then there was only darkness.

20

Katerina strained to open her eyes. A heaviness pushed against her, making her muscles feel weak and tired. The hardness of the ground pressed into her bones so uncomfortably and she could feel her powers being suffocated out of every particle of water within her. She pushed against the cold stone floor to sit herself up and once seated, she scooted away from the wall. She wrapped her arms around her legs and set her head on her knees.

"Why didn't you tell me?" Anthony's quiet voice pierced the darkness.

Katerina lifted her head with some effort and reluctantly opened her eyes. Anthony stood in front of her, leaning tensely against the wall. His eyes were fixed on her with an emotion Katerina couldn't decipher. Her Streaks burned as she recalled revealing them to Anthony. Her stomach turned with regret. Would he still marry her after this confession?

Katerina turned her face away from him to the torches on the walls outside the cell. They flickered unnaturally and there was a chill in the air that she hadn't noticed before. She shivered as a sudden coldness seeped into her. There was something eerie about it and not just because she was in a dark subterranean prison. She stared at the flames on the torches as they danced. The ground rumbled slightly beneath her hands and she thought she could feel a magical presence. There was something happening somewhere close by. Something dark. She hugged her knees closer and continued to be entranced by the flames.

Then it was gone. The torches ceased their flickering and the coldness evaporated. Heat rushed back into her and she took in a gasp of air. She hadn't realized she had been holding her breath.

I must have imagined it, Katerina thought to herself, shaking herself out of her daze.

Anthony came closer to her and knelt in front of her, refusing to let his question hang in the air any longer.

"Why didn't you tell me?" he asked again. "Do you not trust me?"

Katerina dared to look at him.

"I was hoping I would never have to," Katerina said hoarsely. She had to clear her throat, and though it gave her an instant headache, she continued. "I was hoping Liam would find the water stone and I would be cured and that would be the end of it."

He sighed and offered her the leather pouch he was holding. "Here, drink some of this. It's not much, but I'll get us more," he said as he looked over his shoulder to the cell bars.

Katerina thanked him and took the leather pouch. She lifted the water to her lips and felt cool relief as the water slid down her throat. She hadn't realized just how thirsty she was. She could have easily drunk the whole thing, but she stopped. She nearly spilled water all over herself as she tilted her head back up quickly. She wasn't the only one who needed this.

"But the Streaks ..." Anthony said, settling down to sit in front of her. "I saw them and ... well ... they aren't like my uncle's. They signify more than just a sickness, they mean you're a witch, don't they?"

Katerina paused, embarrassment trickling its way into her. He would think she was weak if he even accepted what she was at all, but she couldn't hide this anymore. She had revealed it all already. She kept her eyes on Anthony's as she ran a hand across her chest and the Streaks beneath, and simply nodded, terrified at what his reaction might be.

Anthony's eyes got wide, but she thought he might be holding back a smile. Katerina let herself hope that his reaction was going to be a positive one. She watched as the corners of his mouth twitched up and she saw a glimmer of pride there that tugged on her heart.

"And here I thought Alexander just needed you as a talisman or something," he said with a smile before turning his eyes back to her. "Does that mean you can do something to get us out of here?"

Katerina's hope plummeted. She shook her head and looked away from him. "No. No, I can't do anything to get us out of here," she said quietly, still rubbing the Streaks on her chest.

She turned her head to the side to glance over at the bed in the back of the room. Alexander lay on the bed now, still unconscious, but at least off the cold, hard obsidian stone of the floor. His head was propped up slightly on a wad of clothing and she realized that Anthony must have picked him up on his own to place him in the bed and had done his best to make him comfortable. Her arms prickled with anxiety. He wasn't showing any signs of waking up and she needed him to wake up. She needed him to tell them what to do next. He needed to get them out of here and to the sword.

Anthony's head dropped. "There's nothing you can think of?" he asked, desperation filling his words.

Katerina looked back up at him. "Even if I knew a good spell to try, these walls," she gestured around at the shining black walls that surrounded them, "they are made of obsidian rock. They render us Isavarians quite useless with our magic."

Anthony looked around and then nodded, the hope draining from his eyes. "I see. The obsidian." The look of disappointment stabbed Katerina in the gut. "Well regardless, I still wish you would have told me." Anthony slid across the floor to be next to her and laid his head back on wall behind them.

Katerina hugged her legs tightly and dared to ask him the question she wasn't sure she wanted to know the answer to.

"Does me, being what I am, change things for you? With the marriage agreement?" she asked, unable to keep her eyes on him this time and picking at the bottom of her uncomfortable shoes.

Anthony chuckled softly. "No, no of course not. Why would you think that?"

Katerina's shoulders relaxed as she turned her head to lock eyes with him again. "I always worry about how other people will react when they find out. As I'm sure you know, most people in Esterine hate the witches right now, including my father. He would never claim me as his daughter if he knew. The whole marriage agreement would be a colossal failure." She turned to him with a deadly serious face. "You cannot tell him. Not under any circumstances. Not if you want the marriage agreement to remain intact."

Anthony smiled. "Don't worry, I won't." Then he turned to look her in the face and his smile dropped. "I want the marriage agreement to go through. I really do."

169

Katerina's heart tensed. He was usually so nonchalant and playful, but she could tell he was being serious right now. She quickly nodded and looked away from him.

Anthony sighed. "Your father is missing out on something quite amazing if you ask me. What you can do is … incredible. It's truly a gift."

Katerina managed a crooked smile. "Not everyone thinks that," she said quietly, shaking her head and looking down.

She turned her head away from Anthony and let it rest on her knees. She didn't want to have this conversation anymore. She was too tired and it was all too much. She wished she hadn't told him about her Streaks and she wasn't completely sure why she did. It had seemed like the only thing she could do in the moment, she had been so scared and so disoriented. But that was no excuse. She scolded herself for her weakness.

Anthony was quiet for a moment and then took a deep breath before speaking again. "I would love to be able to do the things Isavarian witches can do. They used to be so important to the Empire, before the Streaks showed up. I can just imagine all the adventures and all the different things I'd be able to see and do if I had those powers."

This is strange, Katerina thought, her expression mirroring her skepticism. Both Liam and Anthony seemed to have no problem with what she was at all. They didn't understand what she could do. They hadn't known her very long, they didn't even know who she really was. They should have been furious with her secret, or at least afraid of what she might do. But they weren't. They had accepted her instantly. *I wish everyone would.*

"And besides that," Anthony continued, "it's a gift from your God, isn't that right?"

Katerina turned to look at him again. "It used to be a gift. But when the Well ran dry, it was clear God was no longer sanctioning the power. To be what I am now is going against the will of God. He doesn't grant us this gift anymore, we take it now through unnatural means."

Anthony sighed and leaned back. "I know people like your father think that, but what do you really think? Do you think you'd be able to do something so astounding without your God's power?"

Katerina paused. She had thought that way, once. When someone else asked her the same question so many years ago. But since then she had accepted that her desires to continue to practice her magic was wrong. She had gone back to the belief that the Well was dry and they were in the Age of Faith; an age that was supposed to be without magic, only faith. She had always felt guilty for her association and fascination with her abilities. But maybe she didn't need to anymore. Maybe she didn't need her father to approve of every part of her.

"I … I don't know," she finally answered. "It used to be different. I was different. And then Streaks …" she fumbled over her words. This conversation needed to be over. She looked over to Alexander and decided he would make safer company. She then pushed her hands against the ground to stand up.

Her head swam immediately with the movement and she stumbled back into the wall. Anthony helped to brace her as he quickly stood up next to her.

She wanted to pull her arm away from him but he held her tightly. "I'm fine," she insisted, tugging her arm against his grip.

"Just let me help you," Anthony said with a sigh. "You don't have to do everything on your own, you know. I'm here."

A heat rose in Katerina's chest. "I'm not trying to do everything on my own," she said. "In fact, I've found I can do very little on my own." She pulled her arm away from him forcefully this time.

"Oh, I doubt that is true," Anthony retorted but stayed where he was. "I see the fire in you. I can tell Destiny has something magnificent planned for you."

"Destiny?" Katerina asked, still avoiding looking at Anthony and walking closer to Alexander.

"Yes, Destiny. The sister god of Lumos and Noxos," Anthony explained briefly. Of course, Katerina already knew this from her Akarian lessons.

"Right. Well it seems Destiny only wants us locked in a dungeon with no way out," Katerina said hotly. This talk of Destiny was ridiculous.

Anthony smirked. "It may seem like that right now, but Destiny … she works in such mysterious ways. We really have no idea what she has in store for us. Not even now when things may seem … rather grim."

He dropped his smile slightly before he continued. "For instance, it appears I was destined to be emperor, just because I was born first and my uncle never married." He backed away from her, peeling his eyes from her with a sigh. "We don't always like what Destiny has for us, but we have to walk our path anyway."

Katerina scrunched her forehead with confusion. "You don't want to be emperor?"

Anthony shrugged. "I don't know. Sometimes I think I do, but other times …" He turned his head toward her again. "I know I shouldn't have snuck along on this expedition, but I needed to get out of Akaria. I needed out of the council rooms, out of the meetings, out of the horrible, every day, mundaneness of it all." He sighed. "I needed something more. Just once. I longed for this adventure. I felt so trapped there."

Katerina's heart sank for him. "I know how that feels," she said quietly, looking at him with sorry, understanding eyes.

Anthony's eyes locked on to hers and Katerina let herself feel for him. She had seen his confidence and admired that he seemed to know what he wanted. She let her heart open, just a little, and the emotions she had been trying to hold back for him washed over her. She let his sadness and longing become her sadness and longing and she didn't pull away when he reached out for her.

He grabbed her around the waist with one hand and put his other hand on her cheek. His eyes peered unwaveringly into hers as he quietly said, "Katerina, I …"

A sudden clamor of chains and footsteps arose outside their cell. Katerina felt a rush of anxiety burst through her chest and she immediately pulled herself away from Anthony and turned to look out of their small cell. Anthony followed behind her, though he seemed reluctant. Someone was coming.

As they watched, two Tykens came into view. They were dragging another figure between them. Katerina's hope faded as she watched the Tykens throw the person into the cell across from them. She tried to focus her eyes in the darkness to see the person more clearly, but they were almost completely hidden in a large black cloak.

Anthony hit the bars with force and yelled to the Tykens, "You know you can't keep us in here! You can't treat us like this! This is going to make my uncle, the Emperor of Akaria very angry! And what have you done with my brother?"

The Tykens continued to ignore Anthony as they locked up the cell with the new prisoner.

"By all that is Good, you MUST tell me!" Anthony yelled as he shook the bars in front of him, his face full of fury.

Finally, one of the Tykens turned to him. With bored eyes, the Tyken spoke, "I don't know who your brother is, boy," he said in a low, rumbling voice.

Anthony gritted his teeth. "I'm not a 'boy.' I am the heir to the Akarian throne. And my brother is the future of the Tykerial Guard of Akaria!"

"The Alumenos is taken care of," the Tyken said as he rolled his eyes. "He's being kept somewhere safe. He's too dangerous to be kept in a simple holding cell like you lot."

Katerina's stomach dropped at the thought of Liam being held somewhere awful. She watched as Anthony's eyes narrowed at the Tykens.

"You can't do this to us," Anthony said in a surprisingly even tone and normal volume, though the words were filled with both desperation and wrath.

The Tyken waved his hand nonchalantly. "Yes, yes, I know. Inola is ready to deal with the consequences, however, and you'll all be put on trial and sentenced in a few days. After the holiday is over."

"Inola has to do the sentencing and she's busy until after the holiday," the other Tyken added.

"So, get comfortable," the first Tyken said before laughing. And with that, the Tykens walked away.

"I am Anthony Farotus, Princep of Akaria and you DARE not turn away from me! There WILL be consequences!" Anthony yelled back at them as they continued to chuckle to themselves.

Katerina turned her gaze to the floor. They didn't believe he was who he said he was, and why would they? It would be entirely too reckless to send the heir of a frail emperor to a Tyken holiday. She squeezed her eyes shut in frustration. She didn't know how long she, or Alexander, could last in here. Her father wouldn't be happy about this and she wondered what he would do.

Anthony continued to yell at the Tykens at the top of his lungs. Spouting his title, his discomfort, his demands. Katerina knew it was all he felt he could do. She tuned out the words and looked up across the corridor again.

The figure that was placed in the cell moments ago sat against the back wall now, looking out toward her. The cloak and the darkness of the dungeon completely shadowed their face. A chill ran through Katerina's body as she felt the invisible eyes boring into her.

21

Katerina stared mindlessly into the blackness of the wall in front of her and lost herself in the shiny swirls of the rock. The Tykens were gone and she had given up trying to see who was put in the cell across from them. Her eyes glazed over as her mind spiraled through a series of bleak thoughts.

How will the Tykens dispose of us? Will it be a peaceful death? Will they make a spectacle of it? How much longer can I live in here with the rock sucking me dry? How much more will it take from me?

"Maybe if I can get their attention again," Anthony whispered next to her, standing up again.

He had eventually calmed down after the Tykens had dumped the new prisoner across from them and had come to sit next to her. He had been whispering plans and shaking his head and intermittently holding his face in his hands as he sat there trying to think of a way out of their predicament. Katerina noticed he had given up on using titles and threats and words, and had moved on to thinking up elaborate plans for escape. He was adamant that they could do it, if they just found the right set of actions, but Katerina had no such hopes.

"So, what do you think?" he asked hopefully, turning toward her.

Katerina dropped her eyes but turned her head in his direction. She hadn't been listening, but it didn't matter. She was sure they were completely at the mercy of their captors at this point.

"I don't know Anthony …" she said weakly, running her finger along the outline of one of the flowers on her gown. She wished he would just give up too.

Then there was a rustling near the back of their cell. Katerina's despondency quickly evaporated as she whipped her head back toward the noise. Her chest swelled with hope and relief as she saw the figure laying on the bed begin to stir.

"Alexander!" Katerina said breathlessly as she scrambled to her feet, nearly tripping over the length of her dress, and hobbled over to his side. Anthony followed behind her. "Alexander, oh thank God!" Katerina cried as she stood over the older man.

"Aw, Xevron take it all," Alexander fussed as he squeezed his eyes shut in a wince at Katerina's exclamation.

"Are you all right?" Katerina asked, whispering this time and hesitating before placing her hands on him.

"Do I look all right?" Alexander complained gruffly. With a loud groan he tried to sit himself up, but struggled. The pain and effort was clear on his face. Katerina grabbed hold of his arm and placed a hand on his back to help him sit, but Alexander shook her off. "Don't you touch me!" Alexander yelled harshly before explaining more softly, "Sorry, the Streaks are quite sensitive. I feel as if my entire body is being pricked with needles."

Katerina gave him space and watched as he sat himself up. The wad of clothing he had used as a pillow unrolled as the weight of his head lifted off it. Katerina saw now that it was the jacket Liam had given Anthony before he entered himself in the contest. Her heart ached at the sight of it.

She turned her attention back to Alexander when his body jolted violently, his lungs contracting in a coughing fit. The deep sound made Katerina cringe and she hated how she didn't know what to do to help him.

"Here," Anthony said from behind her and handed Alexander the canteen of water.

I should have thought of that, Katerina chastised herself.

She watched optimistically as Alexander snatched the canteen from Anthony greedily. He held it to his lips and threw back his head to down the contents. The few sips of water that had been left in the canteen seemed to ease his coughing enough for him to finish sitting up, but small bursts of coughs still escaped him.

Alexander sat on the edge of the plank bed, hunched over and barely able to open his eyes. "Oh holy Tykos," Alexander complained breathlessly in between coughs.

"Place something over his head," a voice bellowed from behind them.

Katerina froze.

The deep timbre of the voice sent a wave of emotions through her, causing memories to surface and conflict to rise within her. Curiosity, longing, anger, and the desire to appear calm and collected all washed through her in a matter of seconds.

"Excuse me?" Anthony asked as he turned to the speaker.

Katerina gathered herself and pushed down the rush of feelings. She turned to look behind her at the figure still sitting calmly, a wrist on one knee, in the cell across from them. Alexander continued to cough and groan behind her. She waited with anticipation for the voice to speak again.

"Cover the man's head with something. It will ease the effects of the obsidian around him," the deep voice explained.

Could it be?

Katerina squinted her eyes in the darkness, trying to make out any part of the face of the man in the cell but it was still too dark.

Anthony paused and then stepped back closer to Alexander. Katerina turned slowly back to Alexander and was immediately struck with a rush of heat through her body at what she saw.

Anthony had removed his shirt and was standing there in front of her completely bare chested. She had of course seen men without shirts, but this time she felt her face blushing with a sudden desire. She took in the shape of his muscles as he argued with Alexander about putting the dirty shirt over his head. She didn't register a word they said as she imagined being held by those arms. She could almost feel how her bare skin against his strong chest might feel.

Then she remembered where she was. She shook herself from her reverie before her mind got out of control and hurriedly stepped closer to Alexander. She very purposefully averted her eyes from Anthony and grabbed the jacket lying on the bed and put it over Alexander's head with authority. Alexander didn't fight her gesture and instead pulled the thick clothing tightly over his head. Alexander's shoulders relaxed and sighed with a sound of relief.

Katerina could see Anthony looking at her in her periphery, but she quickly turned away from him back to the voice from the other cell.

"Thank you," Katerina said cautiously to the mysterious figure. "How did you know …" she began to ask, but he answered quickly.

"I've had some experience with the Isavarian types," the voice said gently.

Katerina's heart beat faster. *It could be him …* she thought.

"Yes, thank you, sir," Anthony said cordially, his shirt now covering his chest again since Katerina had decided to use the jacket instead. "Let's not engage. We don't know what he's in here for," Anthony whispered harshly to Katerina. She could feel the heat of his breath and feel the nervousness in his tone.

"But he might know something that could help us," Katerina whispered back, raising her eyes to meet his, their faces closer than ever.

A chuckle came from the cell across the way. Katerina turned her eyes down and stepped away from Anthony.

That laugh. I know that laugh.

She felt as if she might melt into the floor as her knees buckled slightly beneath her. Anthony grabbed her by the arm to help steady her, but Katerina strode past him and ventured closer to the bars and closer to the mysterious figure, her eyes locked on the man.

"Are you an Isavarian witch?" Katerina dared to ask as she wrapped her hands gently around the bars in front of her, completely focused on the man's every move.

The man paused and then stood up. He walked up to the bars on his cell and Katerina could almost see his chin now.

Was that his chin? Why can't I remember what his chin looked like?

The man grabbed hold of the bars in front of him and pulled back aggressively, testing the strength of the metal. Anthony grabbed Katerina's arm and pulled her behind him.

Anthony stood in front of her now, facing the mysterious man. "What are you doing? Who are you?" Anthony's voice was strong and protective. In the dim light they could see the man remove a ring from his finger. "And what is that you're holding?"

"Oh, this?" the man asked, holding up the small piece of metal in between his thumb and index finger. "Well, with this I plan to save the princess."

Katerina stepped around Anthony just as the man removed the hood from his head. A weight buried itself in Katerina's chest as she took in the familiar face. His classic beauty was still evident in his strong jaw and cheekbones, though his gray eyes looked more tired and worn now. His long white hair was streaked with dirt, but when he smiled at her, she couldn't breathe.

"Mikhal," she said quietly, unable to tear her eyes from him in case he disappeared on her.

It wasn't a question anymore.

It really was him.

"Hi, Kat," he said, his charming smile lighting up the distance between them.

Was he really in here to save her? How did he know she was here? Where had he been? What did he think of her now as she stood here all dirty and helpless in a Tyken dungeon.

"You're here to get us out?" she found herself asking without thinking.

"I am quite experienced at escaping things," Mikhal answered with a mischievous smile. His eyes locked on to hers and she could feel the intensity of his own emotions flowing through them and burrowing into her. He hadn't forgotten her either.

"You know this man?" Anthony asked, the annoyance clear in his voice.

"I …" Katerina hesitated. She couldn't take her eyes from him. Calming her shaky voice, she answered. "I used to."

Mikhal fiddled with the ring in his hand. He pressed down the center of it and a small metal bead popped out of it and into his hand.

"And why would he help us?" Anthony asked quietly, a skeptical tone in his voice.

Katerina opened her mouth to answer, but before she could, Mikhal spoke up. "Let's just say, I owe a debt."

"A debt?" Anthony asked, standing up straighter and a new kind of anger growing in his voice. "What kind of debt?" His eyes bore into Mikhal, daring him to answer.

"Oh for Lumos's sake!" Alexander cried from behind them. Katerina turned to see the older man still clutching the jacket around his head. "Does it really matter right now? Let's just get the heck out of here!"

Anthony took a deep breath and looked back at Katerina. "You're sure we can trust him?"

Katerina nodded, looking directly into Anthony's face. "We can trust him," she answered confidently.

They turned back to Mikhal who had begun to examine the lock on his cell. He pushed against the lock and jiggled it forcefully a few times.

Anthony scoffed. "What is he even going to do? He's been captured just as we have."

"Not just as you have," Mikhal countered, standing up and turning his attention to Anthony. "I meant to get myself captured."

"Why?" Anthony asked incredulously. "And what good does that do us?"

"This place is a lot easier to break out of than to break in to," Mikhal said seriously.

Anthony rolled his eyes and crossed his arms. "All right then, what's your grand plan?"

Mikhal held up the small metal ball in his fingers and then twisted his wrist around to show them the ring he had slipped back on his finger. "The Tykens took most of my possessions, but they didn't take this."

"A ring?" Anthony asked.

"This is much more than a ring," Mikhal said smugly and turned back to Anthony. "I see the Tykens aren't the only ones who lack imagination."

Anthony narrowed his eyes. "What are you going to do with a piece of metal that broke off of a simple, nothing-looking ring?"

Mikhal took the small metal ball and popped it into the lock on his cell. There was a loud pop and Katerina watched as smoke curled upward out of the keyhole of the lock. She smiled, feeling as triumphant as if it had been her own idea. Mikhal had always had the most intriguing trinkets. Mikhal swung the cell door open easily and stepped into the corridor.

"I don't know about this ..." Anthony said to his cell mates as Mikhal approached their cell.

"Do you have a better idea, mister Princep of Akaria?" Alexander asked mockingly from his seat near the back of cell.

Anthony sighed and looked at Katerina.

"We can't just sit here and wait," Katerina said gently to Anthony. "This is our best chance. And I believe we can trust him."

Anthony turned and watched without protest as Mikhal placed a metal ball in the lock to their cell. Katerina's eyes met Mikhal's and she couldn't help but smile at him. Her heart felt warm in her chest.

All their past stolen moments together came rushing back to her in a wave of memories. He had changed her life once and here he was doing it again now. The lock on her cell burst with a loud bang.

Mikhal had set her free.

22

Liam's head pounded steadily and painfully as he wandered around in darkness. He felt like he had been wandering for hours, maybe days, with nothing in sight. His body was beginning to droop and his eyes begged him for sleep. He knew his feet were moving, but the scene always remained the same. He continued shuffling along, unsure of what else he could do.

He had tried to wake himself up from this nightmare, but he couldn't seem to escape. His whole body felt like lead and he felt his limbs were completely paralyzed. What had that Riven done to him? Where was he now? Would he be in this endless dream forever?

Suddenly he heard a splash of water beneath him. His eyes opened wide and looked down. He'd stepped in a puddle. He hadn't stepped in a puddle before. He hadn't even seen a puddle before. This was new. Something had changed.

His body tensed with anticipation as he looked around, but still he could only see blackness. He looked back down and stepped into the puddle again. He stepped both feet into it and walked, the puddle stretched out before him with every step.

He lifted his head and realized he could see far off into the distance something was glowing. He squinted his eyes against the darkness, trying to make out what it was, but he couldn't tell. He quickened his steps closer to the light, refusing to blink so as not to lose sight of it. His feet splashed through water beneath him as he picked up his pace.

He broke into a full run after a few moments, worry ramping up inside him that he might lose this glowing light. Then, suddenly, the ground gave way and the light was ripped from his sight. He was plunged into pure darkness again, his stomach lurching. Liam closed his eyes in frustration, letting his body fall through nothingness.

A calm washed over him and for a few moments he felt at peace. He floated in the dark, letting his muscles completely relax. He felt solid ground underneath his feet again and tranquility trickled out of him. He opened his eyes and there she was—Elyria. A picture of glowing perfection. Liam's body nearly collapsed with relief.

"For Tykos sake, there you are," Liam said, his voice breathless. He hadn't realized he was so out of breath. "What happened? What was all that before?"

Elyria's face wrinkled in torment. Her eyes searched the darkness around him, unable to focus on him. Liam stepped closer as she floated in front of him, like she had before. Finally her eyes found him and her eyes softened a little in relief.

"I'm sorry," she said gently in his mind, her lips still not moving when she spoke. True regret and sadness painted her face. "I didn't mean to keep you in here, in this dream, all that time."

Liam sighed. He wanted to tell her it was all right, but he had no idea if that was true.

"What was that?" he asked again.

She looked down and away from him, fidgeting with her hands in front of her. "I told you before that my powers were unstable, and well … the Tykens have defenses here. They built this dungeon to hold all sorts of magical beings. There are measures put in place to hamper these magical abilities. Using my powers is difficult in here, but I still can. No one has figured out how to turn them off completely. Obsidian doesn't work and not even the vines that are holding you right now seem to do much to my abilities. Rendering me unconscious has proven to be the only sure way to limit me. And sometimes the episodes come on so quickly, that I hardly have time to prepare for them."

"Episodes? So all that shaking and the wind and the sudden darkness, that was because of you?" Liam asked. He wasn't sure if he felt pity or fear.

Elyria nodded. "The Noxenos powers that I hold are too much for one being to possess and it's easy to lose control of them. The power overtakes my physical body and I can do nothing to stop them. My surroundings are affected as well;

lights flicker, temperature changes, the ground can shake, and a number of other things. It's one of the reasons I'm locked up in here and not somewhere else with the Rivens."

Liam nodded slowly, unsure of what to say next. He wanted out of this dream, but he wasn't sure how to ask without seeming insensitive to her plight.

Unsure how to proceed, Liam found himself asking, "You said something about a cure before?"

Elyria nodded. "I knew a witch, before I was thrown in here. She was trying to help me, but nothing worked. She tried spells and potions—the same exact potions that were used all those years ago on the few Noxenos that were not banished with the rest. The potions that drained the older generation of Noxenos of their powers, but in the end, nothing worked. She couldn't help me. Not alone anyway. She told me that there may be a way to rid me of this curse, but it would certainly take immense power."

"Immense power like the power in the Lumos Gems?" Liam guessed with exasperation, massaging his brow.

Elyria bit her lip and nodded. "To do the spell, she would need all four of the Lumos Gems."

Liam squinted his eyes at her. "All of them?" He laughed a little. "Well good luck with that. Finding just one is seeming to be quite impossible."

Elyria didn't waver. "It is still possible. You can still find them all."

Liam's eyes got wide. "Wait, you're expecting me to find them for you? What makes you think I could even do that? I'm locked up in here with you!" He shook his head. "Besides, the earth stone must have been destroyed a long time ago to end up in Katerina's ring."

Elyria shook her head. "The earth stone is broken into pieces, but it is not destroyed. You had to touch the stone to awaken your powers. The power has not been completely released," she explained. "I need the power of the Alumetris." She hesitated and swallowed. "The Lumos Gems are the only things that may work …" she bit her lip sadly as she cut herself off.

Liam shrugged his shoulders and looked away from her. He could see the desperation in her eyes, but he really didn't believe what she was talking about could be done, especially not by him.

"Look, I would love to help you, but I just don't see how I could. First of all, I'm locked up in a dungeon apparently, and I absolutely have to save my uncle first. My family and my country depends on him. And then the Tykerial Guard exam is coming up, then Anthony's wedding, and then I'll probably have my own wedding ..." he rattled off each obligation as he remembered all the plans he had waiting for him when he returned to Akaria.

"If a mountain lion follows turtles into the ocean, he will never reach the peak of the mountain," Elyria said.

"What?" Liam asked, looking back up at the Riven.

Chills ran through his body and he stepped away from her when he saw that her eyes had gone all white.

She didn't appear to be looking at him anymore, but she spoke into his mind again. "Following someone else's plan will only bury you. You must dig down deep inside and free yourself from the weight of the rocks before it is too much." Her voice was sad as she floated down to sit herself on the ground, coiling her tail beneath her.

"Someone else's plan?" Liam asked, still keeping his distance. "It's not like that. I want all these things too. It is my duty to protect my kingdom and stand up as an honorable member of the imperial family. I am very fortunate to have the life I have and ..."

"You are meant for greatness," Elyria said, her milky eyes turning to stare at him. "You can feel that within yourself. You know it must be true. That's why taking the Tykerial Guard exam and courting Caroline has been so difficult for you."

Liam raised his eyebrows in surprise and then furrowed his brow. "Excuse me?" he asked, his mind racing with defensive tactics as his chest filled with the heat of anxiety. How could she know those things had been difficult for him?

He calmed himself down with a big breath before he continued. "And how would following a plan to find all the Lumos Gems for you be any different? I don't even know you! Besides, right now I'm stuck. I have no idea where I am or how to get out of here, nor do I know how I'm even going to manage to get one of the stones, let alone—"

"You have been sent here for a reason," Elyria cut in, a smile growing on her face and then she pointed to something behind Liam.

Liam turned to see a dark hallway in front of him. Without taking a step, the room around him began to move. He watched as Elyria took his mind through the maze of the dungeon. Elyria was showing him something. In his mind, he floated up a long staircase, and took a right immediately once he was up the stairs. Walls of stone with only a few torches passed by him quickly as he continued through the many hallways of the dungeon. Then the torches on the walls changed from just torches to more civilized sconces. It was clear this dungeon was made to be a maze and only a select few would know their way around.

Elyria was one of them.

Suddenly, he stopped. A plain wooden door stood in front of him. Just a plain wooden door with a metal latch. Liam reached out and opened the door. He stepped inside and saw a glorious sight.

The room was filled with a bright, warm light. Liam immediately felt calm as he entered, the tension melting out of his shoulders and his breath becoming more even.

In the center of the room was a white marble pedestal. Liam's eyes widened as he felt a wash of amazement come over him. His stomach fluttered uncontrollably when he saw that floating above this pedestal was a majestic flaming sword. It burned brightly before him, just as he had imagined it would. Liam approached it slowly with awe.

He felt the heat of the magical flames on his face as he came closer. Dancing red-hot flames engulfed the entire blade, but he could see the hilt was perfectly crafted in green alagon material. It was here. Velios was here. It was in this dungeon.

"Velios is here? Is that why …" Liam asked with desperation as he quickly turned around.

However, when he turned around, there was only darkness in front of him. Elyria was gone. Then he noticed the room around him was gone, including the sword. Liam looked around in the darkness, confused. And then Liam felt his body begin to shake.

23

Liam gasped, air flooding through him as his lungs suddenly expanded. The compression around his body had released. He opened his eyes and saw an outline of someone standing over him. He pulled his arms into his chest and tried to roll away from the figure, but only tangled himself further in the ropes that surrounded him. The ropes burned his skin as his weight rolled over them. He winced in pain and, with a closer look, he realized they weren't ropes at all, but some kind of vine. Despite the pain, he continued to try to scramble away from the unknown figure.

"Calm down, it's only me ..." Liam heard a familiar voice say soothingly. He looked up and saw a hand reaching out to him and then a face came into view.

"Anthony?" Liam asked as he squinted his eyes and ceased his thrashing.

Liam's eyes adjusted to the dim lighting and Anthony's face slowly came into focus. Anthony nodded with a smile. He offered a hand and Liam reached up to grab his brother's arm. Anthony pulled Liam up onto his feet with an easy motion, but Liam's legs almost buckled beneath him as he wobbled on his own two feet. His vision faded suddenly and he grabbed the wall to steady himself. An extreme dizziness prevented him from moving further.

"Are you all right?" Anthony asked, holding on to Liam's arm to help stabilize him.

Liam squeezed his eyes shut and nodded.

"What ..." Liam began to ask, but his voice cut through his sore throat like a knife. He winced as he swallowed and tried speaking again. "What happened? Where are we?"

"The Tykens apparently are quite hostile toward magical humans, even though there hasn't been any in Tulneria in hundreds of years, and it would appear this prejudice is stronger than their desire to honor Tykos and the strength he represents and gifted to the Alumenos," Anthony explained with annoyance. "They detained all of us at the games and shoved us in this dungeon. And at the looks of all these obsidian cells … it seems they are quite equipped from when they made a habit of capturing magical humans."

Liam looked around at his own cell. The black walls stretched up all around him, but what bothered him more was the pile of green vines that now laid tangled in the corner. "And those vines," Liam whispered. "Just the touch of them burned my skin."

Anthony nodded and walked over to the jumble of vines. He knelt down and touched the vines. Liam winced at the mere sight.

"They had you wrapped pretty tightly in these," Anthony explained. "These vines must be what they use against Alumenos. To keep you from using your powers."

Liam held his head with one hand as the memory of what really happened at the Tyken games crept back into his mind. He had used too much of his surge strength in the competition. He had made himself too weak to fight against the Tykens when they moved to seize him. Then they had tied him up and knocked him unconscious.

"Anyway," Anthony said, standing up, "we've got to hurry." He grabbed Liam's arm under his armpit to guide him out of the cell.

"But how did you …" Liam began to ask as he looked up to the open door of his dungeon cell and his muscles froze again. A large, imposing figure stood in the doorway, a body flung over his shoulder. Liam couldn't make out his face, but he was sure he didn't know anyone that tall and bulky.

Anthony sighed. "It's all right, he's the one who's getting us out of here," he whispered to Liam. Liam could sense some hesitation in his brother's voice.

"Who is he?" Liam asked in a whisper as he took a step forward slowly. His legs still felt incredibly weak and he had to focus on each step in order to keep upright.

"I don't know," Anthony said, his voice now carrying a tinge of anger. "But Katerina seems to be acquainted with him and he is apparently someone she trusts. She introduced him as Mikhal." He said this last part through gritted teeth.

Liam looked from his brother to the dark figure and then nodded in acceptance. If Katerina knew him, he would trust him as well. Liam hobbled himself farther out of the cell behind his brother and the farther away he came from the insipid vines, the better he felt. When he finally stepped out into the low lighting of the dungeon hallway, he studied the mysterious figure more closely.

The man was tall, more than a foot taller than Liam, and his shoulders seemed especially wide. He looked down at Liam, his long white hair falling slightly into his face and Liam saw now that he held Alexander over his shoulder and a torch light in his other hand. Alexander wore Liam's jacket over his head and Liam averted his eyes from the man's and turned his head to Katerina. She smiled a strained smile, concern clearly written all over her face.

"Well just take your time," Alexander's voice said with irritation from behind the man. "I'm just laying over a bony shoulder like a sack of potatoes!"

Liam opened his mouth to apologize to the old mage, but Mikhal interrupted him.

"Come. We must move."

Without waiting for confirmation from the group, he turned and walked quickly down the darkened hallway. Liam's heart was still pounding from the effects of the strange vine, but he was able to keep in step with the rest of the group as they followed behind the newcomer, trying to stay underneath his torchlight. Alexander propped his head up with his fist and wore a sturdy scowl on his face as his body jostled with Mikhal's movement.

After taking a few steps down the corridor, Liam suddenly remembered his dream. He stopped abruptly and grabbed Anthony's shoulder to stop him.

"Wait, but Velios …" Liam whispered loudly.

"We didn't get the sword."

"No, it's here. It's here in this dungeon!"

"It's here?" Anthony asked in a clearly skeptical tone.

"Yes. We can't leave without it," Liam insisted.

Anthony looked reluctant, but nodded to his brother before running up to grab Katerina's wrist as she followed closely behind Mikhal. Liam limped himself quickly up with the rest of the group as they stopped in front of him and heard Katerina relaying the information to Mikhal.

"Velios?" Mikhal asked, his voice was low and oddly soothing. "Of course, it's here. We've got to keep moving though, the guards will be on us any minute now."

Mikhal turned back around to lead the way again when Alexander coughed and squirm on his shoulder.

"The sword … Velios …" Alexander managed to croak out between coughs. "I didn't come all this way …"

"I know that you need it," Mikhal said calmly. "Where do you think I'm leading us right now? Does this look like a way out? But we *must* hurry."

"You know that we need it? You know it's here?" Liam asked, his suspicions growing. He looked to Katerina, hoping to understand more.

"Yes, he knows. He knows quite a bit about the Lumos Gems too," Katerina explained.

"About all of them?" Liam asked, his stomach dropping at the mention of more than just the water stone.

"We're on the same side, don't worry," Mikhal said through a grunt as he readjusted the body of the defiant older man he was carrying.

Liam dropped his gaze and his mind raced. Who was this man? How did he know so much about them and the Lumos Gems? Then he looked up to see where Mikhal was leading them and saw that Mikhal was at least true to his word that he knew his way around the dungeon. Liam recognized the long staircase in front of them now from what Elyria had shown him in his dream. They ascended the stairs carefully and quietly, but swiftly, and then Mikhal immediately took them to the right. Liam's heartbeat spiked as they continued. He wished he had been able to discern the whole route in his dream. He should be the one leading them to the sword. And then, when he saw the sconces on the walls had change from the simple torch holders into the same ones in his dream, he knew Mikhal really was taking them to Velios.

Liam hurried forward to talk to Alexander, his body humming with adrenaline. "Are you ready with the disenchantment spell?" he asked Alexander, looking into the man's glowering face as he covered another cough.

"Yes, yes, of course we are ready," Alexander said seriously, looking over to Katerina.

Liam turned his head to her and she nodded once in agreement before looking at Mikhal with clear apprehension.

Liam followed behind Mikhal, letting him lead him down the corridors that all looked the same to Liam. He felt more and more confident in Mikhal with every step.

Liam's eyes picked up something strange in the dim lighting and he sucked in a breath. They were approaching a blue door on their right. Elyria. The blue door with the tear drop symbol was the first one he had gone through in his dreams. Elyria was probably right behind that door.

190

All he had to do was open it and she would be there. He could rescue her, get her out of there, away from the Tykens who had imprisoned her. He hesitated in taking another step as he came to the door, but then tore his sight from it and continued. He'd be back for her. He didn't know why, but he felt such a sense of duty to protect her. Maybe it was Destiny. Maybe it was all just in his head. But if what she had told him was true, he knew he would be back for her.

After only a few more steps further down the corridor, Mikhal stopped them. Liam looked up and his whole body hummed with anxiety. The door. The plain door with the metal latch.

"It's behind this door," Liam said.

Mikhal nodded and gestured for Liam to enter. Liam's stomach flopped over itself and he reached within to feel the vibration of his strength, using it to help steady his nerves. Then he nodded and pushed the door open.

He stepped into the room, a warm glow filling the entire space as it had in his dream. Liam felt the coldness of the dungeon melt away and a cozy feeling of safety seep into his muscles as he moved farther into the room.

A massive collection of relics lined the walls. Glass cases and stone pedestals stood around the room holding items as big as shields and as small as jewels and beads. Pottery and statues were placed in between the glittering artifacts. It was full of immense treasures and right in the center, was a sword on fire.

The magical sword, Velios.

Though he had seen the sword in his dream, it was still a stunning sight to behold. He could actually feel the power radiating from it as it rested in a metal bracket, standing over its white marble pedestal, more vibrant and beautiful than it had been in his dream. The flames licked at the air around it, emanating an immense heat. Anthony's eyes glued themselves to the magical sword as the others pushed by him to enter the room.

"Xevron take it all!" Alexander cursed from behind Liam.

Liam watched Mikhal step into the center of the room and place Alexander at the foot of the pedestal before stretching out his back and shaking out his arms.

"What?" Liam asked Alexander. "Are you all right, did he hurt you?"

"I didn't hurt him," Mikhal said with exasperation.

"Well, you weren't very gentle," Alexander complained as he straightened out his clothing and hugged the jacket more tightly around his head. "But more importantly we are all completely doomed."

"Doomed?" Liam asked.

"The walls," Katerina said as she looked around the room. "They are made of obsidian," her voice shook with the words.

"Obsidian?" Liam asked.

"Obsidian," Alexander said grumpily. "The one thing that can render an Isavarian witch completely and totally magic-less."

"We can't do the disenchantment spell," Katerina whispered. Her eyes glazed over when she put a hand to her stomach.

Liam looked around at the walls himself now and noticed the smooth blackness of them. Was this the blackness in his dream?

"So how do we get the sword out of here if we can't break the spell?" Anthony asked in an oddly even voice given the circumstances. His eyes were still transfixed on the glowing flames.

Liam hesitated and looked to Alexander.

"We don't," Alexander said, throwing his arms in the air and throwing the jacket off his head. "It's over. We get re-captured and we just give up."

"Don't say that," Katerina admonished, her voice cracking. "There has to be a way …" she said as she looked around. "There's all kinds of magical things in here, maybe there's something that can help us."

Katerina looked around the room at all the objects on the wall and in the cases. Mikhal began to help her and even Alexander's face softened with hope as his eyes searched the room.

"Maybe there's something we can carry it in," Mikhal suggested as he looked.

Liam turned around just in time to see Anthony reach out for the sword. Liam smacked his hand down.

"What are you doing?" Liam asked Anthony, pushing him away from the sword.

"I was just curious about something. I could hear something …" Anthony said, still fixated on the flaming object.

"You can't touch it. It'll burn your skin off! That's why we need the disenchantment spell," Liam scolded Anthony, trying to get his attention by putting his face in Anthony's line of sight.

Anthony only shrugged. "I feel so drawn to it though. It doesn't feel hot to me …" he said, appearing to be in some sort of trance.

Liam heard shouting coming from outside the room and then a loud commotion before the thundering of footsteps. His stomach twisted into a knot. The

Tykens had discovered their empty cells. They had to get out now if they wanted any chance of escaping.

"We have to go. Now," Liam announced to the others.

"Frachus' bile," Mikhal cursed. "There has to be something!"

Liam closed his eyes. They needed help. Desperately. He didn't know all that Elyria could do, but maybe she could do something to help them. He didn't know what else he could try right now and she had foretold of his victory. She had to help him. They were so close now, maybe he could contact her. He reached out to her, thinking of her face, her bright red hair, her scaly tail, the glow of her body in the darkness.

Elyria, he called in his mind. *Elyria, can you hear me? Do you hear me? Please, please, talk to me.* Liam pleaded in his mind.

The pounding footsteps grew louder and louder as the Tykens drew near. Liam had backed up farther into the room now and could feel the heat of the sword on his back. The heat was so intense as he stood in front of it that he wondered, dramatically, if the heat of the sword or the blade of a Tyken would take him down first.

The footsteps made it to the doorway and Liam's body tensed in anticipation. *Elyria!* He screamed in his mind.

"Anthony! No!" Liam heard Katerina scream.

Liam snapped open his eyes as the heat on his back suddenly ceased and he turned to see Anthony's arm stretched out toward the sword and his hand clasped firmly over the flaming hilt.

24

Katerina felt every muscle in her body tighten dramatically. A sudden strike of fear shot through her entire body as she watched Anthony's arm enter the flames that surrounded Velios, but that fear was quickly disarmed as she witnessed a miracle.

He didn't burn.

To her utter amazement, the flames didn't seem to bother him at all. She could feel the heat from where she was standing, but he seemed completely unaffected. His gaze focused on the sword intensely and he picked it up off the pedestal with one easy motion. Bright flames blazed through his hands as if they were only air as he turned towards the doorway. He lifted the sword out toward the impending flood of Tykens, walking around the marble pedestal and stepping between Mikhal and Liam who stood frozen in shock as they stared at him.

"Holy Aurelia," Mikhal said quietly as he stared.

The door burst open and a cold burst of wind flew through the room. Three armored Tykens bombarded their way in. They piled into the small treasure room, one holding a large hammer, one brandishing a sword, and the other holding a coil of green rope with rocks tied on the end. They raised their voices in a battle cry at the sight of the escaped humans.

Then they froze. The Tykens halted when they saw Anthony holding the flaming sword in his hands. The whole room was still for a moment. Anthony swung the sword back and forth skillfully; swiping it through the air in front of the

Tykens, threatening to burn anyone who got too close. Katerina was surprised, and impressed, by the ease in which Anthony handled the sword as he moved. The Tykens backed up, their faces sneering in frustration and confusion.

Katerina turned her attention to the Tykens and noticed these were not simple guardsman. They wore fitted metal breastplates with massive pauldrons on each shoulder and their horns protruded through dark steel helmets that covered the top half of their faces. Angry eyes, outlined in white primal patterns, peered out from behind the masks. They had sent warriors after them.

"This can't be ..." the Tyken with the rope muttered quietly to the Tyken holding the sword as everyone in the room stared at Anthony.

"Impossible," the other Tyken said.

Mikhal took the opportunity of the pause to step forward in front of Anthony. "You can see it is true!" Mikhal called out and pointed toward Anthony. "You can't deny the rightful owner of the sword. Even Tykens must honor that. After all, you were the ones who made it!"

The Tykens scowled harder at Mikhal.

Rightful owner? Katerina wondered to herself and looked towards her future husband. *Had Anthony known before he grabbed the sword?*

The look on Anthony's face gave nothing away as he narrowed his eyes at the Tykens in front of him. He lowered the sword and stood up straight to face the Tykens. The Tykens stared at Anthony.

"The sword doesn't have a living owner! The line was completely wiped out ..." one of the Tykens said, lowering his own sword.

"This is some sort of trick! Some sort of witchcraft magic!" another one of the Tykens yelled.

"How could it be a trick? We are surrounded by obsidian!" Mikhal said with a presenting gesture.

"Then that would make him ..." the Tyken with the coiled rope said softly, turning to look at his companion next to him.

"... More dangerous than we had originally thought," the Tyken holding the sword finished for his friend as they locked eyes.

The Tyken with the sword suddenly moved to reach for a pouch that hung on his belt and the Tyken with the bolas moved to lift it above his head in a circular motion. Katerina's body tensed and she stepped closer to Mikhal, bracing for the chaos the room would soon fall into. She heard a thump and everyone in the room turned their heads to the sound. Alexander had collapsed and faded into unconsciousness again.

Katerina heard a deep sigh coming from one of the Tykens and when she looked up she watched as the Tyken with the hammer, suddenly swung it into the back of the Tyken with the bolas before he could throw it at Anthony. Her eyes widened in shock as he then kicked the legs of the other Tyken next to him, causing him to yell out and collapse to the ground. The rogue Tyken grabbed the pouch off the other Tyken's belt and dumped the contents on the Tyken on the ground before he could turn to look back behind him.

Katerina remained frozen in shock at what she'd just seen and realized she had been holding her breath. She let the air out of her lungs and felt the coldness of the dungeon prickle through her arms as the Tyken with the hammer turned a scowl on her.

He stepped forward and Katerina saw Mikhal relax his stance out of the corner of her eye as she peered into the eyes of the massive horned figure in front of her. The eyes softened, he removed his helmet and Katerina nearly melted to the floor with relief.

"Kona!" Katerina whispered breathlessly, tears threatening to emerge from her eyes. "I can't believe …"

"I thought I told you to get them straight out of here," Kona said, turning his attention toward Mikhal.

"We needed to get the sword," Mikhal explained, pointing to the flaming sword in Anthony's hands.

"I told you to leave the sword!"

"I think you're forgetting that I don't take orders from you. You know how important the sword—"

"Wait," Liam broke into the argument. "You two know each other?"

"We are recently acquainted," Kona responded, not taking his eyes from Mikhal.

Mikhal, however, turned to look at Liam. "We were brought together by common cause not too long ago," he said.

"And that cause is?" Liam asked, looking between the two.

A common cause. Kona is a magic sympathizer. The thought struck Katerina sharply and she stared at Kona. All those nights he had taken her to see Alexander and the fact that he had kept her secret, it wasn't just because he saw it as his duty. He had believed in what she was doing all along.

Kona sighed. "There's no time to explain. We need to get you all out of here," he said firmly and turned to usher them all out of the obsidian lined room.

Liam took a breath in, likely to try to demand more answers, Katerina thought, but then they heard another parade of footsteps running down the hallway. More Tykens were on their way.

Kona turned to the others. "You must move. NOW!" He motioned for them to hurry. "I'll try to divert them. Take them out the back secret passage," he told Mikhal before he dashed toward the door.

"Kona!" Katerina felt her voice burst from her throat in a sudden desperation to get his attention before he disappeared.

He stopped and turned to look at her.

"Thank you," Katerina said. Her eyes locked with his and she hoped he could feel the weight of gratitude she was trying to express to him now. She wouldn't be here, she wouldn't be this close if it weren't for him.

Kona's deep dark eyes softened. She had never held his gaze this long. Finally, he nodded, put the helmet back on his head, and ran out of the room.

She turned herself to her other companions, shaking off the intensity of the exchange. She saw Liam bend over to scoop up the unconscious Alexander with ease and throw his old jacket over his shoulder. Anthony lowered the flaming sword to his side and they all made their way out of the room.

"This way," Mikhal said authoritatively as he led the group forward.

The tunnels were dark as they ran through them. Only a few torches lit the way. Katerina heard the clamoring of metal and the urgent voices of the Tykens getting closer as they followed.

They continued to follow Mikhal down each hallway, turning when he turned and picking up the pace when they came to long, straight stretches. They moved as fast as they could manage in the darkness. The thumping of the Tykens' feet on the stone floor was getting louder in her ears. She knew they needed to go faster.

Katerina dared to look behind her as they rushed down a long, straight hallway and saw a faint glow of light. The Tykens were catching up with them. She turned her head back to Mikhal and opened her mouth to warn him about how close the Tykens were getting, but instead her voice died in her throat. Her heart dropped when she saw the thick stone wall rising in front of them.

She felt panic starting to rise within her again until she saw Mikhal place his hand on the wall in front of them. He ran his hand across the stones, looking for something. Then he stopped and pushed on one of the stones. The wall gave way to a dark passageway.

"Come on," Mikhal whispered. "Quickly!" He motioned the group through the passageway.

Katerina was the first to run into the tunnel and fear seized her as she delved into the darkness. She couldn't see anything. There was nothing but blackness in front of her. She continued to move forward, one step at a time, one hand out in front of her and the other against the jagged wall. Then a warm glow filled the space behind her. The flaming sword's glow was just enough light for her to be able to see a few steps in front of her. She took in a breath to calm herself and picked up her pace. She could feel the heat of the sword at her back and hear the breathing of the men as they followed her.

Soon she saw a bright speck of light in the distance. Excitement and relief filled her and she picked up her dress to take off in a full sprint. She never should have doubted Mikhal. He knew these tunnels, he knew this dungeon, and he had brought them to safety.

The light got bigger and bigger as she ran, the others following closely behind her. She came to a latticed wooden gate and gripped it with her hands as she looked out. She gave it a forceful push, and to her relief, the gate budged. She kicked it completely down and she ran out into the sunlight.

The glorious, precious sunlight.

It had felt like weeks since she'd seen the sun, though it had only been a day or two. She closed her eyes and tilted her head up to enjoy the warmth. She felt her powers filling up her body again, pouring through her like a gentle tide.

She was warm.

She was alive.

She felt whole again.

"We need a portal out of here," Anthony said sternly, breaking Katerina out of her reverie.

She tilted her chin back down and opened her eyes, hoping he wasn't asking her do it. She saw they had escaped the dark dungeon into a beautiful clearing. Green trees and bushes surrounded them.

Mikhal nodded. "Yes. Try waking Alexander. He should feel better now that we are out of the dungeon and away from all that obsidian. I also might have something to help with that gash on his head."

Mikhal jogged away from the group, over to the trees and bushes.

"Where are you going?" Liam asked as he set Alexander down on the soft ground gently, laying his jacket over the man again.

"I need to get my stuff," Mikhal explained over his shoulder. "Kona said it would be over here somewhere." He wandered through the bushes and began searching and rustling through them.

Kona said he would divert them, Katerina reminded herself, trying to remain calm as the thundering of footsteps continued to get louder.

A group of Tykens came bursting out of the tunnel. Kona wasn't able to distract them all. Katerina saw the fury in the faces of the five Tykens as they rushed into view. They were running toward them with their torches, chains, swords, and ropes raised. There was no way they were getting out of this now. They quickly cornered the group of escapees. Katerina crouched down next to Alexander and looked over at Mikhal as he continued to search. Finally, he seemed to pick something up from the bushes.

Her head snapped back to Tykens, and the boys standing in front of her. Anthony raised the flaming sword and Liam curled his hands into fists, taking a defensive stance behind his brother.

"Don't come any closer!" Anthony threatened and drew the sword across the ground in front of them. Flames ignited in the grass as the sword swept across it.

Katerina turned immediately to Alexander and shook him. "Alexander!" she whispered fiercely at him. "Alexander, please!"

"Here!" Mikhal yelled, rushing over with a leather satchel.

The Tykens closed in, stomping on the fire as they came forward, chains and shackles in their hands. Katerina lifted her hand, hoping to cast a wind spell that would push them back. It was the spell she knew the best, but before she could say the words, Anthony rushed toward the Tykens by himself.

"You idiot!" Mikhal yelled at him as he threw his bag down next to Katerina and rushed after Anthony. "You can't fight them all alone!"

Liam glanced over at Katerina behind him. Then he winced and sighed before leaving her sitting on the ground alone, dashing toward the onslaught of Tykens.

"In the bag!" Mikhal yelled as he disarmed one of the Tykens of their sword with a quick twist of his wrist and taking the weapon as his own.

Katerina quickly opened the leather satchel at her feet. Bottles and trinkets lay strewn freely with bits of food and clothing. *Potions.* Katerina realized with anxious excitement.

"The blue one ... Alexander!" was all she could hear Mikhal yell.

She frantically searched through the bag until she found the small vial of blue liquid. She quickly popped the top off the bottle and carefully held it to Alexander's lips. She lifted his head and tilted the liquid into his mouth. She laid him back down and closed his lips. She closed her eyes and said a prayer.

Then she turned and watched as Velios clashed against the sword of a Tyken and Liam slid into the legs of another, knocking the unsuspecting Tyken off his feet. Mikhal's cloak floated around him as he spun to parry an attack from another one. She knew Mikhal had been trained to fight, but she had never seen his skills in action. She watched with admiration and anxiety as he pushed the Tyken back and slashed his legs.

She darted her eyes away from Mikhal in time to see Anthony thrown onto his back and skid across the ground. Velios had been knocked from his hand and the grass quickly caught fire beneath the sword. Two Tykens made their way toward Anthony triumphantly, while Liam was locked in a battle of strength with another Tyken, trying to wrestle him to the ground like he had in the stadium. Mikhal had the other two Tykens surrounding him, attacking him from different angles. Katerina's heart hammered in her chest as she watched helplessly. She turned back to Alexander, shaking him and begging him to wake up. She hadn't been trained properly to use her magic in a fight like this. Even if she tried, she would likely just hurt one of her allies.

Then she heard a yell and turned to watch a Tyken catch Mikhal's cloak in his grip and tug at it forcibly. Mikhal was forced to release the clasp around his neck before it choked him. The cloak was ripped away from his body, revealing his back to Katerina. She gasped in shock at the sight, her heart sinking and her eyes full of sorrow. She turned her gaze away from him.

She wasn't surprised by two large wings that sprouted from his back. She wasn't even surprised that they were gray and withered, but she was surprised at how painful and pitiful they looked now. They hardly looked like wings anymore at all. Beneath his cloak were two crippled wings, feathers missing and bones showing. She could only imagine the pain he must be in.

When the Tykens saw the dilapidated wings on his back, they lowered their weapons and looked at each other, surprise on their faces. They hesitated to continue the fight until Mikhal picked up his stolen sword again and swung at one of them. Though they seemed reluctant, the Tykens resumed their pursuit.

"Kat!" he yelled toward her. "You can do a wind spell!"

Katerina's heart clenched. He needed her help. She knew he did. Fear threatened to keep her paralyzed, but she had to try to do something. She stood up and concentrated on the wind spell. She could knock all the Tykens off their feet and across the dirt all at once. She knew how to do this spell. She said the words and made the motions, but she only to managed to make a small gust. She tried again, but it fizzled like before. She was only able to cause a light breeze. Determined and on the verge of tears, she lifted a shaking hand.

"*Veter!*" a loud voice called from behind her.

And suddenly all the Tykens fell back, forcefully pushed with focused blasts of wind. They toppled over, one by one as the wind hit each of them.

Relief flooded her body. Alexander was awake. He was propped up on one arm, with the other hand outstretched in front of him. He was breathing heavily and his shoulders slumped as he put his arm down. Katerina crouched next to him and noticed the deep lines under his eyes. This was all too much for him. They needed to get him out of here. She touched his hand before pulling her hand away. The Streaks grew before her eyes, stretching out along his hand, nearly reaching his fingers. If they were lucky, he would only collapse from the strain. He was getting dehydrated and the threat of a DarkHeart was getting very close.

"Alexander, thank goodness you're all right," Katerina said as she put a hand on a part of his arm that was covered.

Her teacher did not acknowledge her concern and instead turned to look at the wall of trees behind them. He pushed himself completely upright with a grunt and threw his arms up toward the trees and took a deep breath, narrowing his eyes in pain.

"Alexander?" Katerina asked. "What are you doing?"

"A portal is best done as a bound spell, but in this case we have no time," Alexander explained, looking at Katerina. "For a portal, you need someone with a memory of where you want to go, a door, and in best cases, a binding object. This is a very advanced, difficult spell. In the future, you'll want to make sure you perform spells like this with plenty of energy and water."

Katerina shook her head. "No, Alexander you're too weak, you'll call forth a DarkHeart if you push too hard. Teach me the spell—"

"I need you to do a shield spell," Alexander said. "I need time."

Alexander looked away from her, back to the trees. "*Misavotive*," he repeated over and over.

A shimmer of light caught Katerina's eye and she turned to look. As she watched, the space between two of the trees sparkled, shimmered, and warped. The spell was already in motion, and it was likely their only hope to get out of there alive. She stood up and stepped back from Alexander. She clasped her hands together and pressed them against her forehead as she prayed that he'd able to complete the spell.

She glanced behind her and saw the Tykens had gotten to their feet and Mikhal's back was covered with his dark cloak again. The Tykens would be coming after them at any minute. She closed her eyes and tried to remember the words for the shield spell. Her mind raced through images of the spell book, searching for the right one. She couldn't remember what the words were. Her mind went completely blank and panic set in. She was completely frozen.

She opened her eyes again. She just needed him to tell her the words. Why hadn't he made her memorize these? She turned back and watched as the air between the trees distorted more and a shimmering circle appeared, starting in the center and then spreading throughout the space. A bright light flashed once the space was nothing but a shimmering curtain, causing Katerina to look away.

"*Veter!*" she heard Alexander yell again and she felt herself being pushed forward with immense force.

A rush of cold filled her entire body. She opened her eyes but could see nothing except whiteness all around her. A completely blank horizon. Then the feeling of the cold, empty space rushed past her and suddenly a tall rock wall came into her view.

She stumbled forward onto gravel and dirt. The coldness left as suddenly as it had come. She stood up slowly, steadying herself as she looked around. Tall rocks and small trees surrounded her now. They had escaped. Alexander had done it!

Katerina turned sharply, giddy with excitement and relief. She saw the portal in front of her, set into the side of a large boulder. She could see Alexander was still on the forest side of the portal. He looked exhausted and his arms shook as he held the portal in place. Anthony and Mikhal were pushed through the portal, Alexander's wind spell forcing and guiding them through. They seemed a little dazed as they stood on the rocky side of the portal.

"Alexander! You did it! You really did it!" Katerina said with glee and excitement, nearly jumping up and down. "Now, come on, let's go!" she said, waving her arm for him to follow them through the portal.

Alexander said one more wind spell and Liam was sent through the portal. Katerina froze. The feeling of happiness beginning to drain from her. Alexander had left himself alone on the other side.

Alexander smiled weakly at her. His eyes were heavy with emotion, making Katerina's smile fade. He never smiled at her, not like this, she realized, and her chest crumbled with worry.

A tear streaked down his face as he looked at her. "Find it. Find the stone and bring it back to Davi and to the many of our kind that suffer. The key must be turned and I have every confidence that this is God's plan for you. You are truly something special in this dark world. Always believe that, and never let go of what your Volkev mother has given you."

And then he dropped his arms.

His body fell forward with the release. Katerina's vision filled with the horrific scene of the Tykens closing in on him, the sides of the portal shrinking as he let himself fall to the ground. She watched a Tyken's sword swinging down toward him as the portal closed into nothing in front of her eyes. She couldn't see him anymore. The portal was gone. Alexander was gone.

25

"No!" Katerina screamed, running toward where the portal had been. A pair of arms grabbed her around her shoulders, stopping her from going any further. "Alexander!" she screamed louder.

Katerina shook herself free from the arms that were holding her and slammed her hands against the large boulder in front of her, but it was nothing but a rock. She yelled for Alexander, pounding her fists against the hard stone, before sinking down to her knees.

And she let the fear in. She let the winds pick up.

"We can't just leave him there!" she shouted as she whipped around to see Mikhal standing right behind her and the other two a few steps back. "How could you just leave him there?"

"We didn't leave him, he pushed us all through," Mikhal said, his face regretful.

"I personally don't think leaving people behind is acceptable," Katerina muttered bitterly loud enough for only Mikhal to hear.

Mikhal's eyes widened for a moment before his whole face fell. His hand gripped his sword again and he sighed, looking at the ground. Katerina scowled and turned back to the wall. She shut her eyes and tried to remember the spell. What were the words he had said?

"We had no choice," Liam said in a serious voice.

Katerina paid no attention to his words, still trying to remember the spell Alexander had used. A pang of nausea crept over her. She didn't know what to do.

But she couldn't just leave Alexander. They needed him. They couldn't find the dragon without him.

"Hey, it's going to be all right," Anthony said soothingly as he approached Katerina.

Katerina whirled around, ready to scream at him for even trying to act like things were going to be all right. But when she turned, she noticed that he still held the flaming sword in his hand. A sudden wave of despair slammed into her like a punch to the stomach. She couldn't help but sink to the ground and let the tears fall.

The nausea intensified and she hugged her arms around herself in an effort to comfort the feeling. The tears came quickly and unwillingly. Crying like this in front of others was her worst nightmare, but she couldn't stop them. They flowed and burned like lava on her cheeks.

Without hesitation, Mikhal rushed over to her, dropping his sword to the ground. He wrapped his arms around her and held her tightly. Katerina knew she should push him away, especially with Anthony watching, but she couldn't fight against the warm, strong arms that she so desperately needed to feel around her. She let herself fall limp into the safety of the embrace. Undignified sobs burst forth from her in full force and she let her whole body feel it.

"You left him …" Katerina said through the pain of her constricted throat. It felt like a ball was stuck in the back of her throat.

"He knew what he was doing, Kat. It was his choice," Mikhal said softly, loosening his hold on her. "Alexander made a great sacrifice for the good of the mission. Without him, we would not have been able to escape."

Katerina squeezed her eyes shut and, though it took an immense effort, she forced herself to push away from him. The warmth and safety and familiarity faded from her bones and left her feeling even more cold and miserable than before. She wrapped her arms around her knees, trying to keep the heat in.

"There wasn't time," Anthony said, crouching down next to her.

Katerina continued to look straight ahead. She couldn't let Anthony comfort her when all she wanted was to fall back into Mikhal's arms. Her eyes filled with tears again and her vision blurred from the water that filled them.

"It's going to be all right," Liam's voice said gently. Katerina's heart wrenched at the words and her chest tightened.

"We can't do this without him. We may have Velios, but we have no idea where the dragon's cave is or how to get there. Not to mention you need someone who knows what they're doing to cast spells," Katerina ranted through her tears, looking directly at Liam now. He seemed to be the only safe place to look.

Liam looked away from her for a moment, clearly uncomfortable, before locking his eyes onto hers again. "It was awful, what happened with Alexander. We'll never be able to replace him. He was a hero, for more than what he did today, and he will always be remembered for it. But we do have Velios and we can figure it out. We have to," Liam said with a hint of hesitation.

Mikhal chuckled and Katerina's weeping lessened as she looked up at him with a questioning look. The morning light shone on him from between the trees and she saw with annoyance that his light eyes and muscular build was just as beautiful as she had remembered.

"Is something funny?" Anthony asked as he stood and crossed his arms.

Everyone turned to look at Mikhal.

"It's just ... I don't think we're going to have a problem finding the cave," Mikhal said and nodded his head to point to something beyond the group.

They all turned slowly to follow Mikhal's gaze. A purple haze was rolling slowly over the ground behind them. Katerina stood up at the sight and craned her neck to see where the haze was coming from.

"Is that ...?" Liam began to ask, but his question trailed off as they moved slowly toward the source of the odd phenomenon.

They followed the haze around a corner of high rocks and up a steep gravel incline. Once at the top, Katerina turned and her eyes filled with a beautiful sight of a sunset over a long horizon. They were high up in the mountains and she could see far off into the distance. The warm orange-red light of the setting sun stretched out in front of her.

She could hardly believe her eyes. She'd never seen anything like it. But her awe was soon traded for a strike of fear when she turned to follow the purple haze again. She saw it pouring out of a dark opening in the side of the mountain. Katerina's stomach lurched with a shot of pure anxiety as she realized what she was looking at.

"So this must be ..." Liam trailed off.

"Yep," Mikhal said eventually. He took a big breath in and placed his hands on his hips, "I do believe we've made it. This is it."

"Alexander," Katerina whispered as she tore her eyes away from the purple fog and dark opening. "He brought us right to it."

"He was the only one who knew the location. It had to have come from him," Mikhal said softly.

This is too fast. Did he think I was ready for this? Are any of us really ready for this? He wouldn't even teach me bound spells. Katerina's mind rushed as she glanced over at the large sword, still flaming at Anthony's side.

"But Velios," Katerina said with a whimper, causing everyone's attention to turn to the sword again. "It's still enchanted."

"That's all right though," Anthony said, lifting the sword up higher. "I can wield it as we fight the dragon," he said with a grin.

"No, we have to break the protection spell on it before it can be used against Garrock. It won't do anything against him while it's still protected by the flames," Katerina explained. She felt numb as the words escaped her.

All her companions lifted their eyes to her. There was a deafening silence as they stared. She knew what they were thinking. She was thinking it too. It was going to have to be her. She was going to have to do the disenchantment.

"I know you can do this," Mikhal said softly as he took a step closer to her.

The other two watched hesitantly, their eyes darting back and forth between the two of them. She saw Anthony lean over to whisper something Liam. Liam's eyes got wide as he continued to look at her, but she could tell he was feigning surprise. He had known what she was, but Anthony clearly assumed he hadn't.

Katerina felt tears threatening to seep through her eyes again. She hated that. She looked down and squeezed her eyes shut. She turned away from the stares and marched back down the incline and into the glen of high rocks they were in before. Her heart raced as her mind tried to think of another solution.

The others followed behind her and were looking at her expectantly again.

"I can't ..." she said quietly with a shrug as she shook her head, avoiding their eyes.

"Yes, you can," Mikhal said again. "Remember what we used to say? Deep breaths ..."

"I believe you can too," Anthony said strongly, cutting off Mikhal. He dropped the sword in front of her. He grabbed her hands in his and she was surprised that his hands didn't feel any warmer than usual. He didn't waver as he looked into her eyes. She felt oddly confident when he looked at her like that.

"You are more powerful than you realize," he said. "Did Alexander teach you the spell?" he asked.

Katerina nodded, keeping her eyes locked on his for a solid moment before taking her hands out of his.

She shook her head. "No, I … I couldn't do anything when Alexander needed the shield in the clearing …" her heart broke to pieces with her next words. "It's my fault. I should have done a shield spell. I could have saved him. He only pushed us all through because I couldn't give him enough time."

"This is different—" Mikhal began to say.

"No, it's not!" Katerina argued, hugging herself, trying to squeeze away the guilt. "And even if I could disenchant the sword. What will we do when we're faced with a dragon?" The thought made her positively sick.

"Hey," Anthony said, standing in front of her again. "We all have moments that we wish we did something different. But this is your next chance to do something right. You decide the way we move forward. I know you can do this." Anthony said this with conviction and stepped back from her. "You probably need some water first though," he said and looked to Mikhal.

Mikhal nodded and reached into his travel sack. He pulled out a leather pouch and handed it to Katerina. She took the pouch from him, but just stared at it.

"What else? What do you need?" Anthony asked.

Katerina didn't answer.

"Kat. Look at me," Mikhal instructed gently and she looked up at him tentatively. "You know the spell. You've learned more than I could have ever taught you before and I believe you could have done this even then. You can do this."

Katerina sighed. Whimpering on the inside, she dropped her head again. She took a drink from the leather pouch, emptying its contents and throwing it down on the ground. She put her hands over her face and thought. She had memorized the spell with Alexander, a pang of grief struck her at the memory. She did know the spell and she would have to at least try. If she didn't, Alexander's sacrifice would be completely in vain. She couldn't let that happen. The Streaks on her chest burned.

She took a deep breath in and looked at the flaming sword on the rocky ground in front of her. "I just need some quiet," she said as she knelt down in front of the sword.

The heat radiated from the sword dangerously as she held her hands over it. She could feel the power that was being held by the object. The sword had held this enchantment for hundreds of years now and she was about to set it free. It had to be her who said these words.

"*Mika helish myvota tenou,*" Katerina muttered as she closed her eyes.

Katerina felt the magic flowing through her veins into her hands as she chanted. She fell into deep concentration as she repeated the words over and over again.

The sword, the flaming sword. Velios. I must quiet the flames.

She felt a tug on her chest. A light pull, coming from the sword itself. It didn't want to be disenchanted. Katerina smiled to herself. She was doing it; it was reacting to her magic. She could feel the resistance.

I am a Volkev witch. This spell belongs to me. I command the flames to cease.

She kept chanting the words. Katerina pushed the magic through her hands and over the blazing hot piece of metal in front of her.

Her head ached, her shoulders throbbed with stress and her hands were almost numb as she fought with the enchantment. She squeezed her eyes shut even tighter. She had to push past the pain. Her mouth was drying out and her head felt light. But still, she chanted.

"*Mika relish myvota tenou.*"

Then, suddenly, a release. Katerina's body hinged forward and she exhaled as power expelled from her. The tension in her head and shoulders and hands lessened, but fatigue set in quickly behind it.

She opened her eyes slowly and looked at the sword on the ground. She smiled weakly when she saw it was no longer on fire. A simple alagon sword lay on the ground now, sparkling with an iridescent hue. She wobbled and braced herself on the ground as she heard the others exhaling in relief behind her.

A feeling of pride flooded through her. A feeling so foreign, a feeling she had chased for years, was suddenly so overwhelming she thought she may burst.

"I had no doubt. Amazing work," Mikhal said and Katerina lifted her eyes up to see him smiling down at her—a smile that once had the power to disarm Katerina completely.

Katerina felt a shooting, horrible pain present again in her shoulder, and she grabbed at it. She felt the burning slowly take over her body. She squeezed her eyes shut as the pain burrowed itself deep within her head.

The Streaks are growing. I just need to keep breathing. The pain is not so bad. It will subside, just ignore it.

Katerina felt the air rush out of her lungs as her chest was filled with a sudden strike of pain. She couldn't hold herself upright anymore and she felt her body fall slowly before slamming into the hard, cold ground.

No ... she thought. *Not now ...* and then strong, warm arms clutched her tightly as the world disappeared.

26

"Over here. Lie her down on this," Mikhal ordered as he threw his tattered cloak on the ground and rummaged in his bag.

Liam's body tensed. He stared at Mikhal's back and what protruded from it. Liam thought he had seen the wings during the fight with the Tykens, but hadn't gotten a clear look. Now, the large appendages were plainly in front of him and he could hardly believe what he was seeing. Mikhal was an Auren.

Liam averted his gaze from Mikhal. It was rude to stare. Liam looked to Anthony as Anthony rolled his eyes and mocked Mikhal's words silently as he held the fainted Katerina in his arms.

"I mean, obviously I was going to lay her down," he muttered.

"Is she all right?" Liam asked, stepping closer to them.

"She'll be fine, she just needs a little rest. The Streaks can flare up like this sometimes," Mikhal explained as Anthony gently lowered her to the ground and pulled out a vial of clear liquid.

"She has the Streaks?" Liam asked quietly. He closed his eyes, disappointed in himself for not putting that together before. But she had always seemed fine.

"She does," Anthony nodded, looking up at him. Concern was clear on his face.

"I've dealt with fainting spells due to the Streaks before," Mikhal said and tilted the contents of the vial onto a cloth. He turned his attention to Katerina and unbuttoned the back of her dress.

"Hey!" Anthony said and pushed Mikhal away. "What do you think you're doing?"

Mikhal looked at Anthony with annoyance. "I'm helping her," he said firmly, holding up the vial and wet cloth.

"With what? What is that?" Anthony demanded, still holding an arm out over the sleeping Katerina.

"It's a potion. It's made with Riven tears, which are very good for healing as I'm sure you know," Mikhal said, clearly trying to bring some cordiality back to the interaction. Then he pushed Anthony's hand away and pulled the shoulder of Katerina's dress down.

Liam immediately looked up at the sky and turned his body away, feeling extremely uncomfortable. "How did you get your hands on a potion made with Riven tears?" Anthony said rather calmly, still hovering over his betrothed.

Interested in the answer, Liam turned back to them, but keeping his eyes down to the ground.

"I have connections to a few Isavarian witches and I have a few Riven friends from childhood. This is a strong healing and pain-relieving potion that I always have with me these days. The pain in my wings has gotten worse recently. Sometimes, it's nearly too much to bear until I take some of this potion," Mikhal explained as he pushed the potion-soaked cloth onto Katerina.

Liam turned back completely now to stare at the tattered wings on Mikhal's back. A gray feather floated to the ground as Liam looked. He cringed at the bones protruding through. The wings seemed to tremble. Elyria had shown him Aurens in his dreams. Had she predicted he would help them? Or was she warning Liam against him?

"It would have been nice to know we had an Auren on our side in the dungeon, you know. You keeping secrets from us is definitely making you look trustworthy," Anthony said sarcastically as he stared at the wings. "Aren't you all supposed to hate us or something anyway?"

Mikhal shook his head as he pressed another piece of damp cloth on Katerina's shoulder. Liam could see traces of the black lines starting to make their way down her arm.

"The Aurens don't hate all humans, no. And I would have thought that my little ring contraption would be a dead giveaway. As far as I know, only the Aurens have things like that," Mikhal said and Liam glanced down at the seemingly

212

normal ring on his hand. "But honestly, I don't go around declaring I'm an Auren because I am somewhat of a fugitive from my people."

"A fugitive?" Anthony asked as he raised his eyebrows. "Oh good, that's great. That's just what we need."

"Aurens are after you? Why?" Liam asked, deciding it was safe to join the conversation. He walked over to them now, trying to keep his eyes on Mikhal and not on the gruesome black streaks that invaded Katerina's arm.

"I used to be part of the Protectorate, the Auren group that took responsibility for keeping the Lumos Gems hidden. That was back when I still went by my given name, Michael. My father was very involved in the original spell that created the Gems and a founding member of the Protectorate. Our family was given great honor for his involvement and I lived a very privileged life when I was young. Of course, when I became of age, I followed in my father's footsteps and joined the Protectorate."

"You're part of the group that wants to keep the Lumos Gems out of the hands of humans?" Anthony asked as he stood over Mikhal, crossing his arms.

"I used to be," Mikhal clarified with annoyance. "As time went on, after about eighty years, I realized I didn't agree with the mission of the Protectorate. I do not believe that humans having magic from the gods is a bad and horrible thing. I made that known by freeing some Isavarian witches we had in custody and now I am on the run. Hunted constantly."

"How long have you been running?" Liam asked. He had forgotten how long the Aurens lived and was genuinely curious about Mikhal's life.

"I've only been running for twenty years now," Mikhal explained.

"Twenty years? So that would make you …" Liam said, more to himself as he tried to calculate how old Mikhal might be.

"I am 203 years old, but that is still very young in the Auren community, mind you," Mikhal explained. "That's equivalent to about twenty-nine years old for humans."

Liam raised his eyebrows at the revelation.

"So you're running from the Auren Protectorate, that's great," Anthony broke in with an unimpressed tone. "Are you just obsessed with magic then? Is that why you came to save us? To get closer to Liam? Or to get back with Katerina?"

Mikhal finished his work on Katerina's shoulder and lifted her sleeve back up over the cloth that he left in place. "I will admit Katerina being involved did weigh into my decision to intervene. I couldn't just let her sit in a dungeon after …" he broke off for a moment before continuing, "… after everything."

He cleared his throat slightly as Anthony's eyes prodded him.

"We met while I was hiding in Esterine. That's when I took, and since kept, the name Mikhal. However, in all honesty, I didn't know she was going to be part of all this at first," Mikhal said, before turning to look at both Anthony and Liam. He stood up and opened his palms to them. "Truth be told, I've been on a mission to find the healing stone as well."

"For your wings," Liam said softly.

Mikhal nodded.

Anthony scoffed. "If you were part of the Protectorate wouldn't you already know all about the healing stone?"

"Unfortunately protecting the healing stone itself was not part of my duties and I was not yet ranked high enough to know all the secrets of the Lumos Gems. There are many secrets about the Lumos Gems that only a select few, like my father, are allowed to know," Mikhal explained.

"So what did you do for the protectorate then?" Liam asked, watching Anthony glare at him out of the corner of his eye.

"I was in the division that oversaw enchanted objects, which included the protection of the magical weapons that are linked to the Gems."

"That's how you knew the dungeon so well," Liam said, putting together the pieces aloud. "There are more magical weapons out there?"

Mikhal nodded. "There is one for each stone. As well as a beast guardian."

"Seems like a frivolous job. Or were there tons of people trying to steal these weapons?" Anthony asked.

"Not usually, not after the hunts died down at least. Most of what I did involved other enchanted items. I would help track them down and confiscate them."

"And now you want to waltz in here to confiscate the stone from us!" Anthony exclaimed, his eyes widened in an accusatory stare.

Mikhal looked down and took a deep breath, Liam thought he saw a flash of anger cross his eyes. "I don't want to take the stone from you. I only want some relief for myself so I can continue to run from the Protectorate and help protect people like your brother here from being captured and imprisoned for their entire short lives," he said sternly, looking at Anthony through a glare.

Anthony stared back at Mikhal, looking very skeptical.

"It has been my life's mission since I left the Protectorate to free all magical humans from persecution and unjust torment due to prejudice. I help them escape the grasps of the Protectorate that are constantly looking for any reason to imprison them. And though Isavarian witches are more or less accepted in Akaria, it's not like that everywhere. Witches are persecuted most everywhere else in the world. Mostly out of fear, or ignorance, but they live in danger all the same. After meeting Katerina, my mission became crystal clear. I have been doing my best to help all those that I can since then. Until the pain became too much to ignore anymore."

"What did happen to your wings?" Liam asked, trying not to look at the sad shape of the wings behind Mikhal.

Mikhal winced as he turned to Liam. "It was a punishment. A punishment that was executed by an Auren I used to call my closest friend. We joined the Protectorate together and even grew up together, which is something quite special in Auren communities. Children are quite rare," he explained. "The pain was manageable at first, but it has gotten gradually worse over the last twenty years and even though I don't know everything about the Water Stone, I do know a little. I was trying to find an Isavarian who could help me work out a way to disenchant Velios when I heard there was another group of humans, with unheard of magical abilities, out looking for it too. So naturally, I was interested."

"Who's out there telling people we're looking for the Water Stone?" Anthony asked angrily.

"The Fairies like to spread rumors," Mikhal said with amusement. "but when I found out who was looking for it and where you guys were going, it all seemed like fate. Destiny was bringing us together."

Liam looked over at Anthony. Anthony had always had a certain devotion to the goddess of Destiny and Liam watched as Anthony scowled, unable to retort.

"Destiny," Anthony mumbled with frustration, clenching his fists at his side.

Mikhal's shoulders relaxed and he raised his hands up, palms showing. "I'm not going to force it on anyone, but I would suggest that you let me help with your injuries."

Liam looked down at himself. He had totally ignored the scrapes on his legs and the cuts on his arms and face. As soon as he acknowledged them, they began to hurt. He looked over to Anthony as he touched one of the cuts on his head. Anthony shook his head at Liam.

"It's the same stuff I use on myself," Mikhal said with an eye roll as he reached back into his bag. "I really do just want to help." Mikhal sat down on the ground and cleaned his own wounds on his arm with a cloth.

"You just want to help yourself," Anthony said.

Liam sighed and decided to sit next to Mikhal. "Will you explain to me what you're doing?" Liam asked, watching intently.

"I'll first clean the wounds with some water, then I'll apply the potion to the outside of the wounds and stitch up any wider gashes. After that I'll apply a bandage and you'll be good to go by morning," Mikhal looked up at Liam. "Maybe sooner for you. I'm not sure what the healing rate would be for an Earth Alumenos."

Liam nodded and rolled up his sleeves. Anthony scoffed from his position away from them.

"I assume you're planning to enter the dragon's cave with us too?" Liam asked as Mikhal gently cleaned the dirt away from Liam's wounds.

Mikhal nodded. "I think you guys could use me."

"What makes you think we'd trust you?" Anthony asked as he rolled a large boulder toward them. "And what good is a crippled Auren to us anyway? We've already got an Alumenos and an Isavarian witch and me with Velios." He sat on the large rock, counting on his fingers. "Do you have any more weapons in that sack of yours?"

"I've got this sword I took from the Tykens," Mikhal said, pointing to the long sword laying on the ground a few feet away.

Anthony huffed. "Just a regular sword though. That won't do anything against a dragon like this. So as far as I know, we only have the one sword," he said crossing his arms.

Liam looked over to Velios, sitting next to Katerina. It gleamed in the bright sunlight. His brother was right. What were they going to do with just one alagon sword?

"Velios is the only sword that can do anything against this dragon, that's true. I'm doing all I can to help you already. I got you out of the dungeon and—"

"You didn't get us out of the dungeon," Anthony said, shaking his head. "We only got out because of Kona. He's the one who saved us from all the Tykens!"

Liam looked to Mikhal. Mikhal looked up at Liam briefly, but sighed and rolled his eyes.

"Regardless, I got us out of the cells and I led us through the maze of the dungeon and out through the secret tunnel. You never would have found your way without me. I also have quite a few helpful potions now," Mikhal continued.

Liam instinctively reached for his wrist, but it was bare. His watch. It was in that jacket that he had left with Alexander. His stomach rolled over in grief. He had lost the most important object he owned.

"Oh yeah? Like what kinds of potions?" Anthony asked, bringing Liam back into the present moment.

"Well, I have mostly healing and pain-killing stuff," Mikhal said, pausing his work on Liam to rummage through his bag. "But I do have some invisibility potion left."

"You have an invisibility potion?" Liam asked shakily, sitting up straighter and trying to get his mind off his devastating loss. It was just a watch.

Mikhal nodded with a smirk. "It helps a lot when you're in hiding."

"Where are you getting all these potions?" Anthony asked, his voice a little less aggressive this time.

"When you help Isavarians, they usually help you back," Mikhal explained with a shrug.

"Is there enough for all of us?" Liam asked before Anthony could press him further.

"There's probably only enough for a couple of us to use, and if it's shared, it won't last very long. We'll need to be fast," Mikhal explained.

"Right yeah, we'll just be quick about defeating an impenetrable dragon in its own lair," Anthony said.

Liam turned to Anthony. He knew it would be better if Anthony didn't go into the cave with them, but he also knew Anthony would fight that idea. An anger rose in Liam's chest as he remembered first seeing his brother's face in the Tyken court. Anthony was going to be nothing but a distraction for them all.

His heart pounding, Liam closed his eyes and spoke. "I'll take Velios and you'll need to stay out here," he said quickly.

"Excuse me?" Anthony asked.

Liam peeked open his eyes to see Anthony's glare turned on him now.

"Anthony," Liam began with a shaky voice before forcing himself into a more serious tone. "I'm the one who's best suited to take down the dragon with it. My strength will—"

"Velios is mine," Anthony said firmly as he stood up and walked over to Liam. "The way it feels in my hand, it feels like a part of me. Besides, you heard what this guy said in the dungeon. The only thing he's said all day that makes any sense, if you ask me." He pointed to Mikhal. "The sword would only let its true owner hold it while it was still flaming."

Liam turned to look at Mikhal.

"That is most likely the only explanation," Mikhal said with a grimace. "The only reason Velios would not burn someone while still enchanted would be because Anthony's ancestry would allow it. Which seems nearly impossible ..." Mikahl tried to explain.

"Well then it would be mine too," Liam said sternly, standing up to meet his brother's eyes. "It's just as much mine then."

Anthony made a face. "It didn't call to you. It was too hot for you to touch and you know it." He looked into Liam's eyes. "We may share ancestry, but it chose me."

Liam rolled his eyes away from his brothers. "You weren't even supposed to be here!" Liam said in a burst of anger.

"Well it's a good thing I was!" Anthony snapped back. "You never would have gotten that sword out of the dungeon if it weren't for me!"

Liam was about to lash back with words about Anthony's irresponsibility and frivolity, but instead he stepped back from his brother and took in a deep breath.

"Fine," Liam said. He knew Anthony would react this way. "You can bring the sword into the cave. But when I ask for it, if it becomes clear I am best suited to take a shot on the dragon, you need to pass it to me." Liam looked into his brother's face seriously.

Anthony glared at him for a moment before responding. "Fine," he agreed through gritted teeth. Anthony couldn't deny that Liam had the best ability to strike the deadly blow to the dragon. "What's this guy gonna do then?" Anthony asked, pointing a thumb over to Mikhal.

Liam heard Mikhal sigh.

"We'll need some distractions," Liam said quickly before turning to look at Mikhal.

"I have some smoke bombs and some light sparklers," Mikhal said patting at his bag again. "I can also fashion a bow and some arrows tonight to—"

"You're going to make your own bow and arrows from twigs and expect that to—" Anthony jeered.

"They will only be used as distraction tools," Mikhal broke in sternly. "Like Liam said. I'll be able to work with Katerina to keep the dragon occupied while you two find a way to get close enough to strike at it."

"You want to work with Katerina, what a surprise," Anthony said mockingly.

Mikhal ignored him. "Katerina's skills will be very crucial to getting us out alive. I've never seen this dragon, but I know there's something different about him. There was always a sort of mystery surrounding this dragon and the other beasts of the Lumos Gems. The witch, she did something to them. Something that has made them vulnerable only to the weapons the Tykens forged. He's not going to be as straightforward to defeat as we might think. He's a mountain dragon, so he's going to be enormous and very strong. You guys will need all the time you can get in order to get close enough safely."

Liam nodded. "Katerina will need to be in position to shield each of us in a moment's notice," he said with a hand on his chin as he thought. "We can discuss this more when she wakes, but I think it does make sense for her to stay with Mikhal while Anthony and I take what's left of the invisibility potion to sneak up behind it. We'll be invisible, Mikhal will work on the distractions while Katerina focuses on shielding the two of you until we make our move." He looked to Anthony. "When I ask for the sword, you will pass it to me and I'll deal the striking blow to bring it down. Velios will be thrust into the dragon's flesh and the guardian will fall," Liam looked up to Mikhal.

"I'll be ready to send an arrow through his eye if needed to finish him," Mikhal offered. "The eyes are a weak point for dragons."

Liam nodded. He looked down to the ground again, hoping for a moment that Anthony would stick to the plan and not cause too much of a distraction for him.

"Anthony, let Mikhal work on those wounds," Liam ordered as he turned away quickly so Anthony couldn't protest. "I'll be back with some sticks and branches for a fire," he said as he walked away from the two of them.

He felt a swell of confidence rise within him as he continued walking away from them. He had never ordered Anthony around like that.

He turned back briefly to see Anthony sitting on his rock and Mikhal cleaning his arm. Anthony was looking at Katerina. A pang of longing struck Liam as he watched Anthony's face turn to genuine concern as he looked over Katerina. Liam wished he had someone to look at him that way. Maybe one day Caroline would.

He hadn't thought about her since they left. Would she be happy at his return? Did he even really care?

Liam was running through the forest. Running from something. Something dark. He turned to look behind him, but he could see nothing chasing him. There was just an overwhelming feeling of something sinister. He turned to look in front again and skidded to a halt.

Elyria laid on the ground in front of him. Her Riven body was sprawled out on the ground. She looked withered and her eyes were closed. Liam's heart dropped with worry.

He hurried over to her and when he knelt down to gently touch her face, she turned to water. He tried to catch the droplets of water, but they all slipped through his fingers. He looked around frantically and shouted her name.

The sun moved below the horizon unnaturally quickly and he saw a pool of water shimmering in front of him in the moonlight. He approached it slowly and Elyria swam up out of it. She smiled at him and rested her head on her hands on the edge of the pool.

Liam felt his body relax. He would finally be able to talk to her. He had so many more questions to ask her. He smiled back at her and moved to sit on the edge of the pool, his feet dangled in the water.

"I'm sorry I couldn't save you," Liam said, his voice echoed.

Elyria looked at him with unconcerned eyes. "It was not time. All needs to be consumed. Anthony doesn't have the stone yet."

Liam furrowed his brow in confusion. "But I thought you said I was the one who needed to find the stone."

Elyria backed away from the edge of the pool. "You won't see it, but it's there. The simplest entry, but the most dangerous threshold. Words are powerful. Expression is key," she said in a silvery voice before her face sank under the water line.

"Wait!" Liam exclaimed, his arm outstretched toward her.

"You must dig deep, Liam. Go within. Break free from your bonds. It is important that you see. I will take you to him," she said cryptically before she let herself be completely immersed in the water.

Liam hesitated before diving into the dark waters after her. The water's icy touch enveloped every part of his body as he pushed himself deeper.

He saw Elyria glowing as she swam farther and farther into the depths of the cold water. He did his best to follow her as she swam away from him and he quickly found that he could breathe in this darkness. It wasn't really water at all. Swimming in this void was easier than swimming through water. Elyria looked back at him and paused for a moment before smiling at him.

A spot of light appeared above them and Elyria swam up to it quickly. Liam followed, but before he could emerge, the bright light filled his vision completely, forcing him to squeeze his eyes shut.

He was then standing at the bottom of a large mountain. He craned his neck upward to view the imposing piece of rock and saw the mountain had a ring of purple smoke around the top of it. The dragon's cave.

He climbed up toward the top of the mountain, but he found it painful on his bare feet. The rocks cut into his bare skin and his feet slipped against the smooth rocks. It was a difficult climb and his muscles tired with effort, but he knew he had to keep going.

When he finally got to the top, he saw a cave opening. He knew this was it. This was where the water stone was. A dragon laid inside and it was up to him to vanquish it. Velios appeared in front of him and he grabbed it out of the air. He stepped forward into the cave confidently.

However, instead of finding himself confronted by a dragon, he found himself in a familiar bedchamber. His uncle's bedchamber with his uncle lying on the bed, coughing and sweating. And dying.

Liam rushed over. "Uncle Philip," Liam said with a shaky voice. "Hold on. Anthony and I will be back soon. Just hold on." He clutched his uncle's hand to his chest but his uncle didn't respond to his presence.

The emperor dropped his head down on his pillow after his coughing ceased and closed his eyes. He whispered something and Liam had to lean over to hear it.

"Time. Time is almost gone," his uncle whispered in his ear.

Liam felt the familiar pain of anxiety work its way through his body. He tried to comfort his uncle by squeezing his hand, but he knew he was right. They were running out of time. His uncle wouldn't be able to hold on much longer.

"Don't touch it ... " his uncle managed to gasp out between a few small coughs.

27

A terrible stiffness in her neck ached as Katerina awoke, and moving it out of the bent position made her muscles scream. She felt the hard ground beneath her and winced, covering her face with her hands and letting out a groan. She didn't want to be awake. Sleep had been such a relief, but her body begged her to move off the solid ground. Pushing herself onto her side so she could sit up, a wash of sharp pains flooded through her entire body. When she blinked open her eyes, she saw a blurry patch of firelight in front of her.

"Oh good, you're awake," a voice said with relief.

Katerina didn't answer and instead grimaced as she held her head in her hands. Her head was swimming and her eyes didn't want to stay open. She heard someone shuffling over to sit next to her.

"Here, drink some of this," the voice told her. They then guided her hand to find the cold tin of a canteen and helped lift it to her lips. As soon as she felt the cool water touch her lips, she grabbed hold of the vessel and drank greedily. She hadn't realized how dry her body felt until now. The refreshing water ran through her like a soothing drug.

After emptying the tin, she put it down and managed to flutter open her eyes again. She was sitting on the ground, surrounded by tall rocks with a small, pitiful fire sitting in front of her, flickering weakly in the chilly night air. She focused her eyes on the figure next to her through squinted eyes.

Mikhal, she thought as the recent memories flooded back.

Mikhal was here. He had come for her. Alexander was gone. They had left him in the clutches of the Tykens. He had used a portal to bring them on top of a mountain and she had disenchanted the sword. The pain in her chest grew and a lump formed in her throat as her eyes brimmed with tears. She didn't know how she was ever going to feel normal again.

Mikhal slid himself closer toward her.

"How are you feeling?" he asked.

"Physically? Mentally? Or emotionally?" Katerina asked with a hoarse voice as she handed the empty canteen back to him.

She glanced around at the makeshift campsite to see Liam and Anthony both lying on the ground a few feet away from her, huddled underneath a small blanket. She looked down to see she had Mikhal's cloak covering her.

"I guess either way, the answer is the same," she admitted and pulled the thin cloak up over her shoulders.

Mikhal nodded, but remained silent.

A trickle of emotion rose within her as she realized she was practically alone with him. She had dreamed of this moment before, but she never thought it would actually happen. After she didn't go with him, all those years ago, she never thought she would see him again.

"Have you been running this whole time?" Katerina dared to ask, looking up at Mikhal.

Mikhal nodded and looked away from her, but she didn't take her eyes from him.

"I'm sorry I had to leave," Mikhal began, looking down at his hands, but Katerina shook her head.

"You would have been caught and imprisoned … or worse," Katerina said, turning away from him, not trusting the tears to stay back.

She would never forget that night. He had asked her to go with him as they stood beneath the great oak tree they often met under, but she wasn't brave enough. She couldn't leave her home, her family, her royal lifestyle. She remembered watching him run and then returning to the castle that was crawling with Aurens searching for him.

"I should have come back," Mikhal whispered. "Once Elijah was off my trail again."

"That would have been very difficult, for us both," Katerina said. The feeling of that last night washed over her and she felt her heart breaking all over again. It took all her strength to will the tears not to fall.

"I just did not know how to get back to you without putting you in danger," Mikhal continued to explain.

Katerina forced herself to look at him, her chest almost bursting with emotion.

"I don't fault you for any of it, Mikhal. I know it may have seemed like it before, but I didn't mean that. I know you didn't abandon me," Katerina said firmly, catching his eyes with her own.

Mikhal looked away and down at her hand. "Your Streaks have gotten much worse," he said as he ran a finger over her bandages.

Katerina hugged her arm and pulled away. "Yes. That's why I sought Alexander out in the first place. I knew the Streaks were growing because I couldn't control my magic. He didn't want to help me at first, but then he found out I was a Volkev. He agreed to help me, but we didn't have much time together before all this water stone stuff started. He seemed to think I was capable of doing something like this on my own."

Mikhal smiled at her. "You are very capable."

Katerina smiled, emotions flooding her body with warmth and tingling. Her eyes searched his face and then fell on the semblance of wings that jutted out from behind him.

"Your wings," she began, her voice and face falling as she looked at them. "They've gotten worse too."

Mikhal sighed. "They have. I was trying to explain to the others that that's what originally got me interested in finding the Water Stone. And by the power of fate, my path to the Water Stone has led me back to you." He looked down at her.

Their eyes locked for a moment and then Katerina looked away. Mikhal leaned away from her and she swallowed the words she might have said. She felt the weight of the engagement necklace, still securely around her neck. She then noticed that Liam had begun to stir. She scooted herself farther away from Mikhal and hugged her knees to her chest as Liam sat up slowly and carefully. He quietly moved himself away from his brother and came to sit on the other side of Katerina, closer to the fire.

"I'm sorry if we woke you," Mikhal whispered.

Liam shook his head. "No, I ..." he began to explain before looking up at them. "I wasn't sleeping well."

Mikhal looked away from them and into the darkness of the night sky. Katerina looked up too and noticed that the moon was waning in the sky. The end of a month was upon them. A time for purging and letting go. She fondled the perfectly cut gems in her necklace. She would be married soon. Most likely by the next full moon. Her heart ached as she glanced at the face of the man she had once hoped it would be with.

Mikhal caught her staring and looked away quickly. He grabbed the canteen next to Katerina and stood.

"We need a few more arrows," he declared.

Katerina only then noticed the pile of wooden arrows stacked next to him.

"And I'll run by that stream we found to fill up on water too. We'll need it tomorrow," he explained without looking at either of them.

Katerina watched as he turned away from her and walked into the darkness. His wings lost a feather as he went and they seemed to shiver in the cold night. She looked away from them, they had never looked that bad before.

"So, you two have quite the history," Liam said, watching Mikhal go.

"That's all it is though," Katerina said. "History."

Liam nodded and came closer to the fire. He added another tiny stick to it and poked at it, trying to get the flames to rise a little more.

Feeling guilty, Katerina looked over to Anthony. His body rose and fell with his sleeping breath. "Is he all right?" she asked, pointing with her eyes.

Liam looked over at his brother. "He's fine. He's annoying, as usual, but he's fine."

Katerina smiled a genuine smile that didn't make her feel guilty. She felt safer and more relaxed as she sat with Liam. She released her hold on her legs and sat cross-legged.

"You really didn't tell him about me, did you?" Katerina asked, squinting her eyes towards Liam.

Liam looked at her seriously. "No. I promised I wouldn't."

Katerina nodded and smiled faintly before looking away from him.

"Are you ... all right?" Liam asked hesitantly, sitting down across from her and away from the fire.

She shrank into herself. Now everyone knew how weak she was.

"I'm all right. Well, I will be, at least."

"Tomorrow ..." Liam said, looking past her toward the path to the mouth of the dragon cave.

Katerina nodded. "I know."

"We're a little bit crazy for doing this aren't we?" Liam asked with a small chuckle.

Katerina smiled back. "Very much so."

Liam looked down at the ground and picked up a handful of small rocks to fiddle with. "But we have to try," he said through a long exhale.

Liam looked back at Katerina, his red curls dipped a little into one of his eyes before he moved it off his face. "We were talking earlier, the rest of us, and we were thinking that you and Mikhal would work on distracting the dragon so that Anthony and I could get close enough to use Velios."

Katerina stared past him and nodded slowly as she imagined the scene.

"But I was thinking, maybe you should have the option to stay out of it," Liam said, his eyes darting away from hers uncomfortably. "If you're not feeling up to it, that is. It would, of course, be really helpful to have you there, but ..."

"I'm not going to just sit out," Katerina said firmly, staring seriously at Liam.

He turned to meet her eyes for a second, before looking away again.

"It's just, well, you could be really hurt and I don't want you to feel like you're being forced ..."

"We could all be really hurt. And I don't feel forced into anything. I can't let this mission fail though. This whole thing cannot fail because of me. Not again. Even if it wasn't supposed to be me," she said and hugged the cloak tighter around herself.

Liam nodded, then smiled slightly.

"I admire your tenacity," he said shyly.

Katerina didn't recognize that word from her Akarian language studies.

"My tenacity?" Katerina asked. "What is tenacity?" She pronounced the word slowly.

"It means determination. It's a kind of courage."

"Oh," Katerina let the information sink in. She shook her head. "I wouldn't say I have courage though. There's a whole lot I'm afraid of still. I would have had a completely different life if I had courage."

Liam shrugged. "I've wanted to be courageous my whole life. I used to think it meant just always stepping up to do the things that scared you, but maybe there's more to it than that."

"Courage is taking the next right step," Katerina explained. "No matter what that means. You have to take that action, no matter how dangerous, no matter how life-shattering, to do that right thing. That's what courage really is. And I'm not sure I truly have that."

"I think you being here right now proves you do."

"I was supposed to go home after we found the sword and disenchanted it. We were all supposed to go home and you guys were supposed to actually prepare for this part. I just fell into this position now. And I don't have a clue what I'm doing."

"I don't either," Liam said, chuckling to himself.

Katerina's shoulders relaxed a little. "I remember feeling a small earthquake in the dungeon … was that you?"

Liam's expression changed from understanding to surprise to confusion to thoughtful all within a few seconds. "I … I don't think it was," Liam admitted.

"But who else could it have been? The walls were obsidian," Katerina asked.

Liam sighed. "Well, I met someone else while I was being held in there. The Tykens had someone else captured in there too … not in the same cell, but …" he broke off. "It's hard to explain."

"You were able to talk to someone else in there?" Katerina asked, trying to make sense of his babbling.

"Yes," Liam said with a sigh.

"Who were they? Did they teach you something?" Katerina asked.

"It was this Riven," Liam said. "I know it sounds crazy, but she … she didn't teach me anything per se, she just … wanted to help me?"

Katerina nodded slowly, but he wasn't making any sense. She could tell he didn't understand what had happened himself. "So you think all that shaking was the Riven then?"

Liam nodded. "I do. I know I'm an Earth Alumenos, but I think I have a long way to go before I'm able to unlock the ability to move the ground and all that. And there's no one to teach me anything about it either …"

He trailed off and Katerina let the words hang in the air. A stab of sadness struck her chest. She didn't have anyone left to teach her either. She had to put all her hopes on this miracle cure now.

"What if it doesn't work?" Katerina blurted out.

"What do you mean? If what doesn't work?"

"The stone. What if it's not real? What if it doesn't actually do what everyone thinks it will do?"

"It will work," Liam assured her without hesitation.

"What makes you so sure?"

Liam shrugged. "Alexander believed in this so much that he came after it twice. He's smart. He wouldn't have come after it again if he didn't have good reasons to believe it would work. And Mikhal believes it will work too. These groups of Aurens and Tykens have spent their lives protecting the secret of this stone and they've been around since its creation. And besides," Liam paused, "it's our only hope."

Katerina took a big breath in. He was right. They had to believe this would work. There was no other option.

"How do you go into this with such confidence?" Katerina asked him.

Liam laughed. "I don't. I really don't have much confidence at all, but I'm flattered that you think so."

"But you do. You really believe we can do this," Katerina said, looking at Liam thoughtfully.

"I believe that I will figure something out, yes. It would be much worse to not even try. This is the only answer for me. The only thing that matters right now. It doesn't matter how scared I am about it."

Katerina zeroed in on his use of "I". *He feels alone.*

"You're not in this alone. We're in this together," Katerina assured him. "No matter how we feel about it." She smiled at him.

Liam nodded appreciatively. "Just two magical humans with barely any knowledge on how to use their powers, a crippled, outcast Auren, and a lunatic with a sword, out to save the world," he said jokingly.

Katerina smiled another warm, genuine smile and an understanding hung in the air between them. There was something about Liam that made her feel safe; not physically safe, but something more. Something deeper.

"And the sword," Katerina said, breaking eye contact, "what made Anthony grab it like he did? It should have burned right through him."

Liam rolled his eyes and took a deep breath. "Apparently it belonged to our ancestors or something?" Liam said with uncertainty. "I guess Anthony could sense that better than I could. I was really distracted at the time though. But he seems to think the sword chose him. And maybe it did. I don't know."

Katerina nodded and then winced as a shot of pain went through her shoulder.

"Does it hurt all the time?" Liam asked, concern clear on his face.

"It does, but I can usually bare the dull pain that is always there. It's the sudden shots of sharp pain that have bothered me more recently. I think they are trying to remind me that they're there. That they are winning and will continue to take over and limit me until they are gone."

"They'll be gone tomorrow," Liam said with a gentle smile.

Katerina let the thought sink in. They really could be gone tomorrow. What would she do then? Who would she be after she was healed? The question was almost scarier for her to try to answer than the dragon fight she had to walk into come dawn.

28

Darkness stared back at Liam as he gazed, unblinking, into the dark opening of the cave in front of him. Purple fog rolled out of it eerily, signifying that they would find what they expected inside. A terrible dragon.

This is absolutely insane, he thought to himself as he dug his fingernails into his palms. *Much more experienced parties have failed. I know we have the sword, but is that really going to be enough?*

"So are we going in then?" Anthony's voice asked.

Liam peeled his eyes from the dark opening to look at his brother as Anthony pointed toward the cave with Velios after swinging it around in a circle with one hand. Liam felt a pinch of annoyance that Anthony was smiling and seemed rather calm about the dangers they were about to step into, while the mere thought made Liam's stomach turn.

Liam glanced at the others and noticed that Anthony was the only one among them who didn't look rundown and tired. They had done their best to wash up in the small stream Mikhal had found, but that did nothing to refresh their energy. They had only managed a few nuts and berries for food this morning and none of them had slept well.

Liam had felt sore and grumpy as they all prepared for the fight in awkward silence. He had been uncomfortable at first when Katerina had fashioned herself a suitable fighting outfit by removing the tattered skirt from her dress, which left her bloomers completely exposed. She tore the ruffles off the underclothes and then took one of Mikhal's shirts and tied it around herself with a sash. The garment was huge on her and covered most of her body, but it did leave her legs free to move. Liam had watched Anthony carefully remove the engagement necklace from her neck this morning and reluctantly trust Mikhal to place it in his satchel that he wore around his body.

"The invisibility potion," Mikhal said, holding out a vial of clear liquid. "You two need to be ready to down it as soon as we come upon the dragon."

Liam reached for the vial, but Anthony's hand swooped in first and grabbed it. Liam made a face at Anthony, but Anthony only smirked. Liam grabbed his wrist again, wishing he had the comforting ticking of his watch with him. He swallowed down the pang of distress he still felt with the item's absence.

"Let's move," Mikhal commanded after rolling his eyes and lit a large torch to lead the way into the cave.

The group moved forward to the dark opening of the cave. Liam watched as Katerina took in a deep breath and walked confidently behind Mikhal. Liam was glad that he had covered his crippled wings again with his cloak. Liam wished they could do this without Katerina. He wished she didn't have to walk into danger like this. He wished none of them had to walk into this, but all he could do now was say a quick prayer to Tykos for protection.

Sunlight faded from behind him as they continued into the pitch-black cave. They walked slowly, deeper and deeper into the cave. Mikhal's torch was the only thing Liam could see. His eyes searched the darkness around them and soon they were walking over piles of bones. Liam's skin crawled and he forced his eyes to stay in front of him and away from the ground. He hoped he wouldn't see if any of the bones were human bones.

Liam's shoulders ached with the amount of tension he was holding in them. He squeezed his hands into fists and ignited his strength, just a little, to make sure it was still there.

Then he felt the pulling.

It was the same feeling he had had in his chest when he first met Katerina and she wore a piece of the Earth Stone in her ring. It was the pulling of the Water Stone. It was here.

"I can feel it," Liam whispered to no one in particular. "It's definitely here."

The sounds of heavy breathing could be heard from deep within the cave. His muscles tensed, his breath became shallow, and his heart rate soared as fear and anxiety coursed through his body.

Numbly, he managed to put one foot in front of the other as they continued through the caverns; they all walked slowly, staying close together. A massive form came into view and they all stopped.

Garrock.

He looked exactly how Liam had always imagined a dragon would look, but at the same time, immensely more terrifying and completely different. Liam could barely believe what he was seeing as his eyes took in the monster.

Garrock was gigantic, with all the expected features of a large mountain dragon. Wings on his back and four legs to walk on, his reptilian shaped head had a clearly menacing look and his teeth were larger than Liam's entire body. But, instead of the scaly, muscular build Liam had imagined, the figure in front of them was missing all of that. The creature was made entirely of bones.

How is this thing alive? Liam thought to himself as he swallowed hard, trying to keep himself together. His mind wanted them all to run, get out of there and escape with their lives, but the pulling sensation in his chest was demanding the opposite.

Liam's eyes studied Garrock as he sat quietly, curled up in the center of a large cavern, his bony wings tucked back behind him. He appeared to be asleep, but it was hard to tell since he had no eyelids. A blue glow emanated from within his eye sockets and throughout his skull. Liam followed the blue glow up to the center of the dragon's forehead.

Then he saw it.

The Water Stone.

It gleamed from the center of Garrock's skull, shining brightly in the darkness of the cave.

Everyone stood for a moment, captivated by what they were seeing in front them. It seemed everyone was waiting for someone else to tell them what came next. It was the calm before the storm. The last moment before all their lives would change forever, either for better or for worse.

Finally, Mikhal cleared his throat. "All right, time to split up," he whispered as he turned back to everyone else. "He appears to be asleep or in some sort of trance or something. Liam, do you think you and Anthony could use that pile of rocks over there to get up onto that ledge?" Mikhal pointed at a pile of boulders off to the left that was piled high enough to reach an upper level of the cave. "I'm thinking if you guys can get up on that ledge, you'll have a pretty good angle to jump on top of him and plunge Velios into his skull to free the stone."

Liam considered the long, narrow ledge near the top of the cave wall. It ran just above where the dragon's head was.

"I suppose that would work," Liam said, his voice shaky and his mouth feeling drier by the second. "We don't want the dragon to know there's anyone here though. As soon as I land on him he'll be aware of our presence. I might need some time to get in the right place."

"We'll be ready with our distractions," Katerina said confidently.

"Time for the potion," Mikhal instructed, looking to Anthony.

Anthony nodded and pulled out the vial Mikhal had given him before. He popped the small cork off the bottle and took a quick sip of the potion. Liam watched eagerly to see if it was going to work. Nothing happened as he passed the bottle over to Liam.

"Give it a minute," Mikhal whispered, reading everyone's thoughts. "The potion will turn your entire body and anything in direct contact with your body invisible."

Then suddenly the outline of Anthony's body disappeared into the darkness. His excited smile faded with the rest of his body until there was nothing visible where he once stood. Even Velios appeared to be gone.

"Amazing," Anthony's voice said.

"Hurry now," Mikhal urged Liam.

Liam nodded, though he felt zero confidence as he stared at Garrock again. Surely other groups have tried this exact thing, using an invisibility potion to sneak up on the monster, but he reminded himself that the others failed because they didn't have the sword, they had Velios and they had him, an Alumenos. They could do this, despite the fact Garrock was nothing like he had expected. Why hadn't Alexander mentioned the creature was this terrifying?

Liam gathered himself and threw the liquid down his throat. He was only half-surprised that it tasted like nothing. He watched as his hands faded from visible sight along with his clothes.

"All right, come on Anthony," Liam said, moving closer to the rocks.

He heard the shuffling of Anthony's footsteps behind him as he quietly pushed aside the bones that covered the floor of the cave as he led the way. They walked in front of the dragon, Liam nearly fainting with each careful step. Finally his hands met the pile of rocks and he very cautiously climbed the boulders.

Together they climbed up the pile of rocks, along the side of the cavern, getting closer and closer to Garrock's head. Liam felt extremely exposed as he continued, but had to remind himself that Garrock couldn't see him. He just needed to be sure to be quiet. He stepped up onto the high ledge and moved over for Anthony's footprints to join his. Anthony made more noise than he would have liked and Liam froze when bits of pebble and dirt tumbled down toward Garrock with Anthony's sloppy movements.

When Garrock seemed to remain unfazed, Liam scooted along the ledge, slowly making his way closer to Garrock. He stopped when he came directly above the sleeping dragon. Liam watched as it laid quietly below him, its breath the only thing visible.

"All right Anthony, hand me the sword, carefully," Liam whispered, extending his arm out to Anthony to feel for the sword.

"It seems far. Are you sure you want to jump down there?" Anthony asked.

"Well, no, I don't really want to …" Liam admitted with annoyance.

"Maybe I should do it then," Anthony's voice suggested.

Anger flashed through Liam.

"You promised you would hand me the sword when I asked," Liam reminded his brother.

Below them, Garrock stirred slightly, alerting Liam.

"I just think …" Anthony began to explain, but Liam was focused on Garrock now.

Terror filled his limbs as the dragon stirred some more and uncurled himself from his resting position. He lifted his head and stood up taller. Liam's adrenaline spiked and he thought he might be sick.

I've got to move now! Liam's mind screamed at him.

He turned his head to demand that Anthony hand him the sword instantly when he heard something landing on bones.

"Anthony?" Liam whispered loudly, but there was no answer.

Liam looked back down at the dragon and was flooded with fury and panic as the dragon screeched. Anthony had jumped.

Frozen in place, Liam's brain spun as he tried to determine what to do next. Anger flashed through him and he scolded himself for even allowing Anthony to come in with them. The anger quickly faded, however, leaving immeasurable fear as his eyes focused on the figure of his brother.

The potion was already wearing off. With every second, they were becoming more and more visible. Liam's stomach dropped. They would soon to be completely exposed. Completely unprotected in front of a very angry, very terrifying dragon. Anthony hung on tightly to one of the bone spikes on the dragon's head with one hand still firmly grasping the sword. The dragon shook its head fiercely, trying to shake Anthony off.

Where are they with those distractions?

Garrock caught sight of Liam as he shook his head and snapped his head toward him as his body faded back into existence. Liam felt his breath stop in his chest as the dragon's eyes narrowed in on him. It glared before letting out a terrifying shriek and turning its body.

Then an arrow came flying out of the sky. The arrow hit Garrock in the back of the head and bounced off. He roared in annoyance, the arrow simply clattering to the ground, but doing its part to draw Garrock's attention.

A bright light flew into the dragon's face as he turned, causing him to roar and shake its head again.

Anthony yelled as he was forced to drop the sword in order to keep his grip on the dragon's head. Liam could tell Anthony would not be able to hold on much longer.

Without a moment of hesitation, Liam jumped off the ledge after his brother. He slid down the side of the wall and flared his power before landing clumsily on the floor. Liam rolled and got up. He looked up to see Anthony barely hanging on. Against all his instincts, Liam ran over to the dragon just as Garrock let out a stream of fire from his gullet toward where Katerina and Mikhal stood.

The blast caused Anthony to release his hold completely and he plummeted to the ground.

Liam's body hummed as he turned on his strength and stretched himself out to break Anthony's fall. Anthony collided with Liam's arms as he jumped out to catch him. They both fell to the ground, rolling and sliding among the bones and dirt.

"Are you all right?" Liam asked his brother through gasps of air.

Anthony groaned. "My ankle."

Liam smacked Anthony on the back of his head. "You idiot! Why did you …" Liam began and then stopped himself. "We don't have time for this now. Where's the sword?" He looked around on the ground near them.

He saw the gleam of the bright metal a few feet away from where they landed.

"Stay here," Liam commanded Anthony.

"Wait," Anthony said, grabbing Liam's shirt. "It didn't work."

"What do you mean it didn't work? What didn't work?"

"The sword. It didn't work. I tried to pierce the stone, it didn't work. I even tried to stab him in the forehead and in the neck. Nothing."

Liam paused, looking into the dirt-covered face of his brother. The sword had to work though. Alexander said it would. Even Mikhal said it would.

"Stay here," Liam repeated and left Anthony behind a pile of rocks.

"You can't just …" Anthony started to say, but Liam wasn't interested in hearing the rest.

He ran and picked up the sword and then bolted over to Katerina and Mikhal right after the dragon completed another blast of fire in their direction. Liam noticed as he ran that the dragon's flames curiously remained alight on the bones around them. He jumped over pieces of bone and slid to a halt next to Mikhal.

"What happened?" Mikhal asked, his eyes wide.

"Where's Anthony?" Katerina asked, worry filling her face.

"Anthony's fine," Liam answered.

Katerina yelled something, making Liam jump, and a blast of light went flying toward the dragon's face.

"There is one problem though," Liam continued, backing up and turning to face the dragon. "The sword didn't work."

Mikhal shot another arrow at the dragon and then both he and Katerina stopped what they were doing for a split second to look at him.

"Did you stab the stone?" Mikhal asked, looking at the sword in Liam's hand.

The dragon shrieked behind him and took a deep inhale. Katerina yelled her shield spell and Liam watched as she held back the blast of fire with an invisible wall, pushing hard against the energy of the fire, her hands outstretched.

"I didn't …" Liam began to explain, but they didn't have time. "Yes, and the forehead, and the neck. I'm telling you, it didn't work. We need to get out of here."

Mikhal shook his head.

"We just need to find the right place," Katerina explained as she blasted another burst of light into the dragon's face. "The sword is the only thing keeping this dragon alive. We just need to find the keyhole."

The dragon blasted another round of intensely hot fire at them. Katerina shielded them from it, but Liam could still feel the heat around them. The fire faded and Katerina let down the shield, dropping her arms. Keeping his eyes on the dragon, Mikhal handed her a small leather pouch. Katerina quickly snatched it from him and drank greedily from it.

Before she could put down the pouch, the dragon's patience with the little humans ran out and he lunged. His mouth opened as his frighteningly large and pointy teeth came straight at them. Katerina screamed and tried to push the dragon back with some sort of spell, but whatever she tried, didn't seem to detour Garrock at all. He looked as if he was smiling as his skull swooped toward them. Liam moved into action. He threw the sword to the side and pulled Katerina behind him.

Liam stood between the others and their certain death as Garrock's jaw widened to engulf them. Liam spread his arms wide, one arm over his head and the other reaching downward, and called upon his strength. Garrock's teeth collided with Liam as he caught the maw in his hands, holding firmly to two teeth above and below him. Liam grunted, flaring his power with everything he could muster. The dragon seemed confused and paused with his jaw held open by Liam's sheer strength.

It was the most terrifying thing Liam had ever done in his life. Failing the Tykerial Guard exam, being made into an outcast, watching his uncle collapse and fight through a terrible disease, discovering his powers, fighting Tykens, being thrown into prison, losing Alexander, all seemed so small as he stared down the throat of the impenetrable, bone dragon.

Then he saw the hole. A normal looking keyhole, as if on a door, flashed above him. The keyhole, the answer to his prayers gleamed above him. It was in the top of the dragon's mouth.

The simplest entry, but the most dangerous threshold.

Elyria's words flashed in his mind.

Words are powerful. Expression is key.

Elyria had hinted at the location of the keyhole. Why she couldn't have just told him, Liam didn't know, but it all made sense now.

Liam could see the searing blue fire building up in the back of the dragon's throat as he struggled against Liam's hold more fiercely, and Liam roared as he used his strength to throw the dragon to one side. Releasing his hold on the teeth, the dragon's bones crashed into the ground and slid into the cave wall. The ground shook violently and bits of rock and dirt broke free from the ceiling, raining down on them.

Liam turned to Mikhal and Katerina. They crouched down behind him, Mikhal shielding Katerina from the falling rubble.

"It's in his mouth," Liam said, his voice shaking with adrenaline.

The other two looked up at him, confusion clear on their faces.

"The keyhole. I saw it, it's in the roof of his mouth," Liam finished explaining as he pointed at Garrock. Fatigue slammed into him and he felt the absence of his power. He knelt down on one knee, trying to catch his breath.

Mikhal jumped to his feet and swiped the sword off the ground as he passed by Liam. He twirled the weapon in his hand before gripping it with two hands, lifting it to his shoulder and then ran for the dragon.

Liam rolled his eyes. *Why does everyone else insist on going against the plan?*

The dragon, still slightly dazed from being thrown across the cave, lifted his head to Mikhal as he approached. Garrock roared at Mikhal, but only sputters of blue flame escaped him. The dragon rolled to get to his feet and as Mikhal approached, the dragon lifted a claw and swatted Mikhal to the side. Mikhal was sent flying across the cave, crashing into a pile of bones and slamming against the hard cave wall. Velios flew from his grip.

"Mikhal!" Katerina screamed.

Katerina pushed a gust of air toward the dragon and Garrock's head snapped back with sudden force. With the dragon briefly distracted, Katerina ran to Mikhal and Liam ran after the sword.

Garrock spun himself around and his tail caught Liam square in the stomach just before he could pick the sword up. The blow surely would have broken his ribs if Liam hadn't been able to flare his strength just in time, allowing him to catch the dragon's tail in his arms.

Something moved out of the corner of Liam's eye and he turned his head to see Anthony running over to the sword now. Liam hurried to push the dragon's tail off him, fear fueling his strength. Liam darted toward the sword. Katerina stood in front of Mikhal, who was still lying on the ground, unmoving. She yelled spell after spell, throwing gusts of wind, bursts of light, and even small bits of rock and flame at the dragon. Liam could see her shoulders start to slump and her cadence slowed. She was running out of energy.

They all were.

Liam raced forward, nonetheless, toward Anthony who had already picked up the sword at this point and stood staring up at the dragon. Garrock's fury peaked

239

and he spread his wings wide in a show of intimidation and warning. The wings smashed into the sides of the cave, causing more of the cavern to crumble. Liam slowed down and lifted his arms above his head to shield himself.

Katerina yelled out a spell again, but stumbled forward and fell to the ground in exhaustion as the magic left her hands. The blast of fire she released veered off course and instead of hitting the dragon, buried into the cave wall right above Anthony.

Liam felt his stomach drop as he watched the cave wall begin to crumble. He sprinted forward with all the energy he had left. Rock, dirt, and ash poured down from the side of the cave in a massive landslide. Anthony ran, but Liam knew he hadn't noticed it fast enough. He would be buried in a matter of seconds.

Liam felt as if he was running in slow motion as he watched the rocks tumble toward Anthony's fleeing body. He knew what he had to do. There was no question that he wouldn't, but the thought still frightened him. This was not only going to be painful, but perhaps even fatal.

Courage is taking the next right step.

Liam stretched out his body as he jumped forward, his hands making contact with Anthony's shoulder just as the rocks and dirt enveloped him. He shoved Anthony out of the way, flaring every bit of strength he had left inside him. Anthony was thrown out of the way just in time and soared toward Katerina and Mikhal. Liam felt a sense of relief even as the rocks fell over him.

He landed on his side and bounced slightly off the hard ground as he hit. He could only lay there with the fluttering of what strength he had left pulsing through him as the rocks flooded over him. They buried him quickly and he was left in complete darkness.

29

*G*o within. Break free ...

No matter how life-shattering ...

You're not in this alone ...

These phrases ran through Liam's head as he laid, paralyzed and helpless in the pitch dark. He had gone unconscious for a few moments, but he was apparently still alive. He tried to move, but he was completely pinned down by the weight of the boulders. He felt within for the vibration of his power. It was only a very faint pulsing.

The weight of the rocks sank into him, suffocating him slowly. The immense pressure pushed on his chest and he could feel the small bit of his power that had kept him alive thus far completely fade. He tried to surge the power again, but it was gone. He had nothing left.

It won't be long now, he thought to himself as the boulders crushed him.

All needs to be consumed.

Break free from your bonds.

He remembered Elyria's words again. They stirred something within him and images flashed through his mind.

He remembered how he had admired Katerina's courage when she agreed to follow him and Alexander on this quest. She never gave up, even when she wanted to. His mind replayed how she had disenchanted the sword. It had taken everything out of her. It had made her faint. She was sick with the Streaks, but still she fought valiantly against the dragon.

He saw Anthony's grin and then the image rushed into his head when he had seen Anthony at the Tyken court in Tykerial Guard armor. But behind all his posturing, Anthony had only wanted to do good. To be the hero. It was something that Liam could understand.

Then he saw his uncle, lying so helplessly in bed. Fighting to stay alive for his nephews and his country. There was so much more he needed to do. There was so much more that Liam needed from him. But his uncle was the one who needed him right now.

Liam heard the crying of Katerina and the shouts from Anthony from somewhere far away. They needed him right now too.

He needed to get up.

For his uncle, for his brother, for Katerina, for Akaria.

He dug his hands into the ground. He grabbed fists of rock and dirt and he could *feel* the earth stir something within him. The element suddenly felt like a piece of himself. He could feel the earth all around him now. Every boulder stacked on top of him, the ground that stretched out across the entire cavern, the stalactites, the rock walls.

He could sense all of it.

The rocks lying on top of him moved. The weight on his chest decreased. He willed the stones to lift away from him and they obeyed. Slowly at first, and then all at once, the boulders flew away from him and he burst out from under all the rubble.

Rocks flew through the air as Liam stood up in the center of the pile. He stretched his arms out wide and slowed the rocks down before they crashed into anything. Garrock turned slowly to look at Liam, as did Katerina and Anthony.

"Liam!" Anthony yelled and fell to his knees.

Katerina simply stared. In shock at what she was witnessing.

Liam turned to Garrock and moved the earth beneath him to drag him away from the others. Liam slammed the dragon against the far wall and then brought his hands down in a forceful motion, commanding the stalactites to fall to the ground around Garrock. They surrounded him, making a fence around him, and then Liam sank the ground beneath the dragon to make a small pit.

The dragon stumbled as the ground sank beneath him. He tried to extend his wings and shoot fire toward Liam, but Liam lifted all the boulders that had once engulfed him and directed them to surround Garrock. The boulders went flying through the air and enclosed around Garrock as the beast shrieked in frustration. He was completely immobilized, buried beneath the rocks and held in place by stalactites. Only the blue glow of his eyes showed through the mountain of rocks.

Liam held the pieces of earth in place around Garrock, his hands stretched out before him and looked over toward Anthony. Anthony and Katerina ran over to his side, sword held tight in Anthony's hand.

"I thought we had lost you!" Anthony said, his eyes red as he approached his brother.

"How did you …" Katerina began to ask, her eyes still wide with amazement.

"I …" Liam stammered. "I'm really not sure how. But I suppose being completely immersed under earth really will unlock the elemental abilities of the Earth Alumenos."

Anthony smiled proudly at his brother and nodded.

"I have him secured for now, but …" Liam said, turning to look at Garrock. "I won't be able to hold him forever. I don't even know how I'm doing this right now," he admitted.

"What do we do?" Katerina asked.

"I need to get to the keyhole. I need to stab him through the roof of his mouth," Liam explained again.

Anthony laughed. Katerina looked at Garrock, her face creasing into lines of worry.

"All right, so I just need to get up there," Anthony said, eyeing the dragon as he struggled against his rocky prison.

"No, Anthony," Liam argued.

"It has to be me, Liam," Anthony said seriously, looking into Liam's eyes as he turned to his brother. "I messed up before, I realize that. I was stupid. I admit it. But this time, it really has to be me. You have to hold him down and I need to stab him."

Liam looked intensely at his brother. His green eyes locked with his brother's blue eyes. He saw his brother begging him to trust him in those eyes. Liam paused for a moment and then he nodded his head once in agreement.

"I'm going to let go of the boulder in front of his face," Liam said, the others looking at him intently. "Katerina, you'll need to shield one last blast of fire, and when that blast runs out, he'll need a few minutes to gather enough fire within himself again before he can shoot any more. I'll release the hold on the boulders around the rest of his body and I expect he'll charge at us like he did before when I found the keyhole. I'll keep his mouth open and Anthony, you get the sword into the keyhole and break this spell," Liam explained.

The other two nodded in agreement, though they looked just as nervous and scared as Liam felt. Liam took a deep breath in and out.

"On the count of three," Liam instructed. "One, two, three!" He released the hold on the boulder that covered the dragon's face.

Garrock stuck his head through the new hole and roared viciously. Liam thought he saw a tinge of red in his glowing blue eyes as he glared at Liam. Garrock fought against the rest of the rocks that surrounded him and Liam had to concentrate to keep them all in place. He could feel the pushing against them and he doubted he'd be able to keep the dragon contained.

Then Garrock's patience ran out and he blasted a stream of blue fire toward them, just as Liam had predicted.

"*Shorovit!*" Katerina yelled strongly as she stepped out in front of Liam. An invisible shield formed in front of them and the fire dispersed around it.

She held the shield in place until the fire disappeared, and then sank down to the ground, catching herself on her hands. Anthony ran out in front of them, sword in hand.

"Please Tykos, let this work," Liam prayed and released his hold on all the earth elements.

A huge strain lifted off Liam's body and the boulders fell from around Garrock. The dragon was freed. Garrock stepped easily out of the shallow pit Liam had dug and swooped closer to Anthony as he ran toward him.

Liam picked up two larger rocks out of the pile that had just fallen to the ground and summoned them quickly. The dragon still charged at his brother, so he directed the rocks toward Garrock's face.

Garrock opened his mouth, like he had before, and made a move to scoop Anthony into it. Liam placed the boulders inside Garrock's mouth and pushed them against the roof and the bottom of his jaw.

The dragon's mouth was held open forcefully as it swung at Anthony. Anthony jumped into the dragon's maw without any hesitation and Liam's hopes soared.

This was it.

Then the boulder holding the top of the dragon's mouth open slipped. Liam had stopped focusing on it for only a second or two and with the dragon still in motion, it slipped out of position.

The dragon's mouth snapped shut and Liam's heart stopped.

"Anthony!" Liam screamed and he tried to use the other boulder to pry open the bottom of the dragon's mouth but the dragon had displaced that one as well.

Garrock straightened himself up, rising high above Liam and stretching out his wings victoriously. He looked as if he was gloating.

Liam's whole body panicked and he raised all the stones into the air around the dragon again.

But the blue glow that sat on top of his head went out. Liam watched as the stone fell from the top of Garrock's head and hurtled toward the ground.

30

Katerina watched as a look of confusion flooded Garrock's eyes. The eyes lost their sinister blue glow and faded into a dull gray. Katerina pushed herself up to watch as Liam released the boulders that he had raised into the air. Garrock staggered slightly and began to sink down. The ground rumbled as he hit the floor, causing rocks and rubble to fall from the ceiling again. Garrock's eyes softened and Katerina felt a pang of pity for the creature.

Then his eyes went completely dark and the bones dispersed from their frame and collapsed to the ground. Bits of bone and dust flew through the cave.

Katerina raised her arm to cover her face to shield herself from the flying pieces of bone. When she slowly lowered her arm and looked around in the dim lighting, the dragon's flames remained burning on the scattered bones and debris in the cave and the silence was suddenly deafening.

A breeze blew through her hair as she recalled how the dragon had looked at her. It had seemed to be smiling as it took her in and prepared to end her with his blast of fire.

She squeezed her eyes shut and let the chills run through her again. But it was over. Anthony had done it. He had put himself in the most dangerous position and placed the key into the lock to end the spell. A pang of guilt shot through her—what had happened to him?

Someone yelled out. "Anthony? Katerina? Anyone?"

Katerina opened her eyes and could barely see the outline of Liam standing in front of her, hunched over slightly and holding his arm to his chest. He looked around the cave and turned toward Katerina. His eyes quickly darted around before he found her. She saw the sharp fear in his eyes dissipate slightly.

"I'm here," Katerina managed to say with a shaky voice.

"Oh thank the gods, Katerina," Liam said with clear relief as he shuffled closer to her.

Then he suddenly turned away. "Anthony?" he called out into the large cave, but there was no answer. Liam called his brother's name again and he limped away from Katerina and shuffled through the clutter of the cave floor, searching through the bones that had exploded around them.

Katerina sat up and turned back to Mikhal. He laid behind on her on his side, his eyes closed.

"Mikhal?" she asked gently and she crawled over to him. "Mikhal, are you …?"

Mikhal groaned slightly and Katerina felt her shoulders relax a little in relief. He was alive.

"Are you all right? How bad are you hurt?" Katerina asked as she put a hand on his shoulder.

He was breathing heavily as he answered. "Hard to say exactly …" Mikhal said through gasps of air. "But I know the pain is exquisite. Are you all right?"

Katerina smiled. "I'm fine," she told him, though she could feel the fatigue pulling her down.

She glanced over his back and her smile was immediately wiped from her face. She saw a piece of his wing dangling behind him. Her body shivered as she realized they were completely broken, nearly shattered now.

"Good," he said. "It would be great if we had some magical healing powers about now though, wouldn't it?"

Katerina smiled slightly and turned back toward where the dragon and the stone had once stood. There was only a pile of bones and rock now and she couldn't see the glow of the Water Stone anymore.

"Anthony!" Liam yelled again, his voice cracking with worry.

Katerina turned and searched behind her for signs of Anthony. Exhaustion crept in deeper as the light in the cave faded. She looked around at the flames that still flickered around them. They were dimming and beginning to go out. They'd never find Anthony or the stone in the pitch black.

Just one more spell, Katerina nearly begged herself.

An ache rose in her chest and her shoulder burned, but she had to push through it. If there was any time to push past the pain, it was now, when she was so close. The stone was there, Anthony was there, just under a bunch of rocks.

They had to be.

Katerina called upon every ounce of strength she had left and lifted her hands out to the sides, over the dying flames.

"*Ogon*," Katerina said softly. She felt the pulling and the draining of her powers through her arm. It was painful this time, burning as it made its way through her.

"*Ogon*," Katerina repeated with more fervor, but still the flames dimmed. She focused on the spell, the heat she wanted to produce, the flames of the fire spell she had done on accident in her chambers with her sister. She had been so frustrated with Anya. Like she always was with her sister ... "*Ogon*," she said confidently, using the remembered anger to fuel her.

The magic ripped through her body and she almost had to scream as the magic rushed out of her. Chest heaving, pain searing, Katerina pushed her intention into the flames around her. The whole cave became luminous again as the flames reignited and suddenly she could see everything clearly.

She wished she couldn't.

Katerina looked around at the dank, dark cave. The smell of musty dirt and charred bones overwhelmed her and she suddenly felt every speck of dirt and ash that caked her face and arms. Bones, rocks, and ash covered the floor of the cave. Large piles of bones stood piled up high in the corner and the pile of rocks that had surrounded the dragon were still strewn in the middle of the room.

Katerina staggered backward. Weakness gripped her and the room spun as she was forced to kneel down to the ground. Her body begged her to collapse, the fatigue close to overtaking her. And when her hair swung in front of her face, she saw she had a clear patch of white running through her hair now. She had never done so much magic in such a short period before and while it had felt so natural at the time, she was paying the price now.

"Anthony!" Liam shouted with elated relief. Katerina watched as he ran over to Anthony who laid on his back, only his boots visible through the rubble and bones.

Katerina closed her eyes, hoping to ease the pain, and sat back on the ground. She could feel the world spin around her even in darkness. She peeked her eyes open slightly and looked down at her arm as she lifted her sleeve. The Streaks crept up to her wrist now, searing and burning with more pain than she thought she could take.

She swayed in her seated position and couldn't keep herself upright anymore. Her torso flopped onto the ground and she could barely keep her eyes open. She heard Anthony groaning and then the sound of bones clattering.

"Ugh," she heard as she managed to direct her eyes up to see Liam pulling Anthony by his arms to sit him upright. They were just a blur. Her eyes wouldn't focus. She felt immediately more relaxed when she realized Anthony was talking.

"Ugh," Anthony repeated. "My back is killing me …"

"You're alive. Thank all the gods! Are you all right besides your back?" Liam asked as his blur moved around Anthony's blur, checking to see if there was anything glaringly wrong with him.

"I think so …" Anthony said. "Is everyone all right? Where's my sword?"

"I don't know where Velios landed, but everyone is hanging in there," Liam said before pausing for a few moments. "The Water Stone is nowhere in sight, but I can feel it's here somewhere."

Liam's blur moved around quickly and the two brother's voices became incoherent. She heard the moving of rocks and bones as they searched through the piles of rubble. Katerina laid her head down on the ground.

She let the doubt creep in. The dragon was just a spell. An illusion. Had they even really seen the Water Stone in the dragon's head or was that just an illusion too?

Katerina began to lose consciousness. The darkness closed in around her. She felt her heart beat in her chest and her breathing became more hastened. She started to sweat and she couldn't move her body anymore. She believed this feeling would never leave as her thoughts spiraled. Maybe she was on the brink of madness, the brink of calling forth a DarkHeart. The stone wasn't even real.

Darkness.

She didn't know how long she laid there before she felt something. A soothing feeling of warmth started to come from her right hand. It traveled up her arm and into her chest like a flow of warm water. The feeling completely engulfed her and seeped into her core. She let herself smile, enjoying the sensation that she was sure her mind was inventing for her.

But then the warmth left and the pain didn't return. Her mind cleared and she felt she could open her eyes again. Fluttering her eyelids open, she turned to look at her arm, fully expecting to see the dark, ugly Streaks, or something perhaps even worse in her delusion, but that's not what she saw.

A swirling blue glow emanated up her arm as the lines, the veins, cracking black scars disappeared. They faded before her eyes. The warm sensation returned and it continued its flow through her entire body. She looked up and saw Anthony sitting next to her, keeping his focus on her arm. He was healing her. He had the stone and he was healing her. They had found it and it was actually working.

Sobs of relief and uncontrollable bouts of laughter began to fight their way out of her. Her chest heaved up and down and tears burst from her eyes. She felt her body shake with all the emotion and she was unable to keep her hands steady as he turned to look at her. She locked on to his beautiful blue eyes.

"Thank you," Katerina said as she calmed her sobs. "I had lost hope for a moment, but you …"

"I wouldn't have jumped into the mouth of a bone dragon for anything other than a happy ending," he said with a smirk. Then he took the glowing blue stone from her palm and stood up.

"Mikhal," Katerina whispered as she sat up. "He needs it, badly."

"No," Mikhal said through wheezing breaths. "No, Liam needs to touch the stone first."

"But Mikhal you're—" Katerina began to argue.

"No, hurry, hand it to Liam," he said almost frantically. She heard a fear in his voice that made her uneasy. "Please, don't make me explain right now."

Confused, Katerina took Anthony's hand and he helped her onto her feet. He handed the stone to her, giving her the choice of what to do next. She wobbled a bit at first as the blood rushed back into her legs and then walked closer to Liam.

His face lit up when he saw what she held before him. She didn't think she'd ever seen such relief and joy on his face before. He had been so stressed and so concerned the whole time she'd known him. She smiled warmly and proudly as she presented the stone to him.

"The Water Stone," she said officially and offered it out to him.

Liam smiled and looked past her toward Anthony. Liam shook his head and exhaled in disbelief before reaching out for the stone.

Then he stopped, his face fell, his eyes narrowed in thought. He pulled his hand back, his lips pressed into a thin line.

"What's wrong?" Katerina asked with confusion.

251

"I don't ..." Liam began to explain, but before he could finish his thought, a brilliant light filled the entire cave.

Katerina squinted her eyes at the artificially bright light and turned around. As her eyes adjusted or the light dimmed, she saw five figures floating through the air above her.

31

"No …" Liam heard Mikhal say as he pushed himself up. "They're here," he grunted out.

Liam looked into Mikhal's eyes and saw pure sorrow there. The bright light dimmed and Liam squinted his eyes as he looked toward it again. Large, shadowed figures came into view and Liam couldn't believe his eyes when he saw who they were.

A group of Aurens with pristinely white, beautiful wings, dressed in shining gold armor, flooded into the cavern with bows drawn.

They've found him.

"Liam! Grab the stone! NOW!" Mikhal cried out.

Liam scrunched his forehead in confusion at the desperate command, but before Liam could even turn his head again, arrows flew through the air swiftly around him. Liam instinctively moved in front of Katerina to shield her from the onslaught. He nearly pushed her to the ground as he clumsily covered her. Liam glanced up and saw that the arrows had landed around them in a perfect circle. They had apparently only shot at them to scare them.

Then he heard cries of agony and snapped his head toward the sound. His knees nearly buckled beneath him as he watched three of the Aurens stand over Mikhal. He writhed in pain on the ground as the Aurens held strange wands, emanating a yellow light, over him.

"What are you doing to him?" Katerina yelled at them, pushing Liam off her. "*Veter!*" she yelled, but nothing happened.

She looked at her hands with confusion before more arrows were shot right at their feet.

Black arrows. Obsidian arrows. Liam's heart sank at the sight as Katerina wavered away from the arrows in front of her.

The Aurens pulled Mikhal's arms behind his back forcefully and pushed his face into the ground. They bound his hands with rope and one of them stood with a foot on his back, pressing him harder into the ground.

Liam could feel the heaviness that he had felt in the dungeon wash over him again. Then he saw one of the Aurens still floating above him, holding a bundle of green rope.

The toxic vines.

He saw Katerina and Anthony glance over to him. They needed him to get them out of this, but his strength was spent. Even if they didn't have some of the vine, he couldn't feel the vibrations within anymore. He should have taken the stone. It surely would have restored his strength.

The Auren decided to take no chances with Liam and released a green net over him. Liam covered his head and then fell to his knees as the vines bit into his skin, the weights on the edges of the vines sank down into the ground around him. He was instantly nauseous and extremely weak. His heart beat loudly in his ears and he fell onto his hands and knees.

Liam avoided looking at Anthony and Katerina and looked back up at the Aurens through the holes in the net. He watched as an Auren with just a simple white tunic and sandals that laced up his legs landed gently in front of him.

"What do you think you're doing? Release them!" Anthony demanded angrily and charged toward the unarmored Auren.

The Auren flicked his wrist toward one of the other Aurens and one of them grabbed Anthony by the shoulders and dragged him backward. Anthony struggled in his grip and started to protest, until the Auren placed a tight gag around his mouth and bound his hands behind him. Liam gave Anthony a sharp, pleading look, asking him not to struggle anymore. Anthony settled himself and scowled at the Auren in the middle as he walked over to Mikhal, who was still being held to the ground by the armored Aurens.

The Auren calmly unhooked a short cylinder from his belt. He expanded the small tube into a long staff by pushing a button on the top of cylinder. Then he shoved the long staff into the ground. He then placed a ball on top of the pole and twisted it into place. He tapped the ball once and an ear-splitting, horrendous noise suddenly emanated throughout the cave.

Liam squeezed his eyes shut and covered his ears. He forced his eyes open to see a dazzling blue light flying away from Katerina. Liam reached through the net desperately for the stone as it flew in front of him, but only managed to get a finger on it before it continued past him.

The Auren caught the stone easily and wiped it clean on his tunic. Liam stared at the artifact. It glowed with a blue light, the magic dancing in silver swirls inside of it. Liam's finger tingled where he had touched it moments before and then a searing pain shot through his arm briefly.

"The stone is ours," Liam said firmly.

The Auren turned the stone over in his hand, looking at it with an unimpressed expression. Then he turned to Liam, a smug smile growing on his face.

"We do thank you for breaking the spell on the dragon. We could not have done that on our own," he said and looked to Katerina next. "Only a Volkev could have disenchanted the sword and I'm sure the strength of an Earth Alumenos was quite handy in fighting the enormous beast."

"That stone is the rightful property of the Akarian empire!" Anthony tried to mumble through his gag as he struggled toward the Auren.

"Michael, Michael, Michael …" the Auren said, ignoring Anthony. A smug smile spread across the Auren's face before he said something in a language that Liam couldn't understand.

"Elijah," Mikhal nearly spat as he wiggled against the arms and feet that held him down. "You're not supposed to be here."

Elijah crouched down next to Mikhal and lifted his chin toward him. Liam watched fury and hatred pour from Mikhal's eyes before Elijah threw his chin to the side in disgust and stood up.

He then examined Mikhal's wings with interest, gliding a finger across them as Mikhal moaned in pain.

"This does look very painful," Elijah said, dragging out the word 'very' as he walked around Mikhal. "Such a shame this had to happen to you. Though what else can you expect me to do when you go against your promises to the Protectorate."

Elijah looked at the Water Stone in his hand again, curiosity gleaming there.

"We always did wonder if the legends were true, didn't we?" Elijah asked and then he waved off the other Aurens that were holding Mikhal down.

The Aurens stepped away from Mikhal and Elijah held the stone up to Mikhal's wings. The stone glowed. A bright blue. Liam was mesmerized by the sight, but found himself in even more awe as he watched the magic work.

From the point where the stone touched his wings, Mikhal's wings began to heal. Blue swirls trickled through the tattered wings and the crippled, decrepit gray wings disappeared one feather at a time, leaving behind the beautifully brilliant white feathers that the other Aurens sported. When the blue swirls reached the last feather, the wings flapped strongly behind Mikhal. Liam watched Mikhal's face fill with relief and elation. He saw the tears lying in the corners of his eyes as he looked down at the ground, ceasing all his struggling and fighting.

He must have been in so much pain, Liam thought to himself as he watched his agony disappear.

With the healing complete, Elijah stepped back from Mikhal.

"So, it does work on Aurens," Elijah said looking intensely at the stone in his hand. "That's interesting. This one is indeed different." He turned his glance back toward Mikhal.

"You kept your word by leading us here and handing over the stone. I shall keep the rest of our bargain beyond your healing," Elijah said as Mikhal picked himself up off the ground. "Your debt is paid. You are now free from the pursuit of the Protectorate."

Liam felt a burst of chills run through his body.

Mikhal did this? He knew they were coming for the stone? He led them here?

He looked to Katerina and watched as she fell to her knees. The emotions of grief and betrayal written clearly across on her face.

Elijah kept his eyes locked with Mikhal's as he handed the stone over to one of his other companions. The other Auren took the stone and carefully set it in a wooden box, latching the box with a click.

Elijah turned away from Mikhal with a smirk and ascended into the air without another glance at the humans. The Aurens surrounding Mikhal blasted him with another jab of their paralyzing wands and the Auren holding Anthony released him by pushing him toward the ground. Then one of the Aurens ripped the net off Liam, the green vines cutting through Liam's skin as it dragged away.

Liam pressed himself up onto one knee, air filling his lungs in gasps. Then he watched as all the Aurens followed behind Elijah, swiftly exiting the cave.

"Elijah!" Mikhal yelled at him as he ran after him. "This isn't what we agreed on!" He tried to use his wings, but they seized up on him, refusing to expand. He threw rocks toward them, trying to get any of the Aurens' attention again, but the Aurens continued out of the cave.

Anthony ran after the Aurens as well, yelling and cursing and throwing stones at them, demanding they listen to the Princep of Akaria.

Two of the Aurens suddenly turned back and raised the tips of their arrows in the air with tightened bows. They shot arrows directly at Liam and Katerina this time, piercing them each through the chest. Liam fell backward, shock gripping his body and watching with horror as Katerina fell beside him.

"You promised I could bring you the stone! They were never supposed to get hurt! You know what those arrows will do to her!" Mikhal continued to yell after the Aurens, falling to his knees, begging with all his heart.

Liam felt a panic rise within him as he watched Mikhal try to take flight once again but failed.

This couldn't be happening.

He hadn't felt this level of deep regret since the fire. He should have done better. He should have been able to stop this. Why did they trust Mikhal? His vision blurred and the shape of the Aurens, who were leaving with the Water Stone, disappeared into the distance.

He felt a wave of coolness wash over him as he let his eyes close.

Then there was only darkness.

ACKNOWLEDGMENTS

I t's quite astounding when I look back at the journey this story has taken and all the people who have had a hand in making it come to life. The characters have changed immensely, some have even come and gone, but the people who have made this book possible were always constant in their support.

First off, I have to thank my parents Jennie and Alfredo. They have always told me I could be anything I wanted to be and I have always believed them. They were responsible for buying me that pair of new shoes that summer before fifth grade that ended up sprouting the imagination branches for the beginnings of this very story. I have never doubted their support and I could not have gone on this journey without knowing they fully believed in me.

My grammy and papa, JoAnn and Mike, had a tremendous hand in this book as well. They nurtured every single ounce of magical playtime in their backyard that the branches of imagination were planted in. I miss my grandma every day, but I know she's smiling down at this accomplishment that she always knew would happen.

And a huge thanks goes to my true partner in life, my husband Scott. He took on the house work, the errands, the cooking and planning for family events, and even the administrative work of setting up the business side and my website. Taking on all these things allowed me the time and energy to focus on the fun stuff—the brainstorming, planning, writing, and editing of this book. Through-out the whole process he was also a reader, a brainstorm partner, and proofreader. He spent countless hours talking about the story and helping me fix plot holes, pointing out the proofreading errors, and most of all—always, always supporting this crazy dream of mine.

Thank you to my sisters, Jacqueline and Jessica, who have patiently waited for their chance to read these words. They have shaped these words more than they know. I wouldn't be the writer or the person I am today without them both. I can't thank them enough for always believing the day would come that my book would be in their hands, even though it took years and me missing family stuff to work on it. A special thank you to Jessica for stepping in for me and sending my final manuscript to the publisher before my deadline when I was unable to.

This book would have never made it into your hands if it weren't for my best friend Carmen connecting me with the most amazing writing coach, Ashley Mansour. Thank you Ashley for pushing me, helping me come up with a concrete plan, training me on mindset, looking over all the versions of my manuscript along the way, talking through plot points, and above all else, truly believing in me and being my safe place and personal Google during this whole process.

To all the people who have never read a word I've written, but believed in my passion and dream anyway—Jack Sharman, Jen Robinson, Javier Roman, Michael Buckley, and Cory Wright. Our happy hour conversations always inspired me to keep going and never give up on the dream.

To my English professor at my engineering school, Dr. Reardon, who told me that I had a gift and that if I ever stopped writing, it would be an affront to whatever I believed had given me this gift. His words have stuck with me to this day.

Thank you to my editors, Susan Barnes and Erin Huntley. The full developmental edit Susan did on the rough first draft, shaped this story and characters more than any other part of the process, and Erin took my final draft and polished it to a shine.

To my Quill and Cup community—I don't know if I would have shown up as much as I needed to to make this book a reality without all of them. Their encouragement and fierce support was just what I needed to keep going when it got tough. Ania, thank you for creating such an amazing community and bringing me into it.

Thank you to everyone at Morgan James for taking a chance on me and not only publishing this book, but being a true partner throughout the whole, crazy publishing process.

Thank you to my amazing beta readers Katelyn Davis, Susan Shepard, Ryan Johnson, and Lauren Youree who helped me clean up some spots and make this book as strong as it could be. A special thanks has to go to Ryan and Scott for reading it all twice and suggesting the big rewrites that have made this story so exciting.

And huge, heartfelt thanks goes to you, you beautiful reader. Thank you for picking up this book and exploring the world of Akaria with me. I hope you come back and stay awhile with me.

ABOUT THE AUTHOR

Photo By Carmen Seda

JoAnna McSpadden is a software developer by day and high fantasy writer by night – giving her a truly eclectic perspective of the world around us. She is a lifelong writer, creative adventurer, bibliophile, and avid fantasy board game enthusiast. When she's not programming e-commerce websites for major household brands, she's writing illustrative literary works of art that inspire readers to dream, embrace their authenticity, and defy the odds to go after whatever it is that they desire – even if it goes against the status quo. JoAnna lives in Kansas City with her husband.

For updates on future releases, fun extras from the world of Akaria, and other news you can visit JoAnna's website at joannamcspadden.com.

A free ebook edition is available with the purchase of this book.

To claim your free ebook edition:

1. Visit MorganJamesBOGO.com
2. Sign your name CLEARLY in the space
3. Complete the form and submit a photo of the entire copyright page
4. You or your friend can download the ebook to your preferred device

Morgan James
BOGO™

A **FREE** ebook edition is available for you
or a friend with the purchase of this print book.

CLEARLY SIGN YOUR NAME ABOVE

Instructions to claim your free ebook edition:
1. Visit MorganJamesBOGO.com
2. Sign your name CLEARLY in the space above
3. Complete the form and submit a photo of this entire page
4. You or your friend can download the ebook to your preferred device

Print & Digital Together Forever.

Snap a photo

Free ebook

Read anywhere